FREEDOM'S
FIGHT

JAKE TYSON

THE VINDICATORS BOOK TWO

FREEDOM'S
FIGHT

AMBASSADOR INTERNATIONAL
GREENVILLE, SOUTH CAROLINA & BELFAST, NORTHERN IRELAND

www.ambassador-international.com

Freedom's Fight

Hardcover ISBN: 978-1-64960-449-1
Paperback ISBN: 978-1-64960-135-3
eISBN: 978-1-64960-185-8
Library of Congress Control Number: 2022930644

Cover design by Hannah Linder Designs
Interior Typesetting by Dentelle Design
Edited by Maggie Platt

AMBASSADOR INTERNATIONAL
Emerald House
411 University Ridge, Suite B14
Greenville, SC 29601, USA
www.ambassador-international.com

AMBASSADOR BOOKS
The Mount
2 Woodstock Link
Belfast, BT6 8DD, Northern Ireland, UK
www.ambassadormedia.co.uk

The colophon is a trademark of Ambassador, a Christian publishing company.

For my grandparents—Denny, Sylvia, Gary, and Beverly.
Thank you for laying the foundations that our family has built on now and,
Lord willing, for generations to come.

ACKNOWLEDGMENTS

As with *Vigilante's Light*, there are so many people I'd like to acknowledge. I couldn't name all of them if I tried, but here are a few who are particularly near to my heart.

Jessica, my wife, for always being there for me, listening to me, encouraging me, and being one of my first readers and my number one fan forever. Thank you for falling in love with my characters as much as I have and for wanting the world to love them, too.

My family—Dad, Mom, Zac, Hunter, and MaKayla—as well as my in-laws and my extended family, for always being supportive of my desire to write, encouraging me to do so, giving me feedback on my writing, letting me bounce ideas off them, asking questions about the writing process, and upselling *Vigilante's Light* to anyone who'll listen!

All the members of the Realm Makers Consortium who helped me figure out things like character names, superpowers, motivation, costume design, and on and on.

Ambassador International, for not only taking a chance on a first-time author by publishing *Vigilante's Light*, but believing in this world I'm creating enough to continue publishing my stories! Thanks also to the editors and cover designers who have helped make these books the best they can be.

Thank you to all the readers of *Vigilante's Light*. I'm so glad that it's out there, and that there are readers enjoying this world I've crafted. Here's to many more (books and readers)!

Most importantly, I couldn't have done this without the desire and the ability to write given to me by my Heavenly Father, and I couldn't have written anything honoring Him if He had not saved me through Christ. Thank You, God, for leading me to this opportunity and for giving me the ideas for Gideon and his friends!

CHAPTER 1

The perpetrator leapt from the rooftop, arms flailing. He landed in a crouch on top of the next building and spared a quick glance over his shoulder. A midnight blue figure, swathed in a flowing cape, was hot on his heels. From his position on a nearby rooftop, Carter Jonson—the Crusader—watched the perp, ready to intercede if he managed to dodge his pursuer.

The man shook his head and continued his escape, raising one of his hands in front of him to shield his eyes from the setting sun. He had to have known that he would eventually run out of time. He couldn't run from the Seraph forever.

Carter and Gideon had been tracking him ever since the footage of Gideon, dressed as the Seraph but unmasked, had leaked to the news. Gideon believed the man they were chasing had flown the helicopter that had taken Luca Serban to Sterling Enterprises. He probably hadn't had a choice—Serban had blackmailed or threatened half the people in this city and paid off the other half. But flying the helicopter wasn't the man's crime. Gideon believed that the helicopter pilot was the same person who had leaked the photo of Gideon to the press. While it hadn't had any negative impact on his life so far, Gideon still wanted the guy off the streets. As a former member of Serban's mob, whether blackmailed or not, he was a potential threat. Carter was just thrilled that he was allowed to tag along.

This guy probably thought he'd gotten away clean. But now the Seraph was on his tail. He'd run for too long, and his past had caught up with him in the form of Sojourn City's own superhero.

The runaway was approaching the Crusader's lookout position. As he ran, he glanced back over his shoulder again. *That's my cue.* The Crusader stepped out from his hiding place, planting himself between the perp and the gap separating this building from the next. The perp turned back around—too late. His eyes widened as he spotted the Crusader, but he couldn't stop his forward momentum. The Crusader raised his arm and clotheslined the man, knocking the perp flat on his back.

Clad in a red-and-black suit with a gray cross emblazoned on the chest and holding the *jo* staff Gideon had given him, the Crusader was sure he cut an imposing image. As the perp scrambled back, Carter twirled the staff and stepped toward him. The Seraph jumped onto the roof and circled around to stand next to Carter.

"Lionel Claremont," the Seraph said. "You have a lot to answer for."

Carter knew this guy. Lionel had been friends with his father, Wyatt Jonson, back when Dad had been job-hopping in the Brooks. Carter's mother had never liked Lionel, but Carter had thought he'd been a nice enough guy. Apparently, Mom was a better judge of character than Carter.

"Uncle Lionel." The Crusader shook his head. "I'm disappointed."

Lionel blinked. *"Carter?"*

"You going to rat my identity to the media, too?" The Crusader twirled the staff and rested it on his shoulder. "I wouldn't recommend it."

The two superheroes hoisted him to his feet and dragged him down a fire escape to the street below. Detective Jolie Anderson, Gideon's girlfriend, was waiting there to slap him in handcuffs.

"You should be relieved, Uncle Lionel," Carter said. "Jail's going to be easy, compared to being under Luca Serban's thumb."

* * *

Gideon Turner stepped into his lair and removed his hooded cape. Two mannequins stood against the left wall, crafted to display Gideon's and Carter's suits when they weren't in use. Gideon hung his cape on one mannequin and ran his hand across the armored chest plate he wore. It still carried the scars of bullets and knife slashes from the night of the Uprising. His best friend and confidante, Dean Sterling, had promised him a new suit of armor before he left on his quest to find the man who'd given Gideon his powers. *Ashcroft.*

But that kind of thing took time. While Gideon waited, he had searched for the man who had leaked his identity to the press. He hadn't expected it to be someone he'd met before. The first time Gideon had encountered Carter's father, Wyatt, Lionel Claremont had been bumming with him on a street corner in the Brooks. Now that he was in custody, Gideon didn't have a reason to put off his quest any longer.

His first stop on his journey would be San Francisco, the home of Joshua, Gideon's cellmate in Venezuela. Gideon had promised Joshua that he would find the older man's family and tell them about his fate just before Joshua gave his life so Gideon could escape.

Once he fulfilled that promise, he would return to Sojourn City, pick up his gear, and head out on his search for Ashcroft. He wasn't sure where to start yet—maybe Romania. It was as good a place as any. Luca Serban, a Romanian crime lord, had told Gideon that he'd worked for Ashcroft before. But Gideon was working almost entirely off hearsay.

"That was fun," Carter said.

Gideon removed his gloves. "They won't all be like that. Most of the criminals in Sojourn City aren't going to roll over at the first sign of a mask."

"I know." Carter twirled his staff. "But you gotta take the easy ones when they come, right?"

"Fair enough. I wish I had more time to train you before I leave, but I think you're doing pretty well. Still, I'd prefer you not get into the thick of it until I get back."

"But what if something big goes down? What if the city needs me?"

That was unlikely. With the Uprising almost two months in the past, the city had settled into a new calm, and good things were on the horizon. Dean, the new CEO of Sterling Enterprises, had ordered construction of a maglev that would run from the Platform, where the city's richest denizens lived, to the Brooks, the worst slums of Sojourn. Dean hoped the maglev, a magnetically-propelled hovertrain, would encourage the upper class to invest in the city since it meant the Platform could no longer be removed from the shore. And with a new police chief just appointed, the cops were cracking down on crime.

But on the off chance anything did happen . . . "Keep in touch with Jolie. If she thinks you're needed, then you can get out there. If not, don't get involved. In the meantime, stick to stopping small-time crimes when and where you can."

Carter nodded glumly. "Got it."

Jolie. Gideon's relationship with his longtime girlfriend was finally beginning to flourish again. After his year in captivity in Venezuela, they'd been out of sync for a while. Tension mounted when he had put on the hood to become the Seraph, and it could have ended the relationship, if they had not decided to put their differences aside for the sake of love. All was reconciled now, and Gideon enjoyed every moment with her. She made him want to be a better man, a better Christian, so that one day he could be the husband she deserved.

"Behold the conquering heroes!" Dean walked into the lair. "Heard you got the guy who snitched on you."

"We did. Of course, that doesn't take back what he did. The whole world knows that I'm the Seraph now."

"Maybe that's the way it should be. People in masks always have something to hide, some reason for keeping their identities a secret. You don't. You are a hero, after all."

Hero. Superhero. The muscles on Gideon's back stiffened whenever he heard those words. Everyone always wanted to apply them to him, but he didn't feel he'd earned them. Superheroes were symbols of hope and prosperity, reminders that humanity could be better. How did Gideon do that? All he'd done as the Seraph was crack skulls and break bones. Any vigilante could put the hurt on someone. It didn't make them a hero.

Wyatt Jonson. Now there was a hero. Without powers, the man stood at the foot of a bridge and fought anyone coming his way, not for the sake of fighting, but to protect those on the other side. He gave his life defending that bridge. Meanwhile, Gideon had duked it out in a pointless fist fight with Luca Serban. While Wyatt died, Gideon could only deliver more punishment. His head knew that defeating Serban had ended the Uprising, but his heart felt his own failure to protect Wyatt too keenly.

Dean would argue, though, so Gideon shunted the thought aside.

"Don't I?" Gideon ticked off items with his fingers. "Where I live, where I work, who my loved ones are, where *they* live . . ."

"Okay, fair enough." Dean walked over to the tabletop computer on the other side of the lair. "I have an idea to help with that. The living part, anyway."

Gideon removed the rest of his armor and placed it on the mannequin, leaving him clad in a midnight blue bodysuit.

Carter still wore his armor and the dark red domino mask that covered his eyes. He stared at his reflection in the glass case that contained the mannequin for his suit and flexed.

Gideon rolled his eyes and chuckled. *Kids.* Gideon was not that much older than Carter; he had about seven years on him. But that felt like a lifetime considering the things Gideon had experienced.

"What's your idea?" Gideon asked Dean.

"We can keep operating from the tower," Dean said, "and convert this whole apartment into a lair. I can buy out the entire top floor. No one will ask any questions. You and I move out to a smaller apartment. That way we're not living in the same place we conduct superhero activities, and if we get attacked, our home and our base won't both be in jeopardy."

"I like it." Gideon walked over to Dean's side. "You get to work on that while I'm gone, okay?"

"No can do. I'm coming with you."

"What? No. There's no reason for anyone to come with me. I'm just going to meet Joshua's family in San Francisco, and then I'm coming right back. I'll be gone a couple days, tops."

"I need to get away, Gid. My dad is in jail, I've just become a CEO . . . It's been a stressful couple of months. And besides, if I really need an excuse, there's a branch of Sterling Enterprises in San Francisco. I can pay them a visit. The new CEO visiting will be good for PR. I've got a private jet, so it won't cost you a plane ticket if I tag along."

He had a point. The trip to San Francisco, while not exactly a vacation, would be a nice getaway. Compared to what they'd gone through the past few months—years, in Gideon's case—this trip might be downright relaxing. And while Gideon wouldn't have minded some time alone, he had experienced plenty of that in a cage in Venezuela. The company would be welcome.

"If you come, then who finds our new apartment?"

"How about Wes? He still lives with your parents; I'm sure he'd like to get out and experience life on his own."

Gideon's brother had been asking if he could move in with him and Dean for the past few weeks. Although Wes was planning to go to law school in August, that was still a few months away. Having some semblance of life on his own before that might be good for Wes. And it would give Gideon more time with him. Between crime fighting and his job at Sterling Labs, Gideon didn't have much time to bond with his brother.

"What about your company?"

"Maddox and Arianna can run the labs, and the board of directors can keep things under control at the enterprise building. They'll be especially willing if they know I'm paying a visit to another branch."

"Maddox and Arianna handle the company, Wes handles the house, and Carter and Jolie handle the crime. Works for me."

"Me, too," Carter said.

"Good." Gideon looked at him. "Now get out of that suit and head home. Your mom will need your help with your siblings."

"Yes, sir."

Before Gideon had agreed to bring Carter on as the Crusader, he'd given him stipulations. Gideon would train Carter to be a vigilante, so long as Carter kept up his duties as man of the house now that his father was dead. He had to take care of his mother and younger siblings first and the city second.

"I'll see you when we get back," Gideon said. "Stay safe."

"You, too."

"Dean, pack your bag. We're going to San Francisco."

* * *

When she received a promotion to detective, Jolie had expected more action to come with the rank. With most of the city's high-profile criminals dead or in jail following the Uprising, being a detective mostly involved dealing with smaller problems. Right now, that meant a flourishing drug trade.

Only in Sojourn City would that be considered small or easy.

She was glad she'd received her promotion before the news had broken that Gideon was the Seraph. If her superiors suspected she knew that her boyfriend was a vigilante, it could have been a roadblock for her career—and it still might be in the future. However, since he was now recognized as an official, citywide superhero, allying herself with him wasn't a crime anymore. They had developed a near-flawless system. He brought down the criminals and turned them over to her, and she collared them. The process, which they'd perfected in the months since tossing Serban in jail, was efficient. No one complained. Not even Captain Andrews, who normally held a strict anti-vigilante policy.

Now, Gideon was leaving. She reminded herself that it was temporary. She understood why he needed to go, but he'd just come back into her life. She hated to see him walk out again, no matter how briefly. She checked her watch. She needed to leave now if she was going to make it to the airport to tell him goodbye. She put her badge and gun in her desk drawer and stood. Her immediate superior, Sergeant Pulaski, glanced at her as she rose.

"Going somewhere, Detective?"

"Taking a break. Gideon's going out of town, and I wanted to tell him goodbye. I don't have any active cases."

"Understood." Pulaski nodded. "Give him my best wishes. The city will miss him while he's gone."

"At least we'll have the Crusader."

"Crusader Jr., you mean. He's no superhero. Not yet, at least."

"I think he's got potential."

"Potential's great, but in the meantime, I'll rely on the officers in this precinct to keep the city safe."

"Whatever you say, sir." Jolie strode past him. "See you later."

She walked outside the precinct and down the steps to where her small, white, decades-old Toyota Camry was parked on the street corner—a street corner that was far cleaner than it had been a month ago. The Brooks still couldn't be called a gentrified neighborhood, but they were making progress. Once, Jolie would've been wary about walking out of the precinct without her sidearm. That wasn't a problem anymore. She still wouldn't go for a leisurely stroll through this neighborhood, but she didn't have to keep her guard up walking to her car. Any improvement was welcome in the Brooks.

Jolie climbed into her car and drove toward the nearest interstate on-ramp. She looked around her as she drove. Buildings that had once been covered in obscene graffiti had been scrubbed clean. Street corners that had once been home to prostitutes and drug dealers were empty. And it was thanks, almost entirely, to Gideon. He would shift most of the credit to her and Wyatt, the first Crusader, but Gideon was the real hero. They'd done their part, but without him, Serban wouldn't have been defeated. That had been the real key to turning things around.

She merged onto the interstate and drove toward the airport. She had considered asking Gideon if she could come to San Francisco with him, but he'd be gone for only a few days. One day a real vacation with him would be nice. She couldn't remember the last time she'd taken one. And whether he would admit it or not, Gideon needed one, too. There had been only six months between his rescue from Venezuela and the start of his career as the Seraph, and in that time he'd had to deal with the stress of starting a new job and watching the Brooks descend into anarchy.

The rest of her drive was peaceful. Rush hour hadn't hit yet, so she wasn't crammed end-to-end with other cars on the interstate. Off to the right, a construction crew put up one of the support beams for Dean's maglev train. Connecting the city like that was a brilliant idea. Jolie was proud of Dean for coming up with it. Now, if he could just pull it off.

Ten minutes later, she pulled off the interstate and into the airport parking lot. Sterling Enterprises' private hangar was around back, and Jolie had to show her ID to a security officer at the gate to get through. She parked next to the hangar and climbed out of her car. The jet had already been wheeled out and was sitting on the tarmac. Gideon and Dean stood next to the hangar doors while the flight crew readied the plane. Jolie approached them.

Gideon saw her coming and waved. "I'm glad you made it."

She pulled him into a hug and kissed him. "I'm going to miss you, but I'm proud of you for keeping your promise."

"Joshua saved my life." Gideon kissed her back and then stepped away. "What else could I do?"

"Be safe." Jolie looked at Dean. "And you take care of him, got it?"

Dean laughed. "I have a feeling he'll be the one taking care of me, but sure."

"The plane's ready, Mr. Sterling!" one of the crew called. "You can board whenever you're ready."

"Thank you!" Dean smiled at Jolie. "See you later, Detective. Take care."

"I will." Jolie turned back to Gideon and hugged him again. "I love you so much."

"I love you, too. Don't worry; we'll be there and back before you know it."

"I know."

"Keep an eye out for Carter, all right? Hopefully he won't need it, but he's young and I think part of him is still treating this crime-fighting thing as a game. I told him not to get involved in anything big without consulting you first. Otherwise, just let him do his thing—take out bank robbers, muggers, and the like."

"Okay. I will."

"Thank you. You're the best."

She squeezed him in a hug one more time, exchanged a kiss, and then stepped back with a soft "I love you" to let him board the plane. He climbed the ramp and turned to wave at her. She waved back as the ramp closed. The plane wheeled away and shot down the runway. Jolie watched the sky until the jet disappeared into the clouds.

CHAPTER 2

The last time Gideon flew on a plane, he'd been on his way home from Venezuela, surrounded by federal agents. This plane was similar in size, but the company was completely different. Other than a stewardess, he and Dean were the only occupants in the main cabin. The soft hum and rumble of the engines created a kind of relaxing ambience—like rain on a rooftop. Gideon struggled to keep his eyes open as he and Dean talked.

"So, the Omer family," Dean said. "What do you know about them?"

"Joshua's son, Mike, is married to Rebecca. They have a son, Patrick. They're Orthodox Jews living in San Francisco, and I've got their address."

"Who doesn't?" Dean asked wryly.

True enough. As Gideon and Dean researched the Omers, they discovered that Patrick Omer was the sole survivor of the infamous San Francisco flu shot epidemic. An entire batch of flu vaccinations had been contaminated, and everyone who received them died, except Patrick. Experts were baffled, protesters were everywhere, and the poor kid had become something of a minor celebrity within the medical community. Gideon was curious himself to find out what made Patrick so special, and what ingredient had caused the epidemic.

"What are you going to tell them?" Dean pressed.

Gideon had been pondering that for days, and he still didn't have an exact answer. He knew what they needed to hear, and what Joshua would've wanted them to hear, so he'd start there.

"I'll tell them what happened to Joshua, why he disappeared from their lives for so long, and that he died saving my life. His dying request was that I tell them about his faith in Jesus."

"Orthodox Jews? They won't like that."

"Maybe not, but I told him I'd do it."

Had the Omers heard about the Seraph? If so, had they also seen the revelation of his identity? Would he knock on the Omer family's door to find them gaping at him like he was a celebrity? He wasn't sure how he'd handle that. But even that would be better than them slamming the door in his face because they were anti-vigilante. It would probably be best if they'd never heard of him before. Just one more thing he'd have to figure out on the go.

"What about you?" Gideon asked. "What are you going to do?"

"I'll visit Sterling Enterprises, give the facilities a tour, shake a few hands, tell them I'm proud of them. The works."

"Sounds easy."

"Should be. Depends on how well the board at this branch has handled news of the power shift. Not everyone's going to be thrilled that a guy in his twenties is running the company, and I don't blame them. I'm not thrilled about it either."

"You can handle it." Gideon smiled. "I mean, look at the maglev train idea you had."

"Yeah . . . I am costing the company millions on a pet project, trying to fix the damage my dad caused to my city. That just screams fiscal responsibility."

"You've got a good head on your shoulders. You're not going to drive the company into the ground."

"I hope not. I majored in science; I don't have an MBA." Dean looked out the window and grew silent. Gideon watched him for a moment. Dean Sterling was a light-hearted jokester, but he was also one of the smartest people Gideon had ever met. To top it all off, he also had a great, big soft side. That would make him a great CEO.

"Any word on a new Seraph suit?"

Dean's attention snapped back to him. "Glad you asked. That's another reason I wanted to come on this trip. One of our research teams overseas discovered a new metal in . . . Italy, I think? They brought it back to the San Francisco labs. It's ultra-light, ultra-strong. They call it aionium. It's from the Greek root—oh, never mind. I won't bore you with the details. But it's really strong."

"You think it would be good for my suit?"

"I do. It won't weigh you down while you're flying, but it's durable enough to protect you from gunfire and bladed weapons—better than the Kevlar weave in your old suit. You won't take three to the chest and fall off a rooftop like you did fighting Monahan. And, hopefully, it'll stand up to any other superhumans you meet."

Gideon cringed at the reminder of the injury. He would've died that night, if not for Wyatt Jonson's help. "Well, I trust your judgment."

"You're set on the whole 'no cape' thing?"

Gideon shrugged. "The cape's a bit . . . theatrical. And I really don't need a mask anymore, either. But if you think it completes the look, you're the costume designer."

Dean made a check mark in the air with his index finger. "I'll remember that. And I'm thinking about rejiggering the color scheme.

I'll keep the blue and gold, but I might brighten it up a bit. You don't have to hide in the shadows anymore, so dark isn't a necessity."

"Sounds good to me. Like I said, you're the designer; just make me a suit, and I'll wear it."

"It will be my utmost pleasure."

* * *

The moon shone down on the streets of the Brooks, its silvery light overpowered by the yellow glow of streetlights. Clad in the Crusader suit, Carter stood atop a drug store rooftop and looked out on his neighborhood. Across the street, the heavy beat of a hip-hop song vibrated from the walls of a club. Neon light escaped from the club's half-open front door as a handful of young adults exited the building, laughing and chattering. Carter watched them disinterestedly. None of them would cause any trouble, unless it was to tumble drunkenly on their faces.

He missed his father. He and Wyatt had always been close. When Dad had returned from active duty in the military, he and Carter had become inseparable. When they'd moved to Sojourn City for a "fresh start" and Carter had struggled to adjust in school, Dad had been there to help him through the transition. When the Brooks had become a festering hole of crime, Dad had been an encouragement to his family— and, as they would later learn, the hero who protected them.

Carter had never thought about going into the military, but he'd tried to emulate his father in just about everything else. He joined the wrestling team, like his dad had in high school. He went out of his way to help others and stand up to bullies at school. He joined the men's Bible study class at church. Heck, he even cut his hair in the same style.

Now he was taking up his mantle in more ways than one. He was the Crusader who fought crime, but he was also the older brother who helped Rhonda and Ellis with their schoolwork, encouraged them in their social lives, and helped Mom gather the family for church on Sundays. He was the man who provided for them and for his mother, Joanna. Trying to stand in the gap Dad had left was the hardest thing he'd ever done, but he was determined to make his father proud.

Since graduating high school, that meant his days were open to work. He already had a job at a corner grocery store in the Brooks, and he upped his hours so he could better provide for his family. He spent the rest of his new, adult freedom serving as the hometown hero, the Crusader. He was glad he didn't have to worry about homework or group projects anymore. It left more time for the important things.

At first, he'd wanted to keep wearing his dad's black leather costume to honor him, but part of Gideon's stipulations for training Carter to fight had been that he had to wear something more protective. Taking one of the Kevlar-lined prototypes of Gideon's suit, Dean had painted it dark red and black, emblazoned a light gray cross on the chest, and added a dark red domino mask. It was a good look.

"You going to stand there all night?"

Carter spun around and raised his staff. Jolie stood on the rooftop behind him, arms folded across her brown leather jacket. She smirked and walked closer. Carter had been standing on the edge of the roof for a long time, and it was hard not to get lost in thought when there was no crime going on in the area.

"No." Carter glanced at the watch programmed into the suit's gauntlet. "I should actually be heading home to check on my family. There hasn't been much activity tonight."

"No, there hasn't." Jolie stepped aside, and Carter walked past her to the fire escape. "Gideon told me to look out for you while he's gone."

"I don't need a babysitter."

"He doesn't think you do. If he did, he wouldn't let you be out here at all."

"Yeah, I guess." Carter split his staff into two truncheons and sheathed them in his belt. "Let me know if you need any help out here."

"I will. Good night, Carter."

He climbed down the fire escape. Did Jolie feel responsible for him? She'd been there when his dad died. Maybe that made her feel like she had to protect him. She didn't, though. He could take care of himself.

* * *

Wes Turner stared at the letter of acceptance from Juncture City School of Law. Being a lawyer had been his dream since he'd been a kid, but lately, he wasn't so sure. Ever since he'd found out that Gideon was a superhero, and then the young Crusader had shown up to save the Turners' lives, he had wondered if there was more than one way that he could help people.

Law school took a long time. Even after he graduated, it would take years to have his own practice or become a senior partner at a prestigious firm. He'd have to intern, work as a junior partner, and climb his way up. It was too much. He wanted to help people right now.

What other options did he have? He had an undergrad degree in criminology that wouldn't get him anywhere close to what he wanted to do by itself. He could always go to the police academy and become an officer. But was that right for him?

He held the letter over the trash can. Over the past few months, he'd stood here just like this dozens of times, weighing the consequences of dropping the letter in and forgetting all about it. But something in him wouldn't let go of the sheet of paper. It was his safety net.

Now that Gideon had asked him to move into an apartment with him and Dean, could he really leave Sojourn City so soon? Maybe. Dean was paying for the apartment, so it wasn't a permanent commitment on Wes' part. He could live there for a few months and then go to law school.

Was that really what he wanted?

He placed the letter back on his desk and shook his head. Whatever he was supposed to do, he would have to figure it out fast. Juncture City School of Law expected him to be there when classes started in less than three months.

Wes grabbed his car keys. He had to get out for a bit and clear his head. A burger and fries from Wally's Diner always helped with that.

CHAPTER 3

"Are you insane?" Mark Garvin, CEO of Garvin Technologies, exclaimed. "The gene splicer matrix is an extremely early prototype. We will certainly not lend it out for use by any outside scientists, let alone those of a competing company."

Artemis Wayans crossed her legs and rested her head against her left hand. She had been in positions of power before, but sitting across the desk from the CEO of one of the most prestigious technology companies in the world was a truly intoxicating feeling. It would mean more if he would cooperate.

"Crowne Pharmaceuticals has made discoveries and breakthroughs that most in the scientific community consider impossible," Artemis said. "Without the proper equipment, Dr. Ashcroft can't further his research. Your splicer is an essential part of our—his—project."

"Ashcroft," Garvin scoffed. "He is a disgrace. A madman."

"I've seen him perform miracles." Artemis leaned forward. "Wasn't Jesus Christ called mad by the Jews? But He performed miracles."

"Discussing religion is not the way to win this argument, ma'am. I'm afraid you've wasted your time coming here; we will not give you the splicer. There is too much research of actual importance, and I won't have the splicer wasted on Ashcroft's musings and whimsies."

Artemis could've easily changed Garvin's mind. It would have taken almost no effort at all. But this was just initial contact, and she hadn't expected him to go along with her first request. She had other options—and a plethora of backup plans in case this didn't work out.

Artemis shrugged fluidly. "What about allowing us to use the splicer under supervision of one of your scientists? It wouldn't be as ideal as bringing it to our lab, but we could still get the job done."

"No. Miss Wayans, I will not lend any device, nor even a single cent, to Crowne or to the so-called 'Doctor' Ashcroft, and I will not be persuaded otherwise."

We'll see.

Artemis leaned forward. "Mr. Garvin—"

Her gaze traveled to the television in the corner of Garvin's office. A news channel was broadcasting footage of a private jet landing here in San Francisco. Reporters mobbed the jet's ramp as the occupants debarked. Both were young, handsome, fit—and the darker-haired one was Dean Sterling, newly-minted CEO of Sterling Enterprises. The other . . .

"I've heard enough, Miss Wayans. You can see yourself out, and kindly tell Ashcroft that he will not find favor with this or any company of decent reputation."

Artemis rose. "Very well. I'm sorry we couldn't come to an agreement. Good day."

She turned and strode from the office. It would've taken only a few words to change his mind. In another moment, she would've done just that. But the splicer could wait. She had other avenues that she could explore, starting with Sterling. His company had another device that would be useful to them. Ashcroft hadn't formally assigned her to retrieve it yet, but a bird in the hand . . .

Garvin would still be here when she was ready to retrieve the splicer. Ashcroft's plan had wheels within wheels, and Garvin

Technologies was only a small cog, one that could easily be replaced. The CEO's belligerence would not stop Ashcroft. Even if he had corporate spies look into Crowne Pharmaceuticals, he'd never find anything. It was a mere dummy corporation, one of many held by Ashcroft. No, they were secure. The plan could be delayed, but never stopped. It was Artemis' duty to see to that.

She took the elevator down to the lobby and walked toward the exit, her high heels clicking against the marble floors. She winked at the guard on duty as she passed him. Her limo waited outside on the curb. Her chauffeur opened the door, and she slid into the soft leather seat.

The small TV across from her cycled through local and nationwide news. She stopped it on one of the channels circulating the footage of Sterling's arrival. Something about the man with him, the blond one, struck a chord in her. She knew him . . . How? Artemis tapped her chin with a forefinger and reached for the remote to turn the volume up with her other hand.

" . . . scion and newly-appointed CEO Dean Sterling arrived in San Francisco yesterday afternoon. Sterling took the reins of his family company after his father was imprisoned for conspiracy. The younger Sterling appears to be traveling the country, making visits to the different branches of Sterling Enterprises."

Nothing about the other man? Pity.

Artemis leaned toward the limo's cab. "Driver, call Sterling Enterprises and make an appointment with Mr. Sterling."

Perhaps he would be more willing to help. After all, young, rich men like him loved the thrill of the unknown.

* * *

The hotel room Dean had reserved for the two of them was almost as fancy as their apartment in Lakeside Central Tower. The living room boasted a scenic view of the San Francisco skyline, two bedrooms with queen beds had private double doorways to their own bathrooms, and a kitchen nook offered a stocked refrigerator. Gideon had seen suites like this only in the movies.

They wouldn't be using it for long. Gideon planned on only one day in San Francisco—long enough to meet Joshua's family and talk to them about anything they might want to discuss. If Gideon needed to stay for an extra day or two while Dean made nice with his company, he was fine with that, but the sooner he could return home and get started on his search for Dr. Ashcroft, the better. He didn't want to be gone from Sojourn City for too long. Carter needed training, and Gideon wanted to catch a few more moments with Jolie before he left again. They were still finding a status quo in their newly-growing relationship. His secret life as the Seraph had nearly ruined what they had. Who knew how far his search for Ashcroft would take him? If he wasn't careful, this mission could become another roadblock. That was the last thing he wanted.

As he had packed for the trip, he found the engagement ring he'd bought what seemed like a lifetime ago. That had been before . . . everything. He still planned to give it to her one day when the time was right. It was crystal clear to him that Jolie was the woman he was meant to marry.

Gideon dried off, dressed in black jeans and a blue short-sleeved Henley shirt, and ran his fingers through his tousled hair. Then he stepped out into the living room.

In contrast to Gideon's casual dress, Dean was clothed in a sharp gray business suit with a deep green tie.

Gideon whistled. "Looking snappy, bud."

"Thank you. And you look . . . "

"Watch it."

"Like how I'd prefer to be dressed right now."

Joshua's family lived in an out-of-the-way suburban neighborhood. Gideon pulled the address up on his phone's GPS as they walked downstairs to the silver sports car Dean had rented for their use. The company had offered a limo, but Gideon didn't particularly want to pull up in front of the Omers' house in a limousine and step out to tell them that Joshua was dead. It would be bad form.

Gideon paired his phone with the car's internal system and hooked it to the console while Dean pulled away from the hotel. Gideon's heart pounded as he silently rehearsed what he would say. If he hadn't learned to control his powers, light would've been shining through his hands as he tried to talk to the Omer family. He took a few deep breaths—four seconds in, hold for four, four seconds out.

Dean pulled off the interstate. "Just call me whenever you're ready to be picked up. If I'm still in a meeting, I'll send a driver."

"It must be nice to be a millionaire."

"Billionaire." Dean laughed. "It is nice, but it's also hard not to get a big head, you know? I have to fight that urge every day."

"I bet. I'm honestly glad I'm not in your shoes."

"You have big feet. You wouldn't fit my shoes."

"Shut up."

They must've had this same conversation a hundred times before. It was familiar. It was normal. Normal was nice. Gideon had almost forgotten what normal felt like.

Being the Seraph is *the new normal.*

He couldn't go back to the way things had been before. And maybe that was a good thing. He didn't know why God had allowed him to develop these powers, but He must've had a greater purpose in mind. At the very least, Gideon had already helped save Sojourn City from a disastrous fate.

Dean parked the car by the curb. Gideon picked up his phone and turned off the GPS. He had a new text from Jolie, telling him Carter had been on patrol last night but hadn't engaged any criminals. The text ended with *Good luck, love you* and a kissing emoji. Gideon smiled, sent her a quick text back, and tucked the phone away.

"Here goes nothing," he said.

"You've got this." Dean leaned over to give him a fist bump. "I'll see you soon."

Gideon stepped out of the car and watched Dean drive away. *God, give me guidance and strength.*

The Omer household was a modest two-story home. A blue economy car was parked in the driveway. Gideon tucked his hands in his pockets and walked up the sidewalk to the front door.

He stopped, his finger hovering over the doorbell. His heart pounded. Gideon wiped a bead of sweat from his forehead and fiddled with one of the buttons on his shirt. His hands shook, and they glowed faintly with traces of his power. He took a deep breath. The light faded; the trembling stilled. He rang the doorbell.

* * *

"Welcome to San Francisco, Mr. Sterling!"

"Please, call me Dean." He shook hands with the chairman of the board. "Mr. Sterling makes me sound old, and that I am not."

The chairman, Max Coleman, smiled and nodded. Max was in his late fifties, and was a longtime friend of the Sterling family. Max always treated Dean like a nephew. It was a relief to see a familiar face. How did Max feel about Dad going to prison? About Dean being appointed CEO?

"Of course not. I was old when you were still a lad, sneaking candies from the saucer on your father's desk. Boy, times have changed, haven't they? The board is ready for you, so follow me, if you please."

"Lead the way." Dean scanned the lobby. It was almost identical to the Sojourn City building. "From the reports I've seen, we're doing well out here."

"We are. Things have been quite promising, especially since the discovery of aionium. Our boys and girls in the lab are quite fond of that stuff."

"As well they should be. Once the board meeting is over, I was hoping to pay a visit to the lab and see some of the miracle metal myself."

"That can be arranged." Max smirked. "You are the boss, after all."

"Right. That is . . . going to take some getting used to."

Max tapped the elevator call button, and they waited for the car to arrive. Dean adjusted his tie, swallowing past the restrictive knot. He was more comfortable in a pair of skinny jeans and a t-shirt or, on the finest of occasions, maybe a polo. He tucked his hands in his pockets.

No big deal. This was just a meeting with the people who ran this branch of his company who had the combined power to vote him out if they didn't like the way he did things.

Yeah. No big deal.

* * *

The boy who answered the door looked about eighteen years old. He had red hair that hung across his forehead, and eyes almost the same piercing blue as Gideon's. He wore a red t-shirt, navy blue joggers, and gray tennis shoes. When he saw Gideon, he looked him up and down, frowned, and opened the door a little wider.

"Can I help you?"

"My name is Gideon Turner. Are you Patrick Omer?"

"Yeah . . . "

"I'm here about your grandfather, Joshua."

Patrick's eyes widened. "You know Grandpa?"

"I . . . yes. Are your parents home? I'd like to come in and talk to you all, if that's okay."

Patrick nodded vigorously. "Hey, Mom! Dad!"

Patrick's father came to the door first. He had black hair, but his eyes were as blue as his son's. He frowned when he saw Gideon.

"Look, we don't want any more reporters or scientists or-or whatever else you call yourselves. We don't know how Patrick survived. We're just glad he did. Can't you just leave us alone?"

Gideon bit the inside of his mouth. Of course, Patrick's father would think Gideon was there about the vaccine.

"This isn't about that." Gideon extended his right hand. Mike Omer took it in a firm grip. "Gideon Turner. I'm here about your father."

If it was possible, Mike's frown deepened. "Come in. Please."

Mike and Patrick stepped aside. The entryway led immediately to a short hallway that opened into the living room. Mike directed Gideon to the couch. A door on the left opened to a bedroom. Gideon saw movement inside, and a moment later, Rebecca Omer joined them. Her hair was red, like Patrick's, and her eyes were green.

Patrick sat down on the couch near Gideon while Mike moved to a recliner across from him. Rebecca stood next to her husband.

"What's going on?" she asked.

"This young man . . . Gideon?" At Gideon's nod, Mike continued, "Gideon says he knows Dad."

Rebecca blinked. "Really?"

Gideon nodded again. "Yes, ma'am."

Rebecca sat down in another chair. Gideon adjusted his position so he could see each member of the family. He opened his mind to sense their emotions. Patrick was hopeful, Mike concerned, and Rebecca surprised. He prepared himself for the coming sadness—and hostility if they didn't appreciate what Joshua had wanted Gideon to tell them.

"How did you find us?" Mike asked. "Did Dad tell you to come here?"

"Sort of. He told me your names and that you live in San Francisco. From there, I just did a search based on that information and found your address."

"Then you should've also found a phone number. Why didn't you just call?"

Well, this is getting off to a great start. He inhaled deeply. *God, let them be receptive.* Leaning forward with his elbows resting on his knees, Gideon began.

"This is the kind of thing I thought would come off better in person than on the phone."

"I see." Mike steepled his fingers. "Go ahead."

"Well, I'm . . . I'm sorry to have to tell you that your father—Joshua—he passed away."

All at once, three waves of sadness washed over Gideon. Much of it came from Patrick, but his parents were also grieved. Mike didn't show it externally. Rebecca covered her mouth with one hand. Tears welled in Patrick's eyes, and Gideon resisted the urge to put a hand on his shoulder to comfort him. He wasn't sure how well that would be received from a stranger.

"I was on a mission trip to Venezuela when I was kidnapped by guerrillas. They threw me in a cage, and that's where I met him—a bald man with a thick beard. He was kind; he had the brightest, most cheerful smile I've ever seen." Gideon smiled at the memory. "We became pretty good friends."

"Sounds like Dad." Mike's lips quirked upward. "So, what happened?"

"We were in captivity for a year, and he told me that he'd already been a prisoner for a year himself when I was first taken."

"What was he doing in Venezuela?" Rebecca asked.

"You didn't know?"

"No," Mike said. "I . . . We weren't close with Dad the past few years. We had some differences of opinion on some important convictions."

Oh boy. Gideon prayed that he would have the right words to say. He didn't want to kill his opportunity to tell them about Joshua's faith before he even got done with his story.

"I'm sorry. He told me he'd taken several such expeditions. He liked to explore."

"He started after Mom died." Mike nodded. "It makes sense."

"How did he die?" Patrick asked.

"We . . . we decided to try to escape. The guerrillas came to get us, and when they did, I rushed them. I managed to knock two of them out and take one of their guns, but their leader nearly killed me. Joshua stepped in and protected me, and he was injured in the process. He said he would stay behind and hold the rest of the guerrillas off so I could escape. He made me promise to come and find you. He wanted me to tell you what happened to him if all didn't go well. I heard him die as I was running. "

Patrick pursed his lips. "He saved you."

"He did. He was a hero."

Rebecca cried softly. A few stray tears drifted down Patrick's cheek, too. So much sadness swirled in the room that Gideon wanted to close himself off from it, but Joshua deserved better than that. He opened himself instead, feeling every raw emotion that washed off the family and picturing the man who had become his hero.

Mike pursed his lips and nodded. "Is that all he said?"

"No, he . . . he also wanted me to tell you about something else. I think you referenced it earlier. Joshua came to believe that Jesus Christ was the Messiah of your religion, and he put his faith in Him. He wanted me to tell you that."

"I thought as much." Mike sighed. "Well. Thank you, Mr. Turner, for coming to us with this. It's good to have closure, at least."

"Yes, thank you," Rebecca said. "Would you care to stay for lunch?"

"Oh, I . . . "

"Please. We may not have been close to Mike's father toward the end, but we still loved him, and hearing about his passing . . . I think it would be easier on all of us if we had someone here who knew him in his last days to tell us more about him."

Gideon looked at Mike. "Is that all right with you?"

"Yes." Mike sniffed, wiping his nose with his thumb. "Yes, that would be fine."

"Then yes. I'll stay."

Rebecca rose and walked to Mike's side. Her husband stood, and the two hugged. Then Rebecca crossed to Patrick and hugged him, too.

"Thank you," she said to Gideon.

She exited the living room. Mike sat back down, as did Patrick. Gideon settled back on the couch and wondered what he should say now.

Mike cleared his throat. "You mentioned you were on a mission trip. I take it you're a Christian, too?"

"I am." Gideon nodded. "My father is a pastor. I am—was—a doctor, a surgeon. I went to Venezuela to help at a clinic sponsored by my church."

Patrick leaned closer, that sharp blue gaze fixed on Gideon. "Why aren't you a doctor anymore?"

"I had to do some things to survive in Venezuela that I'm not proud of, and after that, I didn't think I was worthy of it."

"Oh."

"Where are you from?" Mike asked.

"Sojourn City."

Patrick shifted on the couch. Gideon glanced over at him. There was something in his eyes . . . Did he know about the Seraph? Had saying the name of Sojourn City sparked recognition in the boy's mind? The news had to have spread around the country by now, but Gideon wasn't exactly trending on social media. Not yet, anyway. But from the way Patrick looked at him, the boy might know something.

"What do you do now if you're not a doctor?" Mike asked.

"I work in a laboratory for my best friend, Dean Sterling. He's the CEO of Sterling Enterprises."

"I believe I've heard of it."

"Excuse me." Patrick jumped to his feet. "I've got to . . . use the restroom. I'll be back."

Gideon watched Patrick go upstairs, and then returned his attention to his conversation with Mike. He hoped he'd have another opportunity to bring up his faith. It's what Joshua would have wanted.

CHAPTER 4

The meeting with the Sterling Enterprises board went better than Dean could've hoped. He presented his idea and intentions for the maglev in Sojourn City, knowing that if they didn't like it, his might be the shortest-lived reign of a CEO in company history.

To his relief, they were impressed with the technology that went into the maglev and immediately began discussing how such a mode of transportation could generate revenue in other cities. Places like San Francisco that still used railcars would pay generously to have them replaced by faster, more efficient maglevs. Other cities would follow suit. This one project could be a boon for Sterling Enterprises.

Dean hadn't intended that; he just wanted to help his city. He was paying for Sojourn's maglev out of pocket, and the board loved the publicity angle: their CEO as a benefactor of a downtrodden city. Other cities would see the Sojourn maglev as a demonstration, and when it worked, they would pay to have one for themselves. The CEO would gain public appreciation, and the company would gain business.

Dean left the conference room much happier and less nervous than he had been when he walked in, but he was glad to be out of there. As soon as the large, wooden doors shut behind him, he grabbed his tie by the knot and yanked the green length of fabric free from his neck.

He unbuttoned the top button of his shirt and relaxed his shoulders. That was so much better. He could breathe again.

"Sir?"

Dean turned. A middle-aged man in a lab coat stood nearby. A badge on his lapel displayed the name "Holcomb."

"Yes?"

"Mr. Coleman told me I should take you to the labs to see some samples of aionium."

"Oh! Yes, of course. Lead the way."

Dean followed the older man down the hall to the elevator bank. The scientist called the elevator and looked at Dean.

"It's a pleasure to have you here, Mr. Sterling. I hope you'll be pleased with our progress. We believe aionium could be the next step in military-grade armor."

"That's what I'm hoping for."

The elevator doors slid open, and Dean stepped inside with the scientist. Holcomb clicked the fourth-floor button. When the elevator reached the lab, Dean stepped out—

Into a geek's paradise. The lab was full of cutting-edge tech that Dean had seen schematics for but had never had the opportunity to see in person. Cryo-ray guns, actual hoverboards, magnetic shoes . . . Most of this tech was still years away from distribution. He shook himself from his reverie and fell in behind Holcomb as the scientist strode away toward one corner of the lab.

"This isn't our full lab, of course; only a testing facility," Holcomb said. "Our main lab is at another facility miles away, where most of our research and development is done. This floor is for the technology that is ready to be demonstrated—to someone such as yourself, for example."

"Of course." That was encouraging. If aionium was ready for demonstration, Dean should be able to get his hands on some for Gideon's new Seraph suit. "I'm impressed."

"Thank you, sir."

Holcomb led Dean to a small room in the back corner. Along the far wall was a sheet of metal—aionium, no doubt. A young Asian woman stood next to a table that was loaded with different kinds of weapons, ranging from handguns to assault rifles.

Holcomb waved to the woman. "Dr. Yei, this is Mr. Sterling."

"Hello." Yei extended her hand. "Pleasure to have you with us, sir."

Dean shook her hand. "The pleasure's mine. This place is amazing. That's the aionium, I take it?"

"Yes." Yei picked up a handgun. "I was just about to test to make sure that it retains its durability once it's been refined."

"Go ahead."

Holcomb closed the door behind them. Dean moved against the wall, and Holcomb stood next to him and handed him a pair of earplugs. Dean put them in. Yei checked the handgun, stepped back, and fired. Smoke drifted through the room. When it cleared, Yei approached the sheet of aionium. Dean stepped up next to her. As far as he could tell, the bullets hadn't left a scratch.

He whistled. "Impressive."

"Indeed. But that was only small-arms fire. Let's see how it holds up against some heavier weaponry."

Yei tested the aionium against a shotgun, an Uzi, and a fully automatic assault rifle. None of them left so much as a mark in the metal. Dean scratched the back of his head and blinked.

"I think it's safe to say it lives up to the hype."

"I'd say so," Holcomb agreed.

"I'm very pleased with your work here." Dean shook Yei's and Holcomb's hands again. "I'll send a request for a special project that involves aionium soon. I'd like you two to see to it personally. Very top secret; please don't share the details with anyone."

Yei inclined her head. "Understood."

"I'll keep in touch." Dean opened the door. "Again, good work."

He strode back into the main lab and glanced at the tech scattered around the room. Some of the world's most bleeding-edge advancements were coming from people who worked under him. That *was* pretty amazing.

Dean walked through the lab toward the elevator. He was done here for the day, but Gideon hadn't called him yet. Maybe he'd head back to the hotel and go for a swim. It was uncomfortably warm outside; maybe an hour in the hotel's pool would do him some good. He stepped into the elevator and hit the ground floor button.

His phone rang. Maybe he'd have to stop and pick up Gideon after all. He pulled his phone out, but the number it displayed wasn't Gideon. He frowned and answered it.

"This is Dean."

"Mr. Sterling? I'm sorry to bother you, sir." Dean recognized the voice of one of the chairman's secretaries. "There is a woman here who is requesting an appointment with you."

"Who is it?"

"Artemis Wayans, from Crowne Pharmaceuticals. She says she has a business proposition for you, sir. She didn't specify what."

Crowne Pharmaceuticals? Dean had never heard of them. He checked his watch. "I've got a few minutes. Send her up to the fortieth-floor conference room. I'll meet her there."

"Yes, sir."

Dean didn't recognize Wayans' name and couldn't recall ever hearing or reading it in any scientific or business journals. Who was this unknown woman who worked for a mysterious company and was bold enough to stride into the lobby to ask for an appointment with the CEO?

If she was new on the scene, maybe she didn't fully grasp business protocol yet. But Dean wasn't one to stand on ceremony. He didn't care for the CEO title, and he was not going to get a big head about it. The day he refused someone because of "protocol" was the day he'd ask Gideon to shoot him in the pants with a blast of light—and then he'd retire.

Hearing Wayans out couldn't hurt. Even if her proposition was ridiculous, he had no reason to refuse her until he knew what she had to say. Maybe it would even be worth listening to.

* * *

"So, Gideon, is there anyone special in your life?" Rebecca asked.

Gideon smiled. "Yes. My girlfriend, Jolie. We've dated for a long time, but my year in Venezuela put a few bumps in the relationship."

"I can imagine. But that smile . . . you two are on the mend now?"

"We are."

The room lapsed into an uncomfortable silence. Gideon pressed his lips together and placed his silverware on his empty plate. As kind as they were, he'd only just met these people. There was only so much they could talk about, especially since he didn't want to push Joshua's death in their faces too much. He didn't want to leave too abruptly, nor did he want to linger impolitely.

"Well, Gideon." Mike pushed away from the dining room table and smiled tightly. "Thank you for bringing us news about my father. It's . . . good to have closure."

Thank you. Mike's gratitude brought a sense of finality to the meal. Gideon could excuse himself now. "It was the least I could do for the family of the man who saved my life. Thank you for your hospitality. And thank you, Mrs. Omer, for a great dinner."

"You're welcome." Rebecca smiled. "It was good to have you."

Patrick had been oddly silent for most of the meal. Gideon wasn't sure if it was a cultural thing, if he was sad about his grandfather, or if he really did know more about Gideon than he let on. Gideon probed him with his mental powers, but all he felt was conflict. Patrick was wrestling with something. That was understandable, given what he'd just learned about his grandfather.

"I should probably get going. My friend Dean has to pick me up, and I don't want to keep him waiting." Gideon's phone vibrated. "That must be him now. Thank you again, and if you need anything or have any questions, don't hesitate to reach out. Sojourn City's a long way from here, but if it's within my power, I'll do what I can to help."

"Thank you." Mike extended his hand, and Gideon shook it. "Take care, Gideon. And thank you again."

Gideon wondered if the thank you was also for his presence as a guest who wasn't only there to interrogate Patrick.

"You're welcome."

Gideon stood, told Rebecca and Patrick goodbye, and stepped out into the hallway. He probed each of them one last time with his powers. Rebecca seemed sad, mostly, while Mike was stern and . . . disappointed? He wondered if it was about Joshua's faith in Christ.

Gideon wished he'd had more time to persuade the Omers—but over the course of time, not all at once within a few hours.

He walked outside and closed the front door behind him. Dean wasn't sitting in the car on the curb. Gideon frowned and checked his phone. The notification had indeed been from Dean—a text message. *In a meeting. I sent a limo for you.*

Gideon tucked his phone in his pocket and trod down the steps to the sidewalk. He'd just have to wait here for the car to show up. He looked out at the sky. *Promise fulfilled, Joshua.* He hoped the old man knew he'd done all he could to tell his family about his faith. They hadn't really presented an opportunity at dinner, but he'd left it open for them to contact him if they ever needed him. And he'd told them plainly about Joshua's conversion, too.

The door opened. "Mr. Turner! Gideon."

Patrick bounded down the steps toward him and grabbed him by the bicep, moving him away from the house.

"What's up?"

"I need to talk to you." Patrick started walking down the sidewalk. "But away from my parents."

"I need to wait here so my driver knows where to pick me up."

"We won't go far. Just down the block. Please, it's important."

"How can I help?"

"I've seen the news. You're him, aren't you? You're *that* Gideon Turner. The Seraph."

Gideon closed his eyes. "I was wondering if you figured that out. Yes, that's me."

"Do you think you might be able to help me with something? There's a problem that I've been dealing with recently . . . "

Gideon stopped in his tracks. "If this is about showing up to scare off a bully or to impress some girl—"

"No, no." Patrick held up his hands. "Nothing like that. It's just . . . I . . . watch."

An abrupt gust of wind tousled Gideon's hair. He blinked, and when his eyes opened, Patrick was gone. Gideon's eyes widened, and he looked around. Patrick had vanished in less than a second.

"Over here!"

Gideon swiveled his head around. Patrick stood about a dozen meters from where he had been a moment ago, leaning against a stop sign. A blur rippled through the air, a gust of wind rushed from the opposite direction, and Patrick was again standing next to Gideon.

"What did you just do?"

"I ran. Really, really fast." Patrick's words were coming out rapidly, like an audio file played in fast forward. "It happened a couple months ago, and I haven't really known what to do about it. I didn't tell my parents because I didn't want them to freak out. I've been looking for other people like me, and I'd all but given up when I saw you on the news. I never thought you'd show up at my front door."

"Slow down, kid." Gideon put a hand on Patrick's shoulder. "You're telling me that you have superspeed?"

"Yep. Pretty much."

"And you have no idea how you got it?"

Had Patrick gotten his powers from Ashcroft, too? If so, there might be some clues to the mad scientist's whereabouts here in the city. Gideon could begin his search in San Francisco, instead of traveling to the other side of the world. But what were the chances that Ashcroft just so happened to be in the same city as the family of another man he'd captured? Unless he'd intentionally sought Patrick out, knowing he was related to Joshua . . .

"I have a couple ideas, but they don't really make sense. We can talk about that later. Can you help me? I've been trying to use my powers to help other people, but I'm not very good."

"Patrick—" A limo rounded the corner. "Give me your phone." Gideon entered his number. "Call me tomorrow. I'll see if I can convince my friend to stay in town at least a couple extra days."

"Will do! Thank you so much, Gideon. Or should I say Seraph? It's an honor, by the way. I can't believe I'm talking to an actual superhero . . . "

"I'll talk to you tomorrow."

"Sounds good." Patrick jogged back to his house—at normal speed. "Later!"

Gideon climbed into the back of the limo. This was an unexpected turn of events. But maybe it was all meant to be. Gideon wasn't a big believer in coincidences. Maybe God had orchestrated all this so Gideon could find Ashcroft now, before he did something that a lot of people would regret.

Time would tell. Finding Ashcroft might prove easy compared to trying to teach someone with powers how to use them. For that, Gideon was sure he was unready. *Lord, help me.*

* * *

Dean Sterling was an odd sort. Artemis could tell as soon as she entered the conference room that he was not a typical CEO. She'd read up on him and knew he hadn't been groomed for the role. He'd taken it only because his father had gone to prison. That was interesting enough on its own, and even more interesting was Sterling's companion.

She knew she'd recognized him. Gideon Turner. One of Ashcroft's successes. What would her mentor want her to do about Turner? Artemis would have to ask him later. For now, the mission came first.

Sterling sat at one end of the conference table, dressed in a business suit but missing a tie. His hair was unruly and looked as though it had been finger-combed into place and then subsequently left to its own devices. Not at all the look of the scion of a multibillion-dollar company. More rock star than businessman. She strutted across the room, maintaining eye contact with every step, and extended a hand. She kept her shoulders squared, her expression friendly.

"Hello. I'm Artemis Wayans."

Sterling rose and shook her hand. "A pleasure to meet you, Miss Wayans."

"The pleasure's mine, Mr. Sterling."

The boy smiled. It was not the smirk of a flirtatious charmer, although he had the looks for it. Instead, it was the disarming, boyish smile of an innocent child. The dimple on his chin completed the look. *An odd sort, indeed.* Most scions were arrogant playboys. She'd half expected his eyes to creep leeringly over her body as she approached. Counted on it, almost. She'd picked her outfit with that in mind. Instead, he'd maintained eye contact just as steadily as she had, and continued to do so.

"Just Dean, please."

"Then call me Artemis." She waited for Sterling to sit and took the chair catty corner to him. "I'm impressed, Dean. To be a CEO at your age . . . "

"Not my own doing." His smile faltered. "My father's . . . absence made it a necessity."

"Yes, I heard about Mr. Sterling's incarceration. I'm sorry. It couldn't have been easy to find out that your father was involved in criminal activity."

"No, it wasn't. But he had his reasons. Whether his methods were wrong or not, he accomplished what he set out to do." Dean looked down at the tabletop and then back up at her. "But we're not here to discuss my father. You had a business proposition for me, Artemis?"

"Yes." Artemis clasped her hands and leaned forward against the table. "I represent a movement with access to scientific research and development unparalleled in today's world. We stand on the verge of a great breakthrough, one that could change the course of history, but we lack the equipment to see it to fruition."

She wasn't foolish enough to think that talking so grandly would dazzle the boy. Young and innocent as he was, she could tell he was sharp. There was a bit of skepticism hidden behind the good nature in his eyes, an intelligence that he covered with his wit and charm. Dean was a shrewd man. She wondered what he thought of her. She put on her best smile and continued her pitch.

* * *

Her skin almost obsidian and hair dyed a shade lighter than her complexion, Artemis Wayans was an impressive figure. She was tall—even without the heels she wore, she would've been the same height as Dean. With them, she towered above him. *Subtle intimidation tactic?* Interesting. It wasn't how he would've expected her to approach him.

Her dark eyes never wavered from his. Dean found himself struggling not to blink, lest it be taken as a sign of weakness. She wore a deep blue sleeveless dress with a low neckline, perfectly tailored to her lithe figure. He was sure her outfit, along with everything about her, had been specifically chosen to amplify her presence.

But more than her appearance or her outfit, what impressed him was the way she composed herself. She projected total authority, spoke with passion about her "movement" and their revolutionary ideas, and carried an air of confidence that indicated she was sure he would agree to whatever she asked. It was a business tactic—Dean knew that even without an MBA. She was projecting confidence that he would agree with her proposition so that he would feel unreasonable if he declined.

Her offer left something to be desired. He knew a vague and shady pitch when he heard one. She made no direct reference to Crowne Pharmaceuticals or exactly what her "movement" was working on, nor had she stated the name of her employer. Her confidence might be a decoy, keeping his attention off the research that might be less than altruistic—or even legal. Dean had watched his father shoot down enough similar proposals to know that directness without transparency did not make for good business. Or, too often it did make for good business in a world of sly winks and under-the-table deals. Dean was not going to run his company that way. Honesty was one of the cornerstones of Sterling Enterprises. It always had been, or so Dean had thought until Dad's misdeeds, and he was determined to return to that.

"Sterling Labs has designed a device perfectly suited for our purposes: an aerosol dispersal device that is in its prototype stages, if I am not mistaken. We're not asking for charity. In the end, you would stand poised to reap the benefits of our work."

He pursed his lips. "What exactly are you asking, Artemis? You want us to hand you this device? Its blueprints?"

"Either option would be satisfactory, yes. We are aware that the device will require some time to perfect. We're only asking you to consider loaning it to us so that we may progress with our project."

"And the nature of the project?"

"I'm afraid that's not my place to tell. My employer didn't give me the authority to disclose those details."

"Let me get this straight. You want me, based on nothing more than faith in your word, to turn a prototype, patent-pending device over to you—a representative of a company I've never heard of?"

"Not to me—to my employer."

"You've spoken a lot about your employer, but you haven't said who he is. I also note you've failed to mention Crowne Pharmaceuticals, even though your initial message identified you as an employee of that company."

She settled back in her seat. "I'm afraid you wouldn't recognize his name if I told you. He's somewhat of a pariah among the scientific community, and as a newcomer to this business. I doubt you'd know him."

Dean laughed. "You clearly haven't done enough research. I may be new to the CEO position, but I've been a science geek ever since I've had access to a laboratory. I know pretty much anybody who's anybody in the scientific community—outcasts and heroes alike."

He studied Artemis' face. Her expression remained pleasant and unfazed, but there was something behind her eyes, a flicker of caution . . .

"Jeremiah Ashcroft."

Dean blinked, but otherwise did his best to keep his expression passive. Ashcroft, as in the guy who'd kidnapped Gideon and given him his powers? They didn't know his first name, but what were the odds of that surname popping up here? It would explain her reluctance to divulge the details of their work. "We're trying to give people superhuman powers through illegal experimentation" wasn't going to fly with most CEOs.

"I'm afraid you were correct." Dean shrugged modestly. "Never heard of him."

"As I suspected. What kind of assurances would you need for this deal to happen?"

"Forgive me for asking, Artemis, but why did you choose me? The new CEO is green enough to give up a potential cash cow on the promise of some future reward just because a pretty girl with wavy hair and a tight dress bats her eyelashes at him. Is that it?"

Artemis' smile still didn't waver, but her eyes were all steel. He'd hit a nerve. He was right. She had been trying to take advantage of him. He didn't need Gideon's empathic powers to tell him that. He clasped his hands and placed them on the table in front of him.

"I don't know Ashcroft, but you can go tell him that until he's ready to divulge the details of his projects and provide a concrete proposal, he doesn't need to bother sending anyone else to negotiate with me. Sterling Enterprises will not do business with Crowne Pharmaceuticals." He smiled wanly. "Is that all, Miss Wayans?"

Artemis clenched her jaw, no doubt formulating a response. Dean maintained eye contact with her. She tilted her head as if listening to something, and her expression cleared.

"Very well." Artemis stood and straightened her dress. "I'm sorry we couldn't come to an agreement, Mr. Sterling. Good day."

"Good day, ma'am."

He held his smile until she disappeared through the door. Then he slumped back in his seat and exhaled. Maybe she wasn't powered.

Or maybe she was and had just used her better judgment in deciding that turning Sterling's new CEO into a frog in his own building might not be the wisest course of action. Either way, he was still alive, and now they had a potential lead on Ashcroft. He hadn't expected that when he'd come to the office.

He needed to get the schematics for Gideon's new suit to Yei now. The Seraph might need it sooner than he expected.

CHAPTER 5

Jolie stepped out of her car, examined the chaotic scene in front of her, and shook her head. *Well, I wanted an exciting case.* It was the middle of the day, and a car had wrapped around a streetlight. No one had been injured, but the driver was missing. Two officers and a CSI were gathered around the totaled vehicle. Jolie crossed the street and ducked under a length of yellow crime scene tape to meet them.

One of the officers looked up. "Detective."

"What's the situation?" Jolie asked.

"Witnesses say the driver climbed out of the car right after the accident and ran like the devil was chasing him." The officer shrugged. "My guess is he was drunk."

"No way," the second cop said. "If he was drunk enough to do this in broad daylight, no way he would've been able to run that fast without falling down."

"Get a description?" Jolie asked.

"White or Latino male, late twenties to early thirties, wearing a brown hoodie, blue jeans, and white shoes."

"A hoodie? In this weather?" Sojourn City never got terribly hot, but it was warm and humid. Wearing a hoodie in the summer was all but asking for heat stroke. "Wonder if he had a reason to dress like that."

"To hide his face, maybe?" The officer frowned. "It wouldn't work if you're looking right at him or if a street cam caught his face, but witnesses might not get a good look."

"As evidenced by our only physical description being 'most likely white male.'" She sighed. "So, this guy's in the wind. Put out a BOLO and let me know if you find anything else."

"Yes, Detective."

The officer motioned to his partner, and the two of them returned to their cruiser. Jolie knelt by the CSI, Nate Walker, who was examining the crashed car. It was silver, probably a decade old. The driver's door hung open. Chunks of glass filled the seat and floor; the driver probably sustained some cuts and bruises.

The CSI glanced at her. "Detective."

"Nate, you know you can call me Jolie. What do we have?"

"We might be able to get some blood off these glass shards." Nate scooped them into a plastic bag. "Fingerprints on the steering wheel and door . . . other than that . . . wait, what's this?"

Nate reached down to the car's floor, picked up a gray pill, and studied it. Jolie grimaced. The driver hadn't been drunk—he'd been high. So much for something more exciting than drug dealers. Nate dropped the pill in another plastic bag.

She took the bag from him. "Any idea what kind of drug that is?"

"Not a clue." Nate looked at it through the bag. "Never seen anything like it before. I'll take it back to the lab for analysis and let you know what I find. You have any CIs who know the situation on the streets, I'd talk to them about what's in right now."

"Good idea." Jolie didn't know anyone, but maybe Carter did. "Let me know as soon as you have something, okay?"

"Will do."

Jolie stood, tucked a strand of hair behind her ear, and looked both ways before crossing back to her car. Despite the monotony of drug cases, this one might prove important. If there was a new drug circulating the Brooks, they needed to clamp down on it—fast. The city had already been through a siege. It didn't need an epidemic.

* * *

The more Wes thought about his decision, the more conflicted he became. He really didn't know what he wanted to do anymore. All he knew was that he was going crazy waiting around for a decision to strike him like a lightning bolt.

He studied the computer screen in front of him, scanning listings for apartments in the area. Gideon and Dean had tasked him with finding a place while they were gone, and that offered the perfect distraction to keep his mind off his own indecision. He found several options that he liked and wrote down their addresses to share with his soon-to-be roommates when they returned to the city.

Wes took a bite of a peach and leaned back in his chair. His parents weren't home—Dad was at the church, and Mom was running some errand or another. Wes had the house to himself right now. Despite that freedom, Wes felt completely constricted. He finished off the peach, tossed the core in the trash, and headed out the door.

Wes hopped in his car and drummed his hands on the steering wheel as his mind wandered to his brother's life as a superhero. It had all started with stakeouts in the Brooks. With Gideon out of town, someone had to watch over the Brooks, right? On impulse, Wes drove to Dean and Gideon's apartment, using the spare key they'd lent him to get inside. He rushed up to the lair on the second floor and stared at the Seraph costume.

No, Gideon would kill me.

That wasn't the only uniform. Dean had turned one of the prototypes for Gideon's suit into Carter's Crusader suit, but there was still a second prototype sitting in a heap in the corner. No one would miss it . . .

Wes snagged the uniform, rushed back to his car, and drove toward the Brooks. The farther he drove, the more determined he was to keep going. He could pretend to be a hero for a day. He parked at the East Brooks Refuge Church campus, changed into the uniform, and hit the streets.

It was hard to believe that it had been less than a year since he'd taken a knife wound to the shoulder while defending the church from Romanian mobsters. Although there was still trash and refuse in the streets, the Brooks were safer and cleaner than he ever remembered them. It was a process—and it was working.

"Why am I here?" Wes wondered aloud. "This isn't accomplishing anything."

Maybe he was thinking about this too hard. Law school might really be the answer. The idea of becoming a hero like Gideon was nothing more than a childish fantasy. They were two different people. He had to find his own path. As long as he kept trying to be like his brother, he would never find contentment.

He rounded a corner, and someone toppled into him. Wes grunted and fell to the sidewalk, the other person's limbs flailing around him. Wes tucked his chin to protect his head, and his shoulders smacked against the pavement. Whoever had run into him landed on top and tried to scramble away.

"Watch it!" Wes growled.

"S-sorry." The voice was distinctly male. He sounded panicked. "Sorry."

The man pushed himself off, stared at Wes' outfit with wide eyes, and hurried away. Wes rolled around to watch him go, trying to see beneath his brown hoodie. He didn't catch more than a glimpse of the man's pointed features before he was gone. Wes pushed himself to his feet. As he did, he noticed some gray pills lying on the ground. They must've spilled out of the guy's pocket.

"Nice. Real nice."

He turned and continued walking. *Typical Wes. So busy fantasizing about being a hero that you miss a drug addict running right at you.* He stopped in his tracks and spun on his heel. Maybe that guy hadn't just been an addict. The way he'd been running . . . Maybe he was hiding something. Wes walked after the guy. Maybe he could follow him and find out something about the drug trade in the Brooks. He might even find something useful for the police.

* * *

Carter glanced up from the cash register as the entry bell above the door chimed. Jolie walked in and stepped to the side. Carter acknowledged her with a quick nod and returned to counting the money to hand back to the elderly man in line. He gave the man his change and turned to one of his coworkers.

"Raina, you want to take over for a second?"

"Sure thing."

"Thanks." Carter stepped out from behind the register. "I'll be right back."

Jolie didn't typically visit him at the store. In fact, she'd never done that before. For that matter, she didn't contact him as the Crusader often. This must be important. He wound his way down one of the aisles and stood in a back corner, near a rack of energy drinks. She walked back to him and stepped into the corner.

"What's up?" he asked.

"Looking for a guy. White male, probably thirties, wearing a brown hoodie. Seen him today?"

"A hoodie, in this weather?" He looked down at his own green t-shirt. "I don't think so, but I'll keep my eye out for him. What'd he do?"

"Crashed his car and left it. CSI discovered some gray pills in the car. Which leads me to my second question: heard anything about a new drug on the streets?"

"Not that I can think of. I've got a few coworkers who might; I can ask around."

"See what you can find out, but don't be too obvious. I don't want you getting yourself in deeper than you can handle."

"Girl, I'm the Crusader." Carter grinned. "I'll be fine."

"Maybe, but you're still young, and the drug dealers in this city are hardened criminals. Remember, this isn't a game."

As Gideon constantly reminded him. Carter knew that better than they thought—he'd lost his dad to this life. Sometimes he wondered if they'd forgotten that. They meant well, though, and it wouldn't do any good to argue with her, so he just nodded.

"I'll let you know if I hear anything or see your boy in the hoodie."

"Thank you." Jolie smiled. "You may not think it's exciting, but you're helping me in a big way."

"It's cool."

"Stay in touch."

"Will do."

Carter walked back to the front of the store and stepped behind the register with Raina. Jolie exited the building, the door ringing behind her as she walked out. Raina glanced at Carter and moved aside so he could take over the register.

"What was that about?"

"Oh, nothing. Just a friend."

Raina's eyebrows crinkled. "A detective?"

Man. He'd been hoping Raina hadn't noticed the badge on Jolie's belt.

"Let's just get back to work, Rain. We've got a long day ahead of us."

* * *

After another hour of wandering around the Brooks, Wes was ready to give up for the day and go back to his car. He'd quickly lost track of the brown-hooded junkie, and he hadn't spotted any other suspicious activity. That was probably for the best; he didn't know what he'd do if he *did* see anything. He was strong, and he could throw a mean punch. He knew a few moves that Gideon had taught him, but that didn't make him Seraph or even Crusader material. He was just an average guy.

Still, he wanted to help. That had to count for something.

He kept his hands tucked in his pockets and circled back toward the church. He wished he'd been as lucky as Gideon to have powers. Not that he would take Gideon's for himself if he could; he just wished he was able to do the same kind of thing. He and Gideon could be a great team.

Someone screamed off to his left. Wes tensed and rushed in that direction. As he passed an alley, another scream echoed off the walls. He stopped in his tracks, ducked back, and peered into the alley. Two men had a young woman backed against the wall. One held a baseball bat. The other was reaching for her shoulders with both hands. Wes clenched his jaw and stepped into the alley. *Time to see what you're made of, Turner.*

"Leave her alone!"

The two men spun around, and for a second their expressions were masked in fear.

"Yo." The unarmed man backed up. "Is that—?"

Wes smirked. His resemblance to Gideon was strong, and the armored uniform would only add to the illusion. He strode toward them, hands balled into fists at his sides. The one with the bat looked him up and down and didn't seem quite as impressed. The mugger sneered and stepped toward Wes, raising his bat.

"This ain't the Seraph." The man swung. "Let's pop him!"

This is probably going to hurt. A lot. Didn't matter. He couldn't let them take advantage of that woman. He ducked under the swinging bat and brought his fist up into the man's ribs. The two men had moved away from the woman, and she stood there, trembling. He glanced past them and made eye contact with her.

"Run!" Wes shouted.

Broken from her daze, she sprinted for the other end of the alley. The guy with no weapon growled and took another step toward Wes as his comrade wheezed.

"Who do you think you are, kid?"

"Just a guy trying to help."

The man wielding the bat coughed out a laugh. "You'd better hope that one of the city's real heroes is nearby. Because if not, you're dead."

He ran forward, swinging the bat at Wes' head. Wes ducked under it, and when he stood back up, he jabbed his right fist at the man's face. The bat wielder reeled back and rubbed his jaw. His companion charged in. The thug grabbed Wes' extended arm, spun him around, and shoved him against one of the alley walls.

Wes tried to kick backwards at his assailant, but he couldn't see. The man grabbed the back of Wes' head and reared it back. Before he could slam it into the brick wall, Wes brought his foot over until he found the man's leg, and then stomped down as hard as he could on his foot.

The man screamed and loosened his grip on Wes just enough for him to spin around and punch him in the gut. As the man doubled over, his friend with the bat came in again. Wes raised an arm, and the wooden club smashed into Wes' forearm. The armored gauntlet took the worst of the blow, but it still hurt. Then the unarmed man stepped in and punched Wes. Hard.

Wes went down. His head struck the pavement with a sharp crack. The two men hammered him with blows. He curled up in the fetal position as the unarmed man kicked him in the gut and the face, while the guy with the bat brought his weapon down on Wes' shoulders and back.

"Freeze!"

The blows stopped. Footsteps pounded down the alleyway. Wes looked up. Both men were running away from him. He rolled over. Jolie stood nearby, handgun trained on the men. She looked down at him—and her eyes widened.

"Wes?" She rushed to his side. "Are you okay?"

"Just . . . wanted to . . . help." He tried to stand and grimaced. His back and chest were sore, and his head was throbbing. He touched it, and his fingers came away sticky with blood. "Guess I . . . didn't do too good."

"Come on, we need to get you to a doctor."

Jolie holstered her pistol and wrapped an arm around Wes' shoulders. He leaned into her and wobbled to his feet. Every inch off the ground was agony, but he pushed through it. She walked him out of the alley. Her car was sitting in the middle of the street, the driver's door ajar and the engine still running.

"Thank you."

Jolie opened the front passenger door and helped Wes slide in. "You're lucky I was passing by."

She closed the door and walked around the car to her side. He leaned back in his seat and groaned. Even the soft leather of the headrest didn't ease the pain in his head. Jolie got in and put the car in drive.

"You know we're going to have a long talk about this, right?"

Wes sighed. "Yeah . . . I know."

CHAPTER 6

Following was difficult for someone used to leading. Artemis had been a leader almost all her life. She was class president in high school and editor in chief of her college newspaper. Not long after graduation, she went into local politics and was quite successful. She was the first black woman to serve on her town's city council and only stepped away from the role when Ashcroft recruited her.

She was an idea person, a motivator, a goal-oriented leader charismatic enough to get people behind her. She had always thrived in positions of leadership and felt hampered when she had to follow. It was why Ashcroft had chosen her to be second in command of the Regency, the name behind all the shell corporations. But that also meant that there were times that she had to listen to his instructions.

This was one such time. On any other occasion, she would've stayed and negotiated with Dean Sterling until he acquiesced. As she had spoken with him, Ashcroft had contacted her through the communicator implant he'd placed in her inner ear. She was to back off the hunt for the devices on his list. Instead, she was to watch Sterling and let him lead her back to his superhero friend. She could've easily done both, but Ashcroft didn't like when she argued with him. Reluctantly, she had ceded the meeting with Sterling.

She couldn't follow Sterling in her limo; he would have made her in a second. She ordered her driver to return to her hotel and sat on a bench outside Sterling Enterprises. The parking garage was across the street, so most of the employees would have to pass her to get to their cars. That would provide several opportunities for her to acquire transportation.

A young man—probably an accountant, judging by his dress and the satchel he carried—stepped past her. Artemis rose from the bench and intercepted him.

"Excuse me," she said.

The man's eyes flicked over to her. "Yes?"

Artemis reached out with her mind. "I need to borrow your car."

He reached into his pocket and withdrew his keys. "Second floor of the parking garage, silver Escalade."

"Thank you."

Artemis crossed the street, leaving the dazed accountant standing next to the bench. When he came to his senses, he'd no doubt wonder where his car keys had gone. His memory of her would be so fuzzy he wouldn't be able to give the police her description. They would put a BOLO out on his car, but she wouldn't need it for long.

She pulled out of the parking garage and watched for Sterling. Five minutes later, a silver sports car pulled away from Sterling Enterprises and merged into traffic. Artemis waited for a count of five and drove after it. She drifted back, keeping a reasonable distance between her and Sterling.

The sports car parked outside an opulent hotel. Artemis circled the building once and parked in the front lot. Sterling's friend—Turner—was probably inside. She could have gone in, grabbed him right then, and taken him back to Ashcroft. But Ashcroft hadn't ordered her to do that yet, so she would just watch. She would study Turner. The more she knew about him and his abilities, the easier it would be to bring him in.

And then she could get back to doing things her way.

* * *

Gideon paced in the suite, thoughts spinning through his head so fast he could have lifted off the floor. *How can I teach Patrick? I don't even know how his powers work.* It had been hard enough to master his own powers. How could he understand a stranger's?

Maybe he needed to start with how his own powers worked. When he had first received his powers, they activated without his consent whenever he felt fear or anger. He had taught himself to be more passive and to control how much light he allowed to escape his body. His martial arts training had helped; he'd already been disciplined to slow his breathing and empty his mind of distracting thoughts. Using this training, he had learned to manipulate his powers through visualization. Maybe that was how Patrick's powers worked, too. If not, he didn't know what he'd tell the kid. *What if I screw up?* What if, in trying to teach Patrick how to use his powers, Gideon only confused him and made him more dangerous?

This was crazy. Gideon wasn't ready to be a teacher. He was a vigilante, a solo agent who went out and beat up bad guys. He had superpowers, sure, but he didn't consider himself a superhero, not the way Dean and the majority of Sojourn City did. Gideon couldn't teach Patrick to be what he wasn't himself.

He glanced at the door. Where was Dean? Gideon had been back at the hotel for an hour, and he was still alone. Dean's meeting must have been important.

Gideon leaned against the window and looked out at San Francisco. It was a great view, not unlike the one of Sojourn City from Dean and Gideon's apartment. He could picture Jolie looking up at the sky in Sojourn City. There was something romantic to the idea that they were hundreds of miles apart but seeing the same stars.

Romance. Gideon chuckled. When was the last time they'd had time for that? When was the last time he'd put on a tie and she'd put on a dress, and they'd gone out for an evening together? Far too long.

The door opened, and Gideon turned around. Dean closed the door behind him, walked into the living room, and slumped down on the couch. He let out a long, loud groan.

"You okay?" Gideon asked.

"Long day. And boy, do I have something to tell you."

"Me, too, actually."

Dean closed his eyes. "Why don't you go first? Because when I tell you mine, you're going to want to stay on the subject for a minute."

Gideon raised an eyebrow. "Okay . . . Well, when you dropped me off at the Omers' house, I told them all about Joshua and what had happened to him. They asked me to stay for lunch, so I did. After I left, Patrick followed me out."

"What did he want? Talk more about his grandpa?"

"That's what I thought, too, but no." Gideon sat down across from Dean. "He knew that I was the Seraph. He saw me on the news, and when I told his family I was from Sojourn City, he put two and two together."

"What did he want? Autograph? A cameo at his school to make him popular?"

"Not exactly." Gideon took a deep breath. "He has powers."

Dean's eyes popped open. *"What?"*

"He ran—so fast that all I saw was a blur. He was down the block from me in less than a second."

"Whoa. Where . . . how did he get his powers?"

"I don't know. He hasn't told me yet. He wants me to train him. He says he's not very good at using his speed yet."

"Makes sense, I guess. You're the only known superhero in the world, and you just happened to fall practically in his lap. Of course he'd want you to teach him how to do what you do."

There was that word again. Superhero. What if all Gideon could teach Patrick was how to put the hurt on common criminals? The boy deserved so much more than that.

"What if I can't?"

"Don't think like that. You can do this, man."

"I hope so. All my progress was trial and error—not to mention a bit of help from you."

"Well, I'll help him out, too. We're a team, Gid. We'll do this together. That kid will be speeding through the streets and stopping bad guys in no time."

Gideon chewed the inside of his lip. "This could also mean that Ashcroft has been here, in San Francisco."

Dean's eyes shifted away. "Speaking of . . . The meeting I was in today was with a woman named Artemis Wayans. She wants us to loan out a Sterling Labs prototype distributor to her employer, but she was evasive about who he was and why he wanted it. When I pressed her, she told me his name was Jeremiah Ashcroft."

Gideon leaned back in his seat and blew out a breath. One of Ashcroft's employees was in San Francisco, and so was a young man who had developed superspeed. There was no way that was a coincidence. But if Ashcroft had a hand in this, why was Patrick living with his parents and not in a cage somewhere, like Gideon and Joshua had been?

"What did you tell her?"

"I told her no, and I didn't let her know that I had heard of Ashcroft before."

"That's good." Gideon stood. "Looks like we'll be staying in San Francisco a little longer than we thought. Can you make that new suit here?"

"Yeah. I'll send the schematics to the people working with the aionium and tell them to put a rush on it."

"Thanks. I'm going to call Jolie and let her know what's going on. Then we can talk about where we go from here."

* * *

"So this kid, the grandson of the man you were imprisoned with in Venezuela, happens to *also* have superpowers, and you think they were given to him by the same man who gave you yours?" Jolie shook her head. "This sounds like a lot of coincidences, Gid."

"I know. It's strange. That's why I can't come home yet. If Ashcroft is here, or this Artemis woman who works for him is on the lookout for powered people, Patrick could be in danger. Besides, I was going to search for Ashcroft anyway. Might as well start here, where we've got a lead."

"You're right. Just . . . be careful."

"I will. And I'll be back as soon as I possibly can. Is everything going all right there?"

Jolie looked over at Wes. Doctor Edwin, a member of the Turners' church and one of the few people who'd known Gideon's secret before the news broadcast, had finished applying a cast to Wes' arm and was stitching up the cuts on his head. Even though the suit had taken the shock of the blow to his arm, the impact had still fractured the bone. Jolie wouldn't tell Gideon about his younger brother's activities yet. That should come from Wes himself.

"Mostly. We may have a new drug on the streets—some gray pill. I've got Carter on the lookout for a suspect, and I'll keep an eye on him and make sure he doesn't get into trouble."

"Good. You'll wrap this up in no time. If you can take on the Romanian mob, what can some drug dealers do?"

"Don't tempt fate, Gideon."

"Sorry. I believe in you—you and Carter. Tell him I'm proud of him, okay?"

"I will."

"I miss you. We need to have a date night when I get back—time just for the two of us. A night with no police work, no vigilantism . . . Just you and me out to dinner, maybe a movie, a walk in the park . . . "

"That sounds lovely." Jolie imagined the feeling of Gideon's lips against hers. Butterflies fluttered through her stomach. "I can't wait."

"I love you."

"Love you, too."

Jolie tucked her phone back into her pocket and walked over to Wes' bedside. Edwin finished the stitching and stepped back. The lingering thoughts of Gideon's promised date kept passing through Jolie's mind. It wasn't easy to push them aside and focus on the problem in front of her.

"Nothing too serious," Edwin said. "He does have a bruised rib and a hairline fracture in his arm, and he needs to keep from exerting himself too much for a bit. But I've seen worse. He'll recover quickly enough, so long as he stays out of trouble."

Wes sighed. "I'm right here, Doc. You can talk to me. And don't worry. I'll be more careful."

"Yes, see that you do." He glanced at Jolie. "Thanks for bringing him in."

"No problem." Jolie helped Wes stand. "Let's get you home—and out of that suit. Your parents will freak if they see you in it."

Wes limped a little bit but was otherwise moving just fine. Jolie took it slow and walked beside him in case he stumbled and needed support.

"Did you say something about gray pills earlier?" Wes asked.

"I did. What, you know something?"

"I saw some earlier today. This guy in a brown hoodie ran into me and spilled some of those pills all over the sidewalk."

"Where was he going? Could you tell?"

"He was running back in the direction I had been walking from. I had parked at the East Brooks church. I tried to follow him, but he lost me pretty quick."

"Thank you, Wes. That might be a big help."

His eyes brightened. "Really?"

"Really."

There were few hot spots for drug dealers in the East Brooks. If that was where the guy had been going, then he was likely meeting a dealer in one of those locations. She could narrow her search, and that would save a lot of time. Maybe Gideon was right. Maybe she would get this guy in no time.

"Now, don't get a big head about this, but I am glad you were out there. If you hadn't been, we wouldn't have this lead." Jolie opened the car door for Wes. "That doesn't mean I want you back out there, though."

"I know, I know. Don't worry. I learned my lesson."

Have you? Jolie watched Wes as he eased gingerly into the passenger seat. She'd been through this once already with Gideon. If Wes was anything like his brother—and he was, more than he'd ever care to admit—he had decidedly not learned his lesson.

* * *

"Where are you going to train Patrick?" Dean asked.

"That's a great question." Gideon scratched his cheek. "Obviously I can't teach him to use superspeed in the streets. His identity should stay a secret. He's still a kid; he doesn't need the world to know he's got powers. There's too much pressure—and too much danger."

"Which means he'll need a suit." Dean grinned. "One with different specs than yours because of the nature of his powers. Something aerodynamic that won't hinder him when he runs and will offer protection from the extreme heat he'll experience at high speeds . . . I'll get to work."

"Still leaves us with the problem of 'where.'"

"You can use Sterling Labs. I'll have the testing floor cleared out and just tell everyone it's for a top-secret project. I'll make sure no one disturbs you."

"Sounds good. I'd also like you to run a blood test on Patrick to see if the results are similar to mine."

"Will do." Dean opened his laptop and began typing. "I just sent the schematics for your new suit to Yei. I'll design something for Patrick, and once we get to the lab, I'll run his blood."

Ideally, Gideon would've taken all this a lot slower. He didn't want to push Patrick into something he wasn't ready for, but Gideon couldn't stay in San Francisco forever. He needed to help Patrick and find Ashcroft soon so he could return home.

"When do we start?" Dean asked.

"That's up to Patrick. I gave him my number and told him to call tomorrow. When he does, we'll start. Until then, you may want to get some rest. Once we start, I have a feeling it'll be a while before we stop."

* * *

Patrick stared at his cell phone, the white light of the screen cutting through the darkness of his bedroom. Displayed at the center of the screen was the phone number Gideon had given him—the phone number of a superhero. It was surreal. Never in his wildest dreams would Patrick have believed he would not only know a superhero but be one, too.

It was crazy how quickly all this had happened. One day, he'd been an average high school student. But a random act of chance later, he could run faster than the human eye could track. He could perceive the world around him in slow motion. It was like a miracle.

He tried to keep his mind on his powers so he wouldn't have to think about his grandfather. He and Joshua had been as close as a boy and his grandpa had ever been. His grandpa had been instrumental in teaching him all the traditions that a good Jewish boy should know.

He'd visited their house at least once a week. Then, out of nowhere, his regular visits had stopped.

His father had explained that Joshua's beliefs had changed, that he now followed a false Messiah. That had hurt Patrick. When he had asked his grandpa about it, Joshua told him about Jesus and the stories of the New Testament. The stories had fascinated Patrick, so his grandpa had been more than willing to keep sharing them. Around that same time, one of Patrick's friends, Lucy, had invited him to church with her. Hearing her youth pastor talk about Jesus, it all made sense to Patrick. He wondered why his parents—and other Orthodox Jews—didn't believe what Joshua was saying. Patrick did.

Of course, he couldn't tell his parents about his new faith. Telling them that he believed Jesus was the Messiah would get him ostracized as quickly as it had Joshua. As much as he wanted them to believe, he also didn't want to be cut off from them. He'd never been out on his own, and it was a terrifying prospect.

He turned off his phone, put it on his nightstand, and pulled the covers over him. One advantage of his powers was that he was able to go to sleep very quickly—on days when he used them a lot, anyway. On days when he hadn't used his powers, he would sometimes lie in bed for hours, vibrating as the pent-up energy released itself. He had to find some other outlet for that. But not tonight. Tonight, he was exhausted in a way that had nothing to do with the exertion of his superspeed. The emotions that had washed over him upon finding out about his grandfather's death, followed by the excitement of meeting a superhero, left him utterly drained. He began to drift almost as soon as he closed his eyes.

Tomorrow his new journey would begin.

* * *

Artemis was not a patient person. Waiting in the borrowed car outside a hotel was downright agonizing. She tapped her foot and leaned her head against the steering wheel. These idiots had been in there for hours, and there had been no hint that they'd be coming out anytime soon.

If Ashcroft hadn't ordered her to watch and wait, she would've burst into the hotel, demanded to know which room they were in, and taken the "hero" herself. It would've alleviated her boredom at least.

By the time the sun set, she suspected they weren't going to leave the hotel again that night. She slipped out of the car, and walked toward the hotel. She wasn't going to engage, but she was tired of sitting in the car staring at this boring building. There were other ways to keep an eye on them.

She strode into the lobby and made straight for the front desk. The concierge was an aging man who looked as bored as Artemis had felt. She leaned against the desk. His expression changed from bored to interested as he looked her over. Mentally, she rolled her eyes. She was still wearing the blue dress from her meeting with Dean, and her hair was still stylishly curled. How many women did he give the same look every day?

"How can I help you?" he asked.

Artemis reached into the man's mind and forced her own will past his. This would be a bit trickier than the immediate influence of taking a man's car keys. "Obey my commands."

"As you command."

"There are two men in this hotel I need watched." She handed the concierge a card. "This has my number on it. If Dean Sterling or Gideon Turner leave, you will call me immediately. Do you understand?"

"I understand." The man tucked the card into his coat pocket. "I will do as you say."

"Good. Now you are going to wake up and become yourself again. You will not mention this conversation to anyone, but you will follow my instructions." Artemis snapped her fingers and smiled at him. "Thank you for your cooperation."

The man's brow furrowed. "You're welcome."

Artemis turned and strolled out of the lobby. The post-hypnotic suggestion she had placed on him would remain dormant until he saw Sterling or Turner. When one of them emerged, his memory would be triggered, and he would immediately fall back into a trance and place the call.

Ashcroft had known what he was doing when he'd given her these powers. Because she was used to leading, she could channel the hypnotic energy of her gift naturally. He'd cautioned her to use her powers sparingly because they weren't yet ready for powered people to be exposed to the world at large. He had also warned her that attempting to use her powers against him would end badly for her.

In the grand scheme of things, being the second in command to the future ruler of the world was a lot better than being dead.

CHAPTER 7

Gideon woke to his phone's alarm. His first reaction was to roll over and pull his pillow over his head. He had struggled to fall asleep last night, and he'd lain awake, staring at the ceiling, worried about how he was going to train Patrick. *Just hit the snooze.* Unfortunately, as tempting as the thought was, he didn't have time to waste. Fighting through the fog, he threw his blankets off, stood, and cleared his throat to get rid of the sleep rasp in his voice. Still half asleep, he shuffled into the bathroom and turned on the shower. As the hot water struck his shoulders and back, his focus sharpened. He turned it immediately to Patrick's training.

Patrick's attitude toward his newfound powers was night and day from Gideon's. It was hard to believe that he'd ever considered his powers a curse, but in the beginning he had hated them. Though he now saw his powers as a force for change, he still didn't know much about them. It seemed he learned some new aspect of his powers at every turn, testing their limits. Now, he had to help Patrick find his own limits.

Stepping out of the shower, Gideon dried off and dressed in a white Henley shirt and blue jeans. He stepped out into his bedroom, picked up his phone and wallet, and walked out into the living room. Dean was already there, packing his laptop into a bag. He was dressed in a much more relaxed fashion than yesterday's business suit—a pair of ripped jeans and a Star Wars t-shirt.

"Morning!" Dean said. "I was just getting ready to head down to the lab. I figured you'd get an early start, so I wanted to get all the scientists off the testing floor before Patrick got there."

"Sounds good. I'll call you once I hear from Patrick. If you're set up, we'll meet you there."

"What kind of training are you going to give the kid?"

"Honestly, I'm going to make this up as I go along."

"Lucky for you, I brought some of your gear." Dean held up the bag. "You never know when you might need adhesive beads or concussion gauntlets."

"Leave it to you to prepare for something unimaginable." His adhesive beads, at least, would be a great tool for teaching Patrick; the goop would make escape difficult even for someone as fast as him.

"You know it. I'll leave the car so you can catch up whenever you're ready. Keys are on the counter."

Dean tossed a salute and was out the door. Gideon grabbed an orange out of the complimentary fruit bowl in the kitchen. *God, please help me to be a good teacher for Patrick.* Gideon was uneasy. He was far from perfect and probably unqualified to teach. How many nights had he spent cleaning and bandaging his own wounds? Now Patrick's future as a superhero depended on Gideon's instructions.

Gideon wanted to mentor him spiritually, too. He wanted a chance to tell Patrick about his grandfather's faith away from the disapproving ears of his parents. Patrick's heart might be more accepting than theirs. Hopefully, an opportunity would present itself for him to discuss Joshua's faith while they were honing Patrick's abilities.

Gideon's phone rang. He pulled it from his pocket. The number displayed was not familiar, but it was local. It had to be Patrick. He answered and held the phone to his ear.

"This is Gideon."

"Hey, it's Patrick! I'm up, and I don't have anything going on today. I've already told my parents I'll be out, so whenever you're ready just let me know when and where and we can get started with my training, if that's cool with you."

He talked so *fast*. Gideon took a deep breath and processed the jumble of words.

"My friend Dean is setting up a place for us to practice, but it'll probably be a few hours until he's done. Until then, do you know of anywhere we could meet that would be private enough for us to get started?"

"Sure do. Down by the train tracks a few miles from my house. No one ever goes there, especially when it's this hot out."

"How can I find it?"

"I'll zoom over there and text you my location. Then you can follow it on GPS and meet up with me."

"All right. I'll see you soon."

"Cool! Bye."

The line went dead. Gideon finished his orange and tossed the peel in the trash can. Seconds later, his phone chimed. *That was fast.* Gideon picked up the car keys and headed out the door, checking the location provided. He took the elevator down to the lobby. As he passed the concierge's desk, Gideon's empathic powers spiked. Someone was feeling—he wasn't sure what. It was an odd sensation, like an irresistible compulsion. He looked around. No one was acting out of the ordinary. A moment later, the sensation passed.

* * *

Carter's coworker Raina hadn't known anything about gray pills, but he hadn't expected her to. She wasn't the type of person who would get involved in the drug business. Carter had caught her writing poetry on her break a few times, and he knew her from school. She was probably one of the purest people he'd ever met. Some of his other coworkers, however, might be able provide some information. Carter clocked in and walked to the stockroom. Several of the other employees were back there, unboxing packages of potato chips. Carter picked up a box cutter and joined them.

One was a large man with skin only a shade lighter than Carter's, named Silas Rockwell. Silas wouldn't dare touch any kind of drug. Not anymore, anyway. A sleeve of tattoos—everything from barbed wire to a heart, a skull to a cross—and a few scars hinted at the rougher lifestyle he'd lived in his youth, but now Silas was a family man who worked as a volunteer at an after-school program for troubled boys in the Brooks. He was also a Sunday school teacher at Carter's church. Carter would've trusted Silas with his life. If he knew anything about the current drug trade, it was because of his work with troubled youth, not because of any direct involvement.

The other guy was a different story. A small, pale, wiry man with dark circles perpetually drooping under his eyes, Ethan had a family, too. Unlike Silas, he couldn't shake the chains of his past and still struggled with drug addiction. He had tried to kick it numerous times, and Silas had tried to help.

Who to question first? Because of his work with troubled boys, Silas might know exactly what the gray pill was. He was reluctant to question Ethan about it, because he didn't want to seem accusatory. The guy had

had a rough go of it his whole life, and he didn't need accusations; he needed help. At the same time, he seemed like the best bet.

Silas gave Carter a two-fingered salute. "Mornin', Jonson."

"Morning." Carter picked up a box and sliced it open. "How are you guys?"

"Couldn't be better." Silas grinned and tore into his box. He loaded the bags of chips inside into a shopping cart. "Alicia just called from her appointment. The baby's healthy and growing normally."

"Congratulations." Carter threw several bags into the cart. "This'll be your third?"

"That's right. You know, there's nothing like having kids to motivate you to do your best."

Carter's smile faltered. His father had said something similar on more than one occasion. Silas reminded him of Dad in a lot of ways, from his good-hearted nature to his bulky frame.

"My dad would've agreed with you."

"Your dad was a hero, Carter." Silas broke down the empty cardboard box. Most people in the Brooks knew who Wyatt Jonson really was. The Crusader's identity had been broadcast on the local news in a memorial, and his tombstone bore the title as a badge of honor.

"Thanks." Carter studied his shoes. "I miss him a lot. How's it going with your kids, Ethan?"

Ethan fidgeted with a pallet of sports drinks. "I really want to be a good dad, too. I-I'm trying."

Carter emptied his box and broke it down. He threw it into the pile of flattened boxes next to Silas'.

"Hey, so a friend of mine said she was offered some gray pills. Have you heard about anything like that? Know what they're pushing?"

The two men exchanged glances and went silent for a moment. Silas dropped his gaze to the floor for a moment before he looked at Carter.

"I've heard of it. They call it Shine. I've had to deal with several boys having withdrawals from it in the past few weeks. It's bad."

"Why do they call it Shine?" Carter frowned. "The pill's a dull gray."

"They say . . . " Ethan scratched his arm. "They say it's 'cause when you take it, everything looks really bright and shiny."

"That's the least of its effects," Silas said. "Hallucinations, nightmares . . . the boys I helped were in worse condition than any addict I've ever seen, and most of them had taken it only once or twice."

Carter whistled. "Potent stuff."

"Yeah. I have no idea what's in it, but I've never seen boys cling to a drug so hard, so fast. Your friend was smart to turn it down."

"Thanks." Jolie would be glad to have that much of a lead. "I appreciate it, guys."

"No problem." Silas finished filling the cart and wheeled it to the front of the store. "If we had more kids like you and your friend, maybe the Brooks would be in better condition."

* * *

Patrick looked up at the sound of tires crackling over loose gravel. A silver sports car pulled into the dirt lot next to the railroad tracks. He gawked at it. That was a sweet ride. He wished he had a car like that—not that he really needed a car anymore. But then again, his friends might wonder how he got around if he sped everywhere.

Gideon parked the car and stepped out. He wore a white shirt and Patrick wondered if the slight glow coming off him was the reflection of the sun or his superpower. Gideon put on a pair of sunglasses and walked toward Patrick.

"You weren't lying about the place being remote," Gideon said.

"I told you. It's perfect. So, how do we start?"

Gideon laughed. "Slow down, okay? First things first. Tell me about your powers, starting with how you got them and what you've learned about them so far."

Patrick would've much rather gotten down to business. It was far from the typical superhero origin story portrayed in the movies. But Gideon was in charge here. Even if it took longer than he would've liked to get to the training, Patrick would go along with his methods.

"You're going to think I'm crazy at first, but just hear me out, all right?" Gideon nodded. "I'm sure you heard about the flu shot epidemic. It was all over the news. You probably noticed my dad wasn't happy to see a visitor yesterday. That's why. Lots of people want to see me all the time because of it. What none of them know is, after I got my shot, weird things started happening. I got *really* sick. Like, deathly. My heart was racing all the time and kept getting faster. I was trembling and sweating . . . "

Patrick shuddered at the memory. Even now, the intense cold of the fever, the uncontrollable shaking in his hands, the shortness of breath—his body threatened to lock up just thinking about it. He had no idea what was going on. He took a deep breath and continued.

"After a few days, the symptoms started to go away. I stayed in bed just in case. When I finally did get up . . . "

"You had super speed?"

"Yeah."

"So . . . you think you got your powers from a flu shot?"

"I thought that was insane at first, but then I started looking into it. Every person who went to the same clinic that day started showing the same symptoms. You know the rest. They all died. Their hearts exploded from beating too fast. As far as I can tell, I'm the only one who survived."

Gideon furrowed his brow. Patrick couldn't completely decipher his expression due to his sunglasses. Behind Patrick, the railroad's crossing guard started clanging.

"Most medical professionals thought it was a bad batch of vaccine, but if what you're saying is true . . . " Gideon nodded. "We'll look into that. We'll also run some tests once we get to the training facility. For now, let's see what you've got."

"You want me to run?"

"I want you to race that train." Gideon ascended into the air. "I'll be watching from above."

Patrick grinned and dropped into a runner's ready position. The ground rumbled as the train approached. Its horn split the air, driving knives into Patrick's ears. His heart thumped, and the world around him seemed to slow. He glanced over his shoulder. The train was just yards from the crossing guard. He waited as it passed him, and once the final car was ahead of him—

He ran.

* * *

Even a dozen meters in the air, Gideon felt the gust of wind as Patrick accelerated, passing the train in seconds and kicking up a trail of dust that quickly vanished toward the horizon. Patrick had been gone less than thirty seconds when a fresh cloud of dust appeared in the distance and closed in on Gideon. Patrick came to a stop below him.

Wow. Gideon floated to the ground and stood next to Patrick. The boy's face was red and dirty, but he wore a broad grin. Gideon sensed his excitement. It was near-euphoric.

Gideon shook his head. "That was incredible."

"Thanks. I . . . got into a bit of a mess on the turnaround, but nothing serious."

"We'll work on that."

Gideon considered Patrick's explanation of the source of his powers. Ashcroft must've snuck his super-serum, or whatever it was, into that batch of flu shots. The disaster had been the talk of the medical community in the first few months after Gideon's return. Since it had happened in only one city, and never popped up again, doctors had been baffled. Now, all the pieces clicked together. The rapid, erratic heart rates Patrick had mentioned were consistent with the subjects' bodies trying to adjust to a new homeostasis. They must not have been able to handle it. Patrick's body had adjusted, and the result was super speed. If all the subjects had adjusted, rather than dying, there would have been dozens of speedsters out there today.

Ashcroft's formula was advancing. When he'd given Gideon his powers, he'd hooked him up to IVs, tubes, and a helmet. If he'd condensed it down into a serum that could be mixed with a flu vaccine, then he'd made a breakthrough. Which meant he could give superpowers to whoever he wanted.

Maybe that was why this woman, Artemis, had come to Dean to ask for access to Sterling Labs' dispersal unit. Ashcroft might be ready to mass produce the serum. If that was the case, they had to find him before he got the chance. There were people in the world who could do a lot of good with powers, as Gideon hoped Patrick would. There were others who would abuse their power, and if the luck of the draw gave them an ability that made them unstoppable, like bulletproof skin or Herculean super strength, the world would be in trouble.

"I believe you," Gideon said. "And I think the person who gave you powers is the same guy who gave me mine."

"Really?" Patrick's eyes widened. "Who is he?"

"I know only his name—Jeremiah Ashcroft. He experimented on me while I was a captive in Venezuela." He nearly stopped there, but Patrick deserved the whole truth. "He may have given your grandfather powers, too. Maybe the same powers I have."

"Grandpa had powers?"

"I'm not sure, but it's possible. Once, before I had my powers, he knew someone was coming before I could even hear them. I can pick up on people's emotions, so sometimes I can sense them before I see them. I think that's what your grandfather did. And before he died, while he fought a guerrilla to buy me time to escape, I thought I saw a flash of light when he punched him in the face. It didn't make sense to me at the time, but now I realize it's possible he had powers and didn't know it."

Patrick shook his head. "I can't believe it. If that's true, if this Ashcroft guy is giving people superpowers, then what does he want?"

"I'm going to find that out." Gideon jerked his thumb toward the car. "Come on, let's get to Sterling Labs. We've got a lot of work to do."

Minutes later, Gideon put the car in park. The Sterling Labs building in San Francisco was nearly identical to the one in Sojourn City. Four stories tall, it sat in the middle of a beautiful courtyard lined with canals that flowed into a water fountain in the center of the yard. It was almost eerily similar. If it weren't for the skyline in the distance, he could've thought he was back home.

He climbed out of the car and grimaced at the heat. It was a much different heat than he'd suffered through in Venezuela—dry, not humid—but no more comfortable. At least his shirt wasn't sticking to his body with sweat. He closed the car door and walked up the sidewalk toward the building with Patrick at his side.

Dean stood in the shade near the front door. He waved as they approached. Patrick half-skipped in front of Gideon. For a moment, Gideon thought he was going to speed over to Dean in front of everyone in the courtyard, but the kid contained himself. The three of them met halfway between the parking lot and the fountain.

"Patrick, this is my friend, Dean Sterling. He designed my suit and other gear. He's been backing me as the Seraph since . . . almost day one, pretty much."

"Nice to meet you." Patrick extended his hand. "Thanks for your help. I am psyched to work with you."

Dean shook it. "Pleasure's all mine. I'm looking forward to seeing your powers in action."

"The lab all set up?" Gideon asked.

"Sure is. I just have to clear you with the guard, so he'll know you'll be regular visitors."

Dean led the way into the building. Patrick bounded after him, so Gideon hung back and brought up the rear. He examined Patrick as he walked. He at least had his powers under control. Gideon never saw a hint of a blur or any other indication that Patrick might accidentally zoom around the courtyard unexpectedly.

Gideon sighed in relief as the lobby's cool air conditioning washed over him. Dean walked over to a security officer at a desk and spoke to him. Gideon crossed his arms and waited. Patrick fidgeted, tapping his foot and drumming his hands against his thighs.

"Easy," Gideon said.

"Sorry." Patrick took a deep breath. "It's really hard for me to stand still."

"We're going to try to help you with that. I had to learn how to keep my powers under control, too. They used to randomly kick in whenever I got angry or scared. I had to train myself to keep them contained until I wanted to use them."

"I want to do that, too." Patrick stuck his hands in his pockets. "It's really hard to hide around my parents sometimes. I'll catch my hands vibrating, things like that. I can't keep letting that happen."

"You'll master it with time."

Dean nodded to the guard and walked back over to Gideon and Patrick. "We're good to go. Follow me."

Dean took them up an escalator and down the hallway to the testing lab. The large, open room had the shape of two hexagons pressed together. To the left of the entrance was another door, and next to it a wide window.

Dean pointed to the door. "You two head in there. I've got to grab some things, and then we'll get to work."

Gideon led Patrick inside. The smaller room was furnished with a pair of padded chairs and a computer desk. Patrick took one of the chairs, and Gideon stood to the side of the desk and looked back out at the lab. The vast room was almost entirely empty. The walls were white and made up of countless hexagonal panels. The floor and ceiling were identical. From the look of the panels, Gideon guessed they could withdraw into the walls. There must be sensors or other kinds of technology behind them.

Dean walked into the observation room carrying a needle. "Hey, kid. I need to take some blood. I want to run some tests on it and see if your mutations match Gideon's."

"Okay." Patrick fidgeted. "Don't really like needles . . ."

"I'll be quick."

Gideon moved toward the door while Dean took Patrick's blood. If the results were similar, it would all but confirm that Patrick's powers were from Ashcroft. Patrick hissed as Dean stuck him. A moment later, Dean stepped away.

"All right." Gideon opened the door. "Are you ready to get started?"

"So ready." Patrick jumped to his feet. "Let's do this."

CHAPTER 8

Sitting at her desk at Sojourn PD's twelfth precinct, Jolie pored over the scarce details she had about this case. So far, no one had spotted the brown-hoodie guy since his encounter with Wes the day before. They had tightened their search to the eastern part of the Brooks, but it was still a big area to cover.

Sergeant Pulaski said he would check in with a few of his old CIs in the area. All Jolie had to go on was the description of her suspect and the mysterious gray pills. If the lab would hurry up and get her some information on the suspect—a name would be a great start—then maybe she could finally make a move. But for now, she had almost nothing.

She stepped away from her desk and walked outside the precinct to get some fresh air. A little boy ran by, trailing a blue cape and twirling a branch like a staff. Jolie grinned. It seemed crazy that kids could now play pretend that they were a real life superhero that operated in their neighborhood, not just a fictional one on TV. How would Gideon feel if he'd seen the child? She knew exactly what he'd say: "I'm no superhero. Just a vigilante." He had some weird hangup about that word, and Jolie wasn't sure why. He had powers, he saved people . . . why was it so bad? He didn't like to talk about it, so she respected his privacy.

Seeing the child also drew her mind to an image of her and Gideon, standing in the backyard of some cozy suburban home, watching as their own little one fought imaginary bad guys, totally free of the stresses and evils of the world. Her heart fluttered at the thought. *It could happen . . . one day. But who knew, with everything going on in their lives, when they'd be ready for that?*

Her phone rang. She looked away from the boy and pulled the phone out. Carter. She held the phone to her ear. "Hello?"

"Jolie, I've got something about your pill."

Finally. "What is it?"

"It's called Shine. It's highly addictive, makes the user see everything really bright and shiny, and causes hallucinations and nightmares."

"Any word on where it's sold?"

"No. My only reliable source works in an after-school program and has dealt with some kids with Shine addictions. But he wouldn't know where it's sold."

"Thanks anyway. This will help."

"If you find out where, give me a call. I'm itching to take down some dealers."

"I'll consider it."

"Aw, come on, Jolie—"

"That's the best you're going to get. It depends on how dangerous it looks like it'll be. If I need your help and don't think it'll get you killed, I'll call you."

"Fine."

"Thanks." She started to hang up and thought of something else. "Hey, keep an eye out for Wes, will you? He got beat up yesterday trying to play hero."

"You know he won't listen to me, right? He's like four years older than me."

"I just mean . . . watch his back. If you happen to see him get into trouble, help him out. He means well, but he's not trained."

"Will do. Anything else?"

"That's it. Thank you for your help, Carter."

"No problem."

Jolie hung up and tucked her phone away. Although she'd never heard of Shine, combining the name of the drug with the probable location of the sale, they should be able to narrow the investigation down a lot. But it would still help if she had an ID on her suspect. At least Pulaski's CIs might know where the drug was sold.

One thing at a time. For now, she needed to find out if anyone in the precinct knew anything about Shine.

* * *

From the observation room, Dean activated scanners that had been programmed in the testing lab's walls. The results all concurred—the kid was fast. Faster than fast; with training, he could be supersonic. His heart rate was over twice the rate of a normal person at their peak exertion, and he was running at almost a hundred miles per hour. He circled the lab, visible to the human eye only as a red-and-black streak—the colors of his clothes.

Other than his heart rate, everything else seemed normal. Dean suspected that his blood sugar would drop rapidly after he finished running. He'd likely need a lot more sustenance than an average teenager, which was saying something. Dean would've bet Patrick could eat anyone he knew under the table. Maybe everyone he knew combined.

The computer chirped to signal that Patrick's blood results were in. He opened the file and compared it to Gideon's. Gideon's blood cells had looked normal other than a faint glow. Patrick's appeared normal in structure, but they were constantly vibrating. The two weren't completely consistent. Since they had different powers, that made sense. The main thing he'd been looking for was a massive mutation in the cells, and that wasn't present in either case. This was strong evidence that their powers had come from the same source.

He closed out the files and pulled up the graphic illustrator program he'd used to design both of Gideon's suits. Patrick's suit would need to be much lighter than Gideon's. It would have to withstand extreme temperatures from the friction created while running at high speeds. It couldn't be made of aionium—the metal was light and aerodynamic but still weighed enough to slow a runner down. Good material for a flyer, like Gideon, but not for a speedster. It would be like trying to use a rocket ship's hull for a race car. But the suit had to be protective. As fast as he was, there was always the chance Patrick could take a stray bullet.

Maybe if there were a few strategically placed aionium plates over a bodysuit. Not a full suit of armor, but enough to protect from a grazing shot. The rest of the suit could be made from the hard-fiber material woven in Gideon's first suit. Dean traced out the appearance of the suit and mask. What color would it be? What would Patrick call himself?

Dean grinned and filled in the sketch. *I love my life.*

* * *

Gideon stood in the center of the double-hexagon as Patrick ran the perimeter of the room. He was impressed not only by the boy's speed, but also by his endurance. He had been running for five minutes without stopping, and as far as Gideon could tell, he wasn't slowing down. If his powers were anything like Gideon's, he would crash hard after exerting himself like this.

"Okay, stop!"

The red-and-black blur disappeared, and Patrick slammed into the far wall. Gideon grimaced. That had to hurt. He jogged over to Patrick's side and knelt next to him.

Patrick groaned. "Ow . . . "

"Are you all right?"

"Yeah, I'm fine." Patrick sat up. "That's the little thing I mentioned back at the tracks—it's hard for me to come to a complete stop. I kind of . . . skid. It's worse when I'm running for long periods of time. A quick sprint isn't a big deal, but running for a long time like that really makes it a challenge."

"That could be a problem."

Patrick rubbed his nose. "You think?"

Gideon grabbed Patrick's hand and pulled him to his feet. Patrick wobbled but recovered and stood unsteadily.

"How does it feel when you're running? Describe it to me."

"Oh, I've never had to do that before." Patrick frowned and stared at the floor. "It's . . . it's like . . . okay, imagine you're on a hill. Like the streets here in San Francisco—really steep. You're driving a motorcycle down the hill, full speed. The world around you is in slow motion, but you aren't. Your speed increases as the momentum carries you downhill. Now imagine getting halfway down the hill and realizing you need to stop. You can slam on the brakes, but it's not enough. You're going to fly off the bike and tumble down the hill, and the world's still moving in slow motion around you."

That was a way more vivid description than Gideon expected. When he had first visualized his powers, he'd just imagined the light coming from his hands, and it had. This mental image Patrick had constructed . . .

Is it possible he'll be better at this than I am? "You're starting off with an advantage I didn't have. The mental imagery didn't come that easy for me."

"Really? How will that help me?"

"This visual world you've created, it's all in your head. That means you control it. Next time you run, imagine you're going down that hill full speed, but as you run, imagine the hill is flattening out, becoming a horizontal plane. Instead of running downhill, you're just running in a straight line. It's all in your head. Picture that, and maybe you'll be able to come to a stop instead of slamming into whatever's in front of you."

"I hadn't thought of it that way. Do you want me to try again?"

"In a minute. For now, get some water and maybe a snack. You've probably burned a ton of calories already."

"Will do."

Patrick left the testing lab, and Gideon looked at the window to where Dean sat. "Did you hear that?"

Dean's voice echoed from the lab's speakers. "I did. This kid has some intense mental discipline."

"I'm impressed. This may not be as difficult as I thought. How are his blood samples?"

"I think we can safely say that Ashcroft is behind his powers."

"I figured as much. His vitals?"

"Pretty good. It's amazing how quickly he returned to a resting heart rate."

"His body has adjusted to a new homeostasis. That explains why the other recipients of the shot died."

"Their bodies couldn't handle the stress of the transformation. That was no flu vaccine, was it?"

"No more than I'm a regular family physician." Gideon snorted. "We need to find out where he got the injection and investigate. Maybe a link to Ashcroft will turn up."

"Sounds good." Dean looked down. "I'm going to get back to designing his suit. Let me know if you need anything."

"Right. Thank you, Dean." As Patrick walked back into the lab, Gideon turned to face him. "Okay. Time for round two."

* * *

Artemis' hypnosis subject had reported to her that Sterling left the hotel in his limo earlier that morning. Riding in her own limousine, she had set out after him. Only after she arrived at Sterling Labs had the concierge called again to report that Turner was on his way out. Although Ashcroft had wanted Artemis' eyes on Turner, she decided to stick with Sterling for now rather than running around the city. Turner would show up sooner or later, or else Sterling would leave the lab and meet up with his friend. Either way, she would find him.

Of course, Artemis couldn't just sit outside the labs in a limo and watch for them. She had her chauffeur drop her off two blocks away, and she walked from there to the courtyard outside Sterling Labs. There were dozens of employees and visitors milling about; it wouldn't be hard to blend in. She wouldn't even have to hypnotize anyone.

Artemis had learned long ago that to fit into a place, even where she didn't belong, all she had to do was act like she was supposed to be there. Project enough authority and confidence, and no one would give her a second glance. She had mastered that ability, so no one looked twice when a woman in a black skirt and a blue floral-print top walked into the lobby of a laboratory.

No one except the guard on duty.

"ID, ma'am?"

"I don't have one. I was invited here by Dean Sterling."

"I'll have to call and confirm that." He reached for the desk phone. "If you'll just stay there for a moment—"

Don't resist. "You don't need to check with him; he's probably busy."

"Yeah." The guard frowned. "He probably is. Why don't you head on in?"

"Thank you. Forget I was ever here."

She snapped her fingers and strode past him to the escalator that rose from the lobby to the building's upper floors. She wasn't sure where Sterling was, but she would search until she found him. With any luck, the guard would be the only person she had to hypnotize. Even if there were others, if she was subtle and told them to forget her when she left, it shouldn't be a problem.

Artemis stepped out onto the second floor and walked down the nearest hallway. Like the goddess whose name she bore, she was on the hunt—and she would get her prey. She passed many scientists and employees, but none of them gave her a second glance. She stopped at each door and peered inside.

Artemis rounded the bend of a curved corridor. Ahead, there was a red light over a closed lab door. Several tables and pieces of technology sat outside the lab. She bit her lip. Perhaps this was what she'd been looking for . . .

The light flickered out, the lab door opened, and Sterling stepped out. She ducked into a side room and waited until he had passed. Peering out to make sure he was gone, she smirked. *Target acquired.* She slipped back out into the hall and followed him as he headed for the lobby. Artemis stopped at the top of the escalator and looked down, waiting to see if he was leaving or would return. Sterling went outside and stood in the shade near the door.

Waiting for Turner? Artemis sat down at a small table in a break area where she could watch Sterling. A few minutes later, he returned from the lobby with Turner and a teenage boy in tow. Artemis recognized the boy with a start. Patrick Omer, the only known survivor of the flu vaccine test. She had been watching Omer for some time, but he had never manifested powers that she had witnessed.

After speaking to the guard, Sterling led Turner and the boy upstairs. Artemis picked up a newspaper from the table next to hers and covered her face with it. Once the three men had passed her, she jumped up from her seat and followed them. They returned to the lab with the equipment outside the door.

The light above the door shone red again, which likely meant the lab was in use. If that was the case, there would likely be a passcode required to enter. She stepped up and found a keypad next to the door. She clicked the open button, but the keypad chirped at her and the door didn't budge. Well, she'd just have to wait until they came out.

She pressed her ear to the door. Muffled voices came through the thick metal. She withdrew a small scanner from her pocket. Ashcroft had created this device to detect people who had been altered by his serum. She activated the scanner and pressed it to the door. It beeped and flashed green—a positive.

Then, the scanner beeped again. Artemis raised her eyebrows. It wasn't detecting her powers, not with the sensor pointed away from her. That meant there was another superhuman in the lab. So, the serum had worked on Omer, after all.

Ashcroft had to know about this. She pocketed the scanner and retraced her steps to the escalator. Bringing Turner in would have to wait until she knew what she was up against.

* * *

"Detective? Detective, we've got a positive ID."

Jolie looked up from her desk. Nate, the CSI who'd been casing the scene of the crash when she'd arrived, held out a file. Jolie took the manila folder from him and flipped it open.

"Vince Powers," she murmured. "Age twenty-eight, priors for DUI, distribution, and possession. Sounds like our guy."

"And we've got something else, too. From his car."

"What's that?"

"Come with me."

Jolie rose and followed Nate, leaving Powers' file sitting on her desk. He led her to the crime lab. A gallon-sized plastic bag sat on an observation table in the middle of the lab, filled to the brim with gray pills. Jolie's heart skipped.

"Holy . . . Is all that Shine?"

He nodded. "The pills on the floor of his car had spilled out from a hidden compartment underneath the steering wheel. We found this bag inside."

"Powers was making a delivery. This compartment had to have been an aftermarket modification, right?"

"Yeah."

"There are probably only a few shops in town that will modify a car like that."

"Probably. And I can narrow it further. If you refer to the file I gave you, you'll find that Powers owns an auto repair shop in the East Brooks."

The East Brooks—where Wes had seen Powers just after the accident. Jolie's heart quickened with anticipation.

"I think we've got our guy. Thanks, Nate. Good work."

"My pleasure."

Jolie turned and rushed back to her desk. She needed to set up a task force and raid that shop before they got another shipment of Shine in a car. How many of them were already out there? How many of these pills had already infected the city?

They had to put a stop to it now.

* * *

Dean stared at the 3D rendering of Patrick's suit and nodded in satisfaction. The rendering, along with the detailed notes he'd attached, should be enough for Yei to create the suit. He saved the file, closed it, and looked out at the lab.

Patrick was improving by the hour. They trained until dark the previous night and came back again first thing in the morning. Although Gideon seemed enthusiastic about the speed at which Patrick was learning, Dean could still see the trace of nervousness beneath his optimistic exterior. Gideon was afraid, but that was his own battle to fight, one that Dean couldn't fix with any kind of tech. It was a battle of the heart.

While Gideon worked that out, Dean continued to focus on the technical aspects of Patrick's soon-to-be superhero career. The kid still needed a codename. "The Seraph" was punchy, recognizable, and fit Gideon's powers. Patrick needed something like that. Something distinctly his own.

Thump. Patrick ran into a puddle of goo from an adhesive bead and tumbled to a stop, slamming into a wall and sticking there, coated in the blue-green substance. Dean grimaced. Gideon walked up to Patrick and fired a beam of light into the adhesive to dissolve it.

"You've got to think as fast as you run." Gideon helped Patrick stand. "I threw that bead while you were still halfway across the room, but you still ran straight into it and got stuck. If the rest of the world really moves in slow motion, then you have to be able to react to what you're seeing. It takes discipline, and I've already seen that you have that."

Patrick vibrated his body, freeing himself of the excess gel. "I'll try. Let's go again. I'll see if I can avoid the gooey stuff this time."

Gideon was getting pretty good at teaching, whether he would admit it or not. But if he wasn't careful, he'd wear himself out. He needed to save his energy for hunting Ashcroft. *Speaking of the hunt, I should dig into Crowne Pharmaceuticals . . .*

Patrick circled the room again, leaving a blue-and-gray blur in his wake. Gideon rolled an adhesive bead between his fingers. When Patrick had circled the room eleven times, he threw the bead at the wall. On Patrick's thirteenth lap, the bead struck. The blueish blur swerved. This time, Patrick managed to avoid most of the adhesive, but his trailing foot stuck in the goo. He jerked to a stop and slammed face-first into the floor.

Dean cringed.

Gideon helped Patrick to his feet. "That was better. You're getting there."

"Still got stuck," Patrick grumbled.

"But you avoided most of it this time. You just didn't swerve far enough. Next time, I'm sure you'll have it."

Dean's watch chirped. He activated the microphone on the desk. "Hey, guys, it's getting late. We should probably head out."

"Right." Gideon fired another beam into the adhesive, freeing Patrick. "A night's rest will do you good."

Dean tucked his laptop into his bag, draped it over his shoulder, and walked out into the lab to give Patrick a high five.

"Good work today, kid. Let's get out of here. Dinner's on me."

* * *

For the second night in a row, the trio left Sterling Labs in the late evening, long after the rest of the employees had gone. Artemis watched them from her newly-rented car and focused on Omer.

Ashcroft had planted a case of his serum in a shipment of flu vaccines, and Artemis had infiltrated a clinic and administered the doses of serum herself. The number of deaths had been disappointing, but Omer's survival brought hope. Hope that had been dashed when he didn't appear to manifest powers. Somehow, he'd kept his powers secret from her. Artemis would get a royal chewing out from Ashcroft over this. Her ears burned at her own mistake. Maybe all wasn't lost, though. Turner and Sterling would likely investigate the source of the boy's powers. If they did, that would provide Artemis with a perfect opportunity to grab them.

She tugged on her earlobe, activating her implant. "Somna to base. I'll need backup to complete the plan. Send me Backfire."

CHAPTER 9

Gideon slid into the booth next to Patrick, and Dean took the seat across from them. Since Dean was paying, Patrick had selected an upscale restaurant called Boulevard. Patrick said its standards were up to Jewish customs, but its price point meant that his family rarely ate there. As they settled in, Patrick perused a menu. Gideon glanced at his own and whistled. Good thing Dean was a billionaire. Otherwise, his wallet would be crying after tonight.

Gideon imagined bringing Jolie to a place like this. When was the last time they'd had a nice date? Most of the time, when they got a few hours to go out together, it was for a burger at Wally's. They hadn't been to a place like this since . . . probably since before Venezuela. That had to change. Especially if he was planning a proposal. She deserved someone who could treat her like the wonderful woman she was. He had quite a bit of money saved up from when he'd been a surgeon, money he hadn't used since he'd been living with Dean. Maybe it was time to start using it on her.

"Any word from Wes today?" Dean asked.

Gideon looked up from his menu. "Yeah, he said he's found a few potential apartments. The applications will be waiting for us when we get back."

"Good. And Jolie?"

"She called earlier with a breakthrough on her case. They've found an auto repair shop that is probably involved. It looks like the mechanics are packing drugs into secret compartments before the cars are shipped. She's planning a raid tonight."

"Is Carter joining her?"

"She didn't say, but I trust her to keep him out of harm's way unless it's absolutely necessary."

"Who are Carter and Jolie?" Patrick asked.

"Jolie's my girlfriend," Gideon said. "She's a detective with Sojourn PD. Carter is a . . . "

Dean smirked. "He's Gideon's sidekick."

"He's not my sidekick." Superheroes had sidekicks. Vigilantes didn't. "He's taken up his deceased father's mantle as a vigilante. He is young, though. About your age, actually. I'm trying to keep him out of danger as much as possible."

"Does he have powers?"

Gideon shook his head. "No, he doesn't."

"Did you train him?"

"Some."

"Then I'm sure he can handle himself."

The boy's calm confidence eased the tension that had been building in Gideon's chest for the past two days. He hadn't been able to stop wondering if he was training Patrick correctly, if his methods were even teaching him what he needed to know. What if Patrick was totally unprepared to fight crime? It was the same fear Gideon had for Carter. The two young men were still teenagers. What if they got hurt? Gideon would be responsible, because not only had he encouraged them to fight crime, he'd taught them how—and ineffectively, at that.

Patrick's eyes dropped back to the menu and flitted back and forth so quickly it hurt to watch. "Are you guys ready to order? I'm starving."

Gideon lowered his head to conceal a smile. As he suspected, Patrick had to eat almost constantly to keep up with his enhanced metabolism. He pitied the boy's parents; they must have wondered how one person could eat so much food.

A waiter approached. "May I take you drink orders?"

"I'll have water," Gideon said.

Dean nodded. "Same for me, thanks."

"Hmm . . . " Patrick scanned the menu again. "I'll take a Sprite."

The waiter scribbled the order down and walked away. Dean snapped his fingers.

"That's it!"

Gideon raised an eyebrow. "What's it?"

"Patrick's nickname. His superhero identity. *Spright*. Not like the soda, like the mythical creatures."

"Are sprights fast?" Patrick asked.

"Haven't you ever heard the term 'sprightly'? That's where it comes from. It usually refers to faeries or elves, so yeah, pretty fast. Besides, the name is punchy. It doesn't have to mean fast because it sounds fast. It's perfect."

Patrick tilted his head. "Spright. I like it."

Gideon looked around. Anyone nearby would get an earful of superhero business. But the nearest occupants were three tables away. "On a related note, how are the suits coming?"

Dean grinned. "Yours is almost ready. Yei called me today and said they're slapping on a coat of paint. Patrick's is still a work in progress."

"Do you think we'll get to go on a mission soon?" Patrick asked.

Gideon hesitated. "I do need to start searching for Ashcroft, but I'm not sure I want you to get involved. You're still learning."

"Yeah, but I'm getting better."

"You are, but hardened criminals and superpowered villains won't consider 'getting better' when they fight you. If you're not good enough, they'll kill you. I can't let you out there until I know you're ready."

"I get it. I just don't want to sit around and do nothing."

"At least wait until your suit's ready," Dean said. "That way you'll have some protection when you're out there."

Gideon sighed in relief. A reasonable medium. Before he'd had his first Seraph suit, he'd tried to go into the Brooks as a vigilante and had very nearly gotten himself killed when Katrina Monahan slashed a knife through his jacket and into his gut. Once Dean had designed his armor, it had saved his life multiple times. If Patrick had a suit, Gideon would feel at least a little better about having him in the field.

"Wait for your suit," Gideon agreed. "Then we'll see if you're ready."

* * *

Clad in his red Crusader uniform, Carter stood in the shadow of a warehouse, looking through a chain-link fence at Powers Auto Repair. According to the hours posted in the front window, the mechanic should've closed shop two hours ago, but the exterior lights were still on. The sporadic flashes from the windows told of blowtorches in use. Either someone was pulling the late shift, or something else was going on behind the scenes.

Jolie's voice crackled over the airwaves, breaking the silence. "All units converge."

She'd given him a police radio to wear on his belt so he could hear their comm chatter. Her orders had been specific: watch and listen, and only move in if someone tried to slip out the back door or if it looked like the police were being pushed back. He wasn't a fan of waiting, but it was better than staying at home. He twirled his staff and watched the back door.

Four police cars with blazing sirens pulled up, and Jolie led a group of cops toward the shop. Two officers with rifles stopped outside the door, and a third kicked it in. Those three went in first, then Jolie, and finally the remaining cops. The Crusader tensed, ready to move at a moment's notice. The harsh crack of gunshots pierced the relative silence of the night. Every muscle in his body coiled, ready to spring.

The back door opened, and someone rushed out. The Crusader grinned and leapt at the chain-link fence, clambering over it in seconds. He dropped to the ground and rushed after the runner. The other guy looked back over his shoulder, saw the Crusader, and raised a gun. *Not good!* Carter rolled for cover behind a dumpster. The gun cracked five times. Then, silence.

The Crusader leapt to his feet and continued chasing the man. He was close enough now to make out the shape of a hoodie. Powers? The outfit matched Jolie's description. He pressed forward. Powers, or whoever he was, was fast. The Crusader was determined not to lose him, though. He reached down to his belt with his free hand and grabbed his grappling gun. Its purpose was to scale buildings, but it would probably work as a makeshift tripwire, too.

He aimed the grappling gun at Powers' legs and fired. The high-pressure cord wrapped around Powers' ankles. The dealer tripped over the cord and landed face-first on the ground. The Crusader reeled the line in, hooked the gun to his belt, and twirled his staff. Powers rolled over and fired off a shot with his pistol.

The Crusader flinched, and the bullet grazed off his armored shoulder pad. He stepped forward and raised his staff—

Something hit him on the back of the head. He tried to turn as he fell to see who was behind him but succeeded only in presenting his face as a target for his attacker, who kicked him square in the jaw. The Crusader's ears rang. His kneepads scuffed the ground, and he pressed his hands into the concrete to stay steady. His mystery attacker helped Powers to his feet.

The Crusader pushed himself off the ground. Powers and his accomplice rushed away. The Crusader took a step—and nearly crashed back to the ground. His head spun, and his stomach rose. He leaned against the alley wall and watched them go. The two people running away looked identical. His attacker had been wearing the same clothes as Powers. The brown hoodie, the faded blue jeans . . .

The strangest part was that he was sure that the second man had also shared Powers' face. That surely must've been the blow to his head knocking him senseless, unless Powers had a twin brother. Jolie hadn't said anything about that.

"What the . . . ?"

Footsteps pounded down the alley behind the Crusader. He turned around and raised his staff, but it was just Jolie. She frowned and lowered her gun.

"You all right?"

"Yeah, I would've had him . . . but his brother jumped me."

"It's all right. We got the rest of his gang. We'll get him eventually, too." Jolie patted him on the shoulder. "Brother, you said?"

"Had to be. They looked identical. Even wore the same clothes."

"That's odd. Powers was the only one in the shop wearing a hoodie."

"Maybe his brother was waiting outside?"

"Maybe." Jolie stared down the alley. "Come on, I need to get back to the precinct. And you should probably get some ice on that bruise."

* * *

Gideon wadded his napkin and dropped it on his plate as Dean paid for their meal. Patrick was finishing the last few scraps of food on his plate. He'd been right; the diner had been excellent. He was still partial to Wally's Diner back home, but that might just be nostalgia talking.

As Patrick finished eating, Gideon watched him. It wasn't just the potential of Patrick being in danger that was bothering him—it was his promise to Joshua. Gideon had yet to say more than a few words about Joshua's faith to Patrick or his family. Not only was that falling short of his promise, but if Patrick got killed before coming to Christ, Gideon would feel doubly guilty. And now, away from his parents' influence, was as good a time as any to broach the subject. He took a deep breath.

"Hey, Patrick. I wanted to talk to you about something."

"Sure. What's up?"

"It's about your grandfather's faith. Part of the reason he sent me to talk to your family was because he wanted me to share his faith with you and—"

"Oh, you don't have to." Patrick smiled. "I know all about Grandpa's faith. We talked about it for a long time, and I thought what he was saying sounded true. After he left, one of my friends brought me to a church event they were having. The stuff they said about Jesus compared to the prophecies of the Messiah made so much sense to me. I felt God speaking to my heart, so I put my faith in Jesus."

Relief and joy blossomed in Gideon's heart. Some of the burden he'd been carrying lightened, knowing that Joshua would be elated. "That's great. Your grandfather would be proud."

"I hope so." Patrick wiped his hands on a napkin. "My parents don't know. I'm still trying to figure out what to do about that."

"You should tell them. I know it'll be hard, and you're risking a lot, but they might listen more to you than to me or some preacher."

"Yeah . . . maybe."

Gideon sensed Patrick's fear. He understood why. Staunch Orthodox Jews would ostracize a family member who converted to Christianity. He'd seen the pain of it in Joshua's eyes. Having witnessed it firsthand in his family, Patrick was justified in his hesitation. Whatever happened, even if Patrick's family wasn't there for him, Gideon would be. It was the least that he could do to honor the man who'd saved his life.

* * *

Wes shifted impatiently on the couch and stared down at his phone. He wanted to call Jolie and see how the investigation was going. He was dreading calling Gideon to tell him about what he'd done in the Brooks, even though Jolie wanted him to. Gideon wouldn't approve, and Wes would get an earful. But Gideon had been in the exact same situation a few months ago. Calling Wes out would make Gideon sound like a massive hypocrite.

"It's not going anywhere," his father said.

Mom and Dad had made it abundantly clear that they were unhappy with Wes for looking for trouble in the Brooks. They already had one son who risked his life almost daily, and they were still adjusting to that. To have both sons doing it, and Wes without powers, worried them to no end, he was sure.

But how could he not? If he hadn't been there, that woman would've been mugged, raped, or killed. He'd saved her from that—even though it had cost him a few cuts, bruises, and a fractured arm. In his estimation, it was worth it. If he had to take a beating so someone else didn't have to, then maybe that was his purpose. Wes had always known how to endure punishment. It was why he was such a good football player in college. He wasn't as good at handing it out, but he was resilient. One bad day in the Brooks wasn't enough to discourage him from trying to help people.

And Gideon had to understand that. He couldn't just assume that since he was the family superhero the rest of them were just going to sit and watch TV while he put his life in danger. It wasn't going to happen.

Wes' phone vibrated. He picked it up. It wasn't Gideon, though; it was Jolie. He excused himself and walked upstairs.

"Hello?"

"Hey, Wes. Your information was good. We found the guy in the brown hoodie in the East Brooks."

"Really? I was just thinking about calling and asking you. That's great."

"Well . . . he actually got away. But we shut down the shop he was using to smuggle drugs, and we arrested several of his colleagues."

"Oh." That was disappointing. If the brown hoodie guy was the ringleader . . . "Won't he just start up again somewhere else?"

"Probably, but we know who we're looking for now. We're going to get him."

"I hope you do. Thanks for letting me know."

"No problem. Are you doing okay?"

"The arm still hurts, but I'll survive."

"Take care of yourself, Wes. Gideon would be ticked if he found out you got hurt on my watch."

Wes snorted. "Not ticked at you. Never at you."

There was an awkward silence. He instantly regretted saying it; he hadn't meant it to sound harsh. Gideon was just overprotective and serious at times. That could manifest as anger occasionally, but Wes had never seen it directed at her.

"Sorry, Jolie. I didn't mean . . . "

"It's okay. And you know, I've never seen him get mad at you, either. Certainly not since he's been home. You're his brother, Wes. He loves you."

"I know. I'm just nervous about talking to him about all this. But it'll be okay. Thanks for keeping me updated."

After a quick goodbye, he hung up and stared down at his phone. Maybe he should call Gideon now, after all. As scared as Wes was of disappointing him, he felt equally bad about keeping secrets. Gideon deserved to know. Wes wouldn't know what his brother's reaction would be until he opened up.

* * *

Jolie put her phone down on her desk and rested her head in her hands. The arrests they had made tonight had been significant enough to put a dent in the Shine business, and interrogating their suspects had confirmed that Powers was the mastermind of the group. As long as he was out there, they had no way of knowing how many more dealers were out there.

It wasn't Carter's fault. Powers' brother—or whoever the second man had been—had snuck up on him. It was tempting to say that Gideon never would've been caught in that situation, but Carter didn't have Gideon's powers. He was a normal human being, just like Jolie, and she could've been taken by surprise just as easily as Carter had been.

They'd get Powers soon. That was inevitable. He couldn't hide in the Brooks forever, not with the police and the Crusader looking for him. It still would've been easier with Gideon here. He had his reasons for staying in San Francisco so long, but it was hard all the same.

And even besides needing his help with this case, she just missed him. Their relationship had only recently started to strengthen again, and to have him leave so soon reminded her too much of his year-long absence in Venezuela. She'd always kept faith that he was alive, but it had been the worst year of her life. She looked at the picture of Gideon clipped to the top of her computer monitor.

"I love you."

There was nothing more she could do tonight. Their arrests had been processed and the reports had been filed. She stood, slipped her phone in her pocket, and walked out the door.

* * *

Daylight brought an answer to Artemis' request.

She had just dressed in a comfortable white top, black leather pants, and a red vest when there was a knock on her door. She strode from her bedroom to the front door and opened it. The man who stood outside her luxurious, rented condo was Latino, well-muscled with tightly cropped hair and a full beard. He wore a charcoal denim jacket, despite the heat of San Francisco's sun.

She stepped aside. "Come in."

The man—Alfonso Mendez, codenamed Backfire—was another of Ashcroft's miracles. Recently, he'd been hired as the Regency's head of security. His powers would be ideally suited to draw out Turner and his young, red-haired friend.

"Would you care for breakfast? Coffee?"

Mendez crossed his arms. "Why don't we get down to business, Artemis."

Typical. Mendez had always been a bit of a dull fellow. He hadn't been Ashcroft's first choice for a test subject, and Artemis wouldn't have picked him, either. But Mendez's evolution had been a necessity borne of a lack of subjects at the time. Artemis shrugged and gestured for him to take a seat in a spacious recliner. She lounged on the couch across from him.

"Ashcroft told me you requested my services, *señora*."

"Did he fill you in on the situation with the two superhumans here?"

"Yes." Mendez clasped his hands and leaned forward, elbows resting on his knees. "I know one of them."

Artemis quirked an eyebrow. "Fascinating. Perhaps we can use that to our advantage."

"What do you need me to do?"

"I am going after Dean Sterling, but those two have been sticking to him so tightly I can't risk it. I need you to draw them away, and I know just the way to do it and achieve another objective at the same time. Garvin Technologies has a prototype gene splicer matrix that I—that Ashcroft—need for the experiments. Break into their lab and steal it. Make as big a ruckus as necessary. We want to draw Turner into action."

"Are you sure about this? Ashcroft may not be happy if we reveal ourselves publicly."

"The time for secrecy has passed. Ashcroft will realize that soon enough. Turner has already made himself a public spectacle, and once one superhuman shows up, people would expect there to be more, right? It's time."

Mendez shrugged. "Whatever you say. It's your head if Ashcroft is displeased."

"Just draw them out. I only need them distracted. And if you get the device, so much the better."

"Then I suppose you'll be seeing me on the news." Mendez rose and cracked his knuckles. "I'll go put on something flashy."

"Make a scene, my friend." Artemis smiled. "I'll continue my work behind the scenes."

CHAPTER 10

Dean pulled off his green Mountain Dew t-shirt as he walked from the suite's living room into his bedroom. It had been a productive day. Early in the morning, Yei texted to say that Gideon's suit was ready. When Dean went to pick it up, he dropped off the schematics for Patrick's suit. Then he headed to the lab to watch Gideon and Patrick train.

After a shower, he walked back out into the living room. Gideon was in the kitchen making a cup of coffee. Dean snagged a banana from the steadily emptying bowl of fruit on the counter. He wasn't the superstitious type, but maybe the bowl's emptiness was a sign that they should leave soon.

How were things going back in Sojourn? He trusted Arianna and Maddox to keep the business running smoothly, but he was starting to miss home. The labs here were great, and he loved working with Patrick and designing his gear. San Francisco wasn't home, though, and this branch wasn't the work he loved.

"Patrick's really getting the hang of things." He peeled the banana and took a bite. "You may not be the only superhero for much longer."

"Then maybe reporters will stop crowding outside our front door."

"Unlikely. You're still the only superhero with a public identity."

"Which I would not have chosen."

Dean just didn't understand Gideon's hesitation about the word superhero. He had seen it again at the restaurant, when Patrick had called Carter a sidekick. Gideon refused to talk about it, and from Dean's experience, he wouldn't open up until he was ready. No amount of prying would help. For now, he'd leave it be.

"Yeah, but that's a secret you can't put back in the box once it's out." Dean shrugged. "Sooner or later, the shine will wear off. You'll probably always be a celebrity, but something more interesting will come along."

"*. . . wearing a suit of armor is attacking Garvin Technologies. Police have cordoned off the area and are warning pedestrians to stay away until the unknown powered assailant has been contained.*"

Dean spun around. The TV had been droning softly, ambient noise in the background, but the words snagged his attention away from Gideon. He rushed over to the screen, Gideon right behind him. It showed footage of a man in a rust red metal suit stomping through the front doors of Garvin Technologies. An explosion shattered the lobby's windows, and the camera shook. A security guard hurtled from the open lobby doors and slammed into a car.

This couldn't be coincidental. Between Wayans' appearance at Sterling Enterprises and now this guy hitting Garvin Technologies, something was going down. He turned to Gideon—who was already unzipping the duffel bag containing his new super suit.

"Should I call Patrick?"

"No way." Gideon started changing. "I haven't faced an enemy with powers yet. No way I'm putting him in that kind of danger. Whoever this guy is, I'll have to take him alone."

* * *

By his own estimation, Patrick believed he was improving. That afternoon, he'd dodged the sticky blue-green stuff that came from Gideon's beads twice without getting stuck. Then Gideon shot low-power bursts of light at him. Those were harder for him to dodge. Even though it seemed like Gideon moved in slow motion while Patrick ran, his bursts of light were full speed. It didn't mean they were impossible to dodge—just harder.

Patrick was determined to meet Gideon's standards. He wanted to use his powers for good. It's what his grandfather would've done with his, if he had survived. He just hated that it was taking so long. Sure, it had been only three days, but as fast as Patrick moved, that felt like ages. Gideon was just looking out for his safety. Patrick was fast, but he wasn't bulletproof. If he tripped or didn't move in the right direction at the right time, he could end up dead. But with Gideon's training, he might be ready for that now. He'd learned it was less about his speed and more about how fast he could think while running. It was discipline. And Patrick had that. His family had instilled it in him from the time he could walk. He just had to learn how to apply it to this aspect of his life.

A flash of orange light on the TV caught his attention. Patrick lowered his Bible—he read it only in the privacy of his bedroom, with the door shut and locked, lest Mom or Dad discover his secret—and slid it back under his bed. The news headline warned of an unknown armored man attacking Garvin Technologies.

"No way." He scooped up his phone. "A supervillain?"

He dialed Gideon's number. No answer. Of course not. If Gideon had seen the news, he'd already be on the way. He dialed Dean instead.

"Hey, kid."

"Have you seen the news?"

"Gideon's already on the way."

"Can I help?"

"I'm not sure that's a good idea. You haven't even fought normal criminals yet; you're not ready for a supervillain. Gideon would kill me if I let you go out there."

"Oh, come on! At least let me help get people to safety. I'm fast enough to pick them up and run them away from danger while Gideon fights that guy. I won't even intervene. Please?"

"You don't have a suit. You go out there without a mask, and everyone will know who you are."

"I'll just keep moving. They'll never see my face. If I get tired and can't keep it up, I'll get somewhere safe. Hide in an alley or something. Please?"

Gideon needed him. If he got in a battle with the armored guy, people could get hurt. Between Gideon's powers and the explosions caused by this villain, there was a lot of energy flying around those streets. Civilians were almost guaranteed to get caught in the crossfire.

"Okay. But that's *all* you do. Got it?"

"I promise."

"All right. Then get moving."

"On it." Patrick dropped his phone on the bed. "Mom! I'm going over to Asher's for a bit, but I'll be back before curfew."

Patrick darted out his window without waiting for a response. He channeled his excitement into intense focus. This was a serious situation. He had to treat it like it was.

He had to be a hero.

* * *

Based on Dean's description of aionium, Gideon had expected a suit of Iron Man-style metal armor. Although hardly that bulky, the suit did have heavier armor plates than his previous one had. The black bodysuit contrasted with brighter, royal blue armor plates lined with gold. It came with a pair of gloves, a belt, and boots all done up with gold highlights, and the center of the blue breastplate had a double-winged symbol emblazoned in gold. A similar winged crest, this one with three feathered spikes on either side, adorned the belt buckle. Like his old costume, it had a hood, but it lacked the cape.

Despite the amount of metal that made up the suit, it was so light that he barely noticed the weight as he rocketed across the city.

Gideon still didn't have a measure of how fast he could fly, but judging by the buildings flashing past below, it was fast. He circled around toward downtown. An explosion mushroomed upward between two buildings, lighting up the night. As the orange blossom faded, the buildings shone with red and blue police lights flashing from the street below. *Guess that's where I'm going.* Gideon arced toward the explosion.

The armored man stormed toward a barricade of police cars. The officers stood behind their vehicles, firing at him. The bullets weren't having any effect on the armor; the assailant continued his rampage without so much as a hitch in his step. The Seraph dropped to the street and landed between the police and the armored man. The gunfire stopped, and a murmured awe rose to replace it.

"Who are you?" Gideon demanded.

The armored man rumbled deep in his throat. "Backfire."

A gray blur whizzed past the armored man, and a few pedestrians disappeared, but the assailant didn't seem to notice. The blur appeared and disappeared again. *Patrick?* The kid must have seen the news. *Just stay out of the line of fire.* The Seraph stepped toward the man. He didn't have time to deal with the kid now.

Backfire's dark crimson armor didn't look cobbled together—it was as professionally made as Gideon's. Spikes protruded from his shoulder pads and forearms. His helmet covered his whole face, and the lenses over his eyes glowed a bright red. There were two mandibles, almost like an insect's, curving around the helmet where the man's mouth should be.

"Stand down." The Seraph held out his gloved hands. "Let's talk about this—what do you want?"

Backfire laughed. "I want you, Seraph."

"You know who I am?"

"Of course I know you. We have the same creator."

"What does Ashcroft want? Why is he doing this?"

"You've learned his name? Interesting."

The supervillain picked up the rim of a tire, and the metal reddened as if it was in a furnace. Backfire hurled the rim like a discus. The Seraph extended his right hand and fired a burst of light at the projectile. The rim exploded midair.

"Impressive." Backfire mockingly applauded. "You've honed your powers well."

Backfire stormed toward him and swung a punch. Gideon ducked under the blow and brought a glowing fist up into Backfire's chest. The strike dented his armor. Whatever it was, it wasn't as powerful as aionium—or durable enough to resist the Seraph's powers.

He jabbed with his left fist. Backfire blocked it with his left forearm and crosscut to hit Gideon's jaw with his right hand. Gideon reeled back and fired a burst of light. It caught Backfire on the shoulder and knocked him sideways. The Seraph jumped and spun, kicking at Backfire's head. The blow hit the villain on the cheek of his helmet, cracking one of the insectoid mandibles. Gideon pressed in, punching at the other side of Backfire's head.

The red-armored warrior caught the Seraph's arm and shoved him away. He reached for a piece of debris—and it disappeared just before his hand touched it.

Patrick. He was going to get himself killed.

Backfire stumbled and looked around. The Seraph pressed his hands against the pavement and shoved himself to his feet.

"The other one's here," Backfire rumbled.

"This is between you and me, Backfire." The Seraph fired a two-handed blast that knocked the villain back a few steps. "Last chance. Stand down."

"Not gonna happen."

His fists glowed with fiery energy. The Seraph flooded light from his own fists and rushed in. Backfire swung a backhanded punch that connected with the side of his head. The Seraph flew backward and slammed into a gold minivan. His heart raced, and for a moment he feared his contact with Backfire might make him explode. But nothing happened, and his face didn't feel odd.

Before he could rise, Backfire was on him. The villain swung his fist downward. Gideon rolled aside and came up in a crouch on Backfire's left flank. As the red-armored warrior turned, the Seraph fired two blasts of light—one into his chest, the other toward his mask. Backfire flipped over the van and landed on the sidewalk. Gideon stood and walked toward the villain. Backfire rose and snapped out a kick. Gideon took the blow full in the gut, but his suit absorbed the impact. He grabbed Backfire's foot and shoved him.

Backfire tumbled over, staggered to his feet, and reached out to touch a streetlight. The Seraph turned, hurled himself behind the van, and shielded himself in light. The streetlight exploded.

Before he could rise, Backfire had him by the shoulder. The Seraph cried out as the villain threw him backward and shoved him against the wall. He slammed his fist into the Seraph's face. Gideon pressed a hand against Backfire's chest and shot a burst of light. Backfire flew into the street.

The Seraph stormed toward him. Backfire picked up several objects, heating and hurling them at Gideon. Gideon jumped and floated in the air, flying back and forth to avoid the thrown objects.

"Come down here and fight, coward!" the supervillain roared.

The Seraph floated in front of Backfire, a few yards above him. The villain picked up a piece of the fallen streetlight and heated it. Seraph narrowed his eyes and waited. The metal turned a bright orange. He raised his hand and fired—not at Backfire, but at the shard in his hand. The metal exploded, and Backfire yelled and staggered back. The Seraph floated to the ground and walked toward him. He sensed awe and a tinge of excitement. He glanced up and to his right. Patrick was across the street in an alley. At least he hadn't engaged again. Backfire knelt in the middle of the street, clutching his face. Pieces of his mask littered the ground.

"Surrender now," Gideon said.

"You'll regret this."

Backfire lowered his hand and glared at him, his face illuminated by the crackling light of the fires. His dark features and cruel sneer were marred by the Seraph's last blast, but his visage was burned into Gideon's memory. He halted mid-stride, stunned.

"Remember me?" Backfire laughed. "It's because of you that I have these powers."

Backfire—though that probably hadn't been his name then—had been the captain of the guerrilla forces that had captured Gideon. When Gideon escaped, Joshua had stayed behind to fight Backfire. Gideon had never expected to see him again, let alone here. Or with powers.

"Because I lost you and killed the old man, Ashcroft needed another lab rat. He chose me."

Anger built like a tidal wave in the Seraph's chest, and he struggled to push it down. The villain was down for the count. Gideon didn't need to engage him further.

Backfire raised a glowing hand and pointed it at him. The Seraph generated an energy shield around himself.

A gray blur tackled Backfire to the ground.

"No!" Gideon shouted.

Patrick pummeled Backfire with a flurry of speed-enhanced punches. Before the villain could recover and hurt the kid, Gideon grabbed Patrick by the shoulder and shoved him away. The anger he felt had been only partially his own—much of it had come from Patrick. The boy must've heard Backfire say that he'd killed Joshua. Gideon stared Patrick down. The young man glared back for a moment and then rushed away, disappearing in an instant.

"So that was the other one." Backfire cackled. "Super speed? Neat trick."

"Stop fighting. You know you can't beat me."

"Can't I? How hard do you really think I've been trying?"

Gideon probed Backfire mentally, but he could find no trace of deception. Backfire had been a distraction . . . But for what?

"You can't hold me; you know that. No jail cell can contain what I can do. And I know you won't kill me."

"Won't I?" The Seraph stepped forward. "I killed some of your friends in that jungle."

"And I saw how it tortured you. Now that you have the power to stop people without killing, you won't even consider it."

He was right. Gideon refused to take a life. But he had to do something to stop Backfire. If he just let him go, the villain would be free to hurt more people—and Gideon still had no idea what he'd broken into Garvin Technologies for. He might've already acquired his prize. Footsteps scuffed on the concrete around the Seraph. Police officers swarmed past him with guns trained on Backfire.

"Don't—"

"We'll take him from here," one officer said.

Backfire reached into his belt and removed a small disk, almost like a throwing star. It glowed red. The Seraph threw himself in front of the cops and surrounded himself in a shielding aura. The disk struck his chest plate and exploded. Gideon flew back, hurled by the explosion, and caught himself ten feet in the air. He floated there and looked down.

None of the cops had been hurt; his light shield had absorbed the blast. But Backfire had vanished. The Seraph floated back to the ground. The cops lowered their weapons and walked over to him. The one who had spoken earlier sized him up.

"Seraph, right?" he asked. "Cool suit. What brings you this far west?"

"I just . . . happened to be in the neighborhood."

"Thanks for your help."

"You're welcome. I'm sorry I couldn't catch him."

"You will." The officer holstered his weapon and walked back to his car. "That's what you guys do, right?"

Gideon looked around for Patrick. He didn't blame the young man for being angry. At least he'd obeyed for the most part and gotten his anger under control once Seraph had pulled him off Backfire. It was better than Gideon might have handled himself if their positions were reversed.

He tapped his earbud. "Patrick? Dean? You there?"

Patrick grunted. "I'm here."

"Meet me back at Sterling Labs. We need to debrief. Dean?"

Nothing. Maybe Dean didn't have a comm on him, or maybe he was engrossed in some work. He'd surely meet them at the lab. The Seraph took off and flew over the city. He didn't see any sign of Backfire, so he turned to the lab. He was sure the villain would turn up again. When he did, Gideon and his friends would have to be ready.

He landed on Sterling Labs' rooftop and lowered his hood. Only then did he notice his hands were shaking and light flashed sporadically through his gloves. He closed his eyes, took a deep breath, and concentrated on slowing his heart. Seeing the guerrilla captain again must've shaken him more than he thought. Gideon had been afraid of him back in Venezuela. Now that he had powers, Backfire was a threat again. But he was a threat Gideon could handle.

He just hoped Dean brought him a change of clothes.

CHAPTER 11

As soon as he got off work, Carter hit the streets. He didn't gear up as the Crusader; before sunset, it would be too conspicuous. Instead, he walked the sidewalks in plainclothes, looking for any sign of the Powers brothers. He was still frustrated at himself for making such a boneheaded mistake. Gideon had told him how important it was to watch his back, but he'd been completely surprised by Vince's brother.

If he had been more aware of his surroundings, he might've been able to stop the brother and at least incapacitate one of them. Instead, he ended up injured, and both had escaped. Who knew where they'd go now? If they were smart, they'd be so far underground that no one would be able to sniff them out, and it was Carter's fault.

Jolie wouldn't want him to beat himself up. Gideon, either. Certainly not his dad. But none of them would have made that mistake. Carter was just a rookie who couldn't even hear a guy running up behind him. He'd failed his father's legacy last night. The original Crusader's record wasn't perfect, but he'd always taken down his man in the end. He never would've screwed up something as simple as capturing a drug dealer. Carter was going to make up for it. If Powers thought he could escape justice forever, Carter would show him just how mistaken he was.

Even if he didn't know how yet.

Carter walked to the repair shop where the fight had taken place. It was shut down and cordoned off by yellow crime scene tape. Carter ducked into the alley where he had engaged Vince Powers. A recent rain had caused some dirt in the alleyway to cake, and there were a few shoeprints in the mud. Carter knelt next to them. He recognized one print as belonging to his own thick combat boots. The other print was either Vince's or his brother's.

Carter moved to another patch of mud, close to where Vince had fallen. There was a deep imprint, probably where the dealer's elbow had landed. Next to it was the print of a right shoe, and beside that—an identical right shoe print. Carter frowned. The two had been dressed the same, so it made sense that the prints matched. But it was more than that. Not only were they the same size, but the impression was the same. They were both deeper in the front, as if both brothers had pushed off with their toes as they ran.

It was one thing for brothers to look the same and dress the same, and even to have the same shoe size, but to have the same gait, down to the pressure they applied with their feet as they ran? That was odd.

Carter took a picture of the prints with his phone and walked out to the other end of the alley where the Powers brothers had run. There were tracks where the mud that stuck to their shoes came off on the street. One trail soon disappeared entirely, but Carter followed the other as far as it would go and came to the middle of a sidewalk. He frowned. These tracks just stopped, too—not like the mud was scraped away, but as if the brothers had just disappeared.

He looked out at the street. Some mud near the curb had been disturbed by tires. The brothers could've jumped in a waiting getaway car. If so, maybe some traffic cameras had caught them or could at least provide an image of what their car looked like. He took a picture of the tire tracks and sent it to Jolie along with the earlier photo of the boot prints.

Found these on Russo Street. Possibly Powers' car.

He pocketed his phone and turned to walk back the way he'd come. For now, his search was at a dead end, but maybe some of the clues he'd found could help Jolie. And this time, when she tracked down Powers, Carter was going to make sure the weasel didn't slip away.

* * *

Patrick ran as fast as he could and then pushed harder, circling the lab again and again. Tears welled in his eyes and smeared on his cheeks, spread by the force of his velocity. How had Gideon expected him to react? He'd heard that monster confess to killing his grandfather. He had promised Dean he wouldn't engage, but . . . how could he not?

As soon as Gideon had pulled him free, he felt guilty. He had endangered himself and maybe even Gideon by making him stop long enough to wrestle Patrick away from Backfire. It was not one of Patrick's finer moments. He'd rushed straight back to the lab and started running laps, trying to move faster than his grief could catch him.

Usually he felt free of burden when he ran. That wasn't working so well right now. He rushed past the door to the hallway and saw it inch open a crack. By the time he had rounded the lab three more times, the door had completely opened, and Gideon stepped into the room. Patrick stopped in the center of the room. His breaths came short and choppy, and he put his hands on his head and tried to relax.

"Are you all right?" Gideon asked.

"Look . . . I'm sorry that I got involved. I know it was wrong, but he said he killed Grandpa, and it was like I went into a frenzy and—"

"It's okay. What matters is that you stopped when I told you to. I don't think anyone saw your face." Gideon walked toward the observation room. "Is Dean here?"

"No. I figured you'd gone to meet up with him."

Gideon frowned and went into the other room. Patrick followed.

"He didn't answer on comms." Gideon pulled his phone out. "I don't like this."

Patrick hadn't thought to look for Dean since he hadn't been involved in the fighting. Sterling Enterprises and their hotel were both miles from where the battle had taken place; he should've been safe. So why had he vanished?

"No answer." Gideon stared at his phone. "Where are you, Dean?"

"I'll find him." Patrick turned toward the door.

"Not yet. We need to come up with a plan."

"I can search the whole city in less than an hour, just let me—"

"No. Thank you, Patrick, but we can't afford to split up right now. If something happened to Dean, we have to assume they know a lot about us—our routine over the past few days, where we live, everything."

"They're watching us?"

"They could be, so we need to be on the alert. We don't want to play into their hands."

"Okay." Patrick pursed his lips. "I hope he's okay."

"Me, too."

* * *

Wes had volunteered at East Refuge Church's food pantry since before he went to college. Although most people wouldn't have blamed him for stopping after he'd been attacked by Romanian mobsters while working it last November, he had been determined not to let the encounter scare him off. He continued to volunteer several times a week, usually in the mornings.

It was a simpler way to help, a reminder that sometimes it was the little things that made all the difference. Often, the people who did the most were not mighty warriors, but humble citizens with a heart to serve. That was hard to remember since he lived in a city full of mighty warriors, including his own brother.

All his doubts went away, however briefly, while he was serving food to the people of the Brooks. Their grateful smiles reminded him that he was doing something meaningful with his life.

When the biggest rush of that evening ended, he walked around to the people seated in the fellowship hall to see if any of their patrons wanted something to drink. As he made his rounds, the door opened. Wes glanced at it—and froze.

The man who entered wore a brown hoodie. The same guy who'd run into him the other day? He hadn't gotten a good look at that man's face, but this guy had the same height and lanky build. Jolie's raid must not have gone according to plan if he was here in the church. Wes walked into the kitchen and tapped one of the other volunteers on the shoulder.

"Take over for a minute, would you?" He pulled out his phone. "Jolie, it's Wes. I think I'm looking at that guy you've been hunting . . ."

"What? Where are you?"

"I'm at the church." He peered out into the fellowship hall. "He just walked in, wearing that same brown hoodie."

"Stay there."

"What if he leaves?"

"Just stay put. I don't want you getting hurt, do you understand me? I'll be there soon." Jolie's tone softened. "Thanks for letting me know."

The line went dead. *What now?* Maybe he could stall the guy in the hoodie long enough for Jolie to get there. The guy hadn't even picked up his food yet. If Wes took his time serving it to him, and the guy didn't eat in a hurry, then Jolie should make it. Wes stepped up to the counter and glanced over at his mother, who was running the food line.

"I'll take over. Go on and take a break. You've been at this for hours."

"Okay." She kissed him on the cheek. "Thanks."

As Mom stepped out of the kitchen, Wes scooped mashed potatoes onto a plate. The guy in the hoodie was three people back. Wes added a helping of pulled pork to the plate and handed it to the woman in line. As the next patron stepped up, Wes prepared his plate more slowly. *Every second counts.* Wes served that patron and the next in line.

The man in the hoodie stepped up. Wes avoided his gaze, unsure whether the man would recognize him from the street the other day. But he was being ridiculous. Even if the guy did recognize him, he had no idea Wes was working with the police, or that he even knew the brown-hoodie guy was a criminal. Wes looked up, forced a smile, and handed the guy his plate. Beneath the hood, the man had dark, unkempt hair and a five-o'clock shadow that suggested he'd missed his last shave.

"Enjoy," Wes said.

Over the next few minutes, Wes kept an eye on the suspect. What if he left before Jolie got here? The best move would be to follow him. What were the odds that he'd just fall in their laps like this again? He didn't want to make Jolie mad, but she would forgive him eventually if he led her to this guy.

He forced himself to act casual and not stare at the guy. Another volunteer took over the food line, so Wes weaved his way through the fellowship hall and poured water or handed out packages of food supplies. He looked up surreptitiously when he could to see if the man was still there.

Wes was giving a family a case of ramen noodles and a box of cereal when the guy in the hoodie got up and walked out the door. *No, no, no.* Wes pulled out his phone and darted between people toward the door. He dialed Jolie and slipped outside.

"Jolie, he's leaving!"

"Stay there, Wes. Do not follow him. Which way did he go?"

Wes walked out into the street. The brown-hooded figure was walking down the sidewalk to Wes' left.

"Uh, east. He's headed east."

"All right. Just go back inside and stay at the church."

"By the time you get here, he could be gone! But if I follow him, I can update you on where he is."

"No!" Jolie snapped. "Powers could be armed."

"I won't let him see me. I'll be fine."

"Wes!"

He ignored her and started after Powers. He knew she was going to chew his ear off later, but at least Powers would be in jail.

Powers turned a corner into an alley. Wes picked up his pace. He pressed himself against the building on his side of the alley and peered in. Powers looked around, and Wes ducked back. When he looked into the alley again, Powers had pulled out his phone. Wes raised his own phone to his ear.

"He's in an alley," he whispered, "talking to someone on the phone."

"Wes, you need to back off now."

"I'm just watching him. I—" Powers broke into a run. "He's running. Get here as fast as you can; I'll go after him!"

"Wes, no!"

Wes hung up as he ran and tucked his phone into his pocket. Powers grabbed a ladder to a fire escape and climbed. Wes sprinted across the alley and grabbed the ladder. Powers was already up to the second floor. Wes hoisted himself up and climbed as quickly as he could—not easy with a cast on one arm. He hoped Jolie arrived soon; he had no idea what to do if he caught Powers. He wasn't even wearing the prototype armor.

Why was the guy going to the roof? He'd have nowhere to run. Wes reached the second floor and started climbing the next ladder. Powers was near the roof now. Wes redoubled his speed.

Sirens wailed in the distance. *Please be Jolie.* Wes grabbed the final ladder. He had to detain Powers until Jolie made it here. Wes pulled himself onto the roof. Powers stood at the edge of the building. Wes walked toward him. He wasn't going to jump, was he? Because Wes had no idea how to talk him down if he was.

"Powers!" he called. "Step away from the edge, okay?"

"You shouldn't have followed me."

"I'm just trying to help. That stuff you're pushing is going to hurt a lot of people, including you. You need to back away from the edge. You don't want to hurt yourself, do you?"

"What do you know?" Powers turned to face him and sneered. "You're just an interloper. You don't have a part in this story."

"Story? What story?"

"Where's the Seraph? He's the one I really want. Not you, not the cops, not that powerless wannabe in the red suit."

What did Powers want with Gideon? Wes took another step toward him, his hands raised in a placating gesture. If Wes didn't know better, he would've thought the dealer wanted to commit suicide by superhero. Gideon had never killed a criminal, as far as Wes knew, so Powers would have been disappointed even if Gideon was around.

"None of you are what he is." Powers frowned. "You could be, though. You have the potential."

"What does that mean?"

"Don't let them keep you down, kid. They're going to try to keep you down because you're not a cop, because you don't have superpowers. Don't let them tell you what you can't be."

That switch had been so quick, it could've given Wes whiplash. First, Powers said he was nothing and this wasn't his story. Then he said that Wes had potential and could be whatever he wanted. Maybe Powers was just playing for time. The sirens blared loud and clear now; the police car careened into the alley. Wes took another step toward Powers. If he just kept him talking for a few more seconds . . .

"Look at me," Powers rambled. "A street-level drug dealer, but they gave me purpose. They made me more."

"Who did? What did they do to you?"

"Wes!" Jolie shouted.

He spun around. Jolie pushed herself onto the roof and whipped her gun up, training it on Powers. Wes stepped aside so he wasn't in the line of fire and looked back at Powers. The dealer grinned.

"Welcome to the party, Detective. Sorry I can't stay longer."

"Don't do it, Powers!"

The man took a step over the edge. Wes rushed forward to try to catch him—

The air flickered and a soft *puff* sounded, and then there was a second Powers right behind the first. As the first Powers fell, the second grabbed his hand. The air puffed again, and a third Powers appeared as the second fell. Wes stopped in his tracks and gaped, unsure of what he was seeing. Jolie rushed up beside him, her gun still raised, but she looked as dumbfounded as Wes felt.

The multiple Powers continued to appear and then fall over the edge. The tenth Powers that appeared leaned over the edge, holding the hand of the previous one. He looked back at Wes and Jolie, saluted with the hand not holding his doppelganger, and jumped.

Wes rushed toward the edge with Jolie hot on his heels. He looked over. One by one, the Powers duplicates disappeared until only the one on the ground remained. Jolie pointed her gun over the edge and fired. Powers was already running and disappeared into another alley.

"Did he just create a human ladder . . . out of himself?" Wes asked.

Jolie lowered her gun. "I think he did. We need to call Gideon."

"You're right. We're getting out of our league."

"'We'? 'Getting'? Come on, Wes! You can't keep doing this." She holstered her gun and walked away. "You could've gotten yourself killed."

Wes stayed where he was, staring at the alley where Powers had run. What had he meant when he said Wes had potential? Who had done that to him—made it possible to duplicate himself like that? He said they'd given him purpose. What did that mean?

He turned and walked back toward the fire escape, trying to puzzle it all out and failing. Maybe Jolie was right. He should've just stayed at the church.

CHAPTER 12

Dean's head felt like a watermelon that had been dropped from the top of Sterling Enterprises to strike the concrete far below. As he swam back to consciousness, he gasped—the only sound he could manage to get out. Slowly, his skull began to reform from the fragments that were surely lying all around the room.

His eyes fluttered open. The room was dark, but as his eyes adjusted, the blurred shapes around him solidified into counters, trays, cabinets . . . a medical clinic of some kind? How did he get here?

Something dug into his wrists, pinning him down as he tried to sit up. He struggled against the restraints, but they wouldn't budge. He tried to move his feet—same thing. He slumped back down. His head screamed at him. Whatever had happened, it had done a number on him. Dean thought back. The last thing he remembered was Gideon flying away to fight the armored guy rampaging through downtown. That was it . . .

No. Wait. There was something else.

Dean rushed from the hotel room and toward the sports car. He wasn't sure what to do now. He couldn't help Gideon or Patrick from here, and they didn't have a lair like back in Sojourn City where he could monitor their activity and give updates. The closest thing was their makeshift training room at Sterling Labs. He could go there and wait for them to get done; Gideon was sure to want a meeting when the battle was over.

"Hello, Dean."

Dean turned. Artemis Wayans leaned against the car next to him with her arms crossed, dressed in an attractive sleeveless red vest. What was she doing here?

"Artemis?"

Dean's mind buzzed, like there was some static interference in his brainwaves. He blinked and furrowed his brow.

"You are going to obey me," Artemis said.

Yes, that made sense.

"Sleep now."

Dean's eyes fluttered, and he stumbled, falling to his knees. Part of his brain screamed at him to stay awake, but it was too hard. Artemis had told him to sleep. He had to sleep . . .

What had she done to him? That static, the way he'd followed her commands . . . She had to be a superhuman. She'd hypnotized him and brought him to this clinic. *Is this about the dispersal unit?* Maybe she was going to force him to hand the prototype or the blueprints over to Ashcroft, like she'd originally asked.

Whatever her intentions were he had to escape before she returned. The tight leather of his restraints bit relentlessly into his wrists. A door opened somewhere to Dean's right, spilling light into the room.

"You're awake."

Dean grunted in exertion and shoved himself up. He couldn't completely rise into a sitting position, but at least he lifted his head and shoulders. He looked in the direction of the light. Artemis stood in the doorway, hands on her hips. She reached over, flicked on a light switch, and circled the table so she was standing at Dean's feet.

She wasn't wearing the red vest anymore. She was dressed in a deep green sleeveless leather unitard under a black cape. Gloves the same color as her bodysuit came up to her elbows. A black belt encircled her waist, trailing down to a gun holstered on her right hip.

"Is that your supervillain costume?" Dean asked. "Lame."

Actually, it was pretty cool, but he wouldn't tell her that. Or did she know what he was thinking already? If she had hypnotic powers, maybe she could read minds as well. He'd have to keep his thoughts under control, just in case.

"You think I'm the villain?" Artemis clicked her tongue. "Hardly. What we're doing is a service to the world."

"Oh, the guy trashing Garvin Technologies was providing a public service. That makes sense. Don't get me wrong. They're my competitor, but this is the kind of misfortune that nobody benefits from. And I bet kidnapping me does a whole lot of good for the world, too."

She shrugged. "Sometimes you have to do disagreeable things to reach a goal."

"Is that why you kidnapped me?" Dean yanked on his restraints. "You going to make me give you the dispersal unit, so Ashcroft can keep doing his sick experiments?"

"Sick? That's not what most people would call what we have become. But no, that's not what I want from you. Not right now, anyway. We can get that device anytime we want. No, you will serve us better as bait for your friends."

"No!"

"But, while you're here . . . " Artemis picked up a syringe filled with a greenish liquid. "My friend stole the matrix we needed from Garvin

Technologies. The Seraph may have thought he won that fight, but we still got what we wanted, so in the end, who's the real winner?"

Dean struggled harder. He didn't like where this was going. If what was in that syringe was what he thought it was . . .

"We've mixed our first batch of serum using the matrix, and I need to test it." Artemis walked over to his side and pushed up his sleeve. "Congratulations. You're about to become the world's newest superhuman."

Dean shouted and pushed against her. She pressed a hand against his shoulder and looked down at him, staring into his eyes. That static came back.

"Relax," she said. "Everything's going to be all right."

Dean leaned back. What did he have to be worried about, anyway? She clearly knew what she was doing. She had powers, and her boss had given Gideon his powers. So why shouldn't Dean get them, too? He deserved them as much as anyone else.

He could relax. Everything would be all right. Artemis had said so.

* * *

The first place Gideon and Patrick checked was the hotel. Gideon rushed into their suite and called Dean's name, checking Dean's bedroom and bathroom and then his own, but Dean wasn't there. He changed into street clothes and packed his armor in a duffel bag, and they continued the search.

In the parking lot, they found their first clue. Dean's rented sports car was still in the hotel parking lot, and the keys lay on the ground next to it. Gideon knelt and picked them up.

"Oh, man." Patrick ran a hand through his hair. "You think the bad guys got him?"

"I . . . I don't know." Gideon clutched the keys in his fist. "Come on. We need to hurry." Had Dean left the keys behind intentionally, or had he dropped them in a scuffle?

Their next stop was Sterling Enterprises. If the kidnapper wanted something from Dean, they might have brought him back to the corporate building as leverage to steal something. But the guard on duty said he hadn't seen Dean since that afternoon.

"Are you sure you don't want me to run around the city?" Patrick asked.

"We can't risk it with Backfire still out there. Ashcroft might have other agents in the city, too. He sent some woman named Artemis to talk to Dean a few days ago. Maybe she has something to do with Dean's disappearance." Gideon scratched his chin. "Let's think this over. Where do we know Ashcroft's people have been?"

"Well, the clinic where I got my flu shot, for one."

"Good point. If you're right about the source of your powers, the serum had to get into that clinic somehow. Ashcroft must've sent someone to infiltrate it."

Patrick snapped his fingers. "The clinic's been shut down ever since the incident. It would be the perfect place to lay low!"

"Do you remember where the clinic was?"

"Yeah, of course. It would be hard to forget."

"Great." Gideon dropped into the driver's seat of the sports car and revved the engine. "Give me the address. It might not lead anywhere, but I can at least check it out. Even if no one's there, they might have left a breadcrumb behind."

"Give you the—? No, I'm going with you."

"No way. It's too dangerous. It was hard enough taking on Backfire alone; if he has reinforcements, I can't risk putting you in danger."

"You can't risk fighting alone, either." Patrick crossed his arms. "Like you said, you barely handled one supervillain by yourself. You'll need backup if there's more than him."

He made a good point. But if Patrick got hurt, if something happened . . . How could Gideon ever explain it to Patrick's parents? He'd already had to tell them about the death of Joshua. He didn't think he could bear to deliver the same news about their son. Still, if Gideon didn't have help, he might be the one who died tonight. Or Dean might, if Gideon wasn't fast enough to save him.

He gestured to the passenger seat. "All right, come on."

Patrick climbed in. "What if Dean's not at the clinic?"

"Then at least we've got a lead on Ashcroft, but Dean has to come first. I'm not going to let him get hurt because of me."

* * *

As surprising as it was to discover that Powers had . . . well, powers, it also explained a lot of things that had been bothering Jolie. He didn't have a brother. He'd replicated himself, and the copy had attacked Carter. That was why the shoe prints had been identical, and why Carter said one of the trails had disappeared while the other continued. It could even explain why Wes had run into Powers the same day as the car crash on the opposite side of the Brooks. It could have been a duplicate driving the car, or a duplicate who ran into Wes. There was no way to know which, if either, was the real Powers.

As many questions as this development answered, it raised even more. How had he attained his powers? Who was he working for? What was his goal? Wes had detailed the entire conversation he'd had with Powers before Jolie got onto the roof. He had spoken about purpose, about a story.

If only Gideon were back now. He was more suited to handle a situation like this. As far as superpowers went, at least duplication wasn't the worst thing they could be facing. Powers wasn't bulletproof and couldn't fly. Otherwise he wouldn't have waited around on that rooftop. If it came down to it, shooting the real Powers would probably eliminate the duplicates. Probably.

It would be easier if she didn't have to worry about Wes. He was as bad as his brother. Gideon's drive to help others and stop criminals had been annoying at first, but at least he had the abilities to follow through. Wes . . . didn't. She hated thinking about it like that. He was practically her brother, but he didn't have Gideon's martial arts skills, let alone his powers. He was going to get himself killed.

His encounter with Powers had shaken him. Something about what he said about Wes having potential must've rocked him to his core, because Wes was unusually quiet and pensive. She hoped he was okay. They had returned to the twelfth precinct so she could take Wes' official statement. She wouldn't turn him in for chasing down Powers, even though she technically could for obstruction. That wouldn't help matters. She signed her name on the report and tucked it away.

"Okay." She looked up from her desk. "You're going to go home. You're going to figure out what apartment you, Gideon, and Dean are going to live in when they get back. You are going to forget about Vince Powers. And if I see you getting involved again, I will toss your butt in jail for your own safety. Understand?"

"Yeah, I hear you."

"Thank you for your help today. The more we learn about Powers, the better, and knowing he can duplicate himself will keep us from rushing in unprepared. But please—stay out of it from now on. I can't be responsible for you getting hurt."

"Okay." He stood. "You're welcome."

Jolie leaned her head back and groaned as he walked away. Between him and Carter, she felt like she was babysitting all of Gideon's little protégés and copycats. She had tried calling Gideon three times, and he hadn't answered. As unimportant as it seemed, even hearing his voice would have helped calm her anxiety. What was going on in San Francisco?

It didn't matter. What was going on in Sojourn pertained to her more, and that was what she had to focus on. Whatever Powers' motives and plans were, she had to stop him before he carried them out. The last thing the city needed was an out-of-control supercriminal.

* * *

Artemis sat at a desk behind the operating table and monitored Dean Sterling's vital signs on the computer in front of her. If the matrix had worked correctly, Sterling would wake up alive and powered. If not, he wouldn't be the first person to succumb to the extreme effects of the elixir. His death would be a pity—he could be useful to the cause—but only a minor setback. If it worked, he would be one of few who survived. Maybe with the tool Backfire brought her, the serum could finally be distributed to anyone, free of danger. It would take a larger test group than one man to be sure, though.

Artemis shuddered as she remembered her own evolution. The process had been agonizing. As one of Ashcroft's first subjects, she was hooked up to a table full of tubes and cables and had a thick helmet placed over her head. The serum was even more volatile than when she'd given it to the flu shot patients, so the additional machinery was required for stabilization. When the procedure was done, her head burned from the inside like there was acid sloshing around in her brain. The agony lasted for days. When it finally ended, she had developed her powers.

Ashcroft traveled the world looking for subjects. He spent some time in Romania where one of his subjects, Red Raider, had survived the evolution. From there he returned to the United States, where he met Artemis. Half a dozen of his American volunteers survived the experiment. In Venezuela, a successful subject was killed by Backfire, who Ashcroft had injected as a replacement in a fit of rage. Turner was the only other survivor to come out of that trip.

Not long after Ashcroft returned to the United States, his research had advanced, and he formulated a dose that could be injected via syringe. It killed many of the first recipients. The gene splicer matrix would be a game changer, though. With any luck, Sterling would prove that the serum was stable enough after being run through the matrix to give anyone powers instead of killing them.

Dean's heart rate spiked, and Artemis prepared to resuscitate him if he flatlined. Some of the subjects stabilized after they'd been revived. Artemis rose from her chair, but before she reached his side, Sterling's heart resumed a normal rhythm. That was promising.

The hall door swung open. Artemis swiveled in her chair. Mendez stood in the doorway, dressed in his rust-red armor sans helmet.

Artemis pressed her lips together. "Pity you couldn't bring them in."

"You told me you wanted the matrix and a distraction." He stormed into the room. "I gave you both. For the record, I held back so I didn't accidentally kill Turner."

"Did you?" Artemis raised an eyebrow. "I saw footage of the fight from your armor cam. He was more than holding his own."

"Next time, it won't get that close. You didn't want him dead. If you had, he would be."

She shrugged. "We'll see. Sooner or later, you'll get your rematch. But you still can't kill him. Ashcroft wants him alive."

"What about this one?" Mendez gestured to Sterling. "You've given him powers. What happens if Turner manages to free him? There will be another superhuman on their side."

"I thought you were confident in your ability to take Turner. If that's the case, then we don't have to worry about him freeing Sterling." Mendez growled deep in his throat. Artemis smirked. *So fragile, this one.* For all his muscle and armor, he had a tender ego. "Even if they did manage to free him and escape, we have a backup plan in Sojourn City. We'll get Turner eventually, one way or another."

Mendez stomped toward the door. As he closed it behind him, Artemis walked to Sterling's side. What powers would he develop? The serum Ashcroft had given her for this trip was a different strain than the one she'd used on the flu shot subjects; this one was untested. Even with like strains, they never really knew what powers the serum would give until the subject awoke.

Sterling would no doubt struggle to control his new abilities at first. Artemis had ways around that. If she induced a trance as soon as they woke with their powers, they learned to use them more quickly. That was how Mendez had mastered his.

If only she'd been able to get her hands on the speedster boy before Turner had. He would've been a valuable addition to the Regency. That could still happen, but it would be difficult now that he was in league with Turner. Capturing the boy and realigning his loyalties would be difficult work for Artemis, but not impossible.

Turner and the boy would find out just how futile it was to resist Ashcroft's—and Artemis'—command.

CHAPTER 13

From the street, the clinic looked abandoned. The building was hidden in a shadowy recess, lit only by the vestiges of the golden streetlights. Gideon climbed out of the sports car and pulled his suit from the trunk. As he clipped on his armor, Patrick hopped out of the car and walked up to Gideon's side.

Maybe bringing Patrick along hadn't been the best idea. Patrick wasn't trained to fight, and he still didn't have a suit. His identity would be plain to anyone who saw him, and he'd be in more danger than the chance he could back Gideon up warranted. *What kind of teacher am I, letting him come out here like this?* He should've stood his ground, made Patrick stay behind.

He doubted Patrick would want to stay in the car, but maybe if Gideon told him to watch the perimeter and make sure no one escaped . . . At least the boy would be safe. But if Backfire and Artemis were lying in wait, he might need Patrick's help, as the boy had predicted. It wasn't an easy decision. Why had he been thrust into this role of teacher? He had no idea what he was doing.

"What should I do?" Patrick asked.

"I don't suppose you want to guard the perimeter?" Gideon clipped on his gloves and belt. "It's not exciting, but if anyone tries to run, you're in the best position to stop them."

"Are you sure I can't help you inside?"

"I don't want you to get hurt."

"Look, I don't know him as well as you do, but Dean's my friend, too. Please let me help you. I was useful when you were fighting Backfire in the street; I stole that rubble before he could grab it."

"Yeah, you did." Gideon closed his eyes and pinched the bridge of his nose. "Okay, but you really need to cover your face. I don't want you exposed."

"Hmm . . . well, it's a medical clinic, right? There have to be surgical masks or something. I'll just grab one of those."

It wasn't ideal, but it was something, and Gideon did need him. "You have to listen to everything I say. If I tell you to get out, then you do it. Understood?"

"Yes, sir."

Gideon pulled his hood on. He took a deep, steadying breath and clenched his fists. *It's just another fight.* A fight where his best friend and a teenage boy would be at risk if he failed . . .

He pushed the thought aside. Focusing his mind was one of the first things he'd learned in martial arts training. Doubts would slow him down. His focus now had to be on saving Dean. He strode toward the building, that singular goal burning at the center of his mind. Patrick followed in his wake, not using his super speed yet. Gideon tried the door.

Locked. He blasted the hinge with a beam of light.

"Move in, Spright."

Patrick grinned. "You got it, Seraph."

* * *

Patrick rushed into the clinic and rummaged through drawers and cabinets. Needles, bandages, cotton swabs, tongue depressors . . .

where were the masks? He rushed to the next room over and yanked open a cabinet. The force of his speedy tug knocked several containers down, but he caught them while they were still midair and replaced them. A box of disposable masks sat on the second shelf. He pulled one out and wrapped it over his nose and mouth. He grabbed a cap, too, to cover his shock of red hair. Then he rushed back out into the lobby.

In the time he'd been gone, Gideon had just made it from the front door to the hall that led from the lobby to the exam rooms.

"No sign of him that way," Patrick said. "And all the lights are off down there, too."

Gideon gestured in the opposite direction and walked that way, the soft glow of his fists illuminating the hall. Patrick—Spright—followed in his wake. He could've searched every room in seconds, but he didn't want to run into an ambush without his mentor by his side. He'd take things slow until the fighting started.

He adjusted the mask and cap. Hopefully his identity wouldn't be so obvious with these on. He understood why Gideon didn't want people to know who he was. What would he do if someone went after his parents because they knew his secret identity and wanted to hurt him?

The Seraph pushed open the first door. Spright tensed, ready to move, but Gideon closed the door again and walked to the next. Spright's hands vibrated in anticipation. He tried to still them. The second door yielded the same results.

As the Seraph opened the third door on the left side of the hall, the door opposite him clicked. *Danger.* Everything around Spright slowed to a halt. He rushed forward, grabbed Seraph, and shoved him to the ground.

Time resumed its normal speed as the door finished opening and Backfire leapt out and rammed his fist through the door Gideon had been ready to open.

"Get Dean!" the Seraph called.

Then the Seraph flew—literally—at Backfire, slammed into him, and carried him down the hallway. Spright exhaled, sped up his molecules, and ran inside the room Backfire had just vacated. In the middle of the room was an empty operating table. To its left was a black woman in a green jumpsuit and black cape—the woman who'd given him his "flu shot," although she hadn't been dressed like this then. She didn't see Spright at first; he was still in motion and would be only a blur to her. When he came to a stop, her head swiveled toward him.

"Ah. The speedster." She smirked. "Behind you."

Spright turned—right into someone's fist. He stumbled back into the operating table and looked up. Dean stood over him, fists clenched.

"What—Dean, it's me! Spright, remember?"

Dean lunged at him. Spright sped up again. Dean's fist moved in slow motion. Spright jumped to his feet, stepped around the punch, grabbed Dean by the collar, and dragged him out into the hallway. He slammed him into the wall.

"Snap out of it, buddy."

Dean vanished in a flash of green light. Spright frowned. *What in the . . . ?* Something hit the back of his head. He stumbled forward and smacked his forehead against the wall. As he fell, he turned around.

Dean stood behind him now.

"Oh no." Dean had powers—teleportation, by the looks of it. "Uh, buddy, you've got to wake up. That lady did something to you."

Dean swung a fist at him. Again, Spright sped up so that Dean was infinitely slower than him, and dodged Dean's punch. How could he snap Dean out of this trance? He darted back and forth as Dean swung punch after punch at him. This had to be Artemis controlling Dean. Maybe if Spright knocked her out, her grip on Dean would break. It was worth a shot. As he ran for her again, Dean vanished in a green blink and reappeared in the doorway. Spright managed to slow down and avoid running into him.

"Come on, man. Move." He held up his hands. "I think it's really awesome that you have powers now, but you don't want to be a supervillain, do you? That is so uncool."

Something on the other side of the building exploded—probably from Gideon and Backfire's fight. Spright glanced over his shoulder. That was a mistake. Two hands grabbed him by the collar, there was a flash of green light, and suddenly he was back in the lobby. He looked at Dean.

"Oh. You can teleport other people with you. Cool."

Dean punched him. Spright reeled back and stumbled to the ground. *You've got powers, idiot. Speed up.* He reverse-somersaulted into a crouch, locked gazes with Dean, and then lunged forward and ran circles around his mesmerized friend. He picked up a folding chair as he ran. *Sorry, Dean.* He stopped his cyclonic run when he came around behind Dean and swung the chair at his head—

Dean vanished. He reappeared in the lobby doorway.

"How do you fight someone who can disappear whenever you try to hit them?" This must've been how normal people would feel against a speedster. "I don't want to hurt you, man."

It was eerie how quiet Dean was. Did hypnotized people not remember how to talk, or something? Spright turned toward the hallway. Maybe if he ran at his top speed, he could make it back to the room where Artemis was before Dean could teleport there. He zipped down the hall and rounded the corner into the room.

She was gone. Spright shook his head. Where? Had she just fled, or had she gone to find the Seraph, or—

Dean appeared in front of Spright.

"Oh . . . " Spright panted. "Come on."

* * *

The Seraph grunted as Backfire hoisted him into the air, pulled back, and hurled him. He smashed into a wall and then through it, landing in an exam room on the other side. He coughed and staggered to his feet. The air filled with dust and particles of plaster and insulation. The Seraph's breaths rasped between his teeth, and he coughed as foreign matter tickled his throat. Backfire stepped through the newly created hole in the wall.

"Had enough, *amigo*?" Backfire picked up a chunk of drywall.

"Not even close."

Backfire charged the debris in his hands with his explosive energy and hurled it at the Seraph, who dove to the left. The drywall exploded behind him. Gideon slammed into the door to the hallway. Backfire stepped toward him, swinging a meaty fist at his face. Gideon blocked with his left forearm and swung with his right hand, striking Backfire in the gut. The light-powered punch dented Backfire's armor and knocked him back. The Seraph raised both hands and fired a burst of light into Backfire's chest.

Backfire grabbed a metal tray and hurled it at the Seraph. He generated a light shield, and the tray exploded as it struck the energy field.

Protected by his shield, Gideon stepped toward Backfire and unleashed a series of jabs and uppercuts. Backfire blocked several of his blows, but one caught him on the chin. The Seraph grabbed Backfire's head as he reeled back and brought it down to meet his aionium-clad knee.

Backfire stumbled to his feet, wiped blood from his nose, and grabbed the Seraph around the waist. The Seraph floated into the air, removing Backfire's momentum and leverage. The red-armored former guerrilla held onto the Seraph's waist as he flew. The room was small; he didn't have much room to maneuver. He fired a close-range burst at Backfire, knocking him back to the floor.

How was this guy still fighting? They'd done a lot of damage to each other; only their armor and sheer stubbornness was even keeping them on their feet. Gideon would have to compliment Dean on the aionium. Despite the explosions and constant blows, it was holding up.

But even though bullets and knives couldn't pierce it, it was still effectively a shell. That meant he still felt the impacts of punches and explosions, even though they were reduced. His body ached and screamed at him to rest. He refocused his mind on the fight. It wasn't over yet.

Backfire growled incoherently, stood, and stumbled over to a cabinet. Gideon dropped to the ground and stormed toward him, but Backfire had already lifted the cabinet and, with a shout of exertion, hurled it. The Seraph's eyes widened—*This is going to hurt.* He shielded himself and lifted off, trying to fly to the door.

The cabinet exploded. The Seraph was already in the air, so the explosion hurled him out the door and into the hallway, where he slammed into the adjacent wall. He slumped to the ground. Heavy bootsteps thudded closer. He needed to—

A metal boot smashed into the Seraph's chin. He rolled over onto his back and moaned. Stars filled his vision. Backfire leaned over him, smirked, and reached down to grab him by the collar. The Seraph clutched Backfire's hands and tried to pull himself free.

"I've been waiting a long time for this," Backfire said.

He pulled a fist back. As he did, the Seraph discharged a blast of light from his entire body. Backfire tumbled down the hallway. Gideon dropped to the floor and landed in a crouch. *Hurry up, Spright . . .*

* * *

Was there a way to snap someone out of a hypnotic trance without hurting them? The only way Spright could think of to do it was to hit Dean in the head, which would most definitely hurt. He supposed his friend would forgive him, given the circumstances. The problem was, every time he managed to get close, Dean teleported away.

As far as Spright could tell, Artemis had left the building, so maybe Dean was in a post-hypnotic state. If he snapped him out of it, Artemis might not be able to reassert control. At least, that's what Spright hoped. He just had to figure out how. Maybe Gideon would know. If Spright could find him and help him take out Backfire, then maybe the Seraph could save Dean.

Maybe, maybe, maybe. Too many unknowns. He needed to move.

Spright turned and ran down the hallway where the last explosion had come from—

Dean appeared in front of him. Spright tried to stop, but the teleporter grabbed his shirt and transported them both. Spright looked around. They were outside on the street, between their car and the doors to the lobby.

"You've got to stop doing that." Spright dropped into a runner's crouch. "It's really starting to tick me off."

He zipped around Dean and ran for the door. And again, Dean appeared in front of him, dropped him back in the street, and punched him in the gut. Spright backed up and stopped for a moment, staring Dean down. Maybe this was one of those situations where he'd have to use his mind before his speed.

Whenever Dean grabbed him to teleport him, he had a firm grasp on him. Maybe Spright could use that to his advantage. He'd have a clear shot at him if he took a swing while Dean was still teleporting them. It would be a split second, but if he could move that fast . . .

He had to. This was going to go on forever if he didn't end it now. He took a deep breath, focused on the doors to the lobby, and ran. Just as before, Dean appeared in the doorway and grabbed Spright. He started to teleport them . . .

As soon as Spright's perspective on the world changed, he pulled back his fist and jabbed forward, putting the full force of his speed behind the punch. By the time they landed back in the street, Spright's fist connected with Dean's jaw and flipped him through the air. As he hit the ground, Spright grabbed his head and slammed it down—not too hard, but with enough force to jar him—into the pavement. Dean stopped moving.

Spright put his hands on his knees and panted. That had been harder than he'd expected. Now the question was, should he leave Dean here and go help the Seraph, or should he stay here until Gideon returned? From the sound of that fight, things had been chaotic. His teacher might need him.

Spright put Dean in the back seat of the car and ran back into the clinic. He blazed through the lobby and around the corner into the hallway where the Seraph and Backfire were fighting.

Backfire rose from the floor, and the Seraph crouched down the hall from him. Waves of light emanated off the Seraph's body. As he rose, Spright rushed past him toward Backfire, smashed his fist into the large man's chin—*that's for Grandpa!*—and ran back around him. He grabbed Gideon as he ran and pulled him outside to the street.

" . . . whoa." Gideon looked around. "Do you have Dean?"

Patrick jerked his thumb toward the car. "Sleeping cozy in the back seat. What do you say we get out of here?"

"What about Backfire and Artemis?"

"I couldn't find any sign of Artemis, and neither of us is ready to keep fighting Big Ugly. We should get Dean to the lab."

"The lab?" Gideon's brow furrowed. "Why?"

"He's got powers now. He teleports. And until I knocked him on his head, he was under Artemis' mind control."

It was probably a lot of information for Gideon to process, but they didn't have time to wait. Patrick jerked open the driver's door and gestured for Gideon to enter. He nodded and got in as Patrick circled around to the passenger's side. He just hoped his theory about head trauma snapping Dean out of his trance was solid, otherwise, they'd have a problem on their hands when he woke up.

"We need to make sure Dean's out of the trance first." Gideon swung the car around. "Hotel tonight, lab tomorrow."

As Gideon drove, Patrick removed the mask and cap he'd been wearing and grinned. As intense and stressful as all of that had been, it had also been a rush. The bad guys might have gotten away, but the Seraph and Spright had saved Dean. As far as Patrick was concerned, his first mission was a success.

* * *

How had they evaded her? Artemis had been sure that Sterling's teleportation powers would be more than enough to keep him out of reach of the speedster, no matter how fast he moved. And Mendez . . . that fool's ego had been taken down a peg, at least. Artemis should have known that the brutish thug wouldn't have the tactics necessary to take on the Seraph. It had been her own fault for calling for him instead of one of her other companions.

But all was not lost. Though her connection to Sterling had been broken, there were other ways to get Turner's attention. If she could separate him from his friends, then his greatest advantage would be removed. Mendez had matched him almost blow for blow, and Artemis suspected Turner would've taken the upper hand in the end. But without his sidekicks, the next fight would end completely differently.

Artemis looked out her front window. A muscle car rattled up the driveway. Mendez, no doubt. She opened the door and stepped onto the porch. Mendez climbed out of his car and staggered to Artemis' side. She had left him in the clinic, not particularly caring whether the police came and arrested him or not. He was not nearly as useful as he believed himself to be. Disappointing. His powers gave him such potential, and yet he was still the volatile guerrilla from Venezuela that he'd always been.

"What do you want me to do now?" he asked.

"You're on standby." She went back into the house and removed her cape. "Our backup plan will have to suffice."

Mendez dropped down onto the couch. "Standby? What, you just want me to troll around the city until you have some more orders to snap at me, *mija*? I got you your device. So the *veloz* kid got the drop on me. Doesn't make me a screw up. Besides, you lost Sterling. Remember?"

Artemis narrowed her eyes. "You serve at Ashcroft's command, and he has handed you off to me. So yes, you will wait. You'll have something to do soon enough. For now, lie low. And get out of that ridiculous armor. The police will be looking for you and keeping that on is the perfect way to get caught."

"Whatever you say." Mendez stomped toward the door. "Just remember, you're not the top dog, Wayans. You don't have any actual authority over me. One day, I'll be more useful to him than you are. When that day comes . . . watch yourself."

She watched him as he stormed out. Petty threats didn't concern her; his powers were no match for hers. If he still thought so highly of himself even after he'd been defeated by Turner twice, let him try her. She'd show him real power.

CHAPTER 14

Even though her boyfriend worked there, Jolie rarely visited Sterling Labs. When she was a beat cop, she usually slept the day away so she'd be rested for her night shift. When she was promoted to detective, she worked days. By the time she was off, so was Gideon. She'd been to the labs only a handful of times, and she'd hardly had an extensive tour.

Now that she was up against a superhuman, she needed some scientific help. Since Dean and Gideon were gone, that left her only one option—well, two, really, but they were an inseparable unit. Arianna Serafin and Maddox Odell were Sterling Labs employees who worked in the technology division with Dean. They'd helped "Team Seraph," as they'd called themselves, during the Uprising, and they had studied Gideon's powers in the months since. In today's scientific community, they were likely the most knowledgeable on superpowers, besides Ashcroft. Now they were running the labs until Dean returned from San Francisco. If anyone had an idea of how to contain Powers, they would.

Jolie closed her umbrella as she entered the lab building. The morning summer shower had cooled the air a bit. The guard at the front desk glanced at her, but immediately waved her on when she showed her badge. She found the research and development lab on a floor plan next to the elevator. She rode the elevator to the fourth floor, exited, and followed the hallway to their lab.

Dark-skinned Maddox wore a pair of blue glowing goggles and held a ponderous-looking tube that had the vague shape of a gun. Arianna, blonde-haired and pale, stood to the side, taking notes on a tablet as Maddox trained the huge gun on a sparring dummy on the other side of the lab. Jolie crossed her arms and leaned against the wall to watch. Maddox fired the gun. A net sailed across the room and enveloped the dummy. The net's cords lit up with electrical surges, crackling across the dummy.

Maddox whooped. "Told you it would work!"

"Never doubted you." Arianna typed something into her tablet. "Problem is that thing is huge. The average cop isn't going to want to lug one of those around the streets until they run into a criminal. Kind of takes away the element of surprise."

"She's right." Both scientists jumped at Jolie's statement. She chuckled. "Sorry. Arianna's right about the gun. It's useful, but way too cumbersome. If you could figure out a way to make it more portable, it would be very handy."

"Detective Anderson." Arianna smiled. "To what do we owe the pleasure of this visit?"

"I need your help."

Maddox gestured to a table and three unoccupied rolling chairs. "Take a seat. We'll help however we can."

"We—and by we, I mean myself and the Crusader, plus a little bit of help from the persistent Wesley Turner—have been tracking a drug dealer named Vince Powers. At first, we thought he was just your average street scum. But recently, Wes and I confronted him on a rooftop, and Powers . . . well, he multiplied."

Arianna and Maddox exchanged glances. "Multiplied?"

"Duplicated himself. He jumped off the roof, and then another one of him appeared from nowhere, and then another, and another. He made a human ladder to get to the ground. And then all the duplicates disappeared."

Maddox blinked. "He spontaneously created doppelgangers?"

"Yes."

"I think Sojourn City has its second superpowered occupant," Arianna said.

"Exactly. And while the Crusader is being as helpful as he can, he doesn't have powers. Without the Seraph here, we've got nothing to take on Powers, let alone contain him even if we did grab him."

Maddox scratched his chin. "Interesting dilemma. I'm not sure how to stop someone like that . . . Let me think on it."

"If we could get a brain scan while he's doing it, that might help us figure out a solution," Arianna said. "If his powers are anything like Gideon's, it takes an exertion of will to use them, so any shock that disrupts brain activity should be sufficient to stun him. Hard to think when you've got several thousand volts coursing through your brain. And of course, killing him would theoretically destroy the duplicates. If they disappear at will, they're not real people. Just puppets."

"I don't want to go that far if I don't have to." Jolie shrugged. "So far, he's been relatively nonviolent. Just slippery."

"I concur with Arianna. An electric shock would break Gideon's concentration, so it should do the same for this replicator. It would be a temporary solution," Maddox added. "As soon as his brain rebooted, he'd be able to duplicate again. A brain scan would likely tell us which part of his brain is controlling the duplicates, and thus which part we'd have to keep disrupted. But again, we don't have that."

"We'll brainstorm a solution." Arianna stood up. "If you encounter him, shock him, and keep him sedated. Do remember that this is just a theory, and we can't be held responsible if it doesn't work. We'll try to come up with a more permanent solution."

"Thank you." Jolie rose and shook both scientists' hands. "Keep in touch."

"We will."

She considered asking them if she could borrow that net gun, but as cumbersome as it was, she doubted she'd get a chance to use it on Powers. It would only slow her down. There were other ways to deliver the kind of electrical charge needed to stun Powers without killing him. The *jo* staff that Gideon had given Carter, which could split into a pair of truncheons, had electrified ends. In a pinch, Jolie's taser would also suffice—but the charge in the staff was stronger and would likely incapacitate Powers for longer.

"Oh, and guys? About that shock net . . . ?"

Maddox glanced up. "Got an idea?"

"What about removing the net and compacting the shock into one of those adhesive beads, like Gideon uses?" Jolie held up her fingers to indicate the size of a marble. "Something like that could be even more useful than a taser, potentially. If you can make them excrete that adhesive gel, surely you can come up with a way for them to emit electricity."

Jolie backed out of her lab and walked back toward the elevator, leaving them to ponder her suggestion. She had a solution, however temporary. Now they just had to find Powers. She hoped to bring him down before Gideon returned from San Francisco. To do that, they'd need bait to lure him out—and Jolie thought she had just the thing.

She picked up her phone and dialed.

* * *

"You want me to do what?"

Wes draped a towel across his neck with his free hand. He tucked his phone between his ear and shoulder and removed his boxing gloves. He'd decided to start working on his fighting skills. He'd need them if he was ever going to be of any use to anyone. He draped the gloves on a peg on the wall, waved to one of the employees of Pop's Gym, and headed out the door.

"I want you to be my bait," Jolie said. "You seem to draw Powers to you like a magnet. I don't know why, but it can't be a coincidence that he keeps showing up at the same places as you."

"Did you ever think maybe it's because my brother's a superhero, and everyone knows it? Powers said as much on the rooftop—he wants Gideon."

"Gideon's not here. We can't wait for him to take down Powers. If he keeps distributing Shine in the Brooks, it's going to be a nightmare. And he doesn't even need to hire people to sell it; he can just copy himself and do the jobs of ten men. At least. Who knows if there's a limit to how many copies he can make?"

When Wes had told Jolie that he wanted to help her, this wasn't what he'd had in mind. It was a big change from Jolie telling him to stay away or she'd throw him in jail for his own good. Now, he was supposed to stick his neck out in hopes of catching a self-replicating drug dealer who had shown a creepy interest in him?

"Look, Wes, I'm desperate. So far, Powers hasn't exhibited violent tendencies. He's not a killer. But we still need to bring him in to stop the Shine trade. The problem is, he's gone to ground. The only way to get him to show himself is to bait him—and you might just be the only bait he'll take."

He hesitated for only a moment. "What's the plan?"

"Meet me at the old theater in the Brooks at ten o'clock tonight. You, the Crusader, and I are going to set a trap for Powers."

It wasn't a glorious start to a career in crime fighting, but it was something.

"See you then. And thanks for letting me help . . . even if it is just as bait."

"No, thank you, Wes."

"You're welcome."

He hung up his phone and stuffed it in his pocket. If Jolie expected him to act as bait and then stand aside and let her and the Crusader engage Powers by themselves, she was going to be disappointed. Wes wasn't going to let them put themselves in danger without him. He reached into his pocket and pulled out the spare key to Gideon's apartment. He'd already taken the spare uniform. Surely his brother wouldn't mind if Wes helped himself to a few more of the Seraph's toys that he'd left behind in his lair . . .

* * *

Gideon parked the car across the street and peered out through the windshield. Reporters milled about outside Sterling Labs—no doubt hoping to catch him. Since he'd made a public appearance as the Seraph, everyone and their mother would be scrambling for an interview with him. Before, he'd been the heroic celebrity of one city. Now, he was fighting bad guys across the country.

Patrick ran a hand through his hair. "We'll never sneak Dean inside through all that. What are we going to do?"

Last night, they'd taken Dean straight back to the hotel to clean him up—Patrick's head-smashing technique had broken Dean's nose, causing blood to run down his face and neck—and let him sleep off the trance. By the morning, he still hadn't awakened. Gideon had ruled out a brain bleed, despite Patrick's concern that he might've hit Dean's head too hard. Something was keeping Dean under, and they needed to figure out what. The lab was the best place to do that.

"You can drive, right?"

"Yeah."

"Take the wheel." Gideon unbuckled his seatbelt. "I'm going to give them exactly what they want. Drive around to the loading entrance at the back of the building and take Dean to the lab from there. I'll meet you inside."

"Okay." Patrick unbuckled. "You sure you're up for facing the media?"

Gideon shrugged. "Last night, I fought a guy who almost killed me with an exploding cabinet. What's the worst a few reporters can do?"

He climbed out of the car and tucked his hands in his pockets. They didn't notice him immediately; he was still far enough down the street that they probably hadn't even seen him. He waited until Patrick was driving around the building, and then he hopped up onto the sidewalk and strode toward the front doors of Sterling Labs with all the confidence he could muster.

A woman in her late twenties, dark hair flowing over shoulders clad in a blazer, noticed him first. She yelped out his name and scrambled down the courtyard steps toward him, microphone in hand and cameraman close behind. The other reporters noticed her mad dash and joined her.

"It's him!" someone shouted. "It's the Seraph!"

The first reporter extended her microphone. "Mr. Turner! Why have you come to San Francisco?"

"Who was the armored man you fought in the streets?"

"Are we in danger?"

"Was that man your nemesis? Have you brought a personal grudge to our city?"

"Where did your powers come from? Are you really a superhero?"

Gideon raised his hands. "One at a time, please. Listen, I don't know who that guy was. I just intervened because people were in trouble. I'm in San Francisco for personal reasons. I'm still learning about my powers, and while I wouldn't call myself a superhero, that is what my city calls me, yes. No, I don't believe this city is in danger."

He continued walking. They kept shouting questions at him as he shouldered his way through the crowd, but he ignored them. As far as he was concerned, he'd given them all the answers they were owed. He had more important things to worry about. He pushed his way into the lobby and felt a surge of relief when the reporters didn't follow him through the glass doors.

Now, to check on Dean. He took the escalator up and walked down the hall to their training lab. Patrick was already inside, laying Dean on a fold-out cot. Dean was still unconscious.

Gideon pointed at the cot. "Where'd you find that?"

"Searched the whole building." Patrick shrugged. "Took only a few seconds. Oh, I also brought your suit in. It's in the observation room."

The young man was now wearing a forest green t-shirt with the Sterling Labs logo emblazoned across the right breast pocket in white. He stepped away from Dean.

"So, what do we do now?"

"Artemis' mental powers did this to him. Maybe I can work some magic with mine. While I do that, I need you to find me some things, in case it doesn't work."

Patrick darted away and came back with a notepad and pencil. "Fire away."

Gideon listed off the items he might need, and Patrick dashed away. When the door closed behind him, Gideon knelt next to Dean and reached out mentally. He sensed the same feeling of manipulation that he had at the hotel, days ago. Could this feeling be related to Artemis' powers? Had she been watching them? If he could feel the effects of her powers on others, maybe he could also do something about it. He'd never tried anything like this, but it was worth a shot. He closed his eyes and imagined his mind touching Dean's. He found the manipulation, hanging like a cloud above Dean's mind. He imagined golden light pouring into the cloud and dispersing it.

The cloud vanished. Gideon opened his eyes. Dean was still asleep, but his eyes fluttered behind his lids. He took a deep breath and jerked upright.

"Whoa—what the—?"

The door swished open, and Patrick darted in. "He's awake! What did you do?"

"There was still a trace of Artemis' power in his mind. I just . . . eradicated it, I think."

Dean rubbed his head. "What . . . where am I?"

"Back in the lab," Gideon said. "Are you all right?"

"Yeah, I'm . . . I'm fine. What happened? I remember running out of the hotel, and then I woke up strapped to a table, and now I'm here."

"Artemis. She has mind control powers. She hypnotized you and took you back to the facility where they gave Patrick his powers. Do you remember?"

He didn't want to come out and say, "You have powers." It might freak Dean out and cause him to start popping in and out of places. The last thing they needed was for the world to know that Sterling Enterprises' new CEO had superpowers. Gideon was a virtual nobody, and he had become famous for his powers. Dean was already in the public spotlight, so showing the world his powers would only amplify that fame.

Dean blinked. "She . . . gave me powers. I remember. She called herself 'Somna,' and the guy you fought downtown, his name's Mendez—she called him Backfire."

"Yeah, I fought him again. I know him. He was one of the guerrillas who kept me hostage in Venezuela."

"No kidding? What are the odds."

"Do you remember how to use your powers?"

"I think . . . " Dean vanished. "I do."

The last two words came from behind Gideon. He spun around. Dean stood between him and the door.

"Wow." Dean laughed. "This is so cool!"

"Guess you get to design yourself a suit. For now, get some rest. You've been through a lot."

"Yeah . . . " Dean brushed his nose and grimaced. "I feel like I got hit by a bus."

Patrick scratched his neck. "Sorry."

Gideon and Dean laughed. Patrick blushed and shrugged. Gideon was impressed with the kid. He'd taken Dean out despite his teleportation nearly matching Patrick's speed, and he'd also helped Gideon with Backfire. He was learning quickly. *Maybe I don't need to worry so much.*

"All right," Gideon said. "In a few hours, we'll reconvene and decide what to do about Artemis and Mendez. But for now, let's get out of here."

* * *

Jolie knelt in the rafters above the theater, her right hand wrapped around the grip of her taser. Wes was in position below, pacing at the front of the room, in front of the screen. Through several CI's, she'd managed to leak to Powers that Wes would be there. Now all that remained was to see if he took the bait.

Jolie had given Wes a taser, which he kept tucked in his pocket. He'd shown up wearing the prototype Seraph armor again, but Jolie had told him to take it off. If Powers saw him wearing it, he'd know this was a trap. In the rafters on the other side of the auditorium, Carter crouched in a ready position. He was their Plan A, but Jolie and Wes' tasers would be their backup in case his staff didn't work. The problem was, they had no idea how Powers' duplication worked. Did they have to deliver a jolt to his original body, or would any one of them do? If they did hit one of the duplicates, would it destroy that body? Or would it have any effect at all? Their safest bet was to hit the original, and that's what she'd instructed Carter to do.

But if it came down to it, she'd fight through as many copies as he put out. This was her plan, and she wasn't going to let Wes and Carter suffer for it. She already had misgivings. Had she really been right to bring them in on this? It would've been safer to have a SWAT team here, lying in wait, but the odds of Powers noticing them was too great. They never would've caught him.

Jolie tapped her left index finger against the taser. Her knees ached, and she had a crick in her neck from kneeling in this uncomfortable position and peering down for so long. Was Powers even going to show up? Maybe she'd been wrong about his interest in Wes, and it had been coincidence that they'd run into each other more than once.

Carter shifted. Jolie glanced across the room at him. His deep crimson armor blended in well in the shadows of the rafters. With any luck, he could drop in behind Powers and zap him before the duplicating dealer even knew what was happening.

"How many times do I have to pace the floor before we decide he's not coming?" Wes asked. "I'm starting to wear a hole in the carpet—which, by the way, looks straight out of the nineties. How old is this theater again?"

"We'll wait a few more minutes." Jolie smirked. "And it's not that old. I remember coming to the grand opening when I was a kid."

"Why do you think this guy would come for me?"

"Connection to the Seraph, maybe?" Carter suggested. "If he wants a shot at the big guy, grabbing his little brother as leverage might be the way to do it."

"Or maybe he's one of the last free members of Serban's organization," Jolie said. "He could be out for revenge on Gideon."

"So, it's all about my big brother. That's what I thought."

Jolie felt for Wes. He had always had something of an unspoken rivalry with Gideon, ever since she'd known him. He loved his brother—idolized him, almost—but he also pushed himself to meet Gideon's standards. Gideon had been a doctor, so Wes had been planning to become a lawyer. But having superpowers? That was something Wes couldn't compete with.

It wasn't his fault, and Jolie knew that Wes never had to try to beat Gideon—their parents had loved both boys equally, unconditionally. It must've just been a younger brother's instinct, wired into him. He didn't have to be the best, but he at least had to keep up. And Jolie could tell that he was floundering, searching for a way to do that. He probably didn't even realize it.

Jolie opened her mouth to reassure him when the front door squeaked. She clamped her mouth shut and tightened her grip on the taser. She looked up at Carter and nodded. He was too far for her to tell if he'd seen her or not, but she thought he bobbed his head in return. He moved to his right, crouching directly above the door. Footsteps clacked on the tile foyer and softened as they touched carpet. Wes tensed, almost imperceptibly, and reached into his pocket.

"Mr. Turner." That was Powers' voice, all right. "I heard you'd be here."

Wes turned to face Powers. "What did you mean, back on the rooftop? About me having potential?"

Powers stepped into the auditorium. Jolie moved toward the rope she'd hung off the balcony, ready to slide down to the floor as soon as Carter made his move.

"Look at me." Powers spread his arms. "I was nothing. A two-bit street dealer addicted to my own product. But I became so much more. If I can, think of what you could do."

"Do I have to become a bad guy? Because if so, I think I'll pass."

Jolie put a hand on the rope. Powers took another step down the aisle. Carter hunkered down, preparing to spring. *One more step . . .*

"Bad guy? Come now, aren't you a little old for such a whimsical worldview? Things are rarely as black and white as they seem, Wesley."

Powers took another step, and Carter sprang. The red-clad Crusader leapt from the balcony and flicked the activator switch on his staff. Jolie grabbed the rope and slid down to the floor, keeping her taser ready in her other hand. Carter rammed his staff into Powers' back and the man stumbled forward. At the same time, Wes withdrew his hand from his pocket and hurled something. Powers hit the ground—

And rolled to his feet, leaving one of his duplicates splayed out on the floor. Something struck the doppelganger's body and exploded. A pool of blue-green gel spread over the duplicate's body. *An adhesive bead.* Wes must've helped himself to some of Dean's tech. It hadn't stopped the real Powers.

"Take him down!" Jolie said.

Wes withdrew his taser and rushed toward Powers. Jolie was hot on his heels. As they ran, Powers separated two more copies of himself. One of them lunged at Jolie, and she saw the other rush Carter just before her own adversary was on top of her.

"Hello, Detective." The duplicate grinned wickedly. "Nice to see you again."

Jolie fired her taser. The duplicate's forward motion continued as the volts racked his body, and he slammed into Jolie, knocking her back into a row of chairs. She grunted and pushed him away, but as she grabbed him, he vanished. She turned to face the others. One Powers grappled with Wes. Another charged at Jolie.

She didn't have time to charge her taser again. She pulled her nightstick from her belt and swung it as the duplicate approached her. He blocked the blow with his forearm and grabbed her by her collar. Jolie brought her foot up between his legs and struck him across the head with her nightstick.

As he fell, two more duplicates were already running toward her. One grabbed her right wrist, restricting her use of her nightstick. The other reached for her left hand. She twisted free of his grip and jabbed her fingers into his throat, turning to punch the other copy in the jaw. He loosened his grip on her weapon hand but did not fall.

She jerked free of him and swung the nightstick. He blocked it and retaliated with a left hook. Jolie pulled her head back just in time to avoid the punch. She traded a series of punches and kicks with the clone and finally laid him out when the handle of her nightstick connected with his chin.

This was getting ridiculous. They needed to end it—fast.

* * *

The Crusader brandished his staff as a trio of Powers' doppelgangers rushed him. He struck the center man in the jaw with a backswing. The other two came at him from either side. He split his staff into two shorter batons and twirled them as the copies approached. He snapped out a side kick that struck the leftmost attacker in his kneecap. As he fell, the Crusader raised his batons in a scissor block, catching the rightmost attacker's oncoming arm between them.

"Little make-believe superhero," Powers sneered. "You don't have any powers. You're nothing!"

"I'm more than you'll ever be."

The Crusader shoved the attacker's arm aside and jabbed with the end of his right truncheon, sending a jolt of electricity through the doppelganger. It spontaneously combusted, causing the Crusader to stumble forward. He caught himself and spun around to face the other two duplicates, who were rising from where they'd fallen. One favored his knee as they approached.

"Little Crusader," the one with the injured knee said. "You don't know what you're getting mixed up in, kid."

"If you were smart, you'd hang up the mask and go home," the other agreed.

"Shut up!" Carter shouted.

The first doppelganger swung a punch at his jaw. The Crusader rolled under the blow and came up behind his attacker, jabbing his elbow backward to strike between the Powers clone's shoulder blades. He staggered into a row of seats. The final attacker spun to face the Crusader and kicked him full in the chest. The Crusader's armor absorbed most of the blow, but he still stumbled back a few steps.

As the last doppelganger approached, the Crusader scanned the theater. Jolie was struggling with two more clones, while another had Wes pinned to the ground. If the Crusader could just get to him and take him by surprise . . .

The duplicate in front of him lashed out. He barely ducked under the punch. The doppelganger swung an uppercut that caught the Crusader in the chin. The Crusader stumbled and raised his truncheons defensively.

"Change is coming," Powers' duplicate said. "You shouldn't resist."

The Crusader clicked his batons together and twirled the staff in tight circles. The doppelganger jumped back to avoid being hit. The

Crusader stepped in, pirouetted, and swung his staff at the clone's head. He tried to duck, but the Crusader changed the arc of the staff, coming in from the opposite side. The end of the staff smashed into the doppelganger's jaw and knocked him flat on the ground, where he vanished.

The Crusader turned to the real Powers—but he was gone. Jolie punched her last opponent in the jaw, laying him out, and looked up.

"Where'd he go?"

The Crusader shrugged. "I don't know; I didn't see him . . . "

"Where's Wes?"

"Oh, no." The Crusader scanned the darkened auditorium, hoping they'd just missed their friend in the dim light. "Wes! You here, man?"

No answer. The Crusader stepped over the bodies of the fallen doppelgangers as they began to disappear. Had Powers taken Wes? Or had he fled with Wes in pursuit of him? Either way, they needed to find him fast. The Crusader slung his staff into the sheath on his back and jogged down the aisle, looking for any sign of where they could've gone.

One of the doppelgangers—the one trapped in adhesive goo—laughed. The Crusader spun around to face him, but Jolie was already on him. She grabbed him by the collar and pulled him up as much as his sticky prison allowed.

"You can't help young Mr. Turner now," the doppelganger said. "He's on his way to a higher destiny."

"Where is he?" she demanded.

"Out of your reach. The world is changing, Detective. You are about to become outdated."

The doppelganger faded into nothingness. The Crusader frowned and stepped toward Jolie. She stared down at her empty hands, still curled as if they were holding the doppelganger's collar. He put a hand on her shoulder.

"We'll find him."

"We have to tell Gideon." Jolie lowered her hands. "I made this mess because I thought I could handle Powers without him."

"It's not your fault, Jolie."

She turned and walked toward the exit. The Crusader stood and watched her go. Should he follow and try to reassure her? Should he go home and wait for whatever came next? Or should he go out and look for Wes? Maybe Powers hadn't gotten far. It was possible the Crusader could still catch up to him. One good jolt was all he needed. He just had to do it before Powers knew what was coming so he couldn't repeat his hit-the-ground-and-clone thing. How had he done that? Somehow, he'd channeled all the energy from the Crusader's blow into another body and shunted it out of him. It was a neat trick, but it wouldn't save him a second time.

Even if he could catch up to them, he didn't want to risk Wes getting hurt because of him. And he wouldn't have the element of surprise. Powers would be expecting them to pursue him. He might even leave some duplicates behind to ambush them. No, the Crusader couldn't risk that alone. Jolie was right. If they were going to get Wes back, they needed Gideon's help. But he didn't want to imagine the look on Gideon's face when they told him why his younger brother was in the hands of a supervillain.

* * *

Wes slammed the emergency door open and rushed out into the alley. Powers had knocked him flat and sprinted away from the fighting, but Wes was determined to catch him. Jolie and Carter had been too busy with the duplicates, so it was up to Wes to make sure Powers didn't get away. He leapt over a pile of trash and sprinted through the alley. Powers was just ahead, standing on the sidewalk. Wes slowed down and stopped a few yards away from the drug dealer.

Why had Powers stopped? He was just standing there, hands tucked in his hoodie pockets, looking out at the street. Wes frowned and stepped toward him, keeping one hand on his taser. Was this a trick? Maybe this was one of Powers' doppelgangers, and the real Powers was waiting around the corner to tackle Wes.

"Don't move," Wes said.

"I'm not." Powers turned around. "I'm sorry for all that, but I had to get you alone somehow."

"I—what?"

"They wouldn't understand. Certainly not the detective. Not even that boy. No, he's already been too indoctrinated by his father and your brother. But you . . . you understand."

"Understand what?"

"You deserve to be like him. I can see it in you—you want to be like your brother so badly. To be a hero." Powers removed his hands from his pockets. "I can help you."

"You?" Wes laughed. "You're a drug dealer."

"I was. Now, I have been brought into a much greater plane of existence."

Wes shook his head and trained the taser on Powers. This guy was crazy. Maybe he'd given up drugs, but he was high on something, even if it was his own power.

"You're insane."

"No, I'm not. Let me help you, Wes. I'm not a villain—I just want others to experience what I've been through. If you come with me, you can become much more. You can become a hero like your brother. I told you, you have potential."

Wes lowered his taser. "Why should I trust you?"

Powers backed away. "Because I won't force you. I'm not going to make you follow me; all I ask is that you let me walk. If you're interested in my offer, then put down your taser and come after me. Want to go grab that super suit from your car? I'll wait. If you don't follow, you'll never see me again. But make no mistake, Wesley, this is the offer of a lifetime."

Wes' hands trembled as Powers turned and walked down the sidewalk. Could he really do this? What if it was a trap? The offer sounded good—maybe too good. But on the other hand, if he followed Powers, he could figure out where his base of operations was and lead Jolie back there. Then he'd be a hero, superpowers or no.

He set the taser down on the ground and rushed after the hooded figure.

* * *

Patrick sat in his bed, staring at the wall, long after he should've gone to sleep. He kept replaying the fight at the clinic in his head. He couldn't help it—it had been his first superhero fight, and he had won. They'd rescued the prisoner and beat the bad guys. Of course, the bad guys escaped, but didn't that always happen the first time? They'd catch up with them eventually.

It was so surreal. He'd grown up with movies and TV shows about superheroes. He had fantasized about being one as a kid. He'd even wondered if there might be real ones out there somewhere. But to become one himself? It was more than he ever would've dreamed, and it was amazing.

Something tapped on his window. Patrick swiveled his head around. Lucy Carmichael, his next-door neighbor and longtime crush, sat on the edge of the roof. Patrick grinned and walked over to open the window for her. The seventeen-year-old girl's blonde hair waved gently in the night wind. He'd always thought she was the most beautiful girl he'd ever seen. Her piercing blue eyes and cute button nose made her irresistible, but his connection and attraction to her went beyond the physical. She was the one who invited him to the church event where he'd been saved. He loved her for that.

He stepped aside to let her in, trying not to stare. She wore a gray t-shirt with a Christian band name on the front, blue denim shorts, and her favorite pair of black Vans. She smiled, gave him a hug, and dropped down in a beanbag chair in the corner of the room.

"Where've you been, Omer? I haven't seen you in days."

"I've been busy." He shrugged and sat down on the edge of his bed. "I got an internship at Sterling Labs."

"Oh, hey, look at mister fancy." Lucy grinned. "Kidding. That's awesome! But come on. It's summer. We should get out, have a little fun. Take a day off, huh?"

"I will. But there's a big project they need my help on right now."

"Oh, yeah?" She frowned. "Does it have anything to do with that cut over your eye?"

Patrick cringed. The only visible sign of his fight with Dean was a short gash over his right eye. Less than twenty-four hours, and it was already starting to heal—maybe a benefit of his superspeed. And the cut hadn't been bad to start with; he'd played it off with his parents that he'd just fallen and hit his head. But it was there, nonetheless.

"No, that's just . . . I fell on my way home. Clumsy me."

"Uh-huh." She raised a blonde eyebrow. "Anyway, you coming to church with me tomorrow?"

"Uh, sure."

His parents hadn't been happy with him for being out this afternoon. They gave him a lot of leeway, but being home on the Sabbath was non-negotiable. He'd get an earful tomorrow since he'd missed the day of rest today. He might even get grounded for it, so sneaking out to go to church could be tricky.

"Cool." Lucy stood. "You know, Patrick, I think there's something else going on with you. You can tell me anything. You know that, right?"

Oh, you have no idea how much I want to. He was already keeping from Lucy that he was in love with her. Keeping his superspeed from her, too, was agonizing, but could he trust her with it? How would she react? Gideon didn't think he should tell anyone about his powers but . . . it was Patrick's life, wasn't it?

"I know. 9:30?"

"9:30. See you then." Lucy climbed out the window. "Good night, Patrick."

"Good night."

He sighed as he watched her climb off the roof using the tree between their houses. How was it possible to be so smitten with someone, and they not even know about it? Oh, well. One thing at a time. One day, he'd tell Lucy how he felt. One day.

CHAPTER 15

Gideon's eyes snapped open and his heart pounded as the side table next to his bed vibrated violently. He scowled and buried his head in his pillow. The cursed piece of technology continued to rock the table, filling the bedroom with a grating noise. Growling between his teeth, Gideon rolled over and looked at the offender. His phone screen lit up the darkened room, and the device danced across the small table, causing the vibrations that had awakened him. He rolled out of bed and picked up the phone. *It's two in the morning, who the heck—?*

It was Jolie. His frustration turned to worry. She wouldn't call this late for no reason, and it was even later in Sojourn than here. He answered the phone and brought it up to his ear.

"Hello?" The drowsiness in his voice deepened the word and made it rasp out between his teeth. He cleared his throat and tried again. "Hello?"

"Gideon? I'm so sorry—I . . . "

Although his powers didn't reach across vast distances, he didn't need them to know that Jolie was distraught. He could hear it in her voice. Over years of dating, he had learned to recognize that she had a distinct tone when she was trying to cover up that she'd been crying.

"What's wrong?"

"It's Wes."

Gideon's heart sank. The last time he'd heard from Wes, he'd been gathering applications for a few different apartments. What could've happened?

"He's been kidnapped," she choked out. "It was my fault."

Kidnapped? Who would want to kidnap Wes, and for what? Gideon's stomach tumbled uncontrollably. This had to be about him—someone wanted to get at the Seraph. At least Wes was alive. They could work with that.

"Jolie, I'm sure it wasn't your fault. Start from the beginning."

Gideon clenched his jaw as she explained. A new superhuman in Sojourn . . . cryptic words about a changing future . . . offering Wes a place in it . . .

"It was my idea to use him as bait, Gideon. I'm so sorry. I just thought we'd be able to handle Powers ourselves."

He took in a deep breath through his nostrils and exhaled from his mouth. No need to chew her out. Jolie had done what she thought best; there was no way she could've predicted that it would turn out like this.

"It's okay. They probably took him because of me. The people I've been facing probably sent Powers to get Wes in case their attempt here failed. They already tried grabbing Dean, so it's in their playbook. I'll be home first thing in the morning. We're going to find him, Jolie."

"Okay." She sniffled. "I really am sorry."

"It's not your fault. Just try to get some rest. We're going to figure this out."

"I'll try. I love you."

"I love you, too."

Gideon lowered his phone and hung up. He wouldn't get any more sleep tonight. He rose and walked to the window. The lights of the city shone through the thin curtains. He rolled them aside, stared out at the cityscape, and wondered what to do about Patrick and Dean. Should he bring them to Sojourn with him, or leave them here for the time being?

Whatever he did, he'd have to decide fast. Wes' life could be on the line, and Gideon wasn't going to let his brother suffer on his account.

* * *

As Gideon rushed around the suite, Dean gathered the last of his belongings and stuffed them in his suitcase. It was the middle of the night, and Gideon had awakened Dean to inform him about Wes' kidnapping. Then, without waiting for a response, he'd rushed back to his room to pack.

Haven't I been through enough? Dean was still coming to terms with his superpowers. Just before he'd gone to bed, he'd accidentally teleported out of the bathroom and into the middle of the hallway outside their suite. Luckily, he'd still been dressed, but it was going to take some practice to figure out these abilities. Practice and rest. The latter of which, apparently, he was doomed to never get.

Dean understood Gideon's franticness, but it wouldn't help them. If Gideon was right about the kidnapper's real goal, the bad guys had no choice but to wait for Gideon to return to Sojourn City. They couldn't very well barter Wes' life when Gideon was on the other side of the country.

If Gideon slowed down to think and strategize, they'd be fine. No one had contacted Gideon with a demand yet. But Gideon had made up his mind, and Dean knew better than to try to dissuade him. He'd acted exactly like this when Luca Serban had threatened his family.

Heedless of the advice of Dean, Wyatt, or Jolie, Gideon had rushed off to fight his battles alone. This time, Dean would be there with him.

"What about Patrick?" Dean asked. "If we leave in the middle of the night without telling him, he'll be crushed."

"We'll come back for him as soon as we can. Right now, we don't have time to waste. Every second Powers has Wes, he could be taking him farther from Sojourn City."

"Or he might be sitting on him somewhere in the city, waiting for you to do exactly what you're doing right now."

"Maybe." Gideon hoisted his suitcase. "Doesn't matter. He's my brother."

"Fair enough." Dean finished packing the last of his belongings, clasped his suitcase, and walked toward the door. "I called the pilot. He's very unhappy, but he's standing by. We're good for takeoff as soon as we get to the airport."

"Then let's go."

Dean shook his head as Gideon pulled open the suite door and rushed out into the hallway. Dean followed his friend. He could've stayed, but he wasn't going to let Gideon rush into the fire alone, especially not knowing what he was facing. Right now, he was thinking with his feelings, not his mind. That was going to get him killed.

If he had stopped to think about this, he might've reached the same conclusion that Dean had—that kidnapping Wes made no sense. Artemis had just tried the exact same thing with Dean, and Gideon and Patrick had rescued him. Unless she or Ashcroft were terribly dense, trying the same plan twice was foolish. There had to be more to Wes' kidnapping than they were seeing at first glance. Dean just didn't know what yet.

Unfortunately, that was why he felt the urge to follow Gideon. He had a clearer head, and he'd be able to steer Gideon toward a more logical path. The plane ride would give Gideon time to stop and think, and that was when Dean could hit him with some logic bombs. Still, it was a shame to leave Patrick like this. *I'll send him a text on the way to the airport.* The kid was probably asleep, but he'd see the message when he woke up. That, at least, would be better than waking up to find that his friends had vanished without warning.

Gideon tossed his luggage into the back seat of the sports car and slid into the driver's seat. Dean stowed his own luggage and took the passenger's seat. The bright side about the time of night was that the traffic between the hotel and the airport would be minimal. As Gideon drove away, Dean pulled out his phone and composed a text message to Patrick. *We had to run back to Sojourn City for an emergency. We'll be back soon. Take a few days off, and we'll meet up with you as soon as we can.*

"Are you sure we should leave Patrick?" Dean asked again.

"I don't think his parents would like us pulling up to their house at three in the morning, yanking their son out of bed, and dragging him halfway across the country."

"I know, but . . . "

"I feel just as bad about leaving him as you do. I feel like I'm letting the kid down, but I've got to save Wes. It's not like I'm abandoning Patrick; we just have to leave him for a while."

Dean nodded. Gideon had made up his mind, so Dean would go along for the ride. He sent the text message, tucked his phone in his pocket, and leaned back in his seat. In their hurry, he realized they hadn't checked out of the hotel. *Oh, well.* With any luck, they'd be back before the end of the day—or tomorrow at the latest.

"What if Patrick does want to come with us? Once we come back, I mean. We both know we can't stay in San Francisco forever, and you've been training the kid for only a few days. He needs a lot more training than that—and he needs experience, too."

Gideon's jaw was working overtime. "If he does, maybe you can tell his parents he's part of a Sterling Labs internship program, and he'll have to move to Sojourn City for a few months to complete the program."

"Yeah . . . yeah, that could work. But do you think they'd let him?"

"He's an adult—certainly by Jewish custom, and almost legally. If Patrick tells his parents he wants to come with us, they won't stop him."

"Okay." Dean closed his eyes. Maybe he could get a little rest on the way to the airport. "What are you going to do tonight, anyway? There's not much we can do for Wes until morning."

"I'm not resting until I find him." The steel in Gideon's voice was unmistakable. "I'll search the Brooks street by street if I have to."

Yeah, that'll accomplish a lot. This was the same determination Dean had seen in Gideon when he'd been obsessed with stopping Serban. He'd become a machine—unwilling to rest until his goal had been accomplished. He was going to kill himself if he wasn't careful. But that was why he had Dean.

"I sensed that."

Dean frowned. "Sensed what?"

"You thought something sarcastic. I don't know what, but I sensed the sarcasm."

Dean laughed. Sometimes, he forgot about the subtler aspects of Gideon's powers. He had to be careful what he thought around him—or, more accurately, how he felt around him. It wouldn't ease the situation any if Gideon knew just how skeptical Dean was.

"Sorry. I'm just tired."

"Uh-huh." There was a trace of humor in Gideon's voice. *That's a relief.* "We're almost to the airport. Then you can sleep on the flight."

I don't think so. Gideon didn't know it yet, but the flight would be spent with Dean doing everything in his power to talk some sense into his friend. It was his responsibility, not just as a member of Team Seraph, but as Gideon's best friend. Nothing was going to happen to Gideon, or to Wes. Not on his watch. And now, he had the powers to back that up.

* * *

Almost immediately after dressing down Mendez, Artemis boarded a flight to Sojourn City. Although Turner was still in San Francisco, she wanted to be ready for him when he returned to his home city.

Not long after her arrival in Sojourn, Vince Powers contacted her with the news that he'd successfully persuaded the younger Turner brother to come with him. Artemis was impressed that Powers had achieved something she and Mendez couldn't. But she would withhold her praise until the situation was completely resolved. After all, Wes would serve as an excellent draw for Gideon when the time was right, but the job wasn't done yet.

Artemis walked through the abandoned warehouse owned by Crowne Pharmaceuticals and wrinkled her nose. It was sparsely decorated with crates and pallets serving as chairs and tables. There was a refrigerator and a few cabinets in one room, but other than that the amenities were scarce. The whole place smelled of mildew. She never could've lived here. How Powers could use it as a hidey-hole, she'd never know.

Many of Ashcroft's subjects had once been the dregs of society, used to this sort of life. The man she'd come to know was no exception. Vince Powers had been less than a nobody when Ashcroft found him and offered him a permanent solution to his drug addiction. Powers had taken quite well to his new abilities, but in Artemis' opinion, one could never outgrow their roots. As powerful as he was now, Vince Powers was still a junkie and a street dealer at heart. But at least he could get a job done. Unlike a hardened soldier such as Mendez, apparently.

Wes Turner sat in one corner of the small room with the refrigerator. He had his hands clasped in front of him, elbows resting on his knees. One of his arms was in a cast. He kept looking around suspiciously. He was still cautious—but that was good. He wasn't overly naïve. Just enough to suit their purposes. The question was whether he could be turned against his brother. That would be the real trick, one that Artemis could pull off with some mind games.

Powers—or Fragment, as he was known in the Regency—stood across the room from Turner, leaning against a counter. The dealer smirked at Artemis from beneath the shadow of his brown hoodie. She looked him up and down and shook her head in disgust. Just a hoodlum at heart, as she suspected.

"Go change into a proper uniform," Artemis said.

"What? No 'hello'? No 'job well done'?"

She rolled her eyes. "You performed exactly as you were supposed to. Now please, go put on a uniform. You are part of something glorious—start acting like it."

"Fine."

Fragment sulked away with his hands buried deep in his pockets. Artemis approached Wesley, putting an extra sway in her hips. He looked up as she approached, and his eyebrows raised just a bit. She thought she detected a hint of his pupils dilating. She concealed a smirk. *Just a boy, after all.* She could work with that.

"Hello, Mr. Turner. My name is Artemis Wayans."

"Uh . . . hi."

He didn't seem to know what to do. That was good; it meant he was malleable. Turner's body language told of caution. His shoulders were hunched, his eyes flicking back and forth from her to the door. He was on guard, so she would have to be careful what she told him. She couldn't alienate him.

"I'm so glad you decided to listen to my associate." She gave him her best flirtatious smile. "We've been watching you, Wesley, and we expect great things from you."

"You . . . you do?"

"We do. May I sit?"

Without waiting for permission, Artemis grabbed another crate and pulled it over to him. She sat on it, barely inches away from Wes, and crossed her legs, resting both hands on her upper knee.

"I can tell that you have a desire to do extraordinary things, Wesley. You, like your brother, are destined for greatness."

"You . . . you think Gideon is great?"

"Of course. He's just been misled." She bit her lip in a half pout. "Gideon doesn't realize that we are trying to make the world better—not worse. We don't want to rule with an iron grip or burn the world to the ground. We only want to create protectors, people like Gideon, who can do more to defend innocents than the average police officer."

The best lies are sprinkled with truth. That truism had served her well as a politician. Ashcroft did want to make the world a better place by creating more people like Gideon. However, there would be other steps involved that Wesley might not like as much, so she would leave those out for the moment.

"We want you to persuade your brother of the truth. With both of you on our side, we will achieve our goals far more rapidly. Your brother has become quite famous since his identity was outed. If the superhero of Sojourn City endorsed us, then we would meet far less resistance."

"And you want me to convince Gideon just based on your word?"

"Of course not, my boy." Artemis reached out to touch his good hand—just a brush, barely a caress, but enough. "I will show you what we're planning. I know you want to be like your brother. Let me do that for you."

"You mean . . . you'll give me powers?"

"If that's what you want." Artemis flicked her gaze intentionally to the cast on his arm. "Absolutely."

Wesley studied the floor for a moment, and then the cast, and finally her face. He furrowed his brow, and Artemis could see the wheels of his mind at work. He was no fool.

"That's what I want," he finally said.

"Excellent." Artemis stood and offered him her hand. "Then let's begin."

CHAPTER 16

"Just think about it, Gideon," Dean said. "Would they really try the kidnapping shtick twice in one day? What, they thought it worked out so well the first time that they wanted to go for round two?"

Gideon rubbed his temples. "I thought you were going to sleep."

"I'm not tired anymore."

"Liar." Gideon half smiled. "I can sense how tired you are."

"Will you stop that?" Dean's deep scowl showed his seriousness. "Maybe your senses are wrong this time. If you'll just listen to me for a second, then maybe I can get some rest. I can't sleep knowing you haven't completely thought this through. Going in all without a plan is going to get you captured or killed."

Gideon hated to admit it, but Dean was right. It was odd that another of his loved ones had been kidnapped just hours after he'd rescued Dean. Had they intended for both kidnappings to play out simultaneously, to divide Gideon and Patrick? Or was Wes' kidnapping another play entirely? It had to be part of Ashcroft's schemes, because the odds of another supervillain showing up like Powers had was too big a coincidence. Whatever this was, Ashcroft was coordinating it. Gideon was sure of it.

"What do you think I should do?"

"Slow down and think. Even if they have kidnapped him, remember that they didn't hurt me at all—okay, they gave me superpowers and hypnotized me, but I'm alive and well. If Wes is their prisoner, then the odds are they're probably doing the same to him. That sucks, but we know he's alive. And he will be for some time. If they give him powers, then we have to assume their intent is to add him to Ashcroft's force."

"Okay, that's fair."

"So, here's what I recommend. When we land in Sojourn City, we're going to go back to our apartment and sleep for a few hours. When we wake up, we'll go to the site of Wes' kidnapping, scope it out, and see if we can figure out where this Powers guy took him. If that fails, then we'll dig into his records, search for old haunts, and on and on. We'll find him, Gid. We just have to work smart."

"I hate it when you're right."

"I know." Dean smirked. "Wake me when we land. I'm going to doze now. I'm wiped."

"I knew it."

"Shut up."

* * *

Patrick stared down at the text message in disbelief. "We had to run back to Sojourn City for an emergency. Be back soon. Take a few days off and we'll meet up with you as soon as we can."

They left me.

Okay, so it had been an emergency, and the text had come in at three in the morning. But still. He wasn't even close to ready for Gideon and Dean to leave. He still needed so much training, and Dean hadn't given him his suit yet. *Easy, man. Dean said they're coming back.* As hard as it would be, he'd just have to be patient until then. Besides, he had plenty to keep him busy today. He checked his watch: 9:05. He needed to get ready for church.

He dressed as quickly as he could—which was fast. He tried on a few different outfits and finally settled on a pair of black skinny jeans, a gray t-shirt, and a plaid red and white button-down shirt, open in the front and sleeves rolled up to his elbows. He pulled on a pair of black boots and nodded at his reflection. Not bad. He tamed his hair, brushed his teeth, and ran down the stairs.

"Whoa, where are you going?" his mother asked.

"Lucy and I are hanging out. Gotta go, love you!"

He rushed out the door before she could respond. *That was close.* At least he'd avoided Dad. Patrick bounded off the porch and down the sidewalk to Lucy's house.

* * *

Although brief, Gideon's reunion with Jolie had been a relief he didn't know he needed. She came to his and Dean's apartment early Sunday morning to catch them up on the search for Powers and Wes. She gave them everything the police had on Powers, and that was that. After a too-short hug, Gideon followed her out the door. While Gideon and Jolie searched for Wes, Dean would look for potential hideouts. Thankfully, Dean and Gideon's return in the middle of the night meant that no one realized they were back in town yet. Throngs of Seraph fans had not gathered outside the apartment building, and Gideon and Jolie were able to slip away without notice.

Gideon pulled up next to the old theater, his mind whirling. This building was one of the first places Jolie had seen Gideon in action as the Seraph. She'd called him here to interrogate a member of Serban's mafia. Now, all he could see was a crime scene, the place his little brother had been taken from.

He turned off his Mustang and climbed out. Jolie was already waiting at the front door to the theater. Gideon followed her inside. It was strange, investigating a crime in broad daylight and wearing civilian clothes. His red Henley over a white t-shirt and black jeans seemed entirely too casual for what he was doing, but he didn't need his suit just to look for clues.

"Where's Carter?" he asked.

"At work. Apparently, grocery stores don't let you off your shift just because one of your friends got kidnapped."

Good. Carter shouldn't have been involved in the first place—he wasn't ready to take on a supervillain. Even Gideon wasn't ready for that, considering he'd lost both rounds with Backfire. After Wyatt's death, Gideon couldn't live with himself if Carter got hurt, too.

The auditorium was dark. Gideon stepped forward, and his tennis shoe squished in something. He grimaced and pulled his foot back, revealing a blue-green goo clinging to the sole. *Adhesive gel.* Good thing Dean had designed the gel to gradually break down over time. Otherwise, Gideon would have had to remove his shoe and leave it there.

"Carter used some of his adhesive beads last night?"

"Not Carter. Wes. I think he helped himself to some of the Seraph's supplies."

Gideon raised his eyebrows. "Really?"

"He wants to be like you, Gideon—a lot. He even borrowed one of your prototype suits the other day." Jolie flicked on the lights. "You had to have noticed how conflicted he's been."

"I did. I just thought it was about law school. You mean that he's jealous?"

"Not jealous, exactly. At least, I don't think so." Jolie shrugged. "He just wants to be able to help people like you do."

"He's always had a servant's heart. But that's something to deal with later. For now, what do we have?"

"Wes, Carter, and I confronted Powers here." Jolie waved at the room around her. "Carter hit him with a jolt of electricity, but somehow Powers channeled it into one of his doppelganger bodies, which Wes hit with the adhesive bead. Powers made several more duplicates, and we fought them. When they were all down, Wes was gone."

"Did you see which way he went?"

"It had to have been out the side door." Jolie pointed to the front of the auditorium, near the screen. "Carter was standing next to the main door back here the whole time. If Wes had run by him, he would've noticed. We swept the area around the building, and we didn't see anything. But it was dark, so . . . "

"Let's take a look."

Gideon walked toward the side door, scanning the floor as he did. There was no sign of anything Powers or Wes might've left behind. If it hadn't been for the gel near the entrance, the theater would've looked exactly like what it was—an abandoned building. He pushed the door open and stepped into the alley. A half-skidded footprint smeared the mud near the door. From the shape of the print, he guessed it was from a Converse shoe. *That'd be Wes.*

He held the door open for Jolie and then walked in the direction the print pointed. The alley exited into a side street. Gideon walked toward it and swept his eyes across both sides of the alley, reaching out with his senses at the same time. He didn't detect anything out of the ordinary.

"Look." Jolie rushed ahead of Gideon and knelt in the alley. A small, orange object lay in a puddle. Gideon knelt next to Jolie. A taser—an unfired one.

Jolie picked it up. "It's the one I gave to Wes. He was here."

Gideon studied the ground around the puddle. There was no sign of blood. If Powers had taken Wes from here, he'd done it without hurting him too badly. Gideon touched the taser and focused on his empathic powers. *Confusion . . . inner conflict.*

"Wes was confused about something." Gideon frowned. "But what?"

"Do you think Dean could access the traffic cameras in this area?"

"Probably." Gideon pulled out his phone. "Don't you think someone at the police station could do that, though?"

Jolie looked away. "I . . . don't particularly want anyone there knowing that I used a civilian as bait and then lost him."

"Fair enough." Gideon dialed. "This isn't your fault, you know. As much as I don't like what you did, I probably would've done the same thing if I were in your shoes. This could've happened to anybody."

"Hello?" Dean answered.

"Dean, hey. Can you access footage from the traffic cams in the vicinity of the old theater?"

"On it. Where am I looking?"

"Back alley. We found Wes' taser lying on the ground."

"I'll get right on it."

"Thanks. Let me know when you get something."

Gideon hung up and tucked his phone in his pocket. Jolie stood and wrapped an arm around Gideon's waist. He rubbed her back, squeezed her shoulder, and backed away.

"Come on. Let's start combing the Brooks. Sooner or later, we'll come across something."

"We can start with Powers' old auto shop. I doubt he'd go back there, but maybe he left a clue as to where he might go next."

"Lead the way."

* * *

Jolie swept her flashlight across the interior of the auto repair shop. She was sure the CSIs had already cleaned it out, but if Powers had left anything behind to hint at his location, they had to look into it. The CSIs would've focused on drug-related clues and might've overlooked one that related to Ashcroft. She shook her head. *Supervillains.* What kind of world were they living in?

A warm, golden light filled the room. Jolie lowered her flashlight and glanced over at Gideon. He held his left hand aloft, gentle beams of light spilling from his pores. She pocketed her light and smiled at him. That trick never got old.

"That's kinda hot, you know."

"Technically, it's very hot. Third degree burns hot." Gideon grinned. "But thanks. You're not so bad yourself."

"All right, there'll be time for more flirting later. Promise." She slapped his upper arm and turned away. "Let's see what we can find."

Jolie walked between a few half-dismantled cars. She'd watched as the CSIs had stripped out the hidden compartments that stored the Shine underneath the steering wheels. But maybe those compartments weren't the only secrets these cars held. Jolie knelt next to the front left tire. She went through the trunks, ripped up the pleather seating, scanned the treads . . .

"Hey." She looked up. "I think I've got something."

Gideon darted toward her and shined his hand at the tire. A dull piece of metal was stuck in one of the treads. Jolie pulled it out. It looked like a bolt, but it had been warped. She hung her head. It could've come from anywhere.

Gideon took the bolt from her. "Hey, it's a start. How many of those do you see out in the streets? This had to have come from a specific location."

"Are you sure?"

"No . . . but it's all we've got right now. Where would a warped bolt come from?"

"Maybe a factory or warehouse?" Jolie shrugged. "But there are dozens of those in the Brooks. How would we ever narrow it down to which one?"

"If Dean can get footage from the traffic cameras that indicate which direction Wes and Powers went, then we could single out the factories in that area, research which of them store or manufacture bolts and other metal parts . . . "

"Some start. Gideon, that's a huge stretch. Even if it works, it could take days."

Gideon put his hand, still glowing but not as brightly as before, on her shoulder. It was warm, even through her sleeve. "It's going to be okay. Let's get back to the apartment and see what Dean's come up with. Then we can worry about our next step."

CHAPTER 17

Wes licked his lips and tried to conceal his nervousness as Artemis prepared the serum. After she had promised to give him superpowers, she'd told him that she would have to prepare some things and that she would return in the morning. Wes hadn't been inclined to sleep in the dingy warehouse with only Powers for company, but if he left, that would be it. He'd never find them again.

Knowing that, he'd sucked it up, climbed into the ratty sleeping bag Powers had provided, and done his best to sleep. It hadn't come easy. He was nervous and excited all at the same time. He had to remind himself repeatedly that getting superpowers wasn't the main reason he was here—he was gathering intel that he could give to Gideon later. He didn't have enough yet, so he had to stay. Getting powers was just a bonus. A very attractive bonus, if Wes was honest with himself.

Artemis had made some compelling points, but Wes wasn't completely sold on her cause. She had to be hiding something. Gideon wouldn't oppose her without good reason, and Gideon was a good judge of character. Wes would have to stay on his guard. Once she gave him abilities, maybe he could use them to take down her and Powers, bring them in, and show Jolie and Gideon and everyone else that he could be a hero, too.

Wonder what powers I'll get. It was a thrilling prospect. Having that kind of power . . . the thought was intoxicating.

"Are you ready?" Artemis asked.

"Beyond ready."

Artemis knelt and wiped down his bicep with an alcohol swab. Wes flinched at her touch. She hadn't exactly been subtle in her attempts to flirt with him, which he was sure was to throw him off guard. Still, she was attractive, and her delicate touch had not been unpleasant. Oblivious to his reaction—or pretending to be, maybe—she held up a syringe filled with clear green liquid. Light from one of the warehouse's broken windows shone through the substance. Wes swallowed at the sight of it. What if Artemis was lying, and this was poison or truth serum?

She didn't give him time to protest. She pressed the syringe against his arm. Wes' skin pinched as the needle pierced his flesh. Artemis depressed the pump on the syringe, and the green liquid flowed into Wes' arm. His bicep grew warm, and that warmth spread down into his hand, and then up into his shoulder and through the rest of his body.

The warmth was quickly followed by searing pain.

Wes screamed and dropped from his chair. He convulsed on the ground as the fiery substance worked its way through his body. It felt like it was eating him alive from the inside out. What had she done to him? *I was right—it was poison!*

"Calm," Artemis urged. "The pain will last only a moment."

Wes spasmed as the agony crept through his system. *Nothing could be worth this!* He screamed through clenched teeth. Moments later, the pain subsided. Wes' vision blurred. He rested his head on the ground and let the comforting black of unconsciousness take him.

* * *

Dean studied the design for his suit he had sketched. Although he had training, Dean wasn't as good a fighter as Gideon, and while his powers were useful for sneak attacks, they didn't completely make up for his lack of martial skill like Patrick's speed did. Dean would need something to help balance that out. It would take time for Dean to get to Gideon's level. Until then, he needed a boost. He had the concussion gauntlets. Those would help. But what about a weapon? Gideon had used truncheons until he'd improved enough with his powers that he didn't need them anymore and passed them on to Carter. Dean had never been particularly adept with them or a staff.

Maybe something a bit more stylish, something that could blend with the armor and retract into it when he didn't need it. Nothing lethal, of course; he wasn't going to go around stabbing people with a gauntlet blade, as the assassin Katrina Monahan had done. He needed something he could use defensively and offensively, but non-lethally.

Shields. If he put a small, retractable shield made of aionium in each gauntlet . . . that might work. The shields could be segmented, so they could fold together and slip inside the gauntlets. Aionium was sure to protect him, and it was hard enough to give a good wallop to anyone he hit with the shields.

He sketched the shields and their compartments onto the suit. Now for a mask. Hiding his identity was a necessity; he wasn't sure how Sterling Enterprises' board of directors would feel if they knew their new CEO was a superhero. Not a hood. Maybe a cowl, or a domino mask. And the color? Maybe a dark green . . .

Dean shook his head. He would've enjoyed this more if Wes wasn't in danger.

The lair doors slid open. Dean closed his laptop and glanced up. Gideon and Jolie walked in, and Gideon dropped a warped bolt onto the desk. Dean picked the bolt up and studied it. There were no identifying marks on it—or if there had been, they had been worn off from friction. It was just a hunk of smooth metal now.

"Guys." Dean looked up at them. "I'm flattered by how highly you clearly think of my talents, but you do understand I'm not psychic, right? What do you want me to do with this?"

"Don't know, but it's our only lead," Gideon said. "Anything on the cameras?"

"Not yet."

Jolie looked at the computer screen. "They had to be captured on camera at some point. It would be almost impossible to go anywhere in the Brooks and not be."

"I know, but there's hours of footage. It'll take some time to—" The computer beeped. "Aha. I think we've got something."

Dean pulled up the footage. It showed an empty street corner with little visible traffic. A few seconds passed, and two men crossed the street, one slightly ahead of the other. Dean highlighted their faces and zoomed in. The man in the rear was undeniably Wes. He was carrying a duffel bag.

Jolie leaned against the desk. "That's Powers."

Gideon leaned in on Dean's other side. "Looks like Wes went with him willingly. Why would he do that?"

"Beats me." Jolie shrugged. "When we confronted Powers, he was going on about Wes' place in the story, and about how he had a greater destiny, or something. You don't think Wes would be naïve enough to buy that drivel and go with Powers, do you?"

"No . . . but something is going on. Dean, which direction are they going?"

Dean zoomed back out to get a look at street signs. "That's the corner of Fifth and Markham. They're heading northwest."

"Any warehouses or factories in the vicinity?"

Dean switched over to the program he used to search for the possible bolt factories. He narrowed the parameters down to the northwest part of the Brooks. Five results came up.

"Of those, how many are abandoned?" Jolie asked.

Dean checked. "Two warehouses."

"And of the two, would either of them have stored shipments of metal parts, including bolts?" Jolie tapped the item on the desk. "Like this one?"

"Jackpot. Only one of them stored parts—it's a warehouse on Amherst Avenue. And guess what? It was recently purchased by our friends at Crowne Pharmaceuticals." He looked back at Gideon. "That can't be a coincidence."

Gideon backed away and opened the case containing his new suit. "That's where they've got Wes. Good work, Dean. Now, let's get out there and get my brother back."

CHAPTER 18

The Seraph flew downward as he approached the warehouse, scanning the building for an entrance. Below him, Jolie parked her car across the street, and she and Dean climbed out. They'd cover the exits while Gideon went in and retrieved Wes. Gideon angled toward one of the upper windows of the warehouse, smashed through, and slowed to hover high in the air, near the ceiling. There was no sign of Wes or Powers, but a woman stood in the middle of the warehouse, holding a gun casually at her side.

"Hello, Seraph." The woman smirked. "Why don't you come down here so we can talk face-to-face?"

The Seraph steeled himself as he floated toward the ground. This had to be Artemis. She must've left San Francisco soon after they'd rescued Dean. Which meant, if Wes was here, he might be under her control. The Seraph had been able to clear Dean's mind of her influence, so he knew what it felt like. If she tried it on him, he hoped he would be able to push her out, if he stayed on his guard. He generated spheres of light around his fists, ready to fight.

He whispered, so only his earbud would pick up his words. "Stay outside."

"What?" Jolie asked.

"Somna is here. Can't risk her hypnotizing either of you. Stay out there and wait for my signal."

Static tickled at his mind. Gideon frowned and slowed his advance. She was trying to slip in, hidden behind the static. He closed his eyes, gathered all his mental power, and slammed the doors of his mind shut. No one controlled his mind but him; none were welcome in his soul save for God. This woman would not have a hold on him.

"I'm impressed." Artemis sucked in a shuddery breath and studied him. Gideon sensed her surprise. "I've never met anyone who could resist my hypnosis. Oh, well. Fragment?"

A sense of anticipation, slowly building somewhere behind him, reached a crescendo. The Seraph spun around, bringing up a glowing fist just as a man in a black-and-red jumpsuit leapt at him. He caught the man across the jaw, knocking him flat. When the attacker hit the floor, he disappeared. One of Powers' copies?

Four more men, identical to the first, stepped out of the shadows. Their uniforms were predominantly black, with jagged red lines running down the chest. The gloves, boots, and cowls—that wrapped around their heads and covered everything except their noses and jawlines—were also red.

"This is going to be fun," the four doppelgangers said in unison.

The Seraph dropped into a Brazilian jiu jitsu stance as the Fragments circled around him, each coming in at a different angle. As they rushed in at him, Gideon splayed out his arms and discharged a blast of light in an arc around him. All four duplicates flew back and vanished as they struck the ground.

He took a deep breath. He couldn't manage many blasts like that. Not long ago, just one would've worn him down, but he was building endurance. Even so, a third or fourth blast would render him too tired to fight. He clenched his fists and prepared for another wave of Fragment clones.

They came at him in a horde. He counted six in front of him before they were on top of him, and he heard footsteps from behind. As they mobbed him, he ducked and weaved, bringing his light-encased fists up to meet jaws and solar plexuses. He blocked punches and kicks. But still, they came. A pair of them grabbed his arms and pinned them. The Seraph fought to free himself, but another Fragment stepped in front and struck him across the jaw—one of the few places his aionium suit didn't cover. Blood trickled down his chin from his lip. A third clone wrapped his arms around the Seraph's throat.

"Game over, Seraph."

The Seraph closed his eyes and discharged another repulsing blast. The three Fragments restraining him flew back, and the one who had punched him disintegrated. The Seraph stood and spun around. Where was the real Fragment?

"Gideon, do you need help?" Jolie asked.

"Do I need to teleport in?" Dean pressed.

"Stay there." The Seraph scanned the room. "Somna is still here. Watch the exits; Powers might try to escape."

He rolled his shoulders and looked back toward Artemis. She hadn't so much as raised her gun. Not that her bullets would've left a scratch on his aionium armor, even if she had managed to hit him. He strode toward her and raised a fist, charged with light, ready to blast her.

"Not bad," Somna said. "You lasted far longer than I expected you would. But the time for games is over."

"Where's Wes?" Gideon's shouted query echoed through the warehouse.

"He's right here." She gestured to her right. "He's eager to see you."

Wes walked into the large room. He looked all right. His hair was a mess and dark circles lined his eyes, but he didn't have any obvious bruises. He wore one of the prototypes of the Seraph suit. His eyebrows lifted slightly as he saw Gideon, and his gaze cut briefly over to Artemis.

"Wes?" The Seraph lowered his hand. "What's going on?"

"I—I was trying to gather information for you. I wanted to help."

"Did you now?" Artemis smirked at Wes. "I'm hurt. I'm afraid it's too late for any of that now. Wesley, you know what I told you is true. Gideon doesn't understand the truth—but you do."

"What's she talking about, Wes?"

"Wes willingly volunteered to take our serum. He knows that what we're doing is going to change the world for the better. You should listen to your brother, *Seraph.*"

"What?" The Seraph looked at Wes. "Wes, she's lying. She kidnapped Dean and had a madman rampage through San Francisco just to get to me. These people aren't trying to help anybody; they're terrorists."

"Terrorists?" Somna scoffed. "Hardly. You don't have the full picture of Backfire's mission. His rampage wasn't just some smoke show. And we don't want to terrify anyone. Just the opposite, actually; our goal is to create a safer world."

"Fascists, then. My mistake." The Seraph stepped between her and Wes. "Back away from him. Wes, we need to go."

"You know what is right, Wesley." Somna's voice took on a soothing croon. "Listen to your heart."

"Shut up!" the Seraph shouted.

He could sense the confusion in Wes. He believed Gideon, because he was his brother and he knew Gideon was genuinely good, but he also wanted to believe Artemis. She'd given him the powers he'd wanted, and she had probably been deceptively kind to him.

"I . . . I have to go." Wes stepped toward the door. "I have to—"

"No, you don't," Somna urged.

The Seraph sensed the familiar aura of coercion around Wes as he stopped in his tracks and turned back toward them. She was controlling him. The Seraph spun on her and amplified the energy channeling through his fist.

"Release him now!"

Somna smirked. "No, I don't think so. Wesley? Why don't you show your brother what you can do?"

Wes knelt and touched his right hand to the concrete floor. The Seraph frowned and kept an eye on him, but his fist remained firmly trained on Artemis. As Wes' fingers brushed the floor, the concrete seemed to crawl up his skin and under the sleeve of his uniform. It reached his head and encompassed it. When Wes stood, every centimeter of his body was encased in concrete.

"It's not too late," Somna pressed. "Join us. You and he, fighting together under Ashcroft's command. Wouldn't that be nice?"

"Never." The Seraph took a step back as Wes approached. "Release him, or I'll blast you!"

"If I can't have you, at least I will have him. And we can't have you around, interfering with our business. Wesley, kill him."

The Seraph fired the pent-up blast of energy at Artemis. As the light discharged, Wes grabbed his wrist and shoved it aside. The golden burst flew wide and smashed into a wall, crumbling a baseball-sized chunk of concrete. The Seraph turned to Wes just as his brother swung a concrete fist at his head.

The Seraph ducked under the punch and made a snap decision. He'd have to fight Wes, or they were both doomed. He brought his fist up into Wes' gut—but it was like punching a wall. His skin had turned completely to concrete. The Seraph cried out between clenched teeth and flexed his wounded fist. Wes grabbed the Seraph's shoulder, hoisted him up, and hurled him backward into a support beam.

This isn't good. If Gideon could concentrate for a moment, he could pierce the haze in Wes' mind and free him, but he couldn't focus while Wes was trying to kill him. Maybe if he could take out Somna . . .

He jumped in the air and hovered over Wes' head. His brother looked up and reached for him. The Seraph sailed out of reach and aimed for Artemis. The woman raised her eyebrows in surprise and rushed for the door. Fragment stood in the doorway, waiting for her. The Seraph soared toward them.

"Dean, Jolie, they're heading for the exit!"

Fragment blurred, and two more copies appeared and rushed at him. One leapt in the air and grabbed the Seraph's ankle. Destabilized, he arced toward the ground. He kicked the dangling doppelganger in the face. But by then, the second Fragment was on him—and so was Wes. The Seraph swung a fist, catching the Fragment clone in the gut. A second blow across the jaw laid the doppelganger flat.

Wes grabbed the Seraph's shoulder, spun him around, and punched him straight in the face. The Seraph staggered back, blood filling his nose. Wes swung again. The Seraph blocked with his forearm. The aionium suit took the force of the blow without denting. Wes grabbed his bicep . . . and his skin shifted from gray concrete to the same metallic blue as the Seraph's aionium suit.

Gideon gaped. "Oh . . . great."

Wes kicked him in the chest. Gideon groaned at the force of the impact and sailed backward, using his flight abilities to carry him farther than the strike should've. It gave him distance, which also gave him time.

He floated high into the air, where Wes couldn't reach him, and reached out to his brother telepathically. If he could flood light into Wes' mind the same way he had Dean's, then this fight would be over.

Wes didn't seem content to wait. He looked around, spied a table, and walked toward it. The Seraph focused on the cloud of hypnosis around Wes' mind and imagined it compressing. When it was small enough for him to see clearly, he poured a river of light into it. As he did, Wes reached the table, picked it up, and hurled it at the Seraph.

The Seraph was too distracted by his mental struggle to fly out of the way. At the last second, he moved to the left, but the table clipped him and knocked him off balance. The Seraph grunted and fell toward the ground.

Wes pounced on him. The Seraph raised his arms defensively, and Wes rained down blows on him. The Seraph's gauntlets, made of the same material as Wes' skin, absorbed the blows, but it would be only a few seconds before Wes found an opening. Seraph recalled the image of Wes' brain again and pierced it with light.

One of his arms twisted aside as Wes grabbed it and pinned it to the floor. The Seraph didn't struggle to free it. His only hope now, his only focus, was freeing Wes' mind.

Wes raised a fist, ready to bring it down on Gideon's face. The Seraph pushed with all the power he could muster, hammering a blinding mental light into Wes' mind. Wes recoiled and held his hands to his head, screaming. He fell back off the Seraph and scrambled away. The Seraph rose into a crouch and watched his brother.

"Wes? Wake up, Wes."

Wes pulled himself to his knees and rubbed his head. Slowly, his skin shifted from cobalt back to normal flesh tones. He groaned and shook his head, and then looked around.

"Gideon?" He tilted his head. "What happened?"

"You were captured and mind controlled." Gideon stood and walked toward his brother. "But you're fine now."

He offered his hand, which Wes stared at for a moment before taking. Gideon helped his brother to his feet and led him toward the door. There was no sign of Artemis or Powers.

He tapped his earbud. "Guys? You there?"

Jolie panted. "Yeah. We're here. They got away. Powers threw a bunch of doppelgangers at us and we had to fight them off. By the time we did, he and Wayans were gone."

"It's all right. Get in here. Maybe they left some clues."

He was exceptionally lucky—or perhaps blessed was more accurate—that his powers were able to counteract Artemis' manipulation. What would have happened if he'd gotten there and immediately been hypnotized by her? Dean, Patrick, and Jolie would've been alone in the fight against Ashcroft, and they had little experience against supervillains.

God had been watching out for him. It couldn't have been a coincidence that Gideon had received the exact set of powers he had. Whatever experiments Ashcroft had been running, they clearly affected every person differently. Gideon hadn't really thought about it before, but perhaps his powers hadn't been random—maybe God had given Gideon the powers he had so that he would be equipped to combat Ashcroft and his forces.

Which meant that maybe Wes and Dean and Patrick all had their powers for a specific purpose, too. Maybe it had been more than chance that things had transpired this way.

"What did she do to me, Gid?" Wes asked.

"She has mind control powers. She put you in a trance and made you fight me. But you're fine now." Gideon put a hand on his shoulder. "Cool powers, by the way."

Wes didn't respond, but excitement and joy radiated off him in waves. As Dean and Jolie rushed into the warehouse, Gideon took a deep breath. Another crisis had been averted.

CHAPTER 19

"Are you sure you have to go back to San Francisco?" Jolie asked.

Gideon nodded. "Just for the day. We're going to talk to Patrick's parents about bringing him back to Sojourn City so we can train him here."

"Not that they'll know that's what he's doing," Dean added. "We're going to tell them he's got a Sterling Labs internship. With any luck, they'll buy it."

"Okay." Jolie kissed Gideon on the cheek. "See you soon."

Although they planned to be gone for only a few hours, Gideon found it harder to step out of her embrace than the last time he'd boarded the plane. He wanted to stay here with her, to enjoy her presence. But time would come for that soon enough. He kissed her atop her head, took a deep breath to smell the lavender scent in her hair, and told her goodbye.

Gideon stepped onto Dean's jet. Jolie was not his only reason for wanting to stay. Their search of the warehouse had come up empty. It appeared that it had been used by Powers when he'd been a Shine dealer, but they hadn't been able to find any connections to Ashcroft's organization, even with Dean's confirmation that it was owned by Crowne Pharmaceuticals. It was looking more and more likely that Crowne was a shell company. Now Artemis, Powers, and Mendez were all in the wind.

They'd be gone for only a day. With any luck, they'd be in San Francisco for a few hours—enough time to get Patrick, talk to his parents, pick up the super suit Dean's team had been designing, and get back to the airport. Gideon had already called Patrick and told him they were returning, so he should be waiting for them at the lab when they got there.

Gideon shook his head. A week ago, he'd been the only known superhuman in the world. Now, there were three others on his side, plus three supervillains to top it off. *This is insane.* Would his minimal experience be enough to teach Patrick, Dean, and Wes how to use their powers effectively? They would be a team someday—but for now they were just a bunch of novices. Gideon himself wasn't much better than they were.

But time would change that. It had to. The world was going to need them to stop whatever plot Ashcroft, Artemis, and the rest had been cooking.

* * *

Dean followed Gideon into the lab where they'd been training Patrick. The young speedster was already inside, zipping around the room. He came to a stop as the two men entered, grinning ear to ear.

"You're back! Everything go okay in Sojourn City?"

Gideon tilted his head. "It could've been worse. Artemis is in the wind, though. We'll need to regroup and strategize if we're going to stop them before they make their next move."

"Speaking of . . . " Patrick turned to Dean. "Any word on my suit?"

"I called Yei on the way over here. It should be ready for pickup within the hour."

"Awesome. I can't wait to see it. How long are you guys going to stay here? Are we going to have a public Seraph-Spright team-up?"

Gideon glanced at Dean. "Actually, that's why we came back. We can't stay here forever, but I think we've got a way to continue training you even when we go back to Sojourn City."

"How?"

"Come back with us," Dean said. "I can talk to your parents and tell them that a better internship opportunity opened up there for the rest of the summer. You can stay with Gideon and me until then. That'll give you a couple more months of training before you come back to start school."

"Really?" Patrick beamed. "You'd do that?"

"Only if you're sure it's what you want."

"I am." Patrick stood. "Right now, the best place for me to be is with you guys. I'm not ready to take on supervillains by myself. I need more time with you."

Gideon tilted his head toward the door. "Then let's get to your house. I told Jolie we'd be back before the end of the day."

Patrick grinned. "Thanks, guys. You're the best."

"You're welcome." Dean patted his shoulder. "I just hope your parents go for it."

"Me, too."

Dean followed Patrick and Gideon out of the lab, took one more look around the double-hexagonal room, and turned out the lights.

* * *

Standing in the shadows of the garage attached to the Regency's base, Artemis seethed. What were the odds that Turner had the power to resist her hypnosis—let alone free others from it? Now both Turners were out there, loose cannons, so-called "heroes." They didn't understand that what Ashcroft was doing was for the good of humanity. He was the real hero. If they could only see his genius.

She eyed Fragment and wrinkled her nose. Powers, Mendez . . . choosing these criminals for this operation had been a mistake. She had to own part of that; she'd requested Mendez's help in San Francisco. Still, if Ashcroft had recruited more people like Artemis and fewer curs, maybe things would get done. More than half of the Regency's infrastructure was made up of former criminals.

Things would have to change. They needed a more strategic touch—more mind and less muscle. Artemis was Ashcroft's second-in-command for a reason, and if he was too focused on his experiments to take charge of this operation, then Artemis would do it herself.

Ashcroft had ordered her to return to base with Mendez and Powers for the time being. They would have to reevaluate their strategy from here. Turner didn't respond well to his friends and loved ones being captured, it seemed. Maybe he'd be more compliant if they started killing people he cared about. Ashcroft would've preferred Turner to be on their side when his plan was enacted, Artemis was sure, but maybe even killing his loved ones would not be enough. Maybe Turner was too far gone.

If he wouldn't be persuaded, he was a liability. Ashcroft would just have to settle for Turner's corpse.

CHAPTER 20

Patrick sat on the couch across from his parents and clasped his hands tightly in his lap. While Gideon checked them out of the hotel, Dean gave Patrick's parents an elaborate explanation of Patrick's internship and why there would be more opportunities for him to advance in Sojourn City. He assured them that Patrick would be back by the time school started, and that he could return to visit whenever he wished.

Patrick watched his parents' faces closely. Both looked surprised, but his father was quicker to nod in understanding as Dean spoke. His mom's brow was still furrowed in concern. He knew she'd be the tougher sell—not because she didn't think he was capable, but because she'd miss him.

"Where would Patrick live while he's in Sojourn City?" Mom asked.

"When we first arrive, he can live with my roommates and me in our apartment," Dean said. "We have more than enough room for one more. I also have a second apartment available for rent if he'd prefer to live on his own. But rest assured, wherever he ends up, your son will be well cared for."

Dad looked at Patrick. "Son? Is this something you want to do?"

"Yes. Absolutely. It's exactly what I want."

"Then I see no reason you shouldn't go." Dad stood and shook Dean's hand. "You're an adult, after all. Mr. Sterling, thank you for this opportunity."

"It's our pleasure. Patrick's quite a brilliant young man."

Mom weaved through the room to get to Patrick and crushed him in a bear hug. He grunted and hugged her back.

She kissed his cheek. "I love you. And I'm so proud of you."

"Thank you. Love you, too, Mom."

Dad hugged him, too. His embrace was far more restrained, but no less loving.

"Do good, son. I love you."

"Love you, Dad. I'll do my best."

With that, Patrick rushed up the stairs. He could've easily packed his whole room in minutes, but that would've given some things away to his parents. He pulled his suitcase from his closet and set to work. He packed as many changes of clothes as he could fit, plus toiletries, his Bible, and a few personal items.

He glanced out the window. It would probably be a few minutes before his parents missed him, and Dean and Gideon could keep them occupied. He locked the door, opened his window, and sped across the lawn to Lucy's house. He knocked on the door.

Lucy's mom answered. "Hello, Patrick. Lucy! It's Patrick!"

Patrick smiled and nodded at her as she stepped back inside. Footsteps sounded on the stairs to the second floor, and Lucy appeared a moment later. She bounded out the door and closed it behind her.

"What's up?" she asked.

"I'm leaving for a while."

She raised an eyebrow. "What do you mean?"

"Dean Sterling offered to take me back to Sojourn City with him, so I can . . . uh, continue my internship. I've got to take the offer. There's still so much I have to learn from him—from the company. But don't worry; I'll be back in time for senior year."

Lucy nodded and didn't say anything for a moment. Finally, she touched his shoulder. "I understand. Don't be gone too long, okay? I'm going to miss you."

"Y-you are?"

She leaned in and kissed him on the cheek. Patrick jerked in surprise, then smiled. She smiled back, blushed, and reached for the doorknob.

"I think I figured out what you wanted to tell me. Good luck, Patrick."

The door closed. Patrick stared at it for a long moment, replaying the kiss over in his head. It was just on the cheek, sure. It might not have meant anything. But after long years of unspoken feelings for her, it was a beacon of hope. He grinned, turned, and sped down the street toward Asher's house, and he let out a long, loud whoop as he ran.

* * *

As the jet descended toward Sojourn City, Gideon rolled his shoulders. His muscles protested the motion. The fights with Fragment and Wes, combined with the mental strain of resisting Somna's control and freeing Wes from it, had left him more drained than he'd felt after a fight since . . . well, since the Uprising. The flights to and from San Francisco tired him even further. He was ready to drop into bed and sleep until noon. The pain had been worth it, though. Wes was safe, he had powers, and he was willing to use them for good.

Guess Dean's going to have to design another suit.

The sooner Gideon had backup, the better. Having failed to secure Gideon's cooperation by capturing his brother, Artemis and her allies might go after Jolie or the rest of Gideon's family instead. He doubted Artemis was going to be as merciful with them as she had been with Wes.

Gideon looked out the window at the familiar view of the shores of Lake Superior and the vast Platform jutting out into it. The two-mile bridge connecting the city's economic center to the mainland was now paralleled by the skeleton of the railway for Dean's maglev train. In the days they'd been gone, an impressive amount of construction had gone into the railway.

Patrick leaned toward the window. "Cool."

Gideon smiled. It was easy to forget, after living in Sojourn City for most of his life, that other cities didn't have things like the Platform. This was Patrick's first time seeing it. If only it represented more than the city's corrupt elite. Dean was working to change that, but for now, the symbolism of the Platform was tarnished.

Gideon leaned back in his seat as the jet approached the runway. His stomach lurched a bit, and he loosened his grip on the armrests. One would assume that a superhero who could fly wouldn't get motion sickness on an airplane, but the human body was a funny thing—even if it was superhuman, it seemed. He took a deep breath and waited.

The plane touched down and slowed to a stop. Dean was the first of the passengers to rise. Gideon unbuckled his seatbelt and followed. The transition from the air-conditioned cabin to Sojourn's humid air slapped him unrepentantly. There were no reporters to be seen. Apparently, his arrival at the airstrip had gone unnoticed. That was a relief. Artemis might still be watching them. For the time being, they needed to stay incognito.

Jolie stood across the tarmac with Carter and Wes. Gideon grinned and opened his arms, squeezing her in a hug as she stepped toward him. She buried her head in his shoulder. He ran a hand through her dark hair and closed his eyes, relishing the moment. It was a better reunion than their last one. She leaned back and kissed him. After lingering on the sweet touch of her lips for a moment, he finally released her from the embrace and looked toward Carter.

"Jolie tells me you've been a big help in her investigation," Gideon said. "I knew you were up to it."

"Thanks." Carter smiled, then hung his head. "I'm just sorry I couldn't stop Powers from taking your brother."

"It's okay. We have him back now. That's all that matters."

Gideon put a hand on Carter's shoulder and gave him a reassuring smile. He looked back at the airplane. Patrick exited the plane, carrying his own luggage plus a case with the new super suit Dean had designed for him.

Gideon waved Patrick over. "Jolie, Carter, Wes, this is Patrick Omer. He's a superhero from San Francisco. I'll be training him over the summer."

Carter walked up to him. "Nice to meet you. I'm Carter Jonson—the Crusader."

"Spright." Patrick extended a hand. "I look forward to working with you."

They were around the same age, and although they had far different life experiences, Gideon was sure that working together to fight crime would form a bond between them. They could be a great support system for each other.

Dean's red Camaro pulled up next to them, and he honked the horn. "Let's go! We need to get dinner. I'm starving."

Gideon strode toward the older-model Camry parked nearby. "Wes and I will ride with Jolie. Patrick, Carter, you ride with Dean."

"Wally's?" Jolie asked.

Wally's Diner—their oldest haunt in Sojourn City, a familiar place that had been around for almost as long as the city itself.

"Wally's. We should introduce Patrick to Sojourn City culture the right way."

He climbed into the front seat of Jolie's Camry. As she pulled away from the airport, he glanced over his shoulder at Wes. He was touching the leather seats, the glass window, allowing his fingers to take the form of those materials. It was almost an unconscious act, though, like cracking his knuckles. Wes' attention was elsewhere. He was looking out the window, but his eyes had a distant, glassy look. Gideon probed him mentally. As he suspected, Wes was a boiling cauldron of brood. Maybe getting powers had not satisfied whatever need he thought it would.

Gideon cleared his throat. "You know Artemis controlling you wasn't your fault, right? Your intentions were good—even if your actions were reckless."

"I guess."

"It worked out, didn't it? You've got powers now, and you're free to help me save lives."

"Yeah, you're right." Wes' demeanor brightened a little, and his hand turned to glass from the wrist down. "You know, if I'm going to be a superhero, I guess I need a name, huh? And a costume, too."

"You'll have to talk to Dean about that. It's sort of become his area of expertise."

"What if I had, like, a utility belt made up of different materials? That way, whenever I needed to be something for a specific situation, I could touch that part of my belt and turn into that material."

Gideon raised his eyebrows, impressed, and cast a glance at Jolie. She grinned back at him. He was sure of one thing—Wes was going to be a natural at this.

* * *

Jolie sat at a table with five superheroes, and somehow, she felt right at home. She loved Gideon, had been close with Wes and Dean for years, was growing to consider Carter a friend, and could already tell Patrick was a good kid. This group of people, working together, would change the world.

But where were the girls? There had to be some female superheroes out there. So far, the only female superhuman they'd discovered was Artemis Wayans, and she had no place at this table.

What would it be like to have superpowers? What if Jolie could fly like Gideon, or read minds, or teleport? All her closest friends had powers now. Why couldn't she? Maybe it was for the best. The unfortunate correlation between superpowers and vigilantism might make her job as a detective . . . complicated. Besides, she didn't need powers to make a difference.

She watched Gideon as he talked. Some of the tension of the past year had finally faded away. The constant lines around his eyes and forehead were gone. He had learned how to relax. He'd matured, shaped by his experiences, and though he still radiated the same passion and intensity he always had, it was now under control. She loved him even more for it.

"Dean, Wes, and I will get started on the paperwork for our new apartment," Gideon said. "Until then, Patrick, you can stay with us in the penthouse where we're setting up our lair."

"A penthouse?" Patrick whistled. "Sweet."

Dean popped a French fry in his mouth. "I'll have Arianna and Maddox get to work on suits for me and Wes. Meanwhile, we need to give Patrick's suit a test run."

"We should probably test Wes' powers," Gideon added. "We don't know the full extent of what he can do yet."

Jolie swirled her spoon around in her sundae. All this was well and good, but when were they going to try to catch Powers or Artemis? They were still on the loose, and she had her own problems to worry about, too. Powers hadn't been the only Shine dealer in the Brooks. She needed to find the source of the drugs and bring the whole ring down. Carter might be able to help her with that. His sources had already come through once before.

She was sure the rest of them would help, too. Right now, they needed to focus on learning how to use their powers. As far as Jolie was concerned, they were all making the world a far safer place in their own way.

They needed rest, herself included. It had been a stressful week. Two of them had been kidnapped, and the rest had been fighting supervillains or learning how to use superpowers. Jolie couldn't speak for the others, but she was exhausted. Now that all the people she cared about were home safe, she could really rest. She considered going straight back to her apartment and dropping into bed as soon as her plate was empty.

Gideon balled up his trash and deposited it on his plate. "We'll get all that worked out later. For now, I think we should all try to get some rest."

Jolie wondered if he was feeling as exhausted as she was, if this was a boyfriend telepathy thing, or if he'd picked up her exhaustion with his empathic powers. She didn't care at this point. She just wanted to crash.

"Sounds good to me," she said.

Dean wadded up his trash. "Don't have to tell me twice."

The others murmured in agreement. They paid their tabs and headed out the door. Jolie climbed into her Camry. Gideon slid into the passenger seat.

She smiled at him. "Thank you."

"For what?"

"You could tell how tired I was. You just said that for my sake, didn't you?"

He chuckled. "You yawned five times in the past three minutes. At first I thought you were bored, but I know you better than that."

Jolie backed out of her parking spot and followed Dean's Camaro. "Yeah, you do, Turner."

"What else is bothering you? I'm not a telepath, remember; just an empath."

"It's this new drug, Shine, that's been circulating in the Brooks. Even if Powers is the mastermind behind the drug, we don't know who's making it—or where from. Until we find those things out, the Shine trade will keep growing."

"You'll get your man." Gideon smiled. "You always do. If you need help, let me know, and I'll be there in a heartbeat. But I bet you'll bust these guys in no time, right?"

"Thanks, Gid."

She hoped he was right.

* * *

Artemis refused to hang her head as she stood before Dr. Jeremiah Ashcroft, who ranted about her failure and shouted insults. "Pathetic" and "unworthy" were among the gentler words in his vocabulary. A lesser person would have cringed or shied away from his slew of offenses. She stood proudly, back straight with hands at her side, and steadied her expression to impassivity. His cursing and rambling flowed through her and back out.

He had every right to be frustrated, but she wasn't done. She'd learned. She had seen Turner's strengths, but also his weaknesses.

He would do anything to save his loved ones. She would use that to her advantage.

"I should pull you from this assignment," Ashcroft growled.

He ran his hands through his wild black hair. His teeth gnawed fiercely at his lower lip. Artemis knew he was close to snapping—or returning to his normal, more restrained self. It was always hard to tell which way he'd go.

"But you won't," she said. "You know I'm too valuable; I'm the only one who can bring Turner in."

"Are you? You've failed so far. Perhaps Stormcry, or Red Raider—"

"No." Although either of those two would be more useful at her side than Fragment or Backfire, she wasn't going to give up command of this mission. "Give me another chance. I acquired your gene splicer matrix. I perfected the serum. That's not a total failure. Besides, I've watched Turner in action, and I've seen his blind spots. The others would have to start from scratch. I can do this."

Ashcroft tilted his head and nodded. "One more chance. Don't mess it up. Forget the dispersal unit for now. Focus on eliminating Turner. And this time, for all our sakes, don't give anyone powers if we don't know they'll stay on our side, all right? It just makes things . . . messy."

"It will be done." Artemis hesitated. "Perhaps if one of the others were to help me—"

"You'll get Backfire and Fragment. The others have assignments of their own. For them to succeed, you must as well."

She nodded her head just enough to show she understood. She turned and strode from his chambers. Mendez and Powers stood in the hallway outside, arms crossed.

"Let's go. We've got a job to finish."

CHAPTER 21

One month later

"Sojourn PD!" Sergeant Pulaski shouted. "Come out with your hands up!"

Jolie steadied her gun against the hood of a cruiser and watched the front door of the run-down house where they'd tracked the last cell of the Shine drug ring. It had taken weeks of investigation and coercion of CI's to find this place. In that time, over a dozen teenagers had been hospitalized from overdosing on Shine. Two of them had died. Carter's coworker, Silas, who ran an afterschool program for troubled boys, was despondent. Everyone in Jolie's precinct was chomping at the bit to collar these dealers.

A SWAT team approached the front door with a battering ram. Jolie, along with her old partner, Paul Jordan, and Sergeant Pulaski, stayed behind their cars and kept the breach team covered. One of the house's windows shattered, and the barrel of an AR-15 stuck out and spat fire at the SWAT team. Jolie swiveled her aim to that window and snapped off a series of shots. The shooter, hidden by frilly white curtains, pulled the rifle back inside.

Before the SWAT team could resume their breach, the front door exploded from the inside. The team backed off as gunfire crisscrossed from either side of the doorway. Jolie lined up her sights on a shooter she glimpsed from her angle and fired. The man dropped from his hiding place to the middle of the doorway, clutching his shoulder with one hand and wielding an Uzi in the other. Jolie fired again, catching him center mass.

"Back!" the SWAT team leader shouted. "Get back!"

Her team backed away from the door as Jolie, Pulaski, and Paul continued to provide them covering fire. Jolie ducked down next to the SWAT team leader as she reached the car.

"How many of them are in there?" Jolie asked.

"Didn't get a good look," the woman replied. "At least three or four more, by my guess."

"We need to get in there now." Pulaski loaded a shotgun. "If any of them get away, they can start up their distribution from a new location."

"Roger." The SWAT leader pulled a Crybaby—a Sterling Enterprises sonic grenade—from her belt. "We're on it, sir."

Jolie and the others tucked in their noise-cancelling earbuds. Jolie swallowed, counted to three, and jumped up, opening fire. The SWAT leader hurled the Crybaby through the doorway. As the grenade squealed and the SWAT team rushed in, Jolie pressed a finger to her earbud, opening a line of communication to Carter.

"Crusader, you in position?"

"I'm here."

"We're moving in. Watch the back. Anyone comes out, take them down."

"Roger that."

Pulaski and Paul dashed for the door behind the SWAT team. Jolie rose and rushed in after them, pistol trained on the window that had given way for the AR-15 rifle earlier. There was no sign of the shooter returning. She cleared the doorway and rushed into the house.

Paul went right, toward the kitchen, and Pulaski went left, into the living room, in pursuit of the SWAT team. Jolie stuck with Paul, watching her old partner's back again. The small kitchen, decorated straight out of the seventies, contained a decades-old refrigerator, a circular table, and three folding chairs. Jolie ducked behind the counter with her knee braced on the linoleum-tile floor.

Paul pointed to a door across the kitchen. "Garage."

"Go."

Paul reached for the doorknob, and Jolie trained her sidearm on the door, ready to open fire if anyone was waiting on the other side. Paul yanked the door open—

A large body barreled through the doorway. Jolie squeezed the trigger, but the bulky figure was already on top of her. She grunted and landed flat on her back. Her shot went high, shattering the fluorescent light above her. A second form ran from the door and knocked Paul against the wall. The kitchen's sliding glass back door opened, and the two figures ran into the backyard.

Jolie tapped her earbud. "Crusader, engage!"

She leapt to her feet, shaking glass fragments from her, and sprinted out the door after them. The larger man, the one who'd knocked her down, vaulted the chain-link fence that separated the backyard from the alley behind it. The second man was halfway through the yard. Before he reached the fence, a red-clad form rolled off the roof of a small storage shed in the corner of the yard, came up in a crouch, and leapt forward to tackle him. The criminal, hyped up on adrenaline or drugs, shoved the Crusader off him, stumbled to his feet, and withdrew a switchblade from his pocket.

The Crusader squared off with him. "I've got this one!"

Jolie sprinted past him and his target, kicking up dirt as she pounded through the barren yard. She clambered over the fence and took off down the alley after the runner. He was wearing a white tank top and blue jeans, and a pistol was tucked at the small of his back. In the time it had taken Jolie to vault the fence, he'd already gone too far for her to hit him with her taser. She huffed in annoyance and picked up her pace. The runner came out of the alley and turned left on the street. Jolie reached up to her walkie-talkie.

"This is Detective Anderson, I'm in pursuit of a white male suspect, white tank top, blue jeans, heading south on Washington."

She rounded the corner. The guy was fast, but she was gaining on him. He must have been wearing down. She reached for her taser. She pumped her legs as fast as she could. He was not getting away from her.

He approached Seventh—a busy intersection. Either he'd have to turn to avoid traffic or risk running right into the middle of it. Either way, Jolie should be able to catch him there. Sure enough, his steps slowed as he reached the corner. Jolie stopped a few feet behind him and raised her taser.

"Freeze!"

He turned around and reached behind his back for his gun. Jolie instinctively pulled the trigger on her taser. Spasms racked the man's body, and he dropped to the sidewalk. Jolie rushed to his side, yanked the gun from his waistband, and tossed it aside before handcuffing him.

"You have the right to remain silent."

Her breaths came in heavy gasps, but she grinned despite her exhaustion. She'd done it! The last of the Shine trade had been brought down. She hoisted the man to his feet. Sirens sounded behind her, and a cruiser pulled up. Two officers jumped out and led the dealer over to their car. Jolie holstered her taser.

Not bad for an unpowered detective.

* * *

Patrick looped around the roadblock that slowly ascended from the floor as he circled the training room. He swerved to the side, a little too close to the wall. He fought back a split second of panic and angled his feet, pressing them flat against the wall, and took another step—and another.

He ran parallel to the floor and made another lap. Across the room, a shock cannon crackled. A bolt of electricity flew across the room toward Patrick, and he jumped off the wall, somersaulted into the middle of the room, and dashed away as another shock cannon fired.

This training room was way more advanced than the simple lab back in San Francisco. For the past month, Dean and his friends from Sterling Labs, Arianna and Maddox, had been renovating the top floor of Dean and Gideon's old penthouse apartment. The first floor looked basically the same—a large living room, a kitchen, and a bathroom. But the second floor, which had included several bedrooms and bathrooms, had been completely redone. The walls had been knocked out, and it now consisted of one small bathroom and two large rooms—the training room that Patrick currently occupied and an ops center that looked out on the training room. It held the heroes' suits, gear, computers, and other tech they used to monitor the city for crime.

Patrick's heightened senses warned him of a large aionium sphere, fired from a cannon on the far wall. He ducked under the projectile and sprinted across the room. As he ran, he looked for the deactivation switch on that cannon and the two shock cannons. He heard the slight pulsing of both shock cannons and darted aside as two electrical blasts crossed the path he'd been on a moment before. He came around behind one cannon and switched it off. The other shock cannon and the projectile launcher continued firing.

Another circle around the room, and he'd deactivated the second shock cannon. Two more times around, he spotted the switch for the projectile cannon. He rushed behind it and flipped the switch. Satisfied with his results, Patrick ran back to the center of the room and stopped.

A flash of green popped in front of Patrick's eyes. He flinched back as Dean appeared before him. Dean punched him in the jaw, knocking Patrick flat on his back. Dean winked and teleported away.

Patrick grunted. "End simulation, man!"

He'd forgotten. When he accomplished his objective, he was supposed to shout, "End simulation." When he didn't, Dean surprised him with these unwelcome attacks because Patrick was supposed to "have his guard up at all times." Patrick rubbed his jaw and climbed to his feet.

"Okay." Dean's voice, projected through the intercom, was laced with amusement. He grinned at Patrick from behind the ops room's window. "Sorry. You did great. Just remember to stay on alert the whole time you're in the field, even if it looks like the bad guy is down."

"I know. I'll remember."

Patrick removed his mask and stared down at it. It was black—the same color as the base suit of his costume—with a purple streak on either temple. The armored plates on his chest, waist, knees, forearms, and shins were also purple. For the past month, Spright had rushed around Sojourn City, stopping petty crimes. Nothing even remotely as challenging as what he had faced in the lab had happened yet, but he was making a name for himself.

Dean teleported back into the training room. He wore his own super suit—originally a prototype of Gideon's first suit, which Dean had worn during the Uprising. He'd spray-painted the suit green and emblazoned a darker green "D" over his right breast. "D" for

"Drifter"—his superhero identity. He wasn't wearing his gauntlets or mask.

"That's enough for today, kid." Dean patted him on the shoulder. "Come on, you can take a break."

Patrick nodded. He darted into the ops room, changing out of his suit and into plainclothes in a split second. He placed his suit on one of the mannequins that lined the north wall, between Gideon's Seraph suit and the empty mannequin that normally held Dean's uniform. The fourth mannequin, on the other side of Dean's, wore the red costume of the Crusader. The final suit on display was Wes'. The sleeveless suit was predominantly black, with light blue shoulder pads and vambraces, matching blue lining on the chest, light gray lining on the thighs, and a red diamond emblazoned on the chest. The belt was divided into square segments, each one made of a different material that Wes could replicate with a touch. Glass, wood, steel, rubber, aionium—Dean had included everything he could think of.

The past month had been like something out of Patrick's wildest dreams, and even better. He was part of a superhero team. He got to train with them, learn from their experience, and run around stopping bad guys. Still, Patrick itched for more. Specifically, to track down Backfire. He hadn't forgotten that the villain had confessed to killing his grandfather. That made it a personal mission to find him and put him away for good. He would never vocalize that—not to Dean, and certainly not to Gideon—but it was how he felt, nonetheless.

He was starting to miss his friends. Lucy had been good about keeping in contact through phone calls and texts, but it wasn't the same as seeing them in person. Patrick wondered how long it would take him to run from Sojourn City to San Francisco. A few hours, maybe? He'd never run that far before. Would he even make it? And how would he explain his sudden return to them?

Dean walked over to one of the wide computer screens on the east wall. The screens constantly displayed news feeds from not only Sojourn City, but other major locations around the country. If Ashcroft or any of his followers made a move, they'd see it here.

"You coming to the unveiling?" Dean asked.

"Unveiling?"

"The maglev train. My crew's been working night and day to get the thing done. They've set a record for fastest construction of a citywide transportation system. We're demonstrating it for the public later this week. Thousands of people will be there."

"Oh." Patrick nodded. "Yeah, I'll be there."

"Great." Dean brought up a news feed that showed a local newscaster talking about the train. "In all the movies, bad guys love to attack trains. It might be good to have a few heroes around, just in case."

Patrick chuckled. He related to Dean, even though he was several years younger and several billion dollars poorer than the team's tech whiz. Dean was a geek. Everything they did here was filtered through his vast store of knowledge about superhero movies, TV shows, and comic books. That was pretty much how Patrick had started before Gideon had shown up in San Francisco. Patrick couldn't count the times he'd run through San Francisco, pretending he was Kid Flash or Quicksilver.

"Sounds like a plan." Patrick headed for the door. "I'm going to go grab some lunch. Want anything?"

"Nah." Dean dropped into a chair. "I'll stay here for a bit. Don't forget that Gideon wants everyone to meet here tonight."

"Right. See you then."

Patrick sprinted out of the base, leaving behind everything except the unshakable, burning desire to hunt down the man who'd murdered his grandfather and make him pay.

* * *

Gideon pulled open the door to the police station to allow Jolie to exit. She grinned, kissed him on the cheek, and grabbed him by the shoulder, kissing him harder on the lips. Gideon blinked in surprise before wrapping his free arm around her and kissing her back.

Finally, he pulled back to gasp for breath. "Hi."

He'd come to pick her up for lunch. The two of them *had* grown closer than ever over the last month, but he hadn't expected a greeting this enthusiastic. He smiled. Her eyes were bright, shining with excitement.

"We did it, Gid!"

"Did what?"

"We got them! The last of the Shine dealers. We took them down. Their operation is toast!"

"That's great!" Gideon kissed her again. "Congratulations."

Gently, he wiggled his way out from between her and the wall. He took her hand in his, and they walked toward his car together.

"It's about time," she continued. "They worked their way deep into the Brooks fast. But now that they've been locked up, there will be a lot of addicts going through some very painful withdrawals."

"It'll be worth it, though." Gideon opened the passenger door for her, and she slid inside. He circled around to the driver's side and got in. "Once it's out of their systems, they'll all be in a much better place."

She nodded. "Carter's friend Silas will be happy. That's for sure."

"Silas?"

"Yeah, one of his coworkers, Silas Rockwell. He runs an after-school program for troubled boys. He's been really concerned about Shine, according to Carter."

"Then this will be great news for him." Gideon pulled out into traffic. "Have you heard any rumors about Powers' whereabouts?"

"Nothing. If he's still in Sojourn City, he's lying low."

"He's probably still with Artemis—wherever she went."

It had been a month. Gideon wondered why they hadn't made a move again. Maybe they were reassessing, trying to figure out a new approach. It must've come as a shock to Artemis that he could resist her powers. And while she could influence the others, Gideon had the ability to free them from her control, but it required intense concentration, which would be less than ideal if he was facing more than one opponent.

Dean had been working with Arianna and Maddox to create a neural inhibitor—a device that would block Artemis' brainwaves from affecting others' minds. If the heroes wore them into battle against her, she wouldn't be able to hypnotize them. And if they could place one on Artemis herself, she'd effectively be unable to use her powers until it was removed.

"How are things going with the Junior Team?" Jolie joked, referring to Wes, Patrick, and Carter. Gideon had warned her it was a bad idea to say this around the two superhumans and one skilled vigilante. Ticking them off wasn't a good idea.

"They're making progress. Patrick will probably go back to San Francisco soon . . . "

"You don't sound happy about that."

"I'm not sure it's safe for him to be there by himself yet. Not while Artemis is on the loose. But he's getting homesick, and I can't say I blame him."

"Me, either. Sojourn City's a long way from San Francisco. All his friends and family are there, and sure, he probably considers all of you his friends, but he's known you for only a little over a month."

Gideon nodded. "His true friends are all there, and I get that."

"It's just too bad there's not another superhero in San Francisco who could take over his training."

"Unfortunately, we don't multiply like rabbits."

"And four of the five of you are going to be living here, in Sojourn." Jolie put her left hand on Gideon's right. "Maybe you should start looking for other powered people that you could train to be heroes around the country—even the world."

Gideon concealed a grimace. More teaching. That wasn't what he wanted; it never had been, and though the past month had been disaster-free, it hadn't been easy. His goal had been to protect his city, initially—and then to find Ashcroft and stop him, more for personal reasons than anything. But now he was the de facto leader of a group of superpowered vigilantes, and he was being encouraged to find and train even more of them. *God, is this what You want for me?* It certainly wasn't what Gideon would choose for himself.

"I know they're out there," he said. "Serban said as much, and the past few months have certainly proven it. But it seems like most of them already work for Ashcroft, and if there are any who don't, I have no idea how to find them. It's not like there's a huge genetic difference. I couldn't even find anything in my own blood until I examined it closely. We can't just start picking people for random blood tests, hoping to find evidence of powers."

"True. Maybe someday they'll start showing up on their own. Isn't that usually how it works? Once one person steps forward, the rest follow suit? You were the first superhero to publicly use his powers. Maybe now others will be less afraid to do the same."

That would be nice—even comforting. If there were others out there, maybe even some who'd been around longer than Gideon and just hadn't made themselves known, he might feel less . . . lonely. Even with Dean and Wes and Patrick, he felt like he stood apart because he was the most experienced, which wasn't saying much. He was still learning more about his own abilities, still growing into them. *I just wish they'd all stop calling me a superhero.* Freeing Dean and Wes from Artemis' control felt more heroic than brutalizing criminals, but Gideon was still getting used to that descriptor.

He didn't have time to go on a superhuman scavenger hunt. With Ashcroft, Artemis, Powers, and Mendez all out there—plus who knew how many others—his focus right now should be on training the people already on his side. If there really were superheroes in other cities, they'd show themselves when they were ready.

Gideon snapped back to the present at the sound of wailing sirens. Flashing lights appeared in the rearview mirror. He pulled to the side of the road as a firetruck blasted past. A column of smoke rose from a building several blocks away. As Gideon watched, another firetruck roared past.

Jolie clenched her jaw. "Go."

Gideon pulled out his phone. "Dean, track my phone and get to my location as fast as you can. Bring my suit."

He parked the car on the side of the road. With an apologetic look to Jolie—though her dark eyes were full of understanding—Gideon jumped out and lifted off toward the fire.

CHAPTER 22

Dean pressed his phone between his cheek and his shoulder as he used the computer in front of him to track the GPS on Gideon's phone. It placed him in the Brooks, a few blocks from the police station, moving northeast. Judging from the severity of Gideon's tone, something serious was happening.

"What's going on?" Dean asked.

"Fire. A big one."

Dean patched into the fire department's radio frequency. The fire was at a residential complex—and it was burning fast. This wasn't an electrical fire or an accidental ignition. The speed and size of the fire could only mean arson. Dean pulled on his gauntlets and mask and turned to grab Gideon's suit from its mannequin.

"On my way."

Dean hung up, ran down the hall, and teleported. He appeared in the middle of the air outside the Tower. As gravity took hold, he teleported himself to a rooftop two blocks down, and teleported again. He was still testing the limits of his range of teleportation, but so far, he had been able to make a quarter-mile jump. It wasn't as fast as Patrick could run, but he could move quickly. He would make it to the Brooks faster like this than he would driving a car.

He landed on another rooftop, looked down the road toward the Brooks, and teleported again. Two more jumps, and he saw the column of smoke belching into the sky. It looked as bad as it had sounded on the radio. He jumped off the rooftop he currently occupied and teleported to another one, closer to the fire.

He ran, jumped, and teleported as fast as he could. A minute later, he stood on a rooftop across the street from the burning building. He scanned the streets below. Gideon was running toward the building. Dean teleported down to him, grabbed him, and teleported back up to the rooftop.

"Whoa." Gideon stumbled. "I could've just flown up."

"I know, but we're in a hurry." Dean handed him his suit. "What can I do?"

"Get in, find whoever you can, and get them out. I'll take the upper floors, you take the middle ones. The firemen will have the lower floors under control, hopefully."

Dean looked at the building. He wished he had Gideon's empathic abilities, so he could sense anyone inside who might be afraid. Instead, he'd just have to take it one room at a time. He focused on the fourth floor, ran toward the edge of the roof, and teleported.

His next breath dragged air through his throat like sandpaper. He coughed and forced the smoky air out. Once he had his breathing under control, he listened for any sign of occupants. A cough, a shout for help . . . anything.

A soft cry broke over the roar of crackling flames. Dean turned toward it and wove his way through debris. Smoke stung his eyes and threatened to fill his lungs. Dean held his breath and took another step toward the cry. A doorframe ahead had fallen. He clenched his right fist, and the aionium shield in his gauntlet swiveled out into position. He swung the disk, smashing through the barrier.

"Hello!" he called. "Is anyone in here?"

"O . . . over here . . . "

Dean pushed his way through the remains of the doorframe. A young woman lay on the floor, cradling a child. Both were coughing furiously. Dean rushed to her side and knelt next to her.

"Are you all right?"

She coughed and nodded. "I . . . was on my way out . . . I heard this little boy crying for help."

Dean put his arms around her. "Hold onto me."

He envisioned the sidewalk outside the building, closed his eyes, and concentrated. He felt the air ripple, and the hot, smothering atmosphere of the building was replaced by a crisp summer breeze. The woman gasped. Dean opened his eyes and stepped away from her as she looked around in surprise. Dean glanced down the road. Jolie ran up to his side.

"Anyone else in there?" Jolie asked.

"Not sure. The Seraph's checking the top floors; I'm about to go back in. Keep everyone calm out here!"

"Will do."

Someone cried out and ran over to their side to retrieve the little boy from the young woman. Dean looked back to the building.

"Who are you?" the young woman called.

"Name's Drifter."

He grinned and tossed a salute. Concentrating on the inside of the apartment building, he teleported back in to find more people.

* * *

Gideon smashed through a window and into the top floor of the burning building. He generated a shield of light around himself, keeping some of the smoke and fire at bay. He felt his internal temperature shooting up and cringed. Generating this much light protected him, but it also heated him up. In an already-blazing building, that could be dangerous. He could stay like this for only so long.

He reached out with his empathic abilities, searching for any sign of fear. He felt the determination of the firefighters far below . . . but also from someone much closer, near a source of terror. He frowned and walked in that direction. A lacquered door connecting this room to the next had half-fallen, blocking the doorway. Gideon raised a hand and blasted the door to splinters.

"Hello?" he called. "Is anyone in here?"

"Over here!"

Gideon pressed through the flames toward the voice. A tall, muscular man with rich brown skin, both arms covered in tattoos, stood in an opening where a wall had collapsed. He was trying to lift some debris from the floor. An aging man lay on the ground, pinned by the debris.

"Step aside!" Gideon said.

The man shook his bald head and continued lifting. Gideon sighed and stepped up next to him. He grabbed one edge of the large chunk of debris and lifted. The man who had been pinned slid out. Gideon and the muscular man dropped the rubble.

"Thank you," the younger man said.

"Let's get you out of here." Gideon lifted the older man. "Step away from the wall."

The younger man ducked behind Gideon. Gideon raised a hand and fired a burst of light at the wall. It exploded outward, and sunlight shone in through the hole.

"Grab onto my back."

The younger man did as Gideon had instructed. Gideon lifted off the ground and flew through the hole with both men. He hovered to the ground and set them down. The street was even more crowded now than when they'd arrived; dozens of people milled on the sidewalk across the street from the fire. The younger of the two men Gideon had rescued guided the elder toward the curb to sit down.

Dean appeared in a blink, carrying a soot-stained gray cat. "I think that's everyone."

Gideon reached out toward the apartment building, trying to sense feelings coming from someone other than the firefighters. He couldn't detect any overt traces of fear or worry. He nodded.

"I think you're right."

Gideon looked across the crowd. The building's residents were coughing and covered in soot, but he didn't see any injuries. The elderly man he'd helped save offered Gideon a bright smile. Dean was surrounded by onlookers taking selfies with him and asking for autographs. There were no arrests, no injured thugs to round up. Just rescued civilians. *This is a superhero's work.*

Gideon turned to the tattooed man. "That was brave of you, staying behind to help him."

"I was just doing what anyone would've." The man extended his hand. "Silas Rockwell."

The same Silas Rockwell Jolie had just mentioned to Gideon? He scanned the sidewalk and the street around them. If this was that Silas, then this might've been more than arson. The way Jolie had talked about Silas, he might've made a few enemies in the Shine trade, and now that it had been brought down . . .

Jolie walked up to his side. "Nice work, Seraph."

"Thanks, Detective." Gideon gave her a small smile. "This is Silas Rockwell. He was on the top floor, trying to help this gentleman."

"Silas?"

Rockwell quirked an eyebrow. "Have we met?"

"No, but you run an after-school program here in the Brooks, right?"

He nodded, looking a little puzzled. "That's right."

"You live here?"

"I did. My family had just finished moving into a new home across town. I was here picking up the last of our belongings."

Jolie looked back at Gideon, who nodded gravely. This fire hadn't been an accident, and it hadn't been some pyromaniac's descent into arson. It had been an attempted murder. Whoever had set the fire had been trying to kill Silas, not knowing that he didn't live there anymore.

"You thinking what I'm thinking?" Jolie asked.

Gideon clenched his jaw. "Powers."

CHAPTER 23

Wes walked into the ops room and was assaulted with the smell of smoke. He crinkled his nose as the overpowering scent of smoke enveloped him. It was like someone had started a campfire right in the middle of the room. Where was that smell coming from? Gideon and Dean were at one of the computers, and Dean was typing furiously. Wes walked up to them.

"What's going on?" he asked.

Gideon looked over at him. "There was a fire. Dean and I went to help with search and rescue, and now we think it might've been an attempted murder."

"There have to be better ways to kill someone than burning an entire building to the ground."

"Yes, but how better to make it look like an accident? Whoever did it, they didn't care about collateral damage or civilian casualties."

"Who was the target?"

"We think it was a man named Silas Rockwell, a coworker of Carter's who is outspoken against drugs in the Brooks."

"Is he okay?"

"We got to him in time. But we think the arsonist might be our old friend Powers."

Wes clenched his fists. If Powers was back in town, he wanted the first shot at him. He could've helped Gideon take him down at that warehouse if Artemis hadn't hypnotized him.

Dean glanced over his shoulder. "Not seeing him on any traffic cams or security footage. Doesn't mean he wasn't there, though. He lived in the Brooks long enough that he might know which alleys to take to stay out of sight."

"But why would he come back here?" Gideon asked. "I can't see Ashcroft, or at least not Artemis, being okay with Powers dividing his priorities between their organization and the drug trade."

"Unless the drug trade is just a front. It could serve their purposes for him to be here, or vice versa. Maybe they sent him here, and he took advantage of being in town for an opportunity to get back at Silas."

"Maybe." Gideon scratched his chin. "Either way, we need to find him fast. I'm going to call Carter. I'll have him tail Silas and make sure he's safe."

"I don't suppose odds are good he'd go back to the warehouse?" Wes asked.

Gideon shook his head. "Powers knows that place has been compromised. But he's a weasel. He's bound to have more than one safehouse in the Brooks."

"I'll let you know if anything turns up," Dean said.

"What about me?" Wes asked. "What can I do to help?"

"Just be ready to move." Gideon coughed. "If Powers turns up, we'll need all hands on deck to stop him. Ugh, I'm never going to get the smell of smoke off this armor."

Dean waved toward the mannequins. "Just get undressed. I'll handle the cleaning. Next time you wear it, you won't even notice the smell."

Gideon nodded, patted Wes on the shoulder, and walked out of the ops room. Wes dropped into the chair next to Dean's.

"How are we going to stop Powers?" Wes asked.

"Arianna and Maddox are working on a version of the adhesive bead that delivers a high-voltage shock that might disrupt whatever allows him to duplicate himself." Dean shrugged. "If that doesn't work, then we'll have to do it the old-fashioned way: punch out all the copies until we hit the real deal."

That didn't sound so bad to Wes. He was more than willing to smash in Powers' face dozens of times. In fact, he hoped he got the opportunity to do just that.

* * *

Carter stood in the shadows of an alley and watched Silas from a distance. The man showed no concern and gave no impression that he thought the apartment burning to the ground might've been anything more than an accident. Carter had met few people with as optimistic a worldview as Silas held.

"My wife and kids are safe," he'd said. "That's all I care about."

The big man tucked his hands in his pockets and walked down the street in the direction of Sojourn City West High School. Keeping to the shadows, Carter trailed him. He wasn't wearing the Crusader uniform; if he got caught, he didn't want Silas wondering why there was a vigilante on his tail. Instead, he threw a black hoodie over his work shirt and black jeans and pulled the hood up to shadow his face. His suit and truncheons were in his backpack, just in case he ran into Powers. Experience had shown that even the electrified tips on his batons weren't guaranteed to stop the villain, but Patrick, Dean, and

Gideon could all get to him at a moment's notice if things went bad. Carter could hold Powers off for that long.

Where was Silas going? It was still late summer, and school—and Silas' after-school program—hadn't started yet. Maybe he was just meeting one of the boys he worked with to catch up or something.

Carter was just glad Gideon trusted him with this task. It didn't seem like a lot, but protecting Silas was an important job. If that's what Gideon wanted Carter to do, then he was going to prove that he belonged on Gideon's team, powers or no powers. Lately, he'd felt like the black sheep. Gideon, Patrick, Dean, and even Wes could stop crimes in half the time it took Carter to. If doing this would prove his competence, then maybe Gideon would let him do bigger things.

Silas walked through the school parking lot and toward one of the back doors. Carter frowned, ducked behind a wall, and peered around the corner to watch. What was Silas doing here? Silas unlocked the door, looked around, and went inside. Carter reached inside his backpack and withdrew one of his truncheons. He didn't like this.

A light flicked on inside the school, shining out of a window to Carter's right. Carter dropped to his knees and crawled next to the window. He angled his head next to the glass and strained to hear what was going on.

"You all right?" Silas asked.

"Y-yeah." The second voice sounded familiar. "J-just fine."

"Are you high again?"

"What? No. O-of course not."

Silas' tone took on a warning edge. "Don't lie to me, man. You promised."

"I-I'm sorry. The detox . . . "

Carter furrowed his brow. The voice was that of an older man, not one of Silas' teenage students. Carter tried to peer through the window, but the blinds were drawn.

"I know, man. It's brutal. But I'll help you through it. You got the stuff?"

"Y-yeah."

"Let's see it." There was a moment's silence. "Good job, Ethan. I owe you."

Ethan. That was why the voice sounded familiar. It was Silas and Carter's coworker! Why would Ethan and Silas meet here, instead of at work? He clenched his fist around his baton. None of this seemed right. What had Silas gotten himself involved in?

"W-what are you going to do?" Ethan asked.

"Burn it. It's the only thing to do with it. Is this all of it, Ethan? You didn't keep any for yourself, did you?"

No response.

"Ethan. You know there's not much left; you can either go through withdrawals now or wait a few weeks and then still go through withdrawals. Why not just get it over with?"

"I . . . I'm not strong enough."

Drugs. Silas was acquiring drugs from Ethan and destroying them. No wonder someone had tried to kill him—especially if it was Shine he was destroying. If Powers or another Shine dealer who'd shaken the cops had found out what Silas was doing, there was probably a pretty price on his head.

"Yes, you are." Silas' voice was steady, soothing. "You can do this. I'm here for you. Let me know if you need any help, all right?"

"O-okay."

"Now, give me whatever you're keeping, and let's go."

A few moments later, the light flicked off. Carter edged back toward the corner where he could see the doorway Silas had entered through. It swung open, and Silas walked out with Ethan at his side. The latter was stooped over and jittering, his pale skin waxier than usual. He was high, all right. Carter felt a pang of sympathy for him. The poor guy had been trying to kick the habit for so long . . . He deserved to catch a break.

Carter returned his truncheon to his backpack. It wouldn't be needed in this situation. *Silas looks safe to m—*

A black-and-red blur dropped from the rooftop, landed behind Silas and Ethan, and grabbed the latter man in a chokehold. Silas whirled around and raised his hands in front of him in a placating gesture.

"Let him go. It's me you want."

"Is it?" The assailant peered around Ethan's shoulder, showing his narrow, drawn face. Powers! "You may be the one destroying my drugs, but he's the one giving them to you. I don't approve of snitches."

Carter had to do something fast, or Ethan was going to die. He didn't have time to change into his suit. He dropped his backpack to the ground, pulled on his domino mask, and twirled the one baton he was already wielding. It would have to suffice. He stepped out from his hiding place and flicked the truncheon's activator switch. Electricity crackled from the tip.

"Let him go, Fragment."

Powers glanced over his shoulder. "Ah. The junior vigilante. Missing some of your costume, aren't you, boy?"

Silas swung around. "What—?"

"You're outmatched," Powers leered. "You come at me with a stick?"

"Let him go." Carter repeated, more forcefully this time.

"Very well." Powers dropped Ethan to the ground. "I'll take you instead."

Carter glanced at Silas. "Get him out of here."

Silas helped Ethan to his feet and pulled him away. Carter rushed at Powers. The black-clad villain swung a fist at Carter's head. Carter pulled his head backward. He felt air *whoosh* past his face as the blow barely missed. Powers swung his other fist. Carter blocked it with his forearm. Powers kicked out, catching Carter in the solar plexus. He wheezed and doubled over as the blow shoved the air from his lungs.

Powers punched him in the jaw. Carter stumbled back. *Come on, Crusader, focus.* Carter imagined his father, clad in the black costume and mask he'd worn during his days as a vigilante. His mind centered around that image. He dropped into a ready stance, twirled his baton, and fixed his gaze on Powers.

"Come on!"

Powers reached into his belt and withdrew a collapsible baton. He rushed at Carter and swung. Carter blocked it with his own weapon and retaliated. Powers knocked Carter's strike aside. Carter spun, using the added momentum to increase the force of his blow. He hit Powers on the right shoulder. Electricity crackled. Powers jerked and stumbled back, but part of the charge dissipated throughout his suit.

"Figured you'd try that move." Powers smirked. "Had my uniform altered to counter it."

He brought his baton down in an overhand strike. Carter raised his truncheon to block it, grabbed Powers' wrist with his free hand, and spun it into an armbar. Powers punched Carter in the back. Carter grimaced and struggled to keep his grip on the villain.

Why hasn't he replicated?

Powers struck him again. Carter released his grip on Powers' wrist, spun around, and jabbed with his baton. Powers knocked the blow aside and swung one of his own at Carter's neck. Carter ducked under it and smacked his truncheon into Powers' knee. The joint buckled, bringing Powers down. Carter rose, and as he did, he brought his fist up full force into Powers' chin. The man stumbled backward and landed flat on his back. Carter kicked Powers' baton out of his hands.

"Give it up, Powers."

Powers smirked. "Tell your friends when they want me, they can look at Seattle."

"You're not going anywhere."

"Don't have to. I'm already there."

Powers disappeared. Carter blinked. Powers wasn't even here. Carter had fought one of his doppelgangers sent specifically to get the heroes' attention and, Carter supposed, to settle a personal score with Silas and Ethan. At least Powers had failed on the second account. And as for the first . . . if he wanted their attention, he had it.

Carter picked up his backpack and replaced his domino mask and truncheon inside. He needed to get back to base now. Gideon would want to hear about this.

CHAPTER 24

"Seattle?" Gideon frowned. "Why would he want us to go there?"

"Powers did a stint as a street dealer for an organization in Seattle early in his career." Jolie handed him Powers' rap sheet. "Maybe he's calling you out on his home turf."

Gideon took the folder. It contained everything the police had on the man, plus what his team knew about Powers' abilities and recent activities. He thumbed through the file and nodded.

"Maybe. I'm not sure. Can Powers' duplication abilities really stretch that far? If he's in Washington, how was he able to project a doppelganger all the way in Sojourn City?"

They were gathered in the ops room—the five vigilantes, plus Jolie. She was as much a part of the team as the rest of them. They couldn't do much of what they did without her, and she was benefiting from the arrangement as well. She was often the one who collared the criminals that Gideon or the others caught.

Dean took the folder from Gideon. "We can't make any assumptions. I'll start looking for places in Seattle where he might hide."

"Old haunts," Jolie agreed.

Carter smacked a fist into his open palm. "He's asking for a fight. He'll get one."

"He will." Gideon put a hand on Carter's shoulder. "But not from you. You did a great job tonight, but we can't leave the city without anyone watching over it. That's your job."

Carter sighed, and Gideon sensed his disappointment. He'd known the young man wouldn't like it, but it was the safest place for him to be—and the city really did need someone here. Powers was drawing them to Seattle, if that's where he really was, for a reason, and it wasn't just to settle a score. If he wanted the heroes out of Sojourn City, it might be a trap. Unfortunately, it wasn't an opportunity they could afford to ignore.

Wes, standing in front of his uniform, spoke for the first time. "What are we waiting for? Let's get this guy. Dean, can we take your jet?"

"About that. I can't keep using my private jet for superhero business, or the board might start to get suspicious. But there's a little project Sterling Labs has been working on that I might have sequestered for personal use." Dean tapped on the keyboard, and a sleek black jet appeared on one of the computer screens. "Behold—the Raptor."

Patrick whistled. "Nice."

"It'll be ready for its first flight in the morning."

"I'm still not sure about this." Gideon scratched his chin. "Carter, you said that Powers said we'd find him *at* Seattle, right? Not *in* Seattle."

"That is an odd turn of phrase," Jolie said at Carter's nod. "He could've just misspoken, though. What else could he mean?"

"What else, exactly. Powers might not seem it, but my bet is he's more intelligent than he lets on. And if all of this has been orchestrated by Ashcroft, even more so." Gideon leaned over Dean's shoulder to look at the monitor. "Forget Seattle for a minute. Let's look at places here in Sojourn City that Powers might mean. If he's pointing our attention there, it might be because he doesn't want it here."

"Okay . . . " Dean typed furiously. "Well, there's an old coffee shop in the Brooks that's called Sea Town. It's right near Powers' territory."

"So?" Wes asked. "Is there some reason that stands out?"

"Sea Town is a colloquial name for Seattle. It's a long shot, but maybe."

Jolie leaned in on Dean's other side. "That coffee shop shut down almost two years ago, during Serban's initial rise to power."

"Dean, does anyone own that building now?" Gideon asked.

It was a hunch—Crowne Pharmaceuticals was looking more and more like a shell company. After a month of looking, Dean hadn't found anything on them but a few holdings, and all of them abandoned. Ashcroft had to have more than one front for his true organization, and one of those shell companies might have bought the old coffee house.

"Looks like . . . an individual." Dean frowned. "Jonah Craven."

"Any records on this guy?"

Dean chewed his lip as he searched. "Nothing. I can't find any results for anyone under that name. It's an alias."

"What do you want to bet it's an alias for Ashcroft?" Gideon straightened. "Even if Powers isn't there, we can check it out. Since it's here in Sojourn, Carter, we can use your help—yours, too, Jolie. We need to make sure we're ready for whatever he throws at us; rushing in blind would be dangerous. Dean, have Arianna and Maddox finished the shock beads?"

Dean nodded. "From what Carter said about Powers' suit, it can disperse electrical jolts, but there's a lot more amps in those beads than in Carter's batons. Just one should be able to stun him and hopefully keep him from duplicating himself."

"Good." Gideon looked at the rest of the team. "Gear up. We move in on Powers at sunset."

CHAPTER 25

Patrick knelt in a runner's stance in an alley half a block away from Sea Town. Droplets of rain trickled down his suit. The abandoned streets, covered in a light fog, gave the street an eerie vibe. Patrick's muscles vibrated in anticipation. He took a deep breath through the thin fabric of his mask. *Wait for the signal.*

The plan was simple: Dean would take point, firing an electro-net onto Powers. Patrick would run in right behind him with a pair of electrified handcuffs that Sterling Labs had worked up, slap them on Powers, and with any luck, haul him straight to the back of Jolie's car. They hoped the electricity would keep him from duplicating, so the fight should be over before it started. That was the ideal outcome, anyway. Carter and Jolie guarded the back entrance in case it all went bad and Powers tried to flee that way.

From his position on a rooftop across the street, Gideon said, "He's in there. At least, it's probably him. I can sense only one person."

"I'm going in," Dean said.

"Everybody ready on three."

The vibrations in Patrick's body, initially microscopic, increased as the world slowed around him. Gideon's voice distorted in Patrick's earbud.

"Three . . ."

An eternity waited in the breach between each of Gideon's words. Patrick brought his mind and body into harmony, as Gideon had taught him. He closed his eyes and concentrated. Whatever they encountered in there, Patrick had to be in total control. His powers weren't in charge; he was. He had the power over his own body.

"Two . . ."

This was it. Patrick shifted all other thoughts out of his mind, centering himself only on being Spright.

"One."

Spright pushed off and rushed for Sea Town. He pushed through the glass door and took in the environment at a glance. The single-room coffee house was two stories tall, with a dining area on a balcony overlooking the lobby. The walls and floor were all dark hardwood. Fragment sat to Patrick's left, near the coffee bar, clad in a black-and-red uniform. He had just turned around to look up at the balcony, where Drifter stood with his hand pulled back to toss one of the shock beads. Spright slowed down—not to a complete standstill, but enough that he could observe in real time and react as soon as Drifter's shot hit Fragment.

Drifter released the bead. The device clattered to the ground and unleashed its pent-up charge on the supervillain. Spright sped up and rushed toward Powers as he writhed, pulling a pair of electrified handcuffs provided by Arianna and Maddox from his belt. Fragment hit the ground—

And four more Fragments appeared, two on either side of him. The electrical current still running over Fragment's body spread among the five bodies. He was dissipating the current through his doppelgangers. Spright continued his run toward the center Fragment, the real one, and opened the cuffs. He slammed into Fragment and slapped the cuffs on his wrists, but as he did, a hand grabbed his shoulder and jerked him back. He managed only to clasp the right cuff; Fragment pulled his left hand free and shoved Spright off. Another duplicate planted his heel on the shock bead, crushing it into metal bits.

"Backup!" Drifter called.

Spright jerked his elbow back, striking the Fragment that had grabbed him. As the copy disappeared, he turned back to the real Fragment. But Powers had been busy—the small building was filled with over a dozen Fragments.

"Let's have some fun," the doppelgangers said in unison.

The Fragment doppelgangers swarmed toward Spright. He zipped between them as rapidly as he could in the confined space. As he sped past the clones, he punched them out, the force of his speeding fists hurling them into the air. But for each one he knocked out, there was another waiting to take its place.

The doppelgangers could not catch Spright. Even if they'd been able to, the speed at which he was moving made him impossible to grab without giving them friction burn. But they could confine him, and the more doppelgangers appeared in the bar, the less room Spright had to move. Puffs of air and green flashes of light filled the room as Drifter teleported from place to place, knocking out a duplicate here or tossing a shock bead there, and then moving to a new position before the others could grab him.

The door burst open, and the Seraph flew in, cloaked in a halo of light. Several of the clones rushed at him, and the Seraph laid into them with glowing fists, knocking them down like bowling pins. Wes—as his masked alter ego, Rampart—was right behind him, his body a solid sheet of steel. He jumped into the fray and pounded away at the Fragments.

Where was the real Powers? Taking him out was the key to ending this fight. He was the only one with a handcuff on his right wrist.

Spright pushed through the crowd, scanning desperately for him, but the clones were creating a wall around him. That should make him easy to spot—but in the mass of bodies, everything became a red-and-black blur.

* * *

Rampart brought a steel fist up into a Fragment's jaw and then turned to snap-kick another in the sternum. Something hit him in the back, followed by a pained cry. He smirked and turned to the doppelganger that had punched him, who was clutching his hand.

"I'm made of steel, genius."

He grabbed the doppelganger by the collar, hurled him into the mob of other clones and backhanded another Fragment across the jaw, sending him crashing into a table. Three doppelgangers jumped on Rampart's back. His knees buckled and he went to the ground, but the flurry of blows the trio rained down on him had no effect. He shoved himself to his feet and arched his back, jarring them off. He snapped his foot backward to strike one in the chest.

"He's got to get tired eventually!" he exclaimed.

"Do I?" several dozen doppelgangers mocked.

Fragment swung a punch at Rampart's face. He raised his forearm to block and heard bone crack as the doppelganger's wrist met his metal skin.

No matter how many Fragments they knocked down, he seemed able to generate more. What would it take to make this guy tired? If they could just get to the real Powers and knock him out, the rest of them should disappear. But that was the real trouble.

The Seraph unleashed a blast in a ninety-degree arc that knocked back several of the Fragments around him. Rampart fought toward his brother's side. Maybe if Gideon could discharge a blast big enough to take out everyone in the whole room, they could get to Fragment. The problem was, it would also hit Wes, Patrick, and Dean.

Unless the other two weren't here. Spright could speed out the door, and Drifter could teleport away. Rampart's enhanced skin could take whatever blast the Seraph unleashed. If he could just get to the Seraph's side to tell him that . . .

A purple blur rushed past Rampart, knocking down a row of doppelgangers between him and the Seraph. *Thanks, Spright!* Rampart ran toward his brother.

"Seraph!"

The Seraph pushed his way through the crowd toward Rampart. Fragment's fist bounced off Gideon's shoulder, and Gideon turned and dropped him with a light burst. He stepped to Rampart's side and turned so they were standing back-to-back.

"What is it?"

Rampart blocked a punch. "Can you make a repulse blast big enough to knock out everyone in this room?"

"I've never done one that big before," the Seraph grunted.

What if he had something to amplify his power? If he could channel a light blast through something . . . something like a prism.

"I've got an idea. Spright and Drifter need to get out of here."

"Okay." The Seraph's voice echoed as it came from directly behind Rampart and from his earbud at the same time. "Spright, Drifter, clear out! We've got a plan."

Rampart blocked another blow and brought his fist up into a duplicate's sternum. He grabbed another by the wrist and twisted. The doppelganger yelped as his hand popped out of joint. Rampart shoved him back. A moment later, the purple-and-black blur sped past again and disappeared out the door. A puff of air, and Drifter was gone, too.

"What's your plan?" the Seraph asked. "Because we're really outnumbered now!"

"Hit me!"

"You?"

"Yes!" Rampart shoved a clone away from him. "Full power, shoot a blast of light straight at me—the biggest one you've got!"

"Are you insane? That could melt you!"

"It could if I were steel." He roundhouse-kicked another duplicate. "I'm not going to be. Just do it!"

"All right . . ."

The Seraph leapt into the air and hovered over the ground. All the Fragment clones turned to face Rampart, now standing alone in the middle of the coffee house. As they piled toward him, he touched the glass tile on his belt, and his skin shifted from steel to glass. He looked up at the Seraph, whose hands were glowing a bright gold, the light energy formed in spheres four times the size of his fists.

"Now!"

The Seraph fired straight at Rampart. Rampart braced his knees as the blast of light struck him—and refracted off him. He felt warmth coursing through every inch of his body and wondered if he'd made a terrible mistake. What if this destroyed him completely? His body heated, and he screamed. He planted his feet on the floor and braced himself, struggling to absorb the flow of energy.

The light exploded off him. He grunted and flew across the room, underneath the balcony, and smashed into the back wall. His skin shifted back to flesh, and he groaned as pain racked his body. His shoulders and upper back screamed at him, and his legs felt like he'd just run a marathon without stretching. But he was still in one piece. The room went eerily silent. The Seraph floated down to the floor. Rampart pulled himself to his feet. Dozens of Fragment doppelgangers littered the floor, unmoving, mingled with overturned or smashed tables and chairs. One by one, they vanished until a single Vince Powers remained, handcuffs dangling from his right wrist. He leaned against the bar, his head drooping against his chest. If he wasn't unconscious, he was definitely stunned. Wes staggered toward him. A sharp pain racked his body, but he ignored it.

"That was . . . incredible." Gideon floated to the ground and rested a hand on Wes' shoulder. "Good thinking."

Wes knelt and snapped the cuff on Powers' left hand. "Thanks."

The door opened, and Patrick and Dean reappeared. Wes glanced up at them. Dean's expression was comically stunned. Patrick's was unreadable behind his mask, but he reared back in surprise and turned his head back and forth to take in the emptied room.

"What did you do?" Patrick asked.

"I acted like a prism," Wes said. "Gideon fired a burst of light at me, and it shone through my body and refracted off from every angle. It filled the whole room and knocked out Powers and all his duplicates."

Dean raised his eyebrows. "Are you okay?"

"Yeah . . . a little sore." Wes hoisted Powers to his feet. "But we won. We got this piece of scum. So, I'm good."

Gideon grabbed the villain by the collar. "Where are Somna and Backfire?"

Powers' body rippled, as though he were going to duplicate himself, and the shock cuffs activated. The villain grimaced, and his body stilled. "Heh. Doesn't matter. You're too late . . . "

Uh-oh. Wes stepped toward Powers and touched the aionium tile on his belt just long enough for his fist to transform into the unbreakable metal.

"Too late for what?"

Powers kept his gaze firmly on Gideon, ignoring Wes. "You didn't surrender when she had your best friend—but what will you do now that she has your family?"

Wes clenched his fist. *Mom? Dad?* Who else could Artemis have? She could've even taken Jolie and Carter. Wes shook his head and resisted the urge to crack Powers' jaw with his aionium fist.

Gideon pressed his lips together. "We need to go. Jolie, come get this guy."

No response. Wes' gut churned.

Powers coughed and cackled. "They aren't your only loved ones—and you aren't the only one who has a family." His gaze shifted toward Patrick. "What would an eighteen year old do without his parents?"

Wes couldn't resist anymore. He slugged Powers across the jaw. Something crunched beneath Wes' superstrong metal fist. The villain slumped in Gideon's grasp.

Patrick backed away and pulled his mask off. "They've got our families."

Gideon hoisted Powers onto his shoulder. "Don't worry. We're going to save them—all of them."

CHAPTER 26

They've got my family.

The thought ricocheted around Patrick's mind faster than he could run. If his parents were in danger, if they got hurt because of him, he'd never forgive himself. He'd worked so hard to keep his identity secret, but somehow Artemis had figured it out. If she hurt them because of him . . . One of Ashcroft's people had already killed Patrick's grandfather. If they killed his parents, there would be nothing that could stop him from taking down every single one of them.

"What are we going to do?" He rushed onto the street behind Gideon. "We have to save them!"

"We will. We're going to save both our families." Gideon pulled out his phone. "I'll have Jolie's old partner come down here to take custody of Powers, and then we'll rescue them."

"How?" Wes asked.

"I'm still working on that." Gideon tightened the cuffs and pulled down his hood. "Just take a deep breath. It's going to be okay."

Patrick tapped his foot rapidly against the sidewalk and tried to calm himself as Gideon stepped away to make the call. The thought of his parents being in trouble . . . He pulled his cell phone from a zipped pocket in his uniform and dialed Lucy's number. If she was okay, maybe she could help him figure out what was going on with his family. Gideon seemed to have the same idea about Jolie, because he also dialed.

Dean lowered his own phone. "The Raptor's standing by. Maddox can get you back to San Francisco in no time."

Patrick's shoulders slumped. His phone rang once, twice . . .

"Hello?"

Thank God. "Lucy! You're okay."

"Yeah . . . Why wouldn't I be?"

"Listen, I think my family's in trouble. Have you seen or heard anything strange from my house today?"

"No, not that I can think of. Hold on." There was a long pause. "There's a muscle car outside your parents' house that I don't recognize."

"Thanks, Lucy. Whatever you do, stay inside."

"What's wrong? Patrick, what's going on? Why would your family be in trouble?"

"It's a long story, and I don't have time to explain. Just . . . stay inside. Help is on the way. Stay safe, okay?"

"O-okay. I will. Should I call the cops?"

"No!" He grimaced. "Sorry. No. The cops wouldn't be able to handle this kind of trouble. Stay by the phone. I'll call back in a while."

Patrick hung up and returned his phone to his pocket. Gideon was pacing back and forth, not speaking. Finally, he lowered his phone.

"Officer Jordan's on his way. No answer from Jolie or Carter. Wayans must've grabbed them in the alley." He kicked the brick wall of Sea Town. "This was a setup."

Wes looked up, his lips pressed into a thin line. "Mom and Dad aren't picking up, either."

Patrick exhaled. At least Lucy was safe. They must have studied Gideon longer than Patrick. They took Patrick's parents, but they had everyone Gideon loved, family and friends. What about Carter's family? Jolie's? Did Dean have anyone else in Sojourn City?

Gideon and Dean spent the next few minutes making call after call. Everyone else was accounted for. That made their job easier, if only a little.

"Where do we go first?" Patrick asked.

"I'm thinking!" Gideon's fists pulsed with light. He took a deep breath. "Sorry. We're going to figure this out."

Dean raised a finger. "I've got a suggestion, if you're open."

"Let's hear it."

"The Raptor is fast. If I tell Maddox to really let her fly, we can make it to San Francisco in less than an hour."

Relief flooded Patrick. He felt bad, but he really wanted to save his parents first. But that didn't make sense—they were already in Sojourn City. Logically, rescuing Gideon's family first was the best option.

"We'll split up." Dean pointed to himself and Patrick. "We'll take the plane to San Francisco and save the Omers. Gideon and Wes, you stay here and save Jolie, Carter, and your parents. There are four of us; there's no reason to stay together. If we divide our forces, we can save both families."

Patrick looked to Gideon. *He has to agree.* Gideon had never sent them on a mission without him there to supervise. He'd have to trust that they'd learned enough to handle this on their own—that they could function without his help. Patrick couldn't imagine how conflicted Gideon must be right now.

Finally, Gideon nodded. "It's the best option we've got right now. But I think you should come with me, and Wes should go with Patrick."

"What?" Wes exclaimed. "This is Mom and Dad we're talking about! You're crazy if you think—"

"That's exactly why you should go with Patrick. I'm already doing everything I can to contain my rage, and I'm sure you are, too. If we both go in with tempers flaring, we'll make a stupid mistake. I need someone more level-headed with me, and if you go with Patrick, you'll think more like a superhero and less like a son."

It made a lot of sense, but Patrick didn't really care who went with him. He'd go alone if he had to, but he had to make sure his parents were safe. The others could do what they wanted.

Wes shook his head. "I can't leave them!"

"Wes, I understand, but—"

"No you don't!" Patrick recoiled as Wes surged forward. "It's my fault! If I hadn't been selfish or power hungry, you might have been able to stop Artemis. I never should have tried to be a hero. I only messed it up. Now Mom and Dad could . . . "

Gideon put a hand on Wes' shoulder. "I will protect them. You just focus on rescuing Patrick's family. I'll take care of ours. For the record, I forgive you. I did a long time ago. You deserve to be here as much as the rest of us."

Wes swallowed. "Okay."

Dean crossed his arms. "Sounds like a plan. Don't worry. Everyone's going to be all right. I believe that."

"Me, too." Gideon gestured for everyone to gather around. "But I want to pray over them—and us—before we go out."

Patrick bowed his head as Gideon prayed, but he didn't hear a word Gideon said. Instead, his mind and heart pleaded with God for his parents to be safe. *Lord, I haven't told them about my faith in Jesus yet. Please, let them be okay so I can be a witness to them.*

" . . . amen," Gideon finished.

Patrick opened his eyes. "Amen."

* * *

Jolie tugged against the cuffs binding her wrists to a length of pipe. She had been getting into position behind the coffee house when a woman in a green costume had shown up and knocked her out. Next thing she knew, she was here—not that she was sure where here was. It was a narrow room filled mostly with electrical equipment. In the dim light provided by a few blue-tinted bulbs running along the walls, she could see Carter handcuffed to a pipe on the other side of the room.

"Carter! Carter, wake up."

He groaned and shook his head. "Who got us? Was it Powers?"

"No, a woman. She was wearing green . . . a black cape . . . must've been Wayans."

"What does she want with us?"

"Probably to use us as leverage against Gideon." Jolie struggled against the cuffs. "We've got to get out."

Carter grunted. "I can't move. Maybe if I had some of my gear . . . concussion gauntlets would break us out. But it looks like she took all my stuff."

"It's okay. We're going to be okay."

Gideon would come for them, but she hated feeling like a damsel in distress. There had to be something she could use to get out of here. She slumped back against the wall. For now, at least, she was stuck. But she'd get her chance. And when she did, that woman was going to pay.

* * *

Gideon's anger broke like a tidal wave against the dam of his emotions, threatening to boil over and spread through his whole body. He had to calm himself several times as light shone from his pores. He closed his eyes and prayed for God to help him control his anger.

Powers wasn't helping matters. The villain had been smugly, silently leering at the heroes ever since they made their plan. It was getting to all of them—but especially Wes. Maybe it was because he had the most experience with Powers, but Wes really had a special dislike for that guy. Gideon thought that Wes might just jump up and deck him again.

At least the electric restraints kept Powers' duplicating abilities at bay. It would've been catastrophic for a dozen or more Fragments to suddenly burst into existence. They really needed to figure out a permanent solution for restraining superhumans, something that would dampen their powers to keep them from breaking out. A normal prison cell would never hold someone like Powers.

Gideon rubbed his head. It throbbed from the tangle of emotions bouncing around. He felt everyone's fear, anger, stress, smugness . . . It was overwhelming. It was like hearing half a dozen different conversations all at once, contained inside his head.

"Hey, Gideon?"

He opened his eyes. Patrick had moved to stand next to Gideon. "Yeah?"

"I'm . . . scared. I don't know what I'm up against, and you're not going to be there to coach me through it."

"I understand. It's stressful not knowing who we're going to face. But that's why we have to be adaptable. That's why we train for a variety of scenarios."

"It's just . . . the not knowing part. Get it?"

Do I ever. Gideon was terrified not just of losing his parents, but that Patrick and Wes, or even Dean, would be killed in the fighting. Gideon had been responsible for teaching them, and he was the team leader. If any of them died, it would be on him. But he'd seen their growth in the past month. He had to trust them to fend for themselves. He had to—or he'd go crazy.

"I do. But you're going to be fine. You're quite the hero, Patrick. I think Spright's ready to stop being a trainee and become a hero in his own right."

Patrick's shoulders straightened. "Really?"

"I do. Listen, if you go up against Backfire, just don't let him get his hands on you. And if it's Somna . . . well, Dean will give you the neural inhibitors we've been working on to block her powers. We'll just have to pray they work."

"Okay."

"You two had better move." Gideon thumped Patrick's shoulder as Arianna's car rolled up to the curb. "Good luck."

Patrick nodded and pulled on his mask and goggles. Wes stood, rolled his shoulders, and walked toward the car. As he did, he looked back at Gideon.

"Save them."

"I will." As the car rolled away, Gideon took in a long breath. "Good luck, brother."

CHAPTER 27

Wes swallowed the bile rising in his throat as Patrick sped them across San Francisco. It wasn't only the intense speed making Wes sick—it was the thought of what could be happening to his parents right now. As much as he understood Gideon's reasons for sending him to help Patrick, he still resented not being able to rescue his parents when they were in danger. Hadn't Gideon done the same thing, just months ago? He'd given up fighting the criminals that were overrunning Sojourn City long enough to rescue his parents, knowing that in that time, those criminals could do a lot of damage. Why wasn't Wes allowed to do the same thing?

Whatever the reason, it was done now. The Raptor had dropped them off, leaving Wes stranded in San Francisco with Patrick. The only choice he had now was to do his best to save Patrick's parents and trust Dean and Gideon to do the same for his own.

"We're coming up on the house," Patrick said.

Five seconds later, they skidded to a stop. Wes stumbled, carried forward by the intense momentum of Patrick's speed. His head spun, and he forced himself back to his feet. Patrick stomped toward his house, sliding on the neural dampener Gideon had given him. Wes removed his own dampener from his pocket and slipped it over his ear. He'd been hypnotized by Somna before. He had no desire to repeat that experience. Patrick walked toward the front door, and Wes followed.

He kept a hand near his utility belt, ready to transform into whatever substance would be necessary for the fight ahead.

Patrick put his hand on the doorknob—

The door exploded outward. Spright sailed backward. Rampart touched his concrete belt tile, leapt in the air, caught his friend, and grunted as he slammed into the street. Spright pushed himself to his feet and held out a hand to help Rampart up. He took it and rose. His concrete skin had taken the worst of the hit.

Spright dusted himself off. "Guess we know who we're up against."

Rampart looked up at the house. The doorframe crackled and burned. An armored figure stepped through the opening. A red helmet with insect-like eyes masked his features.

"That's him." Spright's voice was low, menacing. "The man who killed my grandfather. Backfire."

"Welcome, *amigos*! So glad you could join us today."

"Let my family go!" Spright shouted. "You have a problem with me? Fine. Let's settle it between us. There's no reason for them to get hurt."

"No, eh?" The armored man chuckled. "Your *padres* aren't here, boy. Their situation is a bit more . . . precarious."

Rampart reached for Spright—too late. He crossed the yard in a fraction of a second and slammed into Backfire, knocking him to the ground. Rampart rushed toward them. Spright had Backfire pinned down. He raised a hand, which vibrated rapidly.

"Where are they?"

"Remember the clinic? It's scheduled for demolition."

Spright brought his vibrating fist down on Backfire's helmet, cracking it. Then the young speedster rushed down the road, leaving Rampart standing baffled in the front yard. *What am I supposed to do now?* He stepped toward Backfire. He'd never met this guy before; he had no idea how to counter his superpowers.

Backfire groaned and rose, chunks of his helmet falling to the ground. The man inside was Latino, with buzzed hair, scars crisscrossing his face, and a black beard. He looked up and smirked.

"You must be Turner's *hermano*, eh? You've got the same look in your eye. Let's see if you've got the same steel."

Could Rampart get a better lead-in line? He smirked. "If you insist."

He touched the steel tile on his belt, and his skin shifted from dull gray to shining silver. He rushed toward Backfire. The villain charged, and as he ran, swirling red energy appeared around his fists. Rampart leapt when they were a few feet apart and brought his fist down toward Backfire. His steel knuckles slammed into Backfire's face, knocking him to the ground. The villain grabbed Rampart's ankle. He frowned as his leg warmed. With his free leg, he kicked Backfire in the jaw. Backfire released his grip on Rampart's leg, and it cooled back down.

Backfire stood and swung a glowing fist at Rampart's jaw. Rampart backflipped and brought his boot up to kick Backfire under the jaw. He landed on one palm and completed the backflip, coming up in a three-point, foot-knee-fist crouch. Backfire leaned against the porch stairs, rubbing his jaw.

"Like that move?" Rampart strode toward his opponent, pumping his fists. "I've been practicing it for months."

Backfire grabbed a piece of shrapnel from the front door and hurled it. Rampart didn't try to dodge it. The wood should bounce harmlessly off his steel skin. The projectile struck—and exploded into a fireball. Rampart flew backward and slammed into Backfire's car.

Ouch. His skin shifted back to its natural state. Backfire rose and walked toward him. Rampart reached down to his belt. Maybe aionium would be a better option. One thing was for sure—he couldn't let Backfire get his hands on him, or Rampart could explode just like that chunk of wood.

* * *

Spright darted through the streets toward the clinic, pushing himself through traffic and between pedestrians. Several of them cried out, and others photographed or recorded him with their cell phones. He ignored them. All he cared about was saving his parents. If they died, too, there was no force that could prevent him from making Backfire pay.

He pushed himself harder, faster, and let out an incoherent growl as his body protested the speed. He rounded the corner and came to a stop outside the clinic.

What trap had Mendez prepared? Would a bomb detonate if Spright tried to open the front door? There had to be some twist to this. It wouldn't be as easy as grabbing his parents and running out.

Just think, Spright. Think tactically.

He walked toward the front door. Every cell in his body screamed out for him to run in, to just grab them and go. Backfire had said they were running out of time; walking slowly toward them seemed insane. But it could be a trap, and he wouldn't do his parents any good if he got himself killed.

Spright reached for the door and slowly pulled it open. Nothing happened. There was no click indicating an armed bomb, no explosion, nothing. He stepped inside. He didn't see any signs of booby traps. He sprinted down the halls, searching each room for his parents. The right hallway yielded no results. He went left, and—

There they were. His parents sat back-to-back, tied to chairs in the same room where Spright and the Seraph had confronted Dean and Artemis. On the floor underneath their chairs . . .

"Who are you?" Mom asked.

Spright stepped toward them. What should he say?

"I came to save you."

"Don't come any closer!" Dad shouted. "How do we know we can trust you?"

"I'm a superhero. I know who did this to you, and I'm here to help. One of my friends is taking care of him as we speak."

"A superhero?" Mom asked. "Like—like the Seraph?"

"Yes." He took another step into the room. "I'm going to help you, but I'm going to have to look at that device."

Dad clenched his jaw. "He said it's motion-sensitive. If we try to get up, it'll explode."

Spright knelt next to them. He didn't know a lot about bombs. There were wires connecting it to discreet metal plates hooked underneath the chairs. Those were probably the motion detectors. Great—how would he get his parents off the chairs without triggering them? Could he move fast enough to get them outside before the bomb detonated?

"Why did he kidnap us?" his mother asked. "Why us?"

"Because he wants to kill me." Spright studied the wires. "This just might do it, too. I can move fast, but I'm not sure I can outrun an explosion while carrying both of you."

"Then take her," Dad said. "Leave me behind. Just save my wife."

"No!" Mom exclaimed. "I won't leave you!"

"It's not an option anyway. Even carrying one person, I still might not be fast enough."

But what if he could trick the device? Maybe he could make the plates think that his parents were still seated. If he vibrated his hands at the same frequency as the plates, they would remain in place after his parents stood, and if he did that, they could get up and run—he wouldn't have to carry them. And then he might be able to speed away from the blast by himself.

There was only one way to find out.

"I'm going to try something. And if it gets us all killed . . . Well . . ."

His father nodded. "Do it. We've got to try something. He said the bomb is on a timer, so if we just sit here, we'll all die anyway."

Right. No pressure. He grabbed the ropes holding them and snapped them apart. He knelt, took a deep breath, and reached his hands under the plates. He didn't touch them—not yet. He vibrated his hands as rapidly as he could and slowly raised them to touch the plates. He squeezed his eyes shut—

No explosion. Great. So that had worked. He opened his eyes. Now, if his parents could just get up and walk away . . .

"I think I've got it. Get up—slowly—and walk out the door."

"Michael . . . " Mom's voice trembled.

"We've got to do it, hon. We've got no other choice. Just listen to my voice, okay? We're going to do this together. On the count of three. One, two . . . "

Spright braced himself for the extreme heat of a bomb going off in his face.

"Three."

His parents stood—and nothing happened. Spright kept up the vibration, holding the plates in place. Dad laughed in relief and ran to hug Mom.

"Get out of here!" Spright cried.

"Thank you." His mother put a hand on his shoulder. "Thank you."

He nodded and returned his gaze to the bomb, listening to his parents' footsteps fade down the hallway. When he could no longer hear them, he braced himself. His only option now was to release the plates and run like a madman and hope that he was faster than the explosion. He felt his whole body begin to match the vibration of his hands.

Time slowed. The seconds on the clock ticked by at the equivalent of every three seconds, to Spright's perception. There were only five seconds left on the timer—he had to move now. He took a deep breath. *God, please let me survive this.*

He pushed himself away from the chairs with one foot, spun, and booked it for the door. *Click.* The sound of the plates dropping to trigger the detonator reached his ears. He curved into the hallway. *Well, I'm not dead y—*

The bomb went off. A wave of heat washed over Patrick's back. He stumbled forward, rolled, and came to a stop lying on his back. He took a deep breath. Dust and ash fell around him . . . but that was it. He laughed nervously. That had been way too close.

Footsteps clacked on the lobby floor. "Are you okay?"

That was his mother's voice. Spright rolled over onto his hands and knees and looked up at her. She was in one piece. His father appeared a moment later, peering cautiously into the hall. Spright stood and rubbed his head.

"I'm fine. You?"

They nodded. He smiled—which they couldn't see under his mask, he realized—and stepped toward them.

"Who are you?" his father asked.

"I'm Spright."

"No, I mean . . . why did he kidnap us? Who are you really?"

From the tone of his father's voice, it was safe to say that he already had his suspicions. Patrick reached up, pushed his goggles up on his forehead, and pulled down the part of his mask that covered his mouth and nose, so it rested underneath his chin.

Mom gasped. "Patrick?"

"Yeah, it's me." He scratched the back of his head. "I went to Sojourn City to train with the Seraph. I didn't tell you because I didn't want you to worry, and I wanted to keep you safe. But . . . it looks like that didn't work out so well. I'm sorry."

"Where did you get these powers?" Dad asked. "How long have you had them?"

"Can we talk about all that later? I'll explain it all, I promise, but my friend might still be fighting the guy who kidnapped you. He may need my help."

His parents exchanged glances. Dad nodded. "Go."

"Thank you."

Spright replaced his mask and goggles and sped out the door back toward his home. He clenched his jaw as all the rage he'd pent up toward Backfire exploded to the surface. This man had killed his grandfather, rampaged through his city, and tried to kill his parents. It was time to put an end to it.

He blasted into his neighborhood. Up ahead, Rampart and Backfire grappled in the front yard. Spright rushed toward him and slammed into him at full speed. The armored villain crashed to the ground. Spright grabbed him and sprinted down the road, dragging Backfire behind him.

Backfire struggled against his grip. Spright ignored him and sped through the city. He slammed Backfire into a brick wall, adjusted his grip on him, and ran in the other direction. He found a junkyard and dragged Backfire through it, shoving him up against anything with a hard surface. Then he dashed back toward the house.

Rampart stood on the front lawn, looking back and forth for his vanished opponent. Spright darted toward him, lifted Backfire, and slammed him full speed into his own car. The hood collapsed under the weight and force of the armored man. Spright jumped on top of him and rained down punches on him. He restrained them just enough to keep from killing Backfire with the kinetic force of a speed punch.

Rampart made no move to stop him. That was good; Patrick wasn't entirely sure he could be stopped, not yet. He punched again and again, and Backfire jerked and feebly tried to put up a fight. He was too broken. All he managed to do was tug Patrick's mask free of his head. Blood streamed from the villain's nose and mouth, both eyes were blackened, and a large bruise covered his right temple. Patrick punched him again—and again—and again.

"You killed my grandpa! You *killed him!*"

Tears streamed down Patrick's face. He didn't care. All he cared about was this. He punched again.

"Stop!"

Patrick ignored the voice and raised his fist.

"Stop!"

He froze. That wasn't Wes. He looked up. Lucy stood in the yard between their houses, hands covering her mouth as she watched in horror. He looked back down at Mendez, bloody and beaten. The man groaned, and his head sagged to the side. Patrick checked his pulse. He was still alive.

Patrick jumped off the car and dropped to his knees. His throat constricted. *I wanted to kill him.* Backfire had killed his grandpa. *He's gone. I won't see him again until . . . He cut himself off. It didn't matter why he was angry. He'd almost gone too far.* Wes patted him on the shoulder and walked over to Mendez's side, pulling a pair of electrified cuffs from his belt. Patrick didn't dare look up at Lucy. Would she fear him now? Be ashamed of him? Surely, she could never love him, not after seeing what he'd just done.

Suddenly, Lucy's arms wrapped around him. Patrick frowned. How could she hug him after seeing him nearly kill someone? How could she still treat him like this . . . ?

"It's okay," she whispered. "It's okay."

He hugged her back, resting his head on her shoulder, and cried. He was glad she'd shown up when she did. Would he have killed Mendez? He didn't know, but he was relieved that he never had to find out.

"He—he killed Grandpa." Patrick sniffled. "He tried to kill Mom and Dad, and I . . . "

"I know." She gently rubbed his back. "It's okay. You're okay."

"I just . . . felt so angry."

"Let it go, Patrick. You have to let it go. God doesn't want you to hold onto your anger. You have to forgive him."

Tears streamed down his face and soaked her shirt. He sniffled. Forgive the man who'd murdered his grandfather? How could he? He took a deep breath and squeezed Lucy. What was he supposed to say?

"Your grandfather's at peace, and your parents are all right. You have to let it go, or he wins."

She was right. Holding onto his rage at Mendez would only corrupt him, would only satisfy Mendez. It wasn't what his grandfather would've wanted, and certainly not what his parents would've wanted. And she was right—it wasn't what God wanted, either.

"Okay." He raised his head. "You're right."

Lord, please take this burden. Take my unforgiveness and help me to move on. He imagined laying a huge burden down at God's feet. He imagined God picking it up and taking it away. And just like that, the weight pressing on his chest vanished.

"Thank you, Lucy."

"You're welcome." She pulled back and looked down at his costume. "Um . . . I think you have some explaining to do."

Patrick choked out a laugh that was half sob. "Yeah. I know."

CHAPTER 28

The Seraph soared over Sojourn City.

The rainclouds that had blanketed the city earlier were gone, and the sun peeked up from the horizon, setting on the city and casting it in a beautiful orange light. Despite his unique vantage point, Gideon couldn't appreciate the view.

Is this my fault? Gideon's parents were in danger because of his actions as the Seraph—because his identity was publicly known. Worse, it was the second time they'd been endangered in the past few months. If Gideon had never taken up the mantle of the Seraph—or if he'd been a bit more careful before removing his mask on the rooftop of Sterling Enterprises on the night of the Uprising—they wouldn't be in this situation.

Dean looked up at him. "Hey, Mopey. We're going to save them."

Gideon scowled. "I'm supposed to be the one who can read emotions."

"It doesn't take an empath to know why your face is scrunchy."

"I can't help but think this all could've been avoided." Gideon looked down at his friend. He was carrying Dean through the air, his arms hooked under Dean's armpits. "One choice changed everything. Not even a choice—an unconscious action. If I hadn't taken my mask off that night, Artemis wouldn't have known who my parents are, and they wouldn't be in danger now. Heck, if I'd never become the Seraph—"

"Don't talk like that. If you'd never become the Seraph, Luca Serban would be the despot king of Sojourn City right now. And yeah, it sucks that taking your mask off led to all this. But if you hadn't, Patrick wouldn't have known you were a superhero when you went to his house. You never would've trained him. Wes and I never would've gotten powers."

Gideon closed his eyes and took a deep breath, centering himself and clearing his mind of his doubts and worries. Dean was right—a lot of good had come from that one stupid mistake, and it had to have been God's hand at work. The odds of all those things happening at random were too astronomical to calculate.

"You're right. Thanks."

"What're friends for?" Dean's smile faltered. "You sure about this?"

"Absolutely."

They'd figured that the fastest way to get to his parents house was to ascend above the city, and then drop down in freefall, leveling out as they neared the suburban neighborhood. It was risky, but not impossible.

"Okay. Just don't drop me, Turner."

Gideon looked down at the city far below, and his stomach turned. He swallowed the bile that threatened to rise from his throat, tightened his grip on Dean's arm—

And stopped flying.

He nearly lost his grip on Dean as they dropped into freefall, but he jerked his friend close to keep him from sailing away. Gideon closed his eyes and encircled himself in a halo of golden light. They fell . . . and fell . . . and fell. Gideon took as deep a breath as he could manage and angled his body. He lifted himself out of the freefall and soared down a city street.

Dean cackled. "Wooooooooo-hoo!"

Gideon found himself grinning. When he flew, all the fear went away. The wind tickled his face and whipped his hair about. He adjusted his grip on Dean's biceps so he was dangling below Gideon. He descended toward the suburbs.

"Go!" Gideon snapped.

Dean vanished. Gideon put his arms at his side, narrowing his profile, and pushed. His speed increased and he arced toward his parents' neighborhood. Dean popped into their front yard. A few seconds later, Gideon's feet touched the ground, and he stormed toward the front door with clenched fists, feeling the light coursing through him. Dean flexed his arms, and his twin aionium shields ejected from his gauntlets. Gideon reached out mentally, searching for any sign of his parents.

"They're here."

Dean walked toward the door. "Could be a trap. You ready?"

"Let's do it."

Dean tried the doorknob. Unlocked. He raised one shield and pushed the door open. Gideon stepped in after him. He remembered his martial arts training and cleared his mind of distractions. Grief and worry would hinder him in a fight.

The living room looked impeccable. There was no sign of a struggle; no chair or table overturned, no broken lamps, nothing. Mom stepped out of the kitchen, eyes on her phone, and looked up and shrieked.

"Oh, Gideon!" She put a hand to her heart. "Don't scare me like that."

Gideon frowned and rushed across the living room to her. "Mom? You're all right? Where's Dad? Is he okay, too?"

Mom gave him a puzzled look. "Of course we're all right. Why wouldn't we be?"

"I thought . . ." Gideon glanced at Dean, who shrugged. "Wes tried calling you, but there was no response. Someone we were fighting hinted that you and Dad might be in danger."

"We're fine. Dad's out in the garage. It was the oddest thing; our cell signals went out for a few minutes, but they just came back on. No one's come around all day."

"Okay, good." Gideon kissed the top of her head. "I love you. I'm glad you're both safe. I'd love to stay and talk, but there's still someone out there who could be a danger to the city."

"Be safe, dear."

"I will." Gideon led Dean back outside and closed the door behind them. "Well, that was a big distraction. The cell phone lines around the house going out? That's no coincidence. Artemis must have something planned that she wants us out of the way for."

"What's her goal, though?"

"Whatever it is, she's done playing around. She's tried kidnapping my loved ones already and failed—more than once. She doesn't strike me as the kind to repeat a failed plan, and now she has Jolie and Carter. Whatever she wants, if she doesn't get it this time, I think she's prepared to kill them."

Artemis had been humiliated by her repeated failures. Ashcroft didn't seem like the merciful type, based on the brief meeting Gideon had with him in Venezuela. He had punished Mendez for letting Gideon escape by injecting him with his potentially lethal superhuman serum. Artemis might be under some extreme pressure to succeed or suffer the consequences. Dean was right—this was a life-or-death situation. So where would she go? In all of Sojourn City, where was the place that most suited her goals?

"Dean, are there any major public events tonight?"

Dean frowned. "Why?"

"Artemis is a grandstander—she'd want her victories to be public, especially after she's been humiliated. She wants to make a statement. What better way to do that than by publicly holding the girlfriend and teammate of Sojourn City's Shining Knight hostage?"

"That's a good point. Public events, though? I don't—oh no."

"What?"

"The maglev train." Dean stepped toward Gideon. "The public unveiling and first test run are tonight; half the city will be there."

"The train would provide her a convenient place to hold them until she's ready for her moment in the spotlight."

"The unveiling starts in an hour." Dean glanced at his wrist. "Less than, actually. But Gideon, that's not all."

"What? What else?"

"The train—it's carrying the prototype for the dispersal unit that Artemis asked me about back in San Francisco. It's taking it to the airport to be shipped off to our lab in D.C. to prep for a government test."

That had to be it. With that dispersal device, Ashcroft could spread his serum wherever he wanted. If they got a hold of it, he could make superhumans anytime, anywhere. And with an army behind him, Gideon and his friends would be no match for Ashcroft.

* * *

Artemis stood at the front of the maglev train and smiled. The drivers, hypnotized and obediently waiting for her word to start the train, sat before her. She looked out the front windshield and watched as thousands of people congregated outside the railway. Even if Turner and his friends didn't show up, she'd still get her victory—she would get away with the device while the train smashed into a barrier, destroying it and killing Jolie, the Crusader, and a few dozen civilians who'd been privileged to ride the train for its test run. Gideon would be devastated, and the city would see that their superhero wasn't so very heroic, after all.

If he did show up, there was no way to save the train and his friends while stopping her from stealing the device. Even if the other superhumans were with him, Artemis was confident that her plan would go off without a hitch. With the train's conductors hypnotized, they would drive the train into the barrier without question. Even if they were somehow taken out or snapped out of their trance, Artemis had several of Mendez's guerrilla followers standing by to sabotage the engines. She also had several more men guarding Jolie Anderson and Carter Jonson.

No matter what happened here tonight, Artemis would get the victory. While Turner and his friends were distracted fighting Powers and saving their loved ones, Ashcroft's other followers would sneak into Sterling Labs and download intel on the dispersal unit as a contingency. Either way, they'd get what they wanted. All Artemis had to do was ensure the "heroes" were too distracted to interfere. If she killed, captured, or broke them, that was just a bonus—a bonus that she was determined to achieve. This had become personal for her. She couldn't fail her master again. Ashcroft may have shunted her off as a mere distraction, but beating the heroes would put her back in his good graces. He'd remember her worth.

Time would tell if Turner and his superhero squad would show up or not. The train's debut was half an hour away. Artemis drew her gun from its holster, checked it, and holstered it again.

Come and get me, 'Seraph.' Come show me what a superhero can do.

* * *

In the distance, Dean could see the Platform, where the train was stationed. Of all the places Artemis could've held her captives, it had to be the Sterling Enterprises Maglev. Dean shook his head. He and Sterling Enterprises were trying to do good, to better the city, to make it feel more connected. There was nothing sinister, nothing underhanded, about the venture. And yet, a supervillain hijacked the train.

The rainclouds had cleared away, leaving a bright orange sunset in its wake. The distant towers glinted in the light. He teleported two blocks closer, ran, and teleported again to the top of the bridge connecting the Platform to the rest of the city. The maglev's rail was to his right, another bridge merging the parts of the city together. Dean teleported onto the Platform, directly beneath the railway.

Gideon soared by overhead. Dean took a running jump and teleported onto the brick wall that surrounded the entrance to the train station. The crowd was already pouring in—thousands of people squeezing through the security gates and pressing forward to get the best view of the train. The select few who would ride the train for its first journey were lining up. Dean settled into a crouch and scanned the crowd for any sign of Artemis, Jolie, or Carter.

Several people looked up and pointed, and the crowd cheered. Dean glanced up. Gideon hovered high above, looking over the crowd. Dean grinned as Gideon awkwardly waved at the fawning masses. There were perks to being a superhero, but this was one of the downsides—it was hard to do anything without being noticed. At least they hadn't spotted Dean yet. He was behind the crowd, and most of them were looking upward or forward.

Gideon's voice crackled through Dean's earbud. "I don't see them."

"All clear from my angle. Do you sense anything?"

"Too many people. I can't get a good reading on anyone's emotions. It's like sensory overload, but a hundred times worse. I have to close myself off."

"Fair enough." Dean teleported from the wall to the opposite side of the train, where he would be hidden from the crowds. "They might be in the train already. You stay out here and look pretty; I'll search for them."

Dean walked back to one of the rear cars and entered his access code into the door's keypad. It whooshed open, and he stepped inside and looked around. There was no sign of anyone in this car, but through the window to the forward car he saw passengers taking their seats. He crept toward the rear of the train, keeping low and holding his fists tight, ready to eject his shields at a moment's notice.

The train jostled. *Uh-oh.*

"Dean, the train's moving." The sound of the cheering crowd echoed behind Gideon's voice. "I don't think it was supposed to start yet."

"It's not." Dean checked the watch on his gauntlet. "Not for another twenty-five minutes, at least."

"She's here."

"Get in here as fast as you can. I'm in the second car from the back; I'll work my way backward to where the device is being held. You go forward, try to find Artemis. This just got a lot more complicated— there are civilians aboard."

"If it was easy, anyone could do it. Good luck, Drifter."

"Good luck, Seraph."

Dean ejected his shields and walked toward the hatch connecting this car to the one behind it. He wished—not for the first time—that he had Gideon's empathic powers. At least he would be able to sense trouble coming. He opened the hatch and stepped through. This car had no windows, and the warm sunset light that had illuminated the previous car vanished as the door slid shut behind him.

"Welcome aboard, heroes." *Somna*. Her voice echoed over the train's intercom. "I'm so glad you found us in time."

Gideon's voice came through Dean's comms. "Give yourself up, Somna. You're not going to get away with this."

Dean scanned the dimly lit cabin. This one, too, was vacant. Computers, wires, and pipes lined the walls. Dean stepped past them and made his way toward the hatch to the final car. If none of the captives were back there, he'd have to make his way forward.

"Oh, I think I am," Somna continued. "I've prepared for every possible contingency. Even if you manage to save your loved ones—even if you manage to save everyone on the train—you can't catch me, too."

Dean looked up at the ceiling. "We'll see about that!"

The passengers must've been in a panic by now. They had to be hearing all this—at least Artemis' side of the conversation. With the train already rocketing across the city, they were trapped. Should he turn around and help them and worry about Carter and Jolie later?

"Don't bluster," Somna laughed. "You have no idea what you're up against. We can't let you interfere any longer."

"Ashcroft's madness has to come to an end," Gideon said.

"Madness? Is it madness that gave you your powers? What about you, Drifter? Do you think it's madness?"

Dean clenched his fists. "It's madness to force it on people! Not everyone will be able to cope with having powers or make the right decisions with them even if they could!"

"No, but those who do—we'll change the world."

Gideon laughed. "We? You honestly think you're putting your powers to good use, Artemis?"

"It's Somna, Seraph. And yes, I do."

Dean shook his head. She really was nuts. "Heroes don't take captives and threaten innocents."

"I didn't say I'm a hero. I'm a revolutionary. Good luck, gentlemen."

Dean reached for the handle to the next hatch, where the device should be locked down in a storage crate. A revolutionary? Whatever Artemis and Ashcroft were planning, it wasn't going to end well. They had to stop them. He reached out and grabbed the handle—

Something hard struck him from behind. Dean slammed through the hatch and landed in the middle of the rear car. He staggered to his feet, left-hand shield raised to ward off any further blows, and looked back through the hatch. With his right hand, he probed the back of his head. His fingers met a small gash, and he hissed at the pain.

Carter stood in the doorway, clad in full Crusader gear, staff held casually at his side. Both ends sparked menacingly.

"Carter?" Dean stepped toward him. "Snap out of it, buddy; you've got to wake up."

Carter didn't respond. He twirled his staff and rushed toward Dean.

CHAPTER 29

The Seraph fumed as he stormed from one train car to the next. Artemis had clearly gone mad—as mad as Gideon had suspected Ashcroft had been when he'd seen him for the first time in Venezuela. They were going to tear the world apart trying to make it better. They had to be stopped—but first, he had to save everyone on the maglev.

"Seraph!" A mid-fifties businessman jumped to his feet. "Thank God you're here."

"What's going on?" someone exclaimed.

"It'll be all right," another voice soothed. "The superheroes are here."

Gideon closed his eyes. *Right. Superhero. The passengers around him chattered, some nervous, some excited. Cell phone cameras clicked as the civilians snapped shots of him. They needed a hero. That's what he would be.*

"Stay here." He eased the businessman back into his seat. "I'll take care of this."

He pushed open the door in front of him. As he stepped into the next car, anticipation and nervousness—not his—washed over him. He raised an arm to shield his face.

Crack-crack.

Two thugs stepped into the aisle. The Seraph lowered his gauntlet, and a pair of flattened bullets fell to the floor. He closed the door behind him to protect the passengers in the rear compartments from stray fire. As the thugs pulled the triggers, the Seraph extended his left hand and projected a burst of light, knocking both men flat against the far wall. Why did they even try? They had to know they couldn't hit him. He moved forward and grabbed one of them by his jacket collar, hoisting him into the air.

"Where are they?"

The thug shook his head. "D-don't know. We're just hired muscle."

The Seraph threw him to the floor and kicked him in the face, knocking him out cold. These were Ashcroft's people, all right. Their uniforms were identical to the guerrillas who'd kidnapped him in Venezuela. Mendez wasn't the only one the scientist had brought with him. They'd find him more difficult to handle now than he had been in the jungle.

The Seraph pushed open the door to the next car. A hail of bullets greeted him, striking his breastplate and knocking him backward. He glanced down. The onslaught didn't scratch the aionium suit. He stepped into the car and raised a hand, ready to blast the shooter—

But the shooter was Jolie. She stood in the middle of the car. Her eyes were vacant, her pistol held out in front of her.

"Jolie—"

She fired again. Gideon threw up a shield of light, disintegrating the bullet before it reached him. Past her, another guerrilla stood at the front of the car, his rifle trained on Gideon.

The guerrilla swiveled his rifle to Jolie. "Another step and she dies."

Gideon froze. He couldn't fire a blast of light at the thug without hitting Jolie. She was perfectly positioned between them. He had only one other option. He lowered his hands and reached out with his mind. In doing so, he lowered all his defenses. If the thug decided to execute Jolie or take a shot at Gideon's face, he would have no way of stopping him.

But he had no choice. He reached into Jolie's mind and found the cloud of manipulation and confusion surrounding it. He formed his mental light into a hammer and smashed away at the darkness.

The guerrilla swiveled his rifle to Gideon. "Lower your hood and get on your knees."

The Seraph ignored him and continued to push forward with his mind. The cloud of Somna's hypnosis fought back, trying to envelop the Seraph's light hammer. He transformed the weapon from a blunt instrument to a cutting tool and hacked away at the shadows with the imagined sword of light.

That's the secret to beating darkness, Somna. You can have as much shadow as you like, but the funny thing is, no matter how much there is—it can't be all-encompassing if there's a single spark of light.

Jolie's mind contained more than a spark. Her faith in God, love for Gideon, and strong moral compass were a blazing fire. All the Seraph had to do was reach it with his own light. *God, give me strength.* He felt his mental sword grow and brighten. He imagined the blade igniting, a golden flame at the center of the darkness. It was out of his control now; the blade pressed forward of its own accord. It sheared through the shadows like they weren't there. Light exploded outward—

"I said, get on the ground!" the thug shouted. "I will shoot him!"

Jolie spun, her pistol still raised, and fired a trio of shots. The guerrilla staggered back, hit the wall, and slumped to the floor. The Seraph rushed forward and wrapped Jolie in his arms.

"Are you okay?"

"Yes." Jolie lowered her gun shakily. "What happened?"

"Artemis used her powers on you. She's somewhere on this train. I've got to find her."

She pulled Gideon into a passionate kiss. "Thank you."

"You're welcome." He gestured toward the front of the train. "Come on. You want to help me stop a supervillain?"

"Love to."

* * *

Drifter swung his left shield wildly, blocking a strike from the tip of Crusader's staff. Aionium was a non-conductive material, so the jolt of electricity from the weapon dispersed harmlessly off the surface. The Crusader spun and brought his staff down toward Drifter's head. Drifter brought up his right shield and blocked the blow, and then jabbed with his left shield, striking Crusader in the chest.

The younger man stumbled back, wheezing as his breath left him. Drifter dropped into a ready stance, left arm forward and right hand back. He didn't want to hurt Carter, but he had to snap the kid out of his trance. Patrick had accomplished that by hitting Dean in the head. Drifter cringed at the thought of braining Carter with an aionium shield, but he didn't see a way around it.

Crusader rushed in, arcing his staff to strike at Drifter's ribs. Drifter used his left shield to knock the staff to the side and brought the right shield down on top of the staff, jarring it free of the Crusader's grip. Crusader turned and punched at Drifter's face. Drifter teleported out of the way and came back behind Crusader.

"Sorry, kid."

He slammed the face of his shield into the back of Crusader's head. The young man stumbled and tried to turn. Drifter hit him again, this time in the face. Crusader slumped to the floor. Dean retracted his shields inside his gauntlets and knelt at Carter's side. He was unconscious, all right—stone cold. Dean dragged him up against the wall and turned his attention to the dispersal unit.

It sat in a crate in one corner of the car, battened down by several crisscrossing straps. A Sterling Enterprises device normally would've been protected by at least two armed employees; Artemis must've already taken them out. *If she killed them, I'll . . .* He pushed the thought aside. He couldn't do anything about that now. He had to get the device out of her hands. Right now, that meant the best place for it was off this train.

Dean pushed his way out onto the small platform on the back of the maglev. Wind whipped around him as the train bulleted through the city. Strands of his own curly hair blew into Dean's eyes. He grabbed a railing and looked around. They had already crossed into Lakeside, the upper-class part of the city that was on land. From the look of things, they were rapidly passing into middle-class territory— heading for the Brooks, right on schedule.

Refuge Church was just outside Lakeside in a middle-class neighborhood. It sat off to the left in the distance, its steeple rising above the buildings around it.

This was going to hurt.

Dean rushed back inside, freed the device from its straps, and dragged it out onto the back platform. Placing one arm firmly around the crate, he focused on the church, imagining the parking lot and the area surrounding it. He closed his eyes, clenched his fists . . . and teleported. His feet slapped pavement, and he stumbled forward. He opened his eyes in time to see that he was falling face-first toward the ground. He angled himself to roll off his shoulder and came up in a crouch. The crate smashed into the pavement beside him but did not break.

Dean looked back at the train that was already rocketing out of sight. Rolling his shoulders, he strode away from the crate. He'd call someone at the lab—normally, that would be Arianna and Maddox, but they were flying the Raptor right now—and have them come pick it up. He hesitated to leave it unattended. What if Artemis had other agents throughout the city? There were innocents on that train, though. They might need his help. *Okay, inside then.* He grabbed the device again, popped into the church fellowship hall, and returned to the parking lot in two seconds.

Now for the train.

He teleported and reappeared midair several yards behind the train. *Yikes!* He threw his hand out and teleported again. When he reappeared this time, his palm slapped against the railing on the back platform. He wrapped his fingers around it. The train jerked him forward, nearly tearing his arm free of its socket. He thrust his other arm forward and grabbed the railing, pulling himself up onto the platform.

Dean sank to the floor, sitting with his back to the rail, and panted. Sweat beaded his forehead. He reached up and wiped it away.

"Oww . . . " He adjusted his shoulder. That was going to hurt in the morning.

The door to the train car slid open. Carter stepped out onto the back rail. Dean tensed, ready to move if the kid was still hypnotized.

"Dean, are you okay?"

"Yeah." Dean held out a hand, gesturing for Carter to help him stand. "I'm . . . doing all right, kid. You?"

"Yeah, just have a killer headache."

"Huh. How 'bout that? Come on. There's a bunch of passengers that need saving. Let's find Gideon and get this figured out."

CHAPTER 30

Jolie tightened her grip on her pistol as she and Gideon approached the front of the train. They had checked every car so far, and there was no sign of Artemis. The only place left to check was the cockpit.

The neural inhibitor Gideon had given her moments ago itched, but she was glad she had it. Being under Artemis' control had been a disturbing feeling, like being a spectator in her own body and yet also a willing participant. Everything Artemis had commanded had seemed so reasonable. But a small part of Jolie had known it was wrong. She wondered if she would've killed Gideon, if given the chance. She'd fired at him, sure, but she'd also known he was wearing bulletproof armor. If he hadn't been, would Jolie have been able to resist the urge to shoot him? Either way, Somna was going to pay. Nobody made Jolie a puppet and got away with it. She rested her finger over the trigger guard.

"Here we go." Gideon reached for the door to the cockpit. "Ready?"

"Very."

Gideon's fists charged with light, and he slid the door aside. Jolie stepped forward. Artemis stood in the middle of the cockpit, hands on her hips.

"Well, well." Somna smirked. "You made it."

Jolie trained her gun on the woman. "Hands up."

"No, that's not how we're going to play this." Artemis gestured behind her. "The conductors are under my control. I have the power here."

"What's to stop me from freeing them?" Gideon asked.

"My men have orders. If this train stops, they are to open fire on everyone on the maglev platform in the Brooks."

"Witch," Jolie growled.

"Save the people or save the train—and all the passengers on it." Artemis shrugged. "You can't do both, Turner."

"He doesn't need to." Jolie stepped forward. "I'll stop you, and he can go save them. Get out of here, Gid."

Jolie's mind raced. If she shot Artemis, even if it wasn't a kill shot, her control over the conductors might slip. Then they wouldn't have to stop the train—they could just slow it down and be ready to stop as soon as Gideon gave the all clear.

"What do you want?" Gideon asked.

"To see you fail. To see you choose." Artemis smirked. "You can either try to save the people at the station, or try to save the train. You can't do both, and it's unlikely you'll get there in time to save them anyway."

Gideon surged forward, grabbed Artemis, and slammed her into the wall. The villainess cackled. Jolie shook her head in disgust, lowered her gun, and turned her attention to the conductors. Maybe if she took off her inhibitor and gave it to the driver . . . but then Somna could control her again and make her shoot the conductor. Or Gideon. She slammed her fist against the back of his chair.

Gideon dropped her and turned to Jolie. "I've got to go save them. Can you handle this?"

"I'll do my best. Go."

Gideon smashed through the front windshield, soaring away like a rocket. The wind whipped at Jolie's hair. She turned to Artemis and trained her gun on the woman. Artemis laughed. A hand grabbed

Jolie's wrist—one of the conductors. With her free hand, Jolie punched him hard in the jaw. He reeled back. She punched again, and he loosened his grip on her hand. She jerked free and pointed her gun at Artemis again.

Artemis didn't look concerned in the least. "You can't win. If I don't call my men in the next ten seconds, dozens of people will die. I doubt even your boyfriend can get there that fast. But if you let me live, this train will crash into a barrier, destroying it and killing all of us—and likely anyone in the vicinity, as well."

Come on, Jolie, solutions. There had to be a third option besides killing Artemis and dooming dozens of people, or waiting and then dying with them anyway. *Wait a second* . . . There was one possibility. It was a gamble, but Jolie was desperate. She had no idea where Dean was or even if he could help. She was on her own.

Artemis lashed out with her right leg, knocking Jolie backward. Jolie's gun clattered to the floor. She pushed herself up and wrapped her arms around Artemis' waist, tackling her. She punched down at Artemis, but the villainess raised her arms to block the blow. Jolie felt Artemis' right leg hook her own and tried to free herself. Artemis bucked her waist, and Jolie flew over her head and slammed into a console.

Jolie's ears rang from the impact. Groaning, she rolled over and pulled herself to her feet. Artemis reached for the gun holstered at her belt. Jolie dove for her own gun, grabbed it, and fired. Her bullet grazed Artemis' wrist. She flinched, dropping her weapon. Jolie jumped to her feet, grabbed the inhibitor from behind her ear, and jerked it off. Before Artemis could react, Jolie slammed the device down over the villainess' ear and kicked her to the floor. She trained her gun on Artemis' chest.

Did it work?

"What the heck is going on?" the conductor asked.

Jolie glanced at him. "Slow the train down! We're going to crash. But don't stop it—not yet."

"What did you do?" Artemis asked.

"Neural inhibitor. Keeps your powers from working on the wearer—but on you, it keeps you from using your powers at all. Touch it, and I'll put a hole in you."

Artemis' right hand snaked toward the gun lying on the floor. Jolie twitched her pistol and fired at the floor between Artemis' hand and the gun. Artemis recoiled.

"I mean it. Now, you're going to call your men and tell them to stand down."

"Why would I?"

"Because I'll shoot you if you don't."

Artemis scoffed. "I don't believe you."

Jolie lowered her gun and fired into Artemis' right leg. Somna screamed as the bullet tore through her thin jumpsuit, her flesh, and her kneecap. Jolie raised the gun again, training it on Artemis' chest.

"Test me again. Or call your men off. Your choice."

* * *

The Seraph soared toward the train station, light energy blazing around him, a maelstrom of energy propelling him. He flew faster than he ever had, diving between buildings and power lines. He had no idea how long he had before they would start shooting—and he couldn't just take them out. He had to make sure everyone in the station was evacuated before the maglev crashed.

As he approached the station, he probed the area with his empathic abilities. He felt two alert, almost predatory presences. *There.* He surged forward and scanned the area visually. Standing near the end of the platform, close to where the train would strike, two men with AK-47s watched the crowd. The Seraph aimed at the one on the left. He slammed into the man, carried him to the top of the station, and dropped him toward the roof. The thug screamed as he fell. The Seraph turned around to face the remaining shooter. The man raised his rifle—

The Seraph fired a wild burst of energy from his right hand. It struck dead center, sending the man flying back a dozen yards. He hit the ground and lay still. Gideon landed on the platform and put both hands to his mouth, yelling as loudly as he could at the panicking throng of onlookers.

"Get out of here! Get off the platform and clear the station!"

He didn't wait to see if they responded. He leapt back into the air and rocketed away. *God, please, let us stop this train before it's too late.*

* * *

"Juarez, come in." Artemis paused. "Juarez? He's not answering."

"Tell him anyway. You've still got another knee."

"Juarez, if you can hear me, stand down. That's an order." She glared at Jolie. "Happy?"

Jolie nodded. "You can stop the train now."

She lowered her gun slightly and, using her free hand, reached for her handcuffs. They weren't shock cuffs like Gideon and his friends had, but as long as Artemis had the inhibitor on, cuffing her with the good old-fashioned kind should work well enough. Jolie stepped toward Artemis—

The train jostled. Jolie steadied herself against the conductor's chair, frowned, and looked out the window. If anything, the train was gaining speed. Artemis laughed. Jolie glared back at the woman, stormed forward, and slapped the cuffs on her wrists.

"Why aren't we slowing down?"

"Something's wrong!" the engineer said. "I think the engines have been sabotaged."

Oh . . . wonderful.

* * *

The train wasn't slowing down. The Seraph flew toward the front of the train and landed on its nose. Jolie leaned against one wall, her pistol dangling from her right hand. Artemis knelt behind her, hands cuffed behind her back. One engineer sat against the wall; the other was frantically working at the controls.

"What's wrong?" the Seraph asked.

"The engines are sabotaged!" Jolie shouted. "We can't stop the train!"

He glanced over his shoulder. The Brooks station was approaching fast. He had to stop the train somehow—or at least slow it down enough that the impact wouldn't do significant damage. There was only one way he could think of that would accomplish that, and it would probably get him killed. But he had to do something.

"Hey!" Dean stuck his head into the cockpit. "Everyone all right?"

"The train's out of control, and it's going to crash," Gideon said.

"We encountered two guys in the engine room on the way up here. They'd done a number on it."

"You need to get everyone off the train."

Dean looked around—at Jolie, the conductors, and Artemis. He looked behind him, where Gideon saw Carter standing at the ready.

"I can't get everyone out that quickly!" Dean exclaimed. "People are starting to panic. It's a madhouse back there!"

Gideon clenched his jaw. "You've got to try. Crusader?"

The young man stepped forward. "Yeah?"

"Go to the frontmost passenger cabin and release the car from the engine. That will keep the passengers safe, at least. Drifter, you get these people to safety."

The Seraph leapt into the air and soared ahead of the train. He summoned as much light energy as he could muster, letting it crackle and shine around him as it had less than an hour before, when he'd feared for his parents' lives. If Gideon could not stop the train's momentum, and if Drifter couldn't get everyone off, then Jolie and Dean and Carter would all die. The two engineers would die. If his cries hadn't cleared out the station, then hundreds of civilians would die. Even Artemis would die.

He couldn't let that happen. The Seraph looped around and headed straight for the train. His body burned with the power of the light flowing through him. If this didn't work, he would end up splattered all over the railway—but he had to try.

* * *

The Crusader rushed through the first two cars and stopped between the second and third. The passengers were leaning against the windows, exchanging panicked whispers, and even pacing the aisle. A few men huddled around the emergency exit hatch The Crusader stepped into the cabin, and several of them turned to face him.

"Listen up. Everyone needs to sit down and strap in. The engine's out of control. I'm going to disconnect this car from the engine to slow it down. Things might get a little bumpy."

The nervous whispers escalated to a panicked din. Someone started praying at the top of her lungs. One of the men by the hatch shouted for the Crusader to save them. The passengers who were not in their seats hurried to the nearest empty one and buckled up. The Crusader stepped across the line into the third car—no way was he leaving his friends—and reached down for the clamp that connected the cars. He grasped the lever with both hands, tugged on it with all his might—

It snapped free. The Crusader's car, still pulled along by the engine, rocketed ahead, leaving the passenger cars to gradually decelerate. He breathed a sigh of relief and rushed back toward the cockpit. Now, if the rest of them could get out of here alive, they could call this day a success.

* * *

The train bore down. The Seraph flew toward it with extended hands, light pouring off him in blinding beams, closer to white than gold. He braced himself—

At the impact of the train, every bone in his body felt like it had shattered. He screamed and pushed against the engine with all his might, trying to fly at a speed that would counter that of the train and push with enough force to slow the lumbering vehicle. His shoulders and arms protested, and he felt his limbs go numb. Shunting the pain aside, he poured more light energy out of him, surrounding himself in a blazing ball of white light and using the amplified strength it provided to push back.

This wasn't the action of a vigilante, Gideon realized. A vigilante fought in the shadows, hurt people who committed crimes, protected innocents through violence. They didn't rescue innocents from a burning building, reassure panicked civilians, or risk their lives to stop runaway trains. What Gideon was doing right now was the work of a superhero. *I guess they were all right about me.* Now, if he could only survive to tell them that.

God, give me strength.

The Seraph screamed at the top of his lungs and pushed. Every cell was burning with light. He closed his eyes and pushed harder. When he felt like he'd depleted every reserve of energy in his body, he pushed harder still.

And then it was over.

CHAPTER 31

Drifter couldn't carry all five people at once—and that wasn't even counting the unconscious thugs in the car behind them. Maybe if he was fast enough, he could go back and forth and save them all. He grabbed Jolie by the shoulder.

The train jolted. Drifter snapped his head around to look through the shattered viewport. The wind blew hair into his eyes, clouding his vision, but through the strands he saw golden-white light shining from the front of the train.

"Is he doing what I think he's doing?" one of the engineers exclaimed.

"I think so." Drifter tugged at Jolie. "Hold on to me."

She shook her head. "I can't leave him!"

"He's doing this for you. You've got to let me take you out of here now or he's doing it for nothing."

Jolie stared at him, tears welling in her eyes. He nodded at her, pulled her close, and teleported. They landed on the ground just below the railway. Drifter looked up as the train shot past. Gideon was indeed pushing against the front of the train, trying to slow it. Drifter shook his head. *He's crazy.*

He teleported back inside and grabbed the unconscious conductor. The station was getting way too close. He doubted he had time for three more trips. He hoisted the conductor over his shoulder and walked over to the other, who was still furiously working at the controls. He put his hand on that man's shoulder.

"The rear cars are detached!" the Crusader shouted.

Drifter glanced up as the young man rushed back into the cockpit. "Why aren't you with them? Are you crazy?"

"I wasn't going to leave you behind."

"I'll be right back."

Drifter teleported out with the conductors. The man who'd been sitting grunted as he fell from the height of his chair to the ground. Drifter set his companion down next to him and teleported back into the train one last time. Artemis and Carter were the only ones left in the cockpit . . .

He stumbled as he entered the cockpit. He'd prepared his body to adjust to the motion of the train. The problem was, there wasn't any motion. He looked out the shattered windshield. The train had stopped.

"Gideon?"

He jumped up onto the terminal and climbed out through the hole in the windshield. Gideon sat on the rail, his back resting against the front of the train, his head slumped down on his chest. Dean slid off the nose of the train and knelt next to him. Smoke rose from Gideon's body.

"Buddy, you okay?"

You had better not be dead, Gideon Turner. Dean grabbed Gideon by the shoulders and shook him gently. Gideon's head bobbed—a good sign. If he was dead, it would've just slumped, but it had snapped back up for a moment. Dean shook his head and grinned.

"You stupid idiot, you could've killed yourself."

Gideon groaned, and his eyes fluttered beneath his hood. Dean's grin split wide open and he laughed. He laughed in relief, and in disbelief, and in exhaustion. Carter dropped down next to them.

"Is he . . . ?"

"He's alive. Just exhausted. Honestly, I can't believe he pulled that off." He grabbed Carter's shoulder. "Hold on."

Dean teleported them back to where he'd left Jolie and the conductors. Jolie rushed up to them and knelt next to Gideon.

"Is he okay?" Jolie knelt next to Gideon. Tear streaks marked her face. "I'll take care of him. You go get Artemis before she wakes up and gets away."

"Will do."

Dean still felt himself grinning as he teleported back onto the train. Somehow, once again, they had won. It seemed impossible, miraculous—but they'd done it.

* * *

The next day, Gideon stood next to Jolie on the tarmac outside Dean's private hangar and looked up at the sky. The dark, birdlike silhouette of the Raptor hovered overhead, descending toward them. Gideon held Jolie's hand with his left while he fidgeted with his right hand, bound in a sling. He wasn't sure how he had broken only that arm, but it was a miracle the rest of him was intact, save for a few minor sprains and bruises. His powers must've amplified his bones and muscles significantly. He'd feel the injuries for a while, but the damage was far from permanent.

From what he'd heard from Wes and Patrick, everything was all right in San Francisco, too. In fact, the Raptor was bringing Wes—along with the captured Mendez—back to Sojourn. Patrick had elected to stay back in San Francisco. Gideon understood that; his parents had only just discovered his secret identity. And San Francisco needed a hero, too.

Gideon hoped they'd be able to hold Mendez. Artemis was easy enough; they had to keep the neural inhibitor on her. Arianna was working on a portable version of the device that could be installed outside Artemis' prison cell. Even Powers wouldn't be that hard. A quick but strong electric shock scrambled the brainwave pattern required to replicate, so they had installed electric bars in every wall in his cell. Even if he built up an army of Fragments in his cell, they would all end up trapped together behind an inescapable electrical barrier.

But Mendez would be the trick. He could destroy anything he touched. They'd have to come up with some way to keep him contained. Right now, his hands were bound in the blue-green goo from Sterling Labs' adhesive beads—a non-flammable material—but they couldn't restrain him like that forever.

For now, Sojourn City was once again celebrating its heroes. Drifter was recognized as Sojourn's protector, right alongside the Seraph. What damage had been done to the train could be easily repaired, and the only person who'd died had been the guerrilla Jolie had shot on the train. Gideon wished that man could have survived, and mourned his eternal destiny. Far more lives had been saved, though.

He just had to focus on them.

The Raptor settled on its landing gear, and the ramp descended. Gideon released Jolie's hand and strode toward the opening. Wes had changed out of his superhero uniform and instead wore a casual black shirt and blue jeans. He shoved Mendez down the ramp, spotted Gideon, and smirked.

"Welcome to your new home, *amigo*." Wes thumped Mendez on the shoulder. "Hope you like cozy little rooms. Yours will be especially little."

Mendez growled, but did not respond. Gideon smirked. Jolie approached and took Mendez by the forearm. She guided him back to a waiting police cruiser.

Gideon fist-bumped Wes. "Good work, Rampart."

"Thanks. Honestly, Patrick did most of the work. I just held Mendez off while Patrick rescued his parents . . . and then Patrick ran back and whopped the heck out of him."

"Still, not bad for your second supervillain encounter. And by the way, I've been meaning to give you props on that 'prism' move you thought of. Pretty ingenious."

Wes grinned and nodded his thanks. Gideon slapped him playfully on the shoulder, and the two walked toward Gideon's navy-blue Mustang.

"What happened to the arm?"

"Stopped a train with my bare hands." Gideon shrugged. "No biggie."

"Showoff."

* * *

"And that's how I got my powers and became a superhero."

Patrick's parents sat on the couch, staring at him as he paced back and forth in front of the television. Once he had begun explaining his powers, the words tumbled from his lips of their own will. He told them everything—from the moment he'd discovered them, to using them discreetly until he met Gideon, to training with him, and finally becoming Spright.

But there was still one thing he hadn't told them. He felt God prodding his heart to tell his parents about his faith. It was time—but first, they needed to process the bomb he'd already dropped on their lap.

"Well, son . . . " His father sighed. "We're very proud of the work you've been doing. It would have been nice to know before, though."

Mom nodded soberly. "You've been out there putting your life at risk, and we never even knew it."

"I'm really sorry." Patrick interlaced his fingers and put his hands behind his head. "I didn't know how, and I didn't know what you'd say, and I didn't want you to be in any danger, and I—"

"It's okay," Dad said. "Take a breath, son."

Patrick bobbed his head and lowered his hands. He inhaled deeply though his nose and exhaled from his mouth. He felt his heart rate slow ever so slightly.

"We can't stop you from using your powers." Dad stood and walked over to him. "It would be unfair. Clearly, you've been given this gift for a purpose. We couldn't stop you from achieving it even if we wanted to. You're an adult now, Pat. You've got to make your own choices, and this is a big one . . . but it's yours to make."

Patrick hugged his father. He just hoped Dad felt the same way about what he had to say next, because it wasn't likely to be so pleasant.

"Dad, there's . . . there's one other thing."

"Oh yeah? You can fly, too?"

Patrick chuckled nervously. "No, seriously. This is big, and I . . . well, you might want to sit back down, okay?"

His father's expression hardened. Patrick felt his heart race again, and he forced a few deep breaths. *God, give me strength and peace.* He felt it almost instantly, like a gentle trickle of warm water washing through his insides. And he knew it was going to be okay. Dad sat down next to Mom.

"Mom, Dad . . ." He pressed on before he lost courage. "A while ago, Lucy invited me to a church event. I've had a crush on her forever, and so I decided to go with her. I already knew a bit about Christianity from Grandpa, and it all made sense to me. So when the preacher at Lucy's church started talking about Jesus, I just . . . I don't know, I felt God talk to me so clearly that night. It was like nothing I've ever experienced before. I put my faith in Jesus. And I know you're probably disgusted with me and feel like I've betrayed you, but you just don't understand; you can't until you've felt it, too. It's *real*. Jesus is the Messiah; there's no doubt of it in my mind."

He stopped. His parents said nothing. Dad's expression was unreadable. Tears welled in Mom's eyes. Patrick's heart sank. He'd crushed them.

"Thank you for having the courage to tell us, son." Dad stood again. "We love you very much, but . . . maybe it would be best if you spent some time away from here."

Patrick blinked in surprise. A tear rolled down his cheek. He reached up and wiped it away, but it was chased by another.

"Dad . . ."

Go. It was like God spoke the word straight to Patrick's heart. He pursed his lips, nodded, and stepped toward his dad. He hugged him, and then leaned down to hug his mother as well.

"I'm going to leave my Bible here, in my room." Patrick walked toward the stairs. "I'd like it if you would read it. I'm going to come back, okay? San Francisco's my home, and I'm not going to stay away forever."

He walked up the stairs. He didn't have to pack; his things were still in Sojourn City. He'd been afraid of this response, although it had been a worst-case scenario in his mind. He reached under his bed for the second Bible he'd been holding onto in hopes of giving it to his parents one day. He picked it up and set it lovingly on his pillow. Then he walked to his window and climbed out.

Patrick couldn't leave without telling Lucy goodbye. He didn't know how long he'd be gone. He could always find a place in San Francisco, but that would require a well-paying job that he didn't have right now. Maybe what he really needed was some more time in Sojourn City. He hoped Lucy would understand.

Her door stood like a great, forest-green wall in front of him. He raised his hand to knock and froze. Did he really want to tell her his feelings for her and then just leave, possibly for many months? He hesitated.

Just do it.

She'd kissed him on the cheek before he left for Sojourn the first time. Maybe she felt the same way for him. Or had. Could she still, after seeing him nearly kill Mendez? *One way to find out.* He knocked. Footsteps tromped around inside, and a moment later, the lock clicked. The doorknob turned, and the door opened. Lucy stood on the other side in jean shorts and a lime green t-shirt, her hair back in a casual tail.

"Hi, Patrick."

"Hi." He stepped back. "You, uh, you want to come outside for a second?"

She nodded and walked out, closing the door behind her. Was she scared of him? He'd beaten Backfire nearly within an inch of his life, and she'd seen it. She'd stopped him. He wondered what he would've done if she hadn't been there. Would Wes have been able to restrain him? Would he have even tried?

"Are you okay?" she asked.

"Yeah. Well . . . no, but I will be."

"Thanks for your honesty."

"You're welcome. Lucy, I . . . first of all, I'm sorry for what you saw yesterday. I know I almost killed that guy, and I'm not proud of it. Not exactly a great start for a superhero, huh?"

"You didn't kill him, though."

"Because you stopped me."

She shook her head. "No, I know you. You're too good a person. You care about life too much, you love life too much, to take someone else's."

"Thank you." He smiled. "But really, it . . . it was you. It's always been you."

"What do you mean?"

"Lucy, I . . . I like you. I like you a lot, and I have for a long time now, even before you asked me to come to church with you. And it's been so much more since then. I wish that I had told you before, but I was so scared, and I didn't know how. I just thought . . . "

"I like you, too."

Patrick grunted as she stepped forward and squeezed him in the tightest hug he'd ever received. He smiled and hugged her back.

"I'm so glad. But that's . . . there's another reason I came over here to talk to you."

She stepped back. "What's wrong?"

"I told my parents about my faith in Jesus. They were . . . hardly thrilled. Dad suggested that I spend some time away. I'm going to go back to Sojourn City. There's still a lot I can learn from the Seraph and the other heroes there, and they might even need my help. I wanted to tell you goodbye and . . . and I'm sorry that I waited so long to tell you how I felt. But I'm going to come back. I promise."

Lucy's expression stayed strong. "I understand. I'm so proud of you for talking to them. And I'm not going anywhere—I'll still be here when you get back from Sojourn City."

"You will?"

She nodded. "For you? Absolutely."

Patrick hugged her. He felt tears welling in his eyes again. *Why now?* Why had he waited until now to tell her his feelings? Now he had to wait even longer to pursue them.

"Well, I . . . I'd better get going." He chuckled. "I have to tell Asher I'm leaving, and I have a feeling he won't take it as well as you."

Lucy giggled and kissed his cheek. "Maybe you can tell him about your powers, too. Then you'll have Team Spright waiting for you to come home."

"Team Spright. I can't wait."

He backed down the porch stairs, not wanting to break eye contact with her. She waved goodbye. He sighed, waved back, and turned.

And he ran away, as fast as he possibly could.

CHAPTER 32

Dean had been pleasantly surprised when Patrick returned to Sojourn City, asking to stay with the team for a little longer. The four of them—five, counting Carter, and six if Jolie was added to the mix—made a good team. They would've done all right without Patrick, but there was no denying that the speedster added something to the team. They'd need him when they inevitably confronted Ashcroft.

Standing in the lair, Dean looked at the row of five super suits. Blue-and-gold Seraph, black-and-purple Spright, green Drifter, black-and-cyan Rampart, and red-and-gray Crusader. As much as he had enjoyed designing the suits and the tech that the team used, it had never been his ultimate calling. Some part of him had always known that. Maybe that was why it had felt so good to gear up as the Seraph while Gideon was incapacitated, or why he'd suited up again to confront his father on the night of the Uprising. Maybe part of him had always known that his destiny was to be a superhero.

To be Drifter. Dean studied his green uniform. It seemed insane to be grateful that he'd been kidnapped and experimented on, but it had led to this. Artemis had intended his capture for malicious purposes, but God had another plan. Dean had no doubt that, just as Gideon's time as a prisoner of the guerrillas had been part of God's plan for turning Gideon into the Seraph, all the things Dean had gone through in the past few months had been part of God's plan for him to become Drifter.

He would've felt better about it if it weren't for the news he received about a raid on Sterling Labs. During the battle on the train, a woman who flew and a man who shot fire from his hands had breached the security system. The train, the guerrillas, Powers, Backfire, Artemis . . . they'd been there to distract the heroes while Ashcroft's other people made off with the real prize. And it had worked.

"Penny for your thoughts."

Dean turned. Gideon stood at the entry to the ops room, his arm in a sling. He was so much happier than when he'd returned from Venezuela—or even when he'd first become the Seraph. Then he'd been broody, quiet, serious. The weight of being an illegal vigilante had taken a toll on him. Now he always wore a good-natured half-smile, even with a broken arm.

"I was just thinking about fate." Dean crossed his arms and shrugged. "And about how God put all this together for us to have these powers."

"You really believe that's what happened?"

"Don't you?"

They'd talked about it before, but it had been a quick sidebar, not a full discussion. If they were going to do this, Dean wanted it to be with a purpose. His father had mistakenly believed that bringing a mob of criminals into the city was God's judgment. Dean didn't want to replicate his mistakes.

"I do. This can't be an accident. There's a reason we have become what we are." Gideon stepped into the room and paused for a moment. "Superheroes."

It was good to hear him embrace the term. "Agreed."

"Any word on the Sterling Labs break-in?"

"As much data as they stole, it's hard to tell, but one thing lined up: the dispersal device that was on the train had schematics in our archives. They were among the plans stolen. I've already sent the D.C. facility a warning to beef up their security. If they're going to go after that device again, it'll be there." Dean shook his head. "You know, it's pretty crazy that Ashcroft was willing to give up Wayans, Powers, and Mendez just to distract us. Do you think he knew they'd lose, or was he hoping that they'd beat us this time?"

"If they'd won, there would be nothing standing in his way, and Artemis would've brought him the device herself. I think he hoped they would win, to take us off the board, but he hedged his bets by sending the backup team to steal the plans."

"It wasn't a total loss for us, then."

"No."

"Great. Score one for the—" Dean frowned. "What do we call ourselves?"

"I hadn't thought about it. But we probably should have a name."

"Got any ideas? Any snappy team names coming to mind?"

Now Gideon's eyes turned to the super suits. Dean followed his gaze, again studying the five colorful uniforms. Gideon's jaw worked silently for a moment. Then he turned back to Dean and smiled.

"The Vindicators."

A little chill ran up Dean's spine. "I like it. Why Vindicators?"

"Working together, we vindicated the idea that vigilantes—no, superheroes—can be a good thing, a real thing. Against all odds, when the law wanted to bring us down, we stayed strong. And we won."

"Vindicators it is."

* * *

Artemis' cell was a slapdash job put together by Arianna and Maddox in a hurry, but it worked. As far as Gideon could tell, there was no way she could influence anybody outside the cell. The neural inhibitor worked perfectly.

He stood outside the glass wall separating him from her and smirked. She didn't look so threatening in a dull gray prison jumpsuit, especially not with a bandage and brace on her knee where Jolie had shot her. She lay on her back, staring at the ceiling, unmoving. He wondered if she was pouting or plotting her revenge. Maybe both. Gideon had no doubt that Ashcroft would want to come for her eventually. She probably even thought it would be soon. Gideon was determined to be here when that happened.

"What do you want, Gideon?" She practically retched his name.

"I want to know some things. Things like my history." He leaned against the glass with his uninjured hand. "How did Ashcroft create the formula that gave us all powers? Who are you people? I know Crowne Pharmaceuticals is just a front—so who are you really? What are your goals? And where is Ashcroft now? What did your friends want with the DNA splicer that was stolen from Garvin?"

Artemis sat up and faced him. "We call ourselves the Regency. You can't really think I'd tell you our plans, but if you want a history lesson, fine. Knowing how all this started won't help you prepare for how it's going to end."

"Try me."

"Have you ever heard of the Nephilim?"

Gideon had—in biblical history classes. "Ancient beings, half-angel and half-human. They were supposed to be wiped out in Noah's Flood, but legends about them circulated throughout Jewish history, including around the giant Goliath."

"No one knows much about them. The Bible uses the word 'giants' to describe them, but there's debate about whether they were literal giants or just titans of industry and intellect . . . or if they were, perhaps, something more. Something powerful."

"Are you telling me that Ashcroft is trying to create a new race of Nephilim?"

"Precisely." Artemis rose and limped toward the glass. "Ashcroft's father was obsessed with superheroes. He wanted to be one, and he concocted a little formula for himself. But that formula drove him mad. At first, he seemed like the hero our country needed, but over time, his madness led to catastrophe. The U.S. government was forced to bring him down. And with his death, Ashcroft became determined to replicate his father's success, to avenge him. He thought the key to perfecting the serum lay with the Nephilim. He studied folklore, absorbed all the knowledge he could. And then . . . he found them. The original Nephilim."

"What?" That was impossible. The Nephilim were long dead; there were no remaining half-angels on Earth. Their remains would've been long decomposed or, at best, fossilized.

Artemis smirked. "Searching for proof they existed, he stumbled upon a burial site. Five of them, perfectly preserved in chambers like crypts, but far more advanced than any other technology from the time they supposedly came from. The chambers were full of a strange liquid that kept the bodies from decomposing. They were dead, of course. Drowned. But somehow preserved. Lends some credence to the tales of the Flood, no?"

Gideon didn't respond.

"Ashcroft studied them. Their genetics were . . . unique. Not entirely unlike ours, but with some key differences. And he realized that he could use them to create superhumans. He could achieve his father's dreams and more."

Madness. There had been nothing good about the Nephilim. The angels who had sired them had been wicked, fallen from heaven. If the Nephilim really were as powerful as Artemis claimed, they would've been pure evil. Recreating them was insane.

"Ashcroft took blood samples and injected them into human subjects. His first subject died. So Ashcroft experimented—adding different stimulants and other drugs to the blood to distill it, to allow it to reside in a human body. And that, my dear Gideon, is what he gave to you."

Gideon felt his stomach twist. His powers were the result of an abomination, the recreation of a race that God had never intended to exist. A race of evil. He stared down at his hands.

"Ashcroft wants to expand humanity past its potential, to create a safe and perfect world," Artemis continued. "He wants to show them that his father was right all along and make them pay for destroying him. To do so, he will move us to the next step in our evolution. Everyone will have powers."

"But not everyone can survive the formula. Patrick was inoculated as part of a group, and all of them died except him."

"True, but the formula is closer to perfection with every test. The gene splicer Mendez stole from Garvin Technologies brought us a step closer. That's why your friend Dean and your brother took to their powers so readily. Some will die," she shrugged. "But they are the weak, the unworthy. Those who survive will be a part of a new world, a stronger world. Isn't that how evolution works?"

"And I suppose the Regency will be in charge of this strong new world?"

"Naturally."

Gideon pounded his fist on the glass and shook his head. "Never."

"We'll see." She moved back to her bed. "You can't stop it. Ashcroft has more servants than the few of us you've defeated, and more than you have the numbers to counter. He has a contingency plan for every scenario you could come up with. You may fight him if you wish. It'll only get you killed."

Gideon stormed away from her cell, his thoughts a whirlwind of confusion. When he'd first developed his powers, he'd considered them a curse. But through training and understanding, he'd come to look at them as a blessing. The fact that he'd been able to resist Artemis' manipulation powers had reinforced that; he had believed that God had bestowed his exact powers, knowing he'd need them. And his conversation with Dean had doubly reassured him that all this was of God.

Now, he wasn't so sure anymore. Could God really have been a part of something that was an attempt to replicate a great evil like the Nephilim?

And what of this story of Ashcroft's father? Gideon had never heard of it before. Had the government really managed to cover it up so successfully that no one knew that there had once been a superhero in this country? When Gideon had first shown up, everyone had reacted as if he was the first one. How closely was the government guarding this secret? Or was it all a lie by Artemis, meant to garner Gideon's sympathy?

He strode out of the prison. Jolie leaned against her Camry and smiled at him as he approached. He forced a smile and reached out for a hug as he approached. She kissed him on the cheek and settled under his good arm.

"You okay?"

"I don't know." He sighed. "She just dropped a bombshell on me—a few, actually—and now I'm not sure about anything."

Anything except my feelings for you. He looked into Jolie's eyes, so full of concern and love and support, and felt some of his confusion melt away. She was one part of his life that he'd never doubted. Even when he'd been an illegal vigilante and feared how she would react, he had somehow known things would work out for them.

"Whatever she told you, she's a manipulative snake. You can't trust her. Trust me. Trust God. Trust what He's telling you."

"You're right. Thank you."

He thought about how he felt when he used his powers. He knew what the conviction of the Holy Spirit felt like, knew what it was like when God was telling him he was doing wrong. He never felt that when he used his powers. Maybe it was because he used them for good, rather than for evil.

My powers are not a curse. Gideon let the weight of that statement settle on him. He had not sought out this power. He had not greedily searched for something to make him stronger, as Ashcroft and his father had. Gideon's powers had come to him seemingly by accident, but maybe it had been God's providence. God knew what Ashcroft was attempting. Maybe He had allowed Gideon to be captured so someone could stand in the gap. Maybe that was why he'd met Joshua Omer, so one day he could meet Patrick, who had also been given powers. So they could work together, and the world would have two powered protectors instead of one. Now it had four.

Five. Carter might not have powers, but he had proven himself just as worthy of the title of hero as any of the rest of them. He could hold his own in a fight, and he was mature enough to know where he was needed most, as evidenced by his willingness to follow orders on the train. Gideon was proud of him.

And Jolie made six. Maybe she didn't have powers, and maybe she was a detective and not a superhero, but she was still a hero. She—not Gideon—had stopped Artemis. She was smart, and she was strong.

There would be more. Gideon had no doubt of that. Artemis had said Ashcroft was raising numbers of supervillains that Gideon would never be able to match. God knew how many Ashcroft had, and He would more than prepare the side of good to fight back.

Gideon straightened. "Let's go get lunch."

"Wally's?"

"Always." Gideon grinned. "Race you there."

"What? I—"

Before Jolie could climb into her car, Gideon leapt into the air and soared away, her shouting voice trailing behind him.

* * *

"Hey, Carter. Can I talk to you a minute?"

Carter glanced up from shelving a crate of Pringles. Silas stood at one end of the aisle, arms crossed, a casual smile on his face.

"Yeah, just a second."

He finished putting the canisters of chips on the shelves and picked up the empty crate. He walked toward Silas and past him, toward the back of the store. Silas fell in line behind him.

"I never thanked you."

Carter frowned. "For what?"

"For saving my life."

Carter froze. He hadn't exactly been in uniform when he'd confronted Powers outside the school. He'd been wearing his domino mask, but other than that he'd been dressed just as he normally would've. It was possible that Silas had recognized him.

"What do you mean?" Carter asked.

"You know what I mean. I don't know who that guy was, but I've got a good idea why he was after me. If you hadn't been there, I'd probably be dead right now." Silas winked. "Don't worry. Your secret's safe with me."

"Well, you're welcome. And thank you."

"Least I can do for the hero of the Brooks." Silas took the crate from Carter, turned it over, and sat on it. "You're a good kid, you know that?"

Carter sat on another crate. "What gave it away? Me being the Crusader, I mean."

Silas chuckled. "You were wearing the same outfit that night as you'd been wearing at work earlier that day. You just added a hoodie. Not to mention, not long after you asked me and Ethan about Shine, the police and the Crusader hit one of their biggest shipment spots. Besides, your Pops was the first Crusader; everyone knows that. Not a huge leap to think you might be the new one."

"Yeah." Carter laughed. "Guess I wasn't that discreet, was I? Does Ethan know?"

"Nah, he was too busy cowering. It's just me."

"Okay. Well, thank you again. I'm really glad you're not going to turn me in."

"Why would I? I work with troubled kids. With kids like you out there, it gives me hope for the ones who don't seem to have hope right now. If you ever need help, you let me know. Keep doing what you're doing. Even if nobody else ever tells you they appreciate it—I do."

* * *

Wes lay on his bed, staring at the ceiling, and processed everything that had happened over the past couple of months. He'd hardly had time to slow down and realize what it all meant. He was a superhero now. Unlike Gideon, his secret identity wasn't known—but Rampart was. Although he hadn't committed any major actions in Sojourn City yet, he had a feeling it wouldn't be long.

That didn't mean his future law career was over. He still wanted to go to law school, but could he manage that and be a superhero at the same time? Maybe he'd take a year off before deciding. He had all the time in the world.

* * *

Jolie wasn't mad at Gideon, but she was a little irked that he'd gone and flown off like that. The least he could've done was give her a little bit of a head start. He could fly across town in minutes; she had to drive through traffic in her little Camry.

She pulled around the corner and into the parking lot outside Wally's. It was packed, as usual. She expected to see Gideon standing outside the front door, arms crossed and a cocky grin that she was fully prepared to knock off.

But he wasn't there. She parked the car and frowned. Maybe he'd already gone inside to get their seats since it was so busy. She turned off her car and stepped out. As she approached the restaurant, she scanned the lobby through the window. He wasn't at their regular booth, but it was vacant. What was going on?

"Ahem."

Jolie turned around. Gideon stood behind her, hands in his pockets. She tried her best to put on a scowl. It was hard with him.

"I suppose you expect the loser to pay?"

Gideon dropped to one knee and removed a small box from his pocket.

"Gideon . . . what are you doing?"

"Jolie Anderson, I love you so much. I can't believe I've waited this long to ask you—will you marry me?"

Jolie's heart did somersaults through her chest. Tears stung her eyes. She put a hand on his shoulder and smiled.

"Of course I will."

Gideon jumped to his feet and wrapped her in a hug as best he could with an injured arm. Jolie smiled and squeezed him tightly. She would never let go of him again.

* * *

Rebecca Omer walked into her son's bedroom and looked around. The hole in her heart was indescribable; she couldn't begin to understand the depths of her own pain. She felt whiplash from how quickly she'd gone from infinitely proud of her son to horrified and disappointed by his choices.

She sat down on his bed. Patrick was the best boy she had ever known; he was not perfect, but there was genuine goodness and a deep love for others in his heart. In recent months, it had seemed to grow more than she had ever imagined possible. Maybe his newfound faith had more to do with that than she would've liked to admit.

A Bible rested on his pillow. She reached for it, knowing her husband would criticize her for it. But she had to know.

EPILOGUE

Jeremiah Ashcroft was a patient man. His plan to remake the world had been formulated over decades. Forming the Regency had taken time, and they had only begun making strides in the past year. That was not the plan of an impulsive man. His day would come, and he would be ready when it did. Setbacks were inevitable and expected. He would adapt and overcome.

Gideon Turner had sparked a fire of impatience in Ashcroft's heart. How dare one of his own creations turn against him? How dare he inspire rebellion in others like him? Nothing should have been able to stand against his forces, and now four individuals with godlike powers were openly defying him. They had captured three of his top lieutenants, not to mention the squad of guerrillas they'd taken with them.

It was almost time. The world was going to see that Ashcroft was right. The scientific community was going to regret rejecting his ideas. The government would rue the day they had slain his father. He'd have to move the timetable a bit to account for Turner and his cohorts, but doing so would not damage his plan.

He turned to the photograph hanging above his desk. The black-and-white portrait had been captured by some young photographer for a big-city newspaper. It was the only picture of his father's alter ego, Solar Flare, that he had been able to find after the CIA scrubbed all records of Father's existence. The warm, golden glow of his father's hands and eyes had once been a comfort to Ashcroft. The sight of his green-and-yellow costume was a bane to criminals across the United States. Now, they were a bitter reminder. Of all the people to inherit Solar Flare's powers . . . why did it have to be Gideon Turner?

"I will avenge you, Father," Ashcroft whispered. "The one who dishonors your memory will fall."

Ashcroft turned to face his remaining five lieutenants, the last of the command structure of the Regency. They were the finest of his crop, some devoted to his cause out of pure motives and some out of selfish ambition. He didn't care what drove them. He cared about their loyalty. They were strong and intelligent. They knew the plan. And they knew Turner's little team of rebels had to be stopped.

While Somna, Fragment, and Backfire had drawn Turner's attention, the others had used the distraction to procure the data that Ashcroft needed to move into the next phase of his plan. Ashcroft smiled at them.

Heroes always needed something to fight, something to prove their worth. For Turner and his cohorts, that was Ashcroft. But the right threat could draw their attention away from him long enough for him to finish his work.

He had just the thing.

COMING SOON . . .

JAKE TYSON

THE VINDICATORS BOOK THREE

HEROES'
MIGHT

An explosion rocked the aluminum-sided building resting on the corner of a dusty intersection. A pair of cars parked curbside bounced with the shockwave, and a teenage couple standing on the opposite street corner cried out and took off in a full-bore sprint in the opposite direction. Gideon Turner, the Seraph, crossed his arms in front of him in an X, throwing up a shield of golden energy to block the shockwave. His booted feet skidded across the pavement. He stopped in a ready crouch in the middle of the street.

A flicker of green light, and his best friend, Dean Sterling—in his superhero guise, Drifter—was standing next to Gideon.

"First Raven City, then Wichita and Juncture City, now Phoenix?" Drifter shook his head. "Ashcroft's upping his game."

The Seraph lowered his arms and shunted his gathered energy downward to create glowing spheres around his fists. "Any sign of other superhumans in the area, or is it just this guy?"

"Just him for now, but I'm sure Ashcroft didn't detonate a gas bomb just to transform one ex-con." Drifter flexed, and twin peranium shields spun out of his gauntlets. "We'll be hearing of more, sooner or later."

The ex-con in question—the source of the explosion that had just rocked the street—ripped his way out of the chain-link fence surrounding the aluminum building. The tall, muscular con had been rampaging through Phoenix's slums when Gideon and Dean had arrived. He was hyped up on his own power.

"Right." Gideon stepped forward. "Let's get this over with."

Based on the few minutes Gideon and Dean had fought him, Ashcroft's latest superhuman had developed the ability to create shockwaves. Confronting him directly was a no-go, even if Gideon's peranium body armor was probably strong enough to take the brunt of the ex-con's attacks without bending. It was still too risky and was liable to end with more property damage than this guy had already caused.

"You don't want to fight, do you?" Gideon held up his hands in a steadying gesture. "You aren't doing yourself any favors by violating your parole like this. Stand down and let us take you in. We'll testify to your compliance, and when you get out again, maybe you can use your powers for good."

The ex-con sneered. "Why would I do that? I'm too strong for the cops, now. Way I see it, I take you two out? I'm home free."

"Well, it was worth a shot."

As the supervillain brought his hands together to form a shockwave, the Seraph launched himself into the air, flying out of range of the impending blast. He arced around the street and peppered the ex-con with golden blasts of light. The man stumbled back one step, then two. He growled and clapped his hands together—and the air rippled as the kinetic blast split the sky to cannon toward the Seraph. The superhero dropped into a dive, dodging the shockwave, and hit the ex-con with two more blasts. Drifter teleported forward and brought one of his shields down on the criminal's back. The ex-con stumbled forward—

The Seraph slammed into him feet-first, knocking him to the ground. As he hit, the Seraph pressed down and pinned the bigger man, punching him across the jaw with a glowing fist. Drifter knelt and slapped a power dampening cuff onto the supervillain's right wrist.

"All right. That wasn't so—"

Roaring, the ex-con shoved himself upright. The Seraph tumbled back and cushioned his landing with an energy field. The supervillain swung a meaty fist at Drifter, who barely teleported out of the way in time. The Seraph lurched forward and dropped into a crouch, where he snaked his left leg out to sweep the ex-con's feet out from under him. As the ex-con fell, the Seraph threw both hands forward and hit him with a full-force energy beam, hurling him back through the chain-link fence—creating a new hole in the process—and into the side of the aluminum building. He soared in after the villain, dropped to the ground next to him, and brought the cuffs around to connect them to the ex-con's left wrist and activate the dampening field.

"No! Let me . . . go!"

Gideon rose, shook his head, and pulled back his hood. Dean stepped into the building after him, running a hand through his curly brown hair. His green super suit was covered in dust. Gideon looked down at his own blue-and-gold uniform, found it similarly dusty. He chuckled. They were lucky they weren't in worse shape.

"Teach me to underestimate someone." He folded his arms across his chest. "All right. Want to get this guy back to Phoenix PD?"

Dean nodded. "Will do. And then I'll get to work on looking for any other superhuman transformations. With any luck, some of them will be on the heroic side of things. What about you?"

"I'm going to take the Raptor back to Sojourn City." He grinned ruefully. "Jolie and I are taste-testing wedding cakes today."

"Oh, the danger-filled life of a superhero. Go on. Enjoy your day. I have things covered here. If we need help or we're ready to come home, we'll call."

Gideon reached out and clasped his best friend's forearm. "Thanks, buddy. Don't know how I'd do this without you."

"You wouldn't look nearly as fashionable, that's for sure." Dean winked as he hauled the ex-con to his feet. "All right. Get out of here, lover boy. I'll have Maddox prep the plane; he'll be ready for takeoff by the time you get there. I can handle taking Mr. Macho here back to jail."

For more information about
Jake Tyson
&
Freedom's Fight

please visit:

www.creatingforcreator.wordpress.com
www.facebook.com/jaketysonauthor96

For more information about
AMBASSADOR INTERNATIONAL
please visit:

www.ambassador-international.com
@AmbassadorIntl
www.facebook.com/AmbassadorIntl

*If you enjoyed this book, please consider leaving us a review on
Amazon, Goodreads, or our website.*